Sonata
Bass bar
Linings
Sound post
Back plate
Purfling
a Bass bar
b Sound post
c Position of bridge feet
d Curves of bouts, linings
e Blocks
f C-curves
g f-holes
Arching
End button
Tail piece
Bridge
Finger board
Neck
Head
Pegbox
Scroll
Pegs

December 1994

Merry Christmas,

Mom/Mitzi/Grandma,

To a great lover of music, history, and fine writing.

Love,

Elizabeth, Dan, Sarah & Thomas

ALSO BY JOHN HERSEY

Fling and Other Stories (1990)
Life Sketches (1989)
Blues (1987)
The Call (1985)
The Walnut Door (1977)
The President (1975)
My Petition for More Space (1974)
The Writer's Craft (1974)
The Conspiracy (1972)
Letter to the Alumni (1970)
The Algiers Motel Incident (1968)
Under the Eye of the Storm (1967)
Too Far to Walk (1966)
White Lotus (1965)
Here to Stay (1963)
The Child Buyer (1960)
The War Lover (1959)
A Single Pebble (1956)
The Marmot Drive (1953)
The Wall (1950)
Hiroshima (1946; new edition, 1985)
A Bell for Adano (1944)
Into the Valley (1943)

THESE ARE BORZOI BOOKS
PUBLISHED IN NEW YORK
BY ALFRED A. KNOPF

Antonietta

Antonietta

A NOVEL BY

John Hersey

ALFRED A. KNOPF

NEW YORK

1991

THIS IS A BORZOI BOOK
PUBLISHED BY ALFRED A. KNOPF, INC.

Published in the United States by Alfred A. Knopf, Inc., New York,
and simultaneously in Canada by Random House of Canada Limited, Toronto.
Distributed by Random House, Inc., New York.

Grateful acknowledgment is made to the following for permission to reprint previously published material:

European American Music Distributors Corporation: Hindemith Sonata in D, Opus 11, No. 2, Movement 1, measures 1 through 4. Copyright 1920 by B. Schott's Soehne, Mainz. Copyright renewed. All rights reserved. Used by permission of European Music Distributors Corporation, sole U.S. and Canadian agent for B. Schott's Soehne, Mainz.

G. Schirmer, Inc.: Musical excerpts and lyric excerpts from "L'Histoire du Soldat" by Stravinsky. Copyright 1924 (Renewed) by J & W Chester/Edition Wilhelm Hansen London Ltd. All rights for the U.S. and Canada by G. Schirmer, Inc. International copyright secured. All rights reserved. Used by permission.

Library of Congress Cataloging-in-Publication Data
Hersey, John [*date*]
Antonietta : a novel / John Hersey,
p. cm.
Includes bibliographical references.
ISBN 0-679-40194-6
1. Stradivari, Antonio, d. 1737—Fiction. 2. Violin—History—Fiction.
I. Title.
PS3515.E7715A85 1991
813'.52—dc20 90-52905 CIP

Manufactured in the United States of America
First Edition

TO BARBARA

"Cheerfulness keeps up a kind of daylight in the mind, and fills it with a steady and perpetual serenity."

Joseph Addison, *The Spectator*, May 17, 1712

Contents

Musicians and musicologists who read this book will know for certain that it is a novel, because they will find so many "untruths" in it—the peppercorns of fiction, which, a novelist hopes, may give the reader a taste for possibilities that are not found on the everyday menus of fact. This book was written for the fun of it, and I trust that those who know and revere the literal record will find themselves able to read, too, for the fun of it, with forgiving minds. At the end of the book is a note on some of the background sources I have used and abused in writing it.

Antonietta

Act One

1699

An April morning in Lombardy in all its brilliance. Antonio Stradivari, aged fifty-five, stands in the light-filled loggia atop his house examining wedges of maple in order to choose the wood for the back of a new violin. A woman dressed in black, with a huge black shawl drawn around her shoulders, walks alone across the cobbled Piazza San Domenico below. Stradivari's sons Francesco, who is twenty-eight, and Omobono, nineteen, are with him, the one handing him the slabs his father asks for, and the other putting those he rejects back on the overhead racks with great care. All three look down when they hear the sounds of the woman's clogs on the pavement.

The sun is full on the striding woman's face, making it glow like a peach ripened to the edge of readiness—a widow's face, to judge by the weeds, but a face by no means lined by years or ravaged by bereavement. It is an early-morning face, brimming with expectation. The clogs tap a message of vim. The tassels of the shawl swing with the woman's hips from side to side to side to side. Omobono, who is not allowed to speak to his father, draws in his breath and whispers to his brother, "Ai!"

The father, who hears that sound, shoots a glance like a lead ball at Omobono's head. As the tapping and the dance of tassels move on across the piazza, the three men in the airy rooftop space make a vivid triangle of concupiscence, the two sons defining a short base, the father very much at the apex. The loggia is an open gallery with a tiled roof supported by six brick columns, of the sort called in the dialect of Cremona *seccadour*, a place for the drying of fruits and laundry—though in this case it is for the dry storage of precious wood on high racks, and for the slow curing of layers of varnish on violins, three of which now hang by their scrolls up under the slope of the roof. The tittupping of the clogs echoes up under the roof with a fluttering sound around the violins. The woman leaves the square. As the chatter of the clogs diminishes, the geometric tension in the triangle increases. Its filial base shifts uneasily, wrenching the angles.

The father is suddenly flinty. He has been moody for several months, ever since May of last year, when his wife, Signora Francesca Feraboschi Capra Stradivari, whom even her sons knew to be a terror, flickered away like a burnt-out candle after many an agony of imaginary and real ailments. He has made only those three drying violins in the past two months. The sons saw how it pained him, out of the obligation of his position as one of the wealthier men in Cremona, to dole out one hundred and eighty-two lire for a grand funeral of the woman he detested, paying for fourteen priests and a choirboy for the service at the church of San Domenico, and for the procession twenty-six Dominican Fathers and sixteen Franciscans, thirty-one Fathers of San Angelo, twenty-seven of San Luca, twenty-one of San Salvadore, nineteen of San Francesco, hatted orphans, hatted beggars, twelve torch-bearers, six gravediggers wearing capes, a bier and a velvet-and-gold pall, ringing of bells in four parishes, black draperies at the church and the house, and bribes to two magistrates. If he wept at the funeral, his tears were surely those of a penurious man who felt grossly cheated by the need for this splurge.

Yet he has languished ever since, seeming to mourn his wife, or at least to begrudge her having deserted him, as the sons under his discipline all too sorely have known, feeling the sting of his tongue in the shop. Omobono recently suggested to Francesco that their father's eleven-month bad temper was caused by his no longer having a female body aboard which to enjoy *i diritti del marito*—a husband's conjugal rights—for despite his openly declared dislike of his wife, his exercise of these rights had been announced to the five children in the house, over all the years, no less after his passing the age of fifty, by telltale sounds emanating at night from the mother's room on the third floor: clamorous, frequent, energetic. Gentle Francesco was shocked by Omobono's suggestion—as he had also always been by the noises.

Now, as the delectable movements of the tassels of the shawl down there still swish in the triangular memory, the father has become even more finicky than usual. He wants another look at two wedges he has already examined—no, not those! Before! Three and four before that. He remembers the grain of that pair of pieces. The sons have always had to live with this frightening memory. He remembers every one of the scores of slabs of maple and pine that have been aging in the loggia for years—where and when bought, for how much, and how long a-drying. He remembers the exact shape of every violin he has made in nearly forty years, even back to those he made while apprenticed to Nicolò Amati—the archings and tunings of their bellies and backs, the resultant tonal niceties, the patterns of the grains of the wood, and the particular shade of the varnish. Especially he remembers each violin's mode of speech.

He looks, frowning, at the two wedges that Francesco now holds up for his inspection. They are both of maple from Turkey, which he bought from a villainous swindler on a trip to Venice twelve years ago—cut from logs sent to that city as the strongest and most durable wood for the rudders, the interior trim, and especially the oars of gondolas. These wedges were cut on the quarter, from the edge of the log to the heart, perpendicular to the tree's rings, and they show, even in this rough, axe-split state, a promise of the exquisite surges of color, like billowing waves of smoke, that the best quartered maple can yield for the back of a varnished violin. He studies the two wedges for a long time. At one point he looks down from the loggia into the square, his glance sweeping along the line of the woman's recent walk. Brusquely, then, he points to the wedge in Francesco's left hand.

Francesco asks if he wants Omobono to saw the requisite length from the piece, and split it.

To the surprise of both sons, the father says he will do that work himself. But first he wants to choose the pine for the new belly.

Again he takes his time, looking at many slabs. He chooses for the belly, at long last, a board four and a half inches wide of red pine, of the variety known locally as *azarole*, cut from the south side of a tree on the south slopes of a mountain in the Tyrol where the pines get a heavy salt seasoning in the air from nearby saltworks. He bought it at a bargain in a consignment from a Milanese cheapjack, who didn't know how good it was. Its grain is straight, even, and fine but not tight. The board has been cut on the slab—tangent to growth rings.

Later, Omobono asks Francesco:—Did you notice how long the old man took today, choosing? He hasn't been that particular for months, has he?

Francesco says:—Thanks to God.

Omobono:—Thanks to the woman in black.

—What do you mean?

—The way she walked. Did you see his face?

—You have a filthy tongue.

—I saw your face, too, Francesco.

Now they descend to the ground floor, to the shop. As the three enter, Carlo Bergonzi, the father's only apprentice aside from his sons, leaves off whisking the maestro's workbench with a feather duster. That bench and those of Francesco and Omobono and the narrower one of the apprentice are immaculate. The father tyrannously insists on this. There is not one wood shaving on the floor.

The tools have all been wiped and are at parade rest in their racks or on their hooks at the backs of the benches. The father thinks of these as his greatest treasures on earth, his beloved trinkets, the jewels of a *liutaio*. No, they are much more than that, they are capable of being brought to life as extensions of his hands, for when he holds them they quiver, as if on perfect pitch, in unison with the vibrations of his personality. His great gift is matched precision of mind and hand; the tools are the faithful messengers of his precision to the wood he shapes. He is a rather casual Christian, but he takes the trouble to pray over these objects the first thing every morning. Indeed, he has taught Francesco and Omobono and Carlo to revere their tools as if they were sacred, as hallowed as relics of martyrs of the church.

There they all are: chisels for scooping, for shaving, for cutting mortises, for incising purflings; gouges and gauges; razor-edged half-moons of steel for scraping; calipers to measure thicknesses; sharpeners; wooden-handled knives for shaping *f*-holes; clamps of various sizes; bending irons; delicate tiny double-cut files—flat, half-round, rattail, three-square. Most beautiful of all are the parades of small elliptical metal planes, all laid out in processions of varying sizes, down to no bigger than the first joint of a forefinger, their hungry little blades set by wooden wedges into convex feet. On the maestro's bench there is, besides, reposing in a chinaware cup, a small piece of hematite in the shape of a human eyetooth, which the father likes to use for burnishing.

Before the three came down from the loggia, the father cut the two slabs he had selected to a length of fifteen and a half inches, and he split each exactly in two with a hatchet as sharp as a fortune-teller's tongue. He announced upstairs that he intends to make this violin entirely himself, every step of the way, with no help from the sons, and in order to give them work to do in the meantime he has less painstakingly chosen slabs for two more backs and bellies on which they can do the usual preliminary work.

Francesco and Omobono now see that their father meant what

he said, for he even lights a fire himself for the gluepot—a chore the apprentice has always done—and sets some hide-and-hoof glue to melt. He uses a flat plane to face down the wedges for the back and the slabs for the belly, and when the glue is ready he joins and clamps the pieces together, so that when they have been shaped for the finished violin, both belly and back will have halves that more or less twin each other.

Something else unusual: he hums as he works, popping his lips on staccato notes. This is bizarre; he is usually broodingly silent at his bench. But hearing the humming, Omobono nods, as if he knew this was going to happen. Francesco, with his sensitive ear, recognizes a sprightly theme from a violin trio they have recently heard* by a promising young redheaded Venetian priest-violinist—"*il prete rosso*," as he is nicknamed. The composer's father, a friend of Stradivari from Brescia, proudly sent the violinmaker a hand-copied score of the piece.

Two whole days pass before the father, seated at table *a pranzo* with his sons and Carlo Bergonzi, looks up from his plate, where he has been attacking a delicious pope's-eye of veal with diced ham that Feliciana the cook knows to be his favorite dish, and says to no one in particular:—Do you know who the woman was?

Francesco says:—The woman?

The father says:—The one in the early morning, the widow.

Omobono, who is not allowed to speak to his father, says to Francesco:—Tell him it was the widow Zambelli.

Francesco dutifully tells his father that it was the widow Zambelli, as if his father had not been able to hear Omobono.

The father says very sharply to Francesco:—Ask him how he knows.

Francesco asks the question.

---

*Gavotta from Opus 1, No. 1, by Antonio Vivaldi.

Omobono lazily sops up the gravy on his plate with a piece of Feliciana's peasant bread made from a mixed meal of corn, rye, millet, and beans, lifts it and bites into it, and then says, with his mouth full and a dribble of gravy on his chin:—Tell him that I inquired.

Having received this answer, the father shifts in his seat, obviously wanting to ask another question, but Feliciana comes in with a plate of fruit and cheese, and he waits until she has put it on the table with a clatter and has gone back to the kitchen. Then he says to Francesco:—What inquiries? Ask him.

Francesco to Omobono:—What inquiries?

Omobono:—After work, last evening, just before sunset, I took a walk.

The father's face is red. He swallows a sip of half-and-half wine and water. Then he says angrily to Francesco:—What business did he have gossiping?

Without waiting for Francesco's transmission, Omobono looks his father directly in the eye and with great audacity says straight to him, as it is forbidden to do, in a melting tone of voice:—I did it for you, Babbo.

The father's face looks like a sky in which peculiar, turbulent winds are blowing clouds this way and that. What will there be, hailstones and trees bent by gusts, or patches of blue and then sharp shadows on the grass? Suddenly the eyes soften, the frown becomes unstitched, and Antonio Stradivari, speaking to Omobono for the first time in more than two years, says:—I forgive you, son. I forgive you. It has been long enough. Now tell me what you learned.

And Omobono, showing neither pleasure nor excitement at having been released from his father's long censure, says that her name is Antonia Maria Zambelli. He learned this from an apprentice of the Guarneris who was at Leopoldo's billiards last evening. He says that there were seven or eight men around the tables, and he casually mentioned the woman's passage through the piazza and tried as carefully as he could to describe her face, but no one could think whom he meant. Then—another swipe with the bread at the gravy—he told the players as exactly as he could how she walked, and in fact he began to go swaying across the floor himself in mimicry of her walking. He had not taken more than three paces when the fellow from the Guarneris said Zambelli. Then at once others chimed in, agreeing.

Omobono:—They all said *Sì, sì*, Zambelli! Zambelli! Then I asked some questions.

The father waits, but Omobono offers no more. The father is forced to ask:—What did you learn?

Omobono says her husband died ten months ago of pellagra complicated by a weakness of the lungs.

The father:—How old is she?

Omobono says that the guess of those who know her was that she is in her middle thirties.

The father:—Reputation?

Omobono sops up more gravy. Then, looking down at his plate with the birth of a smile on his face, he says:—Friendly!

—Children?

No children, Omobono says. Who could know whether it was the husband's fault or hers?

The father, in a sudden fury:—What were you doing at Leopoldo's? You know that place is off limits. You had better swear to me that you were not playing billiards.

Omobono:—Babbo! How could you think that of me? . . . I sometimes watch.

The father:—You have no business in such a place. They have brawls. You could hurt one of your hands. You should stay away from those people.

Omobono:—Yes, Babbo.

The father:—Have you forgotten why I would not speak to you?

Omobono:—No, Babbo. I was home before dark—you saw me come in.

Now the weather on the father's face breaks slightly for

the better again, and he searchingly says:—When you say "friendly"—

Omobono:—I was listening very carefully. There was no suggestion whatsoever . . .

Omobono leaves his answer hanging. The father says nothing.

He is at his bench, with a large rectangle of thick white paper spread out in front of him. Omobono nudges Francesco and jerks his head in their father's direction, calling attention to the stillness, the rigidity of the back. No humming this morning. The father is tall and slender; the power in his shoulders, arms, and hands has always intimidated the slighter sons. He is wearing, over a rough linen shirt and wool pantaloons, a white leather apron that reaches well below his knees. He also wears a knitted, cone-shaped white wool hat, which will be replaced at the summer solstice by an exactly similar one of cotton. The sons and Carlo move around on tiptoe.

He is about to draw the design for the new violin.

What matters to the man at the bench is the voice of the finished and ripened instrument. The crucial thing in life is not to repeat oneself. Repetition dries up the springs of one's energy, leads to sameness and dullness, and dullness tends toward death. Thus every violin must be an invention. There must be changes each time, even if they are slight—in the arching under the bridge and on the back, in the swirl of the *f*-holes, in thicknesses, in the shapes of the C-curves and the bigger bouts and the sides and the corners, and in the final ensemble of the fifty-eight various parts. All the parts work together to give each violin its unique tone of voice, never to be matched, any more than a given diva's lovely singing can ever be heard from anyone else's throat.

Moreover, its physical beauty must also be its very own, thanks to the unrepeatable grain and waves of the plates of wood, to tiny variations in the purfling at the points, to changes in the swoop of the scroll at the head, to modulating glints of varnish—to ever-shifting mixes of the feminine and the masculine in the look of the whole. For the man at the bench realized years ago that a violin's tone is not spontaneous: it has to be coaxed out by a violinist, and a violin that is loved by its player—for its beauty as well as for its freedom of speech and richness of voice—will give up sweeter sounds than it will if it is not so loved. He knows this to be true. He has heard it again and again: the same instrument responding differently to different expert violinists. A fine violin, he knows, is a sensitive, animate creature.

He picks up his pen, dips it in the inkwell, draws an axis down the middle of the page with a ruler, marks off certain spaces on that line and several symmetrical measurements on either side of those marks. Then he begins to draw the shape of the bouts: the curves of the upright sides of a violin. As always, the sons are amazed, watching him—dismayed, for they know they will never be able to do what he is doing. He draws freehand, yet the curves on either side of the axis are perfect mirrors of each other. He outlines the *f*-holes.

He looks for a long time at what he has done. Then he gets up and goes to the latrine to piss.

As soon as he is out of the room, Francesco and Omobono and Carlo crowd around the bench. They see the shape of a woman's round shoulders, close waist, and broad hips.

Francesco whispers:—Omobono, *osservalo!*

Omobono whispers:—*Dio!*

Carlo asks in a whisper why they are excited. Francesco tells him that there is not a question here of minor changes from the last violin. This is new. This is a radically different basic pattern from that of the violins the old man has been making for almost a decade. No! No! For longer.

—This is something new, Omobono.

Omobono whispers:—He is out of his head.

. . .

It is Omobono who dares to ask the father, when he comes back, about the new design. Omobono has pretended not to care whether his father spoke to him or not, but since Omobono's release Francesco has already seen a subtle rounding off of the hard edge of indifference his younger brother has held up to the world for so long. That "manliness," as Omobono must have thought of it, only made things worse in the house. It enraged the father and made him shout—at Francesco, who was supposed then to pass the shout on in a very loud voice to Omobono.

Here is what caused the trouble, more than two years ago, between Omobono and his father.

Omobono had just celebrated his seventeenth birthday. He hated the work in the shop, because at that time Carlo had not been bound and he was the factotum, the one who had to tidy the benches and clean the gluepot and take the wood shavings to the kitchen to be burned, and the rest of the time his father made him stand at his shoulder, watching every move of his hands, for hours on end. This was how he was supposed to learn the craft. As his mother grew sicker and sicker, his father became more and more overbearing.

What was more, apprenticeship was a kind of imprisonment. In the sons' earliest years, their father had laid down a strict rule that they were never to go out into the city alone after dark until they were men, until they were twenty-one. The father said that his master, Nicolò Amati, had had this rule. The apprentices could go out during the day to run errands or even to play, if they wished, during the siesta—though the father said a *liutaio*'s life is one of work, siesta was a time to regain hand strength in rest. As for the one daughter, Catterina, the poor thing would never have the good fortune to make violins, so in a sense she had nothing to save herself for in life, yet she was forbidden to go out even during daylight hours, unless accompanied by Feliciana the cook or Marisa the mother's maid or Gianna the chambermaid.

At dusk one June evening, Omobono told Francesco he was

going to sneak out—to breathe air that doesn't stink, he said. Francesco tried to talk him out of it—all very well for *him*, who was by then over twenty-one, to preach caution. After the father retired to his room, Omobono slipped out through the back courtyard.

The summer twilights were long and soft. Men and women walked in the narrow streets. Life was hard. Lombardy was a worn-out toy of the Spanish Viceroys. The countryside had been ravaged for decades by famine, plague, war. Omobono's young friends were cynical. What future could there be, except one of cheating, lying, cutting corners? Name a magistrate and whoever you were talking with would rub his thumb and fingers together, meaning: a greased wheel turns. Cremona's cultural glories: cheese, sausages, mustard! Priests like flocks of jackdaws. Confess, sinners, confess!

Yet there was laughter in the streets in the evenings. You could hear mandolins.

That evening Omobono ambled alone across the piazza, gazing at girls. He strolled through side streets, walked past the cathedral and its campanile. Looking up at the tower, he grew dizzy: the tallest phallus in Italy, against a magenta sky. His chest was like a stove full of smoke, its flames smothered by wood shavings from the shop: the smoke was the pain of resentment. He had forgotten to sharpen the scrapers that morning, and his father had treated him badly all day. A girl looked him right in the eye as she came toward him—shiny dark irises, with glints of magenta in them from overhead, asking his eyes the only question that matters in life; but of course she was chaperoned—by her fat mother. They swept past him.

On an impulse, as it grew dark, Omobono went into a tavern, on a corner across from the Palazzo del Comune, called in mockery Il Ridotto, after the foyer of a grand theater or opera house, where the gentry would gossip and flirt between acts. Here workingmen, still in their sweaty work clothes, drank and laughed and gambled away their last soldi, then went home tipsy to their furious wives.

Omobono heard his name called. Paolo Mandelli, an apprentice with the Ruggieris, about nineteen, a boastful, edgy fellow, very short and therefore careful to speak with the calm voice of a tall man. He was playing zara with several other young men on a table with a raised board at one end to bounce the dice against. He invited Omobono to join in. Omobono shook his head, no. Mandelli said a Stradivari ought to be able to cough up a few chick-peas, come on, play.

Omobono:—My father would kill me.

Paolo Mandelli:—Does your father drink at Il Ridotto?

Omobono declined again and watched the others. They were having such a good time. No one minded losing two soldi; he would get them right back. Bursts of laughter like fanfares. The loser slapped the money down as if losing were an act of defiance. The winner grinned. The dice bounced, glistened. Omobono felt something like sexual desire; his chest still hurt, but now it was more the pain of yearning. And finally he said he would play one game.

He won from a stranger.

He thanked Mandelli's friends, and stepped back to watch. Mandelli said a winner couldn't not play again. Omobono said no, he shouldn't have played at all. The others began storming at him. Knowing that he shouldn't play made him want to all the more, and finally he took the two spotted cubes from Mandelli on the palm of his right hand. He closed his fingers and shook the dice in the hollow of his hand. Just as he was about to throw, he had a prickling sensation at the back of his neck.

He turned his head.

His father stood in the doorway looking like a ghost, for he was still in the outlandish white wool cap and white apron he wore at his bench. What could he possibly be doing at Il Ridotto? Omobono did not need to ask himself that question, because it was obvious that his father had seen his restlessness at table and had grown suspicious and had searched for him in the house and had come out looking for him. Who but his father would have the instinct to come to exactly the right doorway?

The fierce eyes raked just once at Omobono's figure, frozen as it was leaning forward to roll the dice. Then the father turned and left—and because of his son's defiance of the curfew would not speak to him, or be addressed by him, for more than two years.

But now Omobono's tongue has been set free, and he is more gratified than he will admit—he is trying to appear less sulky, as Francesco has seen, less loutish, though he is still brash. He boldly says that he and Francesco have noticed a sharp change in this new design. What does it mean?

It is a question of tone, the father says.

—How tone?

The father sits at his bench. He takes up a pine board three-quarters of an inch thick, about ten inches by twenty, on which he traces the new design. With a scroll saw he begins to cut out the mold on which to build the violin's sides. As he works, he starts talking to his sons, with his back to them. They have never heard him talk like this at his bench.

—You were not born yet. Long before you were born, when I started out. Of course I made the violins I had been trained as an apprentice to make. From twelve years old. You think I am hard on you. Nicolò Amati never swore, understand that he never struck me, but he made me sweat. He made me swallow my spit, I tell you. He had eyes like two of these. [*He picks up an awl.*] Oh, how grateful I am to him! I could make a violin by myself when I was seventeen. You have never seen my early violins—all sold, *grazie a Dio*. I was still working in Maestro Nicolò's shop when I married your mother. I worked on shares, you know. It was not easy. Your mother wanted Spanish-style hooped skirts from Milan. An expensive bed for her room—we were in the Casa del Pescatore in Santa Agata parish then. You were born on that bed, you unlucky little frogs. I was making violins by choice all that time from the Amati family's "small pattern"—they were easy-speaking, you know, easy to play because they tucked under your chin and were manageable. High curves in the belly and the back. These gave a silky, bright, small tone, part soprano, part oboe—lovely. I was proud of that sweet tone. Then you came, and Catterina. Your mother wanted a bigger house, so we moved here, you know. And then four years later Maestro Nicolò died, eighty-eight and a steady hand to the very end, that was my heartbreak. After that I was completely on my own. And at that very time your mother changed. I don't want to talk about that. I was on hot coals. I wanted to shout—wanted to make violins that would shout. A bigger tone. So for about six years I went to the Amati "grand pattern," a bigger box—but the tone was not enough bigger. I changed each violin in detail, you know, but the strong voice that I wanted never quite came. So—when?—nine years ago—the year of your mother's disgrace—that was when I started making my long and narrow violins, my *stretto-lungo* pattern. You know them. You two have chopped at them every day. I remembered the Maggini violins, from Brescia. But I made them flatter, that was the secret. And yes! They had more carrying power, you have played them, Francesco, they throw sound to the rafters at the far end of the cathedral, even when you play pianissimo. Deeper—contralto, chest tones. More difficult to play, I know, not so quick in response to the bow. But a full tone. . . . *Ohimè!* I have felt so restless. Your mother is gone. The other night I was awake all night. I rolled from side to side, I was so high-strung it seemed to me I could hear the spiders making their webs. But do you know something? I was happy! I had been so stale. In the middle of the night I visualized an entire violin. How to catch it all: the purity of tone of the Amati "small," but also the best of the "grand," you know, with the brilliance and fullness of my own long violins, but with less reach and easier to play, new tuning of the belly and the back, entirely new, it all came to me, you'll see, silver on the high notes, a woodwind sound on the D and G strings, but equal value from all the strings. Everything: sweetness, power, roundness, woodiness—without having to attack like a butcher with the bow. Everything. With this! Wait and see. [*He shakes the already almost cut-out mold over his shoulder.*]

Something of the old "manliness" turns over with a sigh in Omobono's head. He says:—You lay in bed and saw the tassels on that black shawl waving to you the other morning from down in the piazza, didn't you, Babbo? Each little tassel called out Antonio! Antonio!—didn't it, Babbo?

The father slams down the mold, turns in his seat, looks awls at Omobono, and then, as blood fills his cheeks, gives way to a sheepish grin and says:—Why did I give you back your tongue? If you let a goat in the house, he will bleat you deaf.

Goat. His wife's name from her previous husband was the word for goat: Capra. He met Francesca Feraboschi Capra only once before he married her. The scene is all too sharp in his memory—a Sunday afternoon in April, thirty-two years ago. His father and mother, Alessandro and Anna, were sitting as stiffly as glazed pottery figures in straight oaken chairs in the small "formal" room of their house in Santa Cecilia parish. He remembers pacing back and forth along the south side of the room, moving each way through brilliant cubes of sunshine that poured in at two tall windows; he even still sees in his mind the motes dancing in those boxes of light. His three much older brothers, Giuseppe Giulio Cesare, Carlo Felice, and Giovanni Battista, indulging their maddening curiosity about the woman who will be produced for the baby brother, leaned at ease against the opposite wall. His older sister Angelina Teresa had the kindness not to join this awful jury.

Sunday afternoon was the only time off for an Amati ap-

prentice. Antonio's work was beginning to be noticed; just the year before, he had put his own label, complete with the little woodcut monogram he has been using ever since, a double circle containing a cross and the letters A and S, inside a violin he had made, under the left-hand *f*-hole:

Antonius Stradiuarius Cremonenſis
Faciebat Anno 1667

At twenty-three he was earning, by family standards, good money, passed on to him by Maestro Nicolò in shares, in accordance with the contract that bound him. His father had insisted, since Antonio was by then making his own instruments and already had a strong reputation, that it was time for the boy to be married, and he had hired the notary Tomasino Androtti as a go-between to find a suitable bride.

During his quest, Androtti had given reports. The most suitable possibilities, he had said, were two in number. First choice, from the point of view of bloodlines and dowry: a maiden, Rosalba Greppi, daughter of a merchant of sausages, aged twenty, unfortunately *extremely* plain. Second choice: Francesca Feraboschi Capra, daughter of il Signor Dottore Francesco Feraboschi, eminent mathematician. This candidate was widowed and had a passable dowry from the estate of her late husband, who died in April, two years back, of a bullet wound inflicted by a harquebus late one night in Piazza Santa Agata. Two slight disadvantages, perhaps, in that she was three years older than the applicant bridegroom, and in that there were insistent rumors suggesting that her late husband had been shot for dubious reasons either by Francesca's brother or by his own hand—a crime in Heaven's eyes in either case. However, this candidate was less plain than the other one. Antonio's father had said he didn't want his son to have to marry a frightfully ugly woman; Androtti had better pursue the second possibility.

He had done so, with success, and now the Stradivaris' one

family servant, Luigia, a bent old woman, came to the door of the room and announced that guests had arrived. Here they were. The notary pushed a young woman through the doorway in front of him. Behind them came the parents, the mathematician with a pointed beard, the mother as thin as a broom handle. They were beaming with joy, presumably at the prospect of a liaison with the respectable Stradivari family.

All home eyes peered at the candidate, who seemed not to share her parents' euphoria.

Antonio's first impression was of a nose. Its shape had not been blessed by God, and it was inflamed. The woman darted the glances of a hunted rabbit around the room, evidently wanting to see which young man's snare was to catch her by the leg, and she sneezed three times. She had a cold. Antonio heard his brother Carlo snicker. Signor Androtti was flourishing contract papers before Antonio's father, who called for a pen and ink. And in a few minutes, after a brief but spirited quarrel over the amount of Androtti's fee, without anyone having asked him what he, Antonio, thought, the marriage contract was signed.

He is gluing up the tiger-striped maplewood bouts of the sides, and the dark red-brown willow blocks and linings. He has cut the four corner blocks and the two end blocks, keeping them as light as possible, so that in the finished violin the sides will vibrate as freely as can be, contributing extra overtones to each sweet note. He has planed the strips of maple for the bouts to a uniform thickness of one twenty-fourth of an inch. He curves them to fit the mold with heated bending irons and glues them to the blocks. He has cut mortises in the corner blocks for the short sections of the sides in the C-curves, and he glues the strips in, carefully wiping away the excess semen-like glue. Once the sides are fitted to all the blocks, he soaks the narrow strips for linings in hot water and bends and glues the upper set of them into place.

All this is exact and ticklish work, done by hands that are both delicate and powerful. Let's look at one of them: the right hand.

The hand as a whole is large. The fingers are slender, tapering, but the pad on the outer phalanx of the thumb is broad and curls outward for some distance, like the graceful beak of a pitcher. The narrow fingernails, pale as candle wax, with little white moons at their bases, are trimmed to the quick. The skin on the back of the hand is like that of a twenty-year-old girl. One large ungirlish vein, full and warm-looking, runs sinuously along the center of the back, doing a Turkish dance on the underlying tendons as they open the fingers or let them be closed by the muscles in the palm. There is dark hair on the wrist but not on the hand. The primary knuckles, as the fingers close, are as big as chestnuts; they, and those of the fingers, show no signs of the gnarling of age.

As Stradivari turns up the underside of his hand, we can see the huge swelling of the flexor of his thumb and the equally huge one of the palmaris brevis and flexor of the little finger. Across the upper end of the palm is the mound of the other flexors. Thus the palm is a crater of power. Its fateful wrinkles are shallow, clean. The life line is very long and unwavering. The love line is broken once.

There is not a hint of perspiration on either side of the hand. The palm is as dry as a page of the ancient Cremona census book in the Palazzo di Città.

What is most important about the hand we cannot see but must take on faith, judging by the precision of the work it does. The degree of sensitivity of each fingertip can only be imagined by comparing it with a supernatural ear that is able to pick out the sound of someone whispering on the far side of the Piazza San Domenico on an evening when there are a hundred people strolling about. The second knuckle of the second finger is the precious tool with which the maestro taps to tune the plates of his violins' bellies and backs.

It is this hand that now with tender care adjusts a padded clamp to hold a segment of lining in place in the new violin.

A few days later. He has slipped the shaped sides out of the mold, has glued in the second set of linings, has traced the outline of the sides onto the plates of maple and pine for belly and back, has cut these out with allowance for overlapping edges, and has started the crucial scooping that will shape them to do their heavenly work. All through these stages, the sons have been struck by his restless excitement; on this particular morning, the blows of his hammer on his gouge are like the eager syncopated knocking of a woodpecker's beak. The sons are amazed, after the siesta, to go back down to the shop and find their father's chair unoccupied. He has always been there ahead of them in the afternoons.

Antonio Stradivari is just then hurrying across the Piazza San Domenico. In his single-mindedness he has not bothered to take off his apron and cap. The apron flaps at his knees. He is an ambulatory scarecrow. Pedestrians turn their heads to look at him. Along with their astonishment, they get a lift from this figure's headlong vigor and from the craggy, burning face. With his long gait, lifting himself high on the ball of each foot at the end of each step, he strides to a house across from the church of San Sigismondo, climbs to the second floor, walks into an office without knocking.

Signore Apostolo Agnesi, banker and accountant, has someone with him. Stradivari is forced to wait on a bench. He crosses and recrosses his legs. At last a man leaves, looking crestfallen. Stradivari is admitted to the inner room.

Agnesi handles Stradivari's financial affairs; money for violins is deposited with him, and he invests it for the *liutaio*, hoarding it as jealously as if it were his own, for he knows this client to be stupendously tightfisted. The banker is a fat, genial man, dressed in the latest of embroidered suits, with a gold chain at the neck, from Paris. To do business with this client, he customarily calls at his home—in the evening, after work. Being visited by Stradivari, who almost never stirs from his house during the working day, is so unusual that it makes Agnesi anxious.

Stradivari clears his throat. He looks at the floor. He clears his throat again.

Agnesi:—Is there some trouble?

Stradivari shakes his head, no.

Agnesi is not reassured. Two more questions. Two more headshakes. Agnesi waits. A long silence.

Stradivari, finally, with a kind of gasp:—I need your help.

Agnesi, on guard:—Anything. Please.

Painfully, Stradivari gets it out that he is in need of help with a discreet investigation. Very quiet. Confidential. He needs to have a full report on a certain person.

Agnesi's eyes are hooded with caution. Are there perhaps legal difficulties? A lawsuit? Blackmail? He asks:—What person?

Stradivari squeezes out some words. The banker leans forward. He has not heard. Please repeat.

This time the banker jumps, because Stradivari repeats in a strangled shout:—Signora Antonia Maria Zambelli!

Agnesi is in a transport of relief and prurience. *Eccomi qua!* he says, at your service! Signora Zambelli happens to be in his parish, San Sigismondo. He does not know her except—*che gioia!*—by sight! His face radiant with malicious curiosity about his old friend and valued client, he adds:—I will do the best I can.

He roughs out the back, cutting the outside first. The arching is relatively flat.

Now he reaches the hilltop of his excitement. He will marry the vision of the new violin that he had in the night to the reality of the wood in his hands. In the next few days of shaping will lie the fate of the final tone, for it is in the interplay of vibrations of belly and back that the violin's timbre and power will have their genesis. And the back, being of stiffer wood, will bear a special burden of responding to the resonances passed down to it through the sound post from the belly.

When he has roughed both surfaces of the wood, he starts shaving at them, using, turn by turn, various of his little elliptical convex-footed planes. Over this work he takes days. He is constantly elated. He feels joy in every delicate scoop of the iron of a plane. Here is where the hypersensitivity of his fingertips comes into play. He has metal calipers he can use to measure how thin the wood is becoming, but amazingly to his sons he is able to loop his forefinger and thumb around the edges of the plate and feel differences of thickness of as little as one sixty-fourth of an inch. And here, above all—as, after three days' work, he puts away the planes and uses the half-moon scrapers on both faces of the plate, and as the plate grows thin enough to flex with his hands—here is where a radical innovation of the vision of that sleepless night is made real.

The departure is this. In all the violins he has made to the Amati patterns, and in his own long violins, the back was slightly thicker along the longitudinal axis and tapered off toward the sides, so that when the plate was flexed, there were two lengthwise wings of wood, so to speak, on either side. This time he is dividing the plate horizontally. He cuts the waist, between the C-curves, to a thickness of twelve sixty-fourths of an inch, leaving a fraction thicker a circle around the place where the sound post will stand, and then he tapers the wood toward each end down to a thickness of eight sixty-fourths of an inch. Eventually, when he grasps the two ends and flexes, new wings bend, this time, in the upper and lower bouts. He feels sure that these will be the wings of a new kind of sound.

All the while, as he has gouged and planed and scraped, he has periodically lifted the plate to his ear and tapped on it with the second knuckle of his right hand. He detects, with his acute sense of hearing and his gift of perfect pitch, the note of the scale that each section of the plate yields with its vibrations. With minute differences of thickness he tunes the plate so as to sound a rising chromatic scale through an octave from A-sharp to A-sharp as he taps upward diagonally from bottom to top. When he has finished, after a week's work, the back as a whole rings with precisely the fundamental, central pitch that he wants: F-sharp.

What is more, he can see that this back is going to be surpassingly beautiful. Under varnish it will glow with a glorious mirrored array, never seen before, never the like to be seen again, of waves of maple—each wave like a caress in color.

The day of the wedding he saw that Francesca had other features besides the nose. Seen dimly through her veil, her lips seemed thin and ungenerous to him. Her eyes rode above bruise-like half-moons. She brought to the church for their wedding a hacking cough, each blast of which billowed the veil out like the sail of a felucca in a sudden puff of wind. He discovered that night that she had a strong, healthy body, which wrestled him so fiercely that it took much of his reserve of power in his shoulders and arms to subdue her to his will. Her coughing in his face was a challenge to his ardor. By nine o'clock he had tupped her.

Having been inculcated since childhood with the strict rules implicit in the marriage contract, she managed his household, saw to his needs, ordered up his meals, and—though not without a vigorous self-defense that made him think of her as something like a criminal resisting arrest—submitted to his servicing of her. But nowhere in the contract, or in the mythology surrounding it, did she find a requirement that she must have tender feelings toward him. Bearing six children of his seed—the first of two Francescos died at six days of age—she made it clear that she was willing to be proud of his growing fame but that she regretted her life with a brute who sat at his workbench all day long and had not a word to say to her that did not have to do with violins.

Yes, her body was young and stocky and strong, but her mind soon became a prosperous factory of imaginary illnesses. She was to lay claim to headaches, rheumatism, dropsy, pox, scrofula, typhus, malaria, rashes, pellagra, liver failure, consumption, and many other ailments, including unspeakable venereal diseases which she said she could only have caught from *him*—but, he said, why not from the goat she had been married to before? Perhaps that hairy one had shot himself in shame at having got sick from whoring. This was the kind of bickering that went on over Francesca's complaints, few of which proved to have any substance at all. Once, she even said she thought she had a bubo of the plague under her arm, though Antonio shouted at her that there had not been a trace of the plague in Cremona since the devastating scourge of it fourteen years before he was born. Nor, in fact, was there a trace of actual swelling in her armpit.

She insisted from the first, in their house, the Casa del Pescatore, on having a separate bedroom. Scattered on the tops of its furniture were scores of boxes and bottles of pills, syrups, spices, oils, powders, plasters, unguents, electuaries, and poultices. She could not get a good night's sleep without taking a powder of opium, dried garlic, henbane, and papaverine. An apothecary whom she trusted supplied her with special prophylactics for each month of the year:

January: an unguent of pork fat reduced in rose-hip syrup rubbed on the skin; boiled bone marrow taken internally.

February: a brew made from licorice.

March: a powder of dried bark of the roots of black elm, ash, mulberry, poplar, willow, elder, and tamarisk, moistened with the tears that drip from clipped stems of violets and borage.

April, the cruelest month: frog flesh cooked in oil, roast

swallows, a stew of sparrow's brains. Dew gathered in the morning.

And so on. July was awful, with, among other things, an oily broth made from ants, scorpions, and vipers.

Antonio had to admit to himself that in spite of all her rituals of survival, she remained, during the years when her four living sons and her daughter were little children, a sturdy, energetic, and faithful mother, giving each child in turn a full measure of warmth of breast and heart. Much as he came to dislike Francesca, he grew jealous of his own children as they luxuriated in her open love for them.

On the eighth day he begins to shape the belly. Here the task is to match exactly the arching he has given the back. Unlike the back, the belly has practically the same thickness throughout, six sixty-fourths of an inch.

After three more days, he is ready to glue the bass bar to the underside of the belly—a delicate wand of pine tapered toward both ends and shaped to fit the curve of the belly plate. It is nine and a half inches long, a quarter of an inch high at its highest point, and three-sixteenths of an inch wide. He places it so it will be under the left foot of the bridge, where it will reinforce the vibrations of the deep tones produced on the G and D strings.

Now Marisa the maidservant comes to the door of the shop. The maestro is bent over, his whole body clenched into a fist of concentration. He is tuning a chromatic scale into the belly—taking feathery shavings from the new bass bar and dusty scrapings from the plate, tapping again and again with his knuckle to hear the tones. Marisa is terrified, because the maestro has shouted a thousand times, as if he truly means it, that any woman who touches shoe leather to an inch of the shop floor will be assassinated. She announces in a voice just above a whisper that there is a man at the front door, wanting to see the maestro.

Stradivari, shaken from his concentration, says:—Tell him to go away and come back after dark.

Marisa:—He said you would say that. He said to tell you it is Signor Dottore Agnesi.

Without another word Stradivari puts the belly plate down, drops his scraper on the bench, wheels out of his chair, the blood draining from his face, and brushes past Marisa on his way to the street door. Francesco and Omobono hear his cordial greeting, and then they hear him leading the banker upstairs, on the way to the loggia on the roof, where only the slabs of wood have ears.

Agnesi says:—What a beautiful day! *Ecco! Guarda!* The mountains look as if you could reach out and touch them!

Stradivari, sounding a little out of breath:—Yes, yes.

Agnesi, extending a hand up toward one of the three slowly drying violins:—Magnificent!

Stradivari:—*Amor del Gesù!* Keep your dirty fingers off that!

Agnesi:—Antonio, calm yourself.

Stradivari:—What have you come to tell me?

Agnesi, turning away:—How high your house is. I didn't realize you could see the river from here. [*Now he wheels back and looks right at Stradivari, and he says, with a twitch in his right eye that may be a wink*:] She is twenty years younger than you.

Since Agnesi seems to have nothing more to add, Stradivari almost shouts:—What else?

The report is thorough:

Antonia Maria Zambelli was born in September, 1664, which would put her on the road to thirty-five at the present time. Since the father, who had a small business of making and bottling mustard, died when she was nine, her mother, overburdened with five younger children, put her in the Convento delle Vergini Spagnole, a filthy establishment with notoriously cruel nuns. There she was taught, after a fashion, how to manage a household: how to light lamps, set the table in the breakfast room, make bread, cook veal and *minestra*, wash linen, sweep tile floors, mend clothes, and arrange flowers. She was also given thoroughgoing instruction in ways to keep the tinder of the flesh damp and fireproof.

According to one informant, she came out of the convent, at age sixteen, *una candida oca*, a naïve goose. The lessons as to tinder were apparently forgettable; she was reported to have had a series of passionate crushes on older men. A priest who took her confessions at the time, lured away from his solemn priestly duty of confidentiality by Agnesi's offer of a ducat, told him that she used to come sobbing into the confessional box about what she imagined might happen in the arms of this and that man. So far as the priest could tell, these partners had no interest in her; their imaginary fondlings and strokings, which she described to perfection, gave her ecstasies of guilt which it was a great pleasure to absolve with the assignment of a few *ave Marias*. She confessed no real sins—although, the priest said, it is very hard to know how truthful a clever girl of sixteen or seventeen will be in the booth.

By the time she was eighteen, her body—Agnesi got *this*, he says, from an old woman, a cousin of Antonia's mother who moved in to help out in the crowded house, and whose tongue was well whittled by the knife of gossip—the girl's body was as lithe as that of a young roe. Her breasts, the crone said, brought to mind exquisite goblets blown at Murano, and her thighs were so firm that when she ran it looked as if she could bound effortlessly six feet into the air. At nineteen she ran away from home—an escapade still a mystery to all who know her. It is not clear whether she was chasing a man on those strong legs with the intention of spreading them. She was back, at any rate, in three weeks.

When she was about twenty or twenty-one, she had a reputation of dressing up whatever she said; some had the opinion that she was a rudderless liar, that she couldn't help herself; one person said he had caught her changing a lie (which he had previously heard her tell) right in the midst of it. Her mind, in other words, was a grasshopper.

Perhaps because her dowry was meager, she was not married until she was twenty-four, at which age most women give up and take holy vows and are never seen again. Her husband, Vittorio Zambelli, a decade older than she, was a nondescript clerk, working in the household of a marquis. She kept a tight grip on him by slavish attention to his wants and, as if by coincidence, got from him whatever *she* wanted—a blissful marriage, it seemed to outsiders, though the old aunt says she made eyes at every man who came in the house. Zambelli died last June, of pellagra followed by consumption.

People all say that Antonia Maria Zambelli has an empty head. That she has a gait like a harlot's. That she is eager to agree with whatever is said. That she cries when criticized. That if you ask her a question, she stops and thinks and then, very often, says nothing.

Agnesi concludes, eager to find out what is behind all this: —So you see, Antonio, this is a shallow, negligible, weak woman. If there is trouble from her, there should be no difficulty in taking care of it. I would be glad to help. Just say the word.

Stradivari:—How much do I owe you?

Agnesi:—Please! Do not insult your old friend. It has been a pleasure.

Stradivari:—You paid a ducat to the priest.

Agnesi:—Are you trying to put a price on friendship? [*One last try*:] Let me know if I can help.

But Stradivari is already on his way downstairs.

He returns to the shop with shining eyes. At his bench he picks up the belly and goes back to work on it. He starts to hum—the same melody as before, with that same popping of the lips on staccato notes. Omobono throws a significant look at Francesco, who shrugs. Then, as he resumes tuning the belly plate, he stops the humming, and the sons hear him sounding the notes of the chromatic scale he is working up, but not through his nose as usual—this time tripped off his tongue: ta-ta-*ta!* ta-ta-*ta!* The scale runs in this case from G-sharp to G-sharp, and the plate, when he finishes it toward evening, yields a fundamental pitch of E—exactly one whole tone lower than that of the back.

This difference of pitch is by no means an error. For over a century before this, violinmakers have somehow intuited—one of their many miracles of intuition—that a difference in pitch between belly and back would help to yield a generous bundle of harmonic overtones: the eerie, echo-like bouquet of sympathetic vibrations that gives any musical note its true richness. The Amatis settled on exactly one whole tone as the interval that yields the most abundant harvest of these harmonics, and Stradivari follows their lead—although, thanks to his vision in the night, the zones yielding the notes of the scales on his plates are slightly different this time, for the first time, from theirs. These new zones, he feels sure, will make for new tones.

At the light evening meal—fish and bread—he is in a tumult of good will. Never in their lives have the sons seen him drunk, but this night Omobono wonders, Has the old man been tippling at a wine bottle?

In his early thirties his name became known wherever music was played, not only in the principalities of Italy but also abroad. For a few years he decorated some of his instruments with inlays as twined as the tendrils of grapevines, which dilettante noblemen were proud to show off to guests as the filigreed violins were sawed at by their court musicians. Serious virtuosos praised the quality of sound his other violins gave out. Orders poured in.

This was when he began to accumulate—and to love—money. And here for the first time was established at least one kind of reciprocity of love with his wife, for Francesca loved money even more than he did, and with a more active heart. That is to say, he was satisfied to have it stored away to grow, like mushrooms in a damp box in a cellar; she wanted to use it —to eat the delicious mushrooms!

When Omobono, the fifth surviving child, was born, Francesca began to clamor for a larger house. Nine human beings— seven in the family, and two servants—were all over each other in the tight little Casa del Pescatore, which she had always said smelled of stale sex because of gurry that must have been strewn around by its ancient fishermen owners. The next year, the wife of one of the violinmaking Guarneris told Francesca about an ideal house belonging to a Picenardi family, at No. 2 Piazza San Domenico. It was a bit narrow, but it had three floors and an attic, with space for a shop for the maestro on the ground floor, and with a *seccadour* on the roof—perfect! Soon Stradivari, pale as a wounded man losing spates of blood, made a down payment of two thousand lire imperiali, and promised with gritted teeth to add within four years five thousand more, less ten lire excused by Picenardi because Stradivari agreed to pay the canons of the cathedral the annual tithe on the owed sum: six imperial soldi.

Two years later, when the banker Michele Monzi of Venice ordered a quartet of instruments, ornamented with inlays, for King James II of England, for one hundred ducats, Francesca, without telling her husband in advance, ordered a vast Spanish bed for her own room, with satin draperies arranged over it like a Moroccan nomad's tent.

Two years after that, when the Grand Duke of Florence bought a number of instruments, she *had* to have a farthingale from Barcelona, glistening with a design in silver thread, and she also hired a second chambermaid, to be her personal servant.

The following year, when Cardinal Orsini, Archbishop of Benevento, ordered three instruments, she went wild over two enormously expensive ivory-sticked fans made in Trieste, one with a scene, painted on silk, of naked maidens and clothed youths picnicking in a glade, the other with four panels depicting delightfully wicked assignations.

Later that same year, when Victor Amadeus II, Duke of Savoy and King of Sardinia, bought an instrument for thirty golden pistoles, she purchased a dress with an oval neckline *alla francese*, and with oversleeves cut short to allow for elegant puffs at the wrists.

The year after that, when the Marquis Michele Rodeschini and the Marquis Nicola Rota both bought instruments, she spent a great deal on a dress with a neckline decorated with Milanese lace, and with a *marsina*, a slit cover-skirt that gave glimpses of gorgeous laced petticoats.

And the next year after *that*, when the King of Spain ordered a quartet of instruments, she went too far—bought a dress in a new French style, with a stiff bodice down to the waist embroidered with gold thread, which cost half the entire amount the Spanish King's violins had brought.

Each time Stradivari was presented with a bill for one of his wife's extravagances, previously unannounced to him, he threatened to kill her, and she took to her bed for a week.

He is cutting the *f*-holes in the belly with a small wood-handled knife. This work is his greatest pleasure. These beautiful swooping gashes, from which sound will one day pour, take on the marks of his personality, as true to him as a signature. Today, however, he is restless. Suddenly he puts the knife and the belly plate down, gets up from his bench, and rushes out of the house with a look on his face that seems to Omobono to be one of terror, as if he were being pursued by a werewolf.

He hurries across town to the neighborhood of the Palazzo Fodri, where, after a somewhat confused search, he finds the house in which Signore l'Avvocato Benedetto Zucchi carries on his business. Admitted at once to the inner room, the wild-eyed figure in his white apron blurts out to the attorney his commission: to approach the family of the widow Antonia Maria Zambelli, of San Sigismondo parish, and open negotiations for a marriage contract.

After this for several days he is calm. Both Feliciana and Marisa remark on his unusual sweetness to them. At work he is patient and steady. He is gentle with his sons and Bergonzi. He cuts the graceful neck from the same maple slab that he chose for the back; it almost seems that the violin will come to life in the form of a swan. Next he shapes the wedge of the fingerboard and veneers it with thin pieces of ebony, perfectly mitred at the corners.

And now comes the only part of the violin that will contribute nothing to its sound but will make its appeal to the eye alone: the head on the end of that neck. If a violin is to be a work of art, it must have sensual bouts, a stunning back, perfect purfling, and, above all, a head with an exactly symmetrical scroll that dares to challenge God's ingenuity in having designed all curving things: the snail's helix, the whorls of a fingertip, the poised lips of breaking waves, the glowing swirls at the shoulders of thunderheads in summertime—and, more to the point, the delicate convolutions of all the human ears that will listen, one day, to the finished violin's song.

He rough-cuts the form of the head, and with a newly drawn template to guide him, uses a needle-like awl to prick into each side of the wood the spiral curves he means to carve. In the next two days of this work, he constantly hums, and it seems as if he is trying to cut the sound of the notes in his throat into the wood. The scroll, when he is done with it, is a melody by young Vivaldi.

In Cremona they were beginning to say:—As rich as Stradivari. Francesca was putting on airs. One night, after she had surrendered with unaccustomed passivity to her husband's exercise of his rights, she said, as he got up to leave:—I want a *cicisbeo.* I want to hire a manservant.

She expected a terrible quarrel. Instead, Antonio simply said:—To wait on *you?*

She said:—I need a trained *cavalier servente.* Advice about what to wear. I feel unsure of my taste. You never go out in the evening. I need to go to concerts, the theater. I need an escort. We get scores of invitations. And you—nothing but work, work! We never stir out of the house. I'm being stifled. *All* the women have lady's men.

—All the women? What are you talking about?

She broke into tears and began to cough and to beg and to sniffle, and in disgust he said he cared nothing about her or what she did. He left her to go to his room.

She took his indifference as permission, and two days later she went by coach to Milan. There she called on wealthy women friends and asked their advice about finding a manservant. On her third visit, she struck gold. Yes! A splendid man, belonging until recently to the Marquesa Maria Gaetana Pannini, who had suddenly died of cholera, just three days ago, at the age of thirty-one. The man had impeccable training, a spotless record. Rather expensive, though.

Signora Stradivari:—With my husband, money is not a question!

And the very next day the man answered a summons to the inn where she was staying, and the day after that he rode with her in the coach back to Cremona.

When she told her husband what the man's wages would be, she thought he must not have heard what she said. He merely shrugged.

Her *cicisbeo*'s name was Giovannini. He was five years younger than she. With his hooked nose and his high forehead (some would have called this baldness), his frizzled sideburns and his pigtail hanging down behind to his waist, his neck in a choker with lace from Torino, his frock coat with embroidered borders hanging free, his right arm cocked with the back of his hand to his hip, his left hand raised with the thumb and forefinger making a circle, his long muscular calves snug in silk stockings with clocks at the ankles, and his feet in pointed shoes with toes angled outward—he was elegant from scalp to sole!

And how much he knew! He was with her all day long, from the moment she woke up to the time of her last yawn before retiring. He was a shadow—tactful, discreet, alert to her every need. Appearing in her bedroom every morning to advise her about what to wear and how to dress her hair, he firmly guided her toward what was impeccably French—no longer Spanish!—and up-to-the-minute. Going to and from mass with her, he explained doctrines of the church she had never understood. On one of their walks together in the city, he took her to the church of Santa Margherita and opened her eyes to the frescoes of Giulio Campi. He taught her to play piquet and basset and faro with elegant cards he produced, decorated with gnomes and unicorns, and tactfully he lost to her every time. He could dance a minuet as lightly as the winged seed of a dandelion on June air. He read her the fables of La Fontaine, and recited at length, from memory, frisky verses by Francesco Redi and patriotic sonnets by Vincenzo da Filicaia. At a *commedia dell'arte* he whispered in her ear what Harlequin was going to say in an improvisation before the actor even opened his mouth. He hummed, falsetto, themes of Corelli.

There was nothing he did not know or could not do. In his company she had not an instant of boredom.

Stradivari was delighted. His wife no longer whined, and she suddenly seemed to have been cured of every "illness."

Now—most rewarding of tasks—he glues up the body of the instrument. The violin at last begins to take shape. First he fastens the back to the sides, then he glues the belly on—very lightly, because he is going to have to remove it when he attaches the neck. He makes both plates fast to the sides by driving tiny pegs through them into the end blocks, precisely centered.

When the glue has set, he is ready for a task more exacting than any he has yet performed: the insertion of the purfling, the narrow lines of inlay just inside the rims of the belly and back. These will give those rims exquisite accents—and more, for by reinforcing the fibers of the grain all round they will protect the thin outer edges of the violin from splintering. The first step is to use a gauge to mark a line seven thirty-seconds of an inch from the edges; then another line five thirty-seconds in. At the corners, above and below each C-curve, he stops using the gauge and works freehand, making the points aim not at the exact center of the corners but swooping them inward, in a loving embrace of the shape of the C.

With his powerful right hand he next wields a razor-thin knife to make shallow cuts exactly along the marked lines. The joy of his heart lies in the precision of his hand. He works steadily, without a sound now, leaning intently forward. When the pairs of lines are finished on both plates, he begins to pick out the wood from between them with a purfling chisel, making channels one-sixteenth of an inch wide and one-twelfth of an inch deep. His concentration is as hot and tight as a beam of sunlight focused through a magnifying glass.

There are sounds of a knocking at the front door, and of Marisa the maidservant answering. Stradivari holds the chisel in midair, waiting for silence. Instead, Marisa comes to the threshold of the shop and says:—A letter for the maestro.

Stradivari, annoyed by the interruption, resumes cutting the purfling channel and says:—Read it to me, Francesco.

Francesco takes the letter from Marisa, opens it, and pauses. Then, to his father:—It is very short. It is from your attorney. It says, I have bad news for you. Shall I come to you, or will you come to me? It is signed "Avvocato Zucchi."

When he heard the first sentence, the father jumped as if hit from behind, and now a groan comes from his chest as from a tomb. He sets the box of the violin down and raises his hands in a tragic gesture, signifying, God in Heaven, see what you have done to me now! He flings out of the room and out of the house.

The sons go to the bench to see what has happened. It is clear that the chisel slipped; there is a nasty nick at one side of the channel. There will forever be a legendary flaw in this violin.

Avvocato Zucchi is expansive, almost jovial. He says:—There are other suitors. Four in number. The Zambellis want to know why their Antonia Maria should marry an old man. You must understand, this is a widow, who has a mind of her own. This is not a virgin. The suitors have been active. She knows them. She prefers the one who is a notary, he is a giant, he could lift you up with one hand, Stradivari. The parents prefer the one who is a docent of philosophy, used to be a priest. I have seen him, he is as ugly as a goat's hind leg. Nevertheless, he is preferred. They do not know you, Stradivari; they said I had come to them like a fork of lightning, unexpected and unwelcome. They spoke of your wife's scandal, seeming to think it was your fault. Why should their daughter be put at risk to a husband who, after all, must have had something to do with his first wife's loins catching fire? I praised you to the skies. They shook their heads. And they said, Antonia's year of mourning is not over yet—what is his hurry? [*Leans forward and whispers:*] *Senti!* It is possible that my saying that she "knows" the suitors was an understatement. [*Aloud again*:] Do you follow my drift? All four! That's what I heard. I realize one should not slander a poor widow. However. You should think it over, Maestro. Is this woman worthy of you?

Stradivari:—How much do I owe you?

Zucchi:—Four ducats.

Stradivari, over his shoulder as he goes out the door:—You thief, you will be paid.

. . .

When he reappears in the shop, he looks a hundred years old. He sits at the bench, staring at the nick on the white box of the new violin for a long time; then with a sigh he goes back to work on the rest of the purfling channel. Having finished that, he starts trimming fine small strips of maple, two stained black and one still white, down to unbelievably tender yet perfect little whiskers of wood, uniformly one forty-eighth of an inch thick and one-twelfth of an inch wide, to be sandwiched, black-white-black, into the purfling channels. His hand trembles. He cries out, leans back, picks up the body of the violin and raises it above his knee, and Francesco, looking across at his father from his own bench, has a terrified moment of thinking that he is going to smash the box into a thousand slivers on his own thigh. Francesco dares not speak.

But Omobono says:—Is there something I can help you with?

At this the father abruptly puts the box down and once again rushes headlong out of the house. The brothers look at each other like men who have lost their way in a forest.

He is at the banker Agnesi's rooms. Never having been taught properly how to write—he has a scraggly hand and spells poorly—Stradivari has for years had a discreet arrangement with his old friend Apostolo Agnesi to write all letters for him having to do with his sales of violins. He has long since overcome all embarrassment about telling Agnesi what he wants to say and watching him put it all down, and this time, though somewhat winded from his haste in the streets, he seems as calm and businesslike as ever. Agnesi is thrown into an ecstasy of ribald guessing by what the maestro dictates. He writes:

> *Antonia Maria Zambelli, come to my shop at 2 Piazza San Domenico. I have something I want to show you.*
>
> *I remain respectfully and cordially your servant,*
>
> *Antonio Stradivari*

Back in the shop he spends the afternoon gluing in the filaments of purfling with a steady hand.

Omobono later asks Francesco if he noticed that the old man had not bothered to glue a tiny patch of pine into the nick he had made.

Omobono:—I saw him smiling this afternoon when he looked at his mistake.

In the next four days, the sons see that their father will work for a time, then stand up and pace back and forth, then return to his bench. Sometimes he walks all the way to the street door and back. The work he does is no less careful than usual. With a leaf-thin knife he removes the belly and attaches the neck to the body, getting it exactly centered by lining up the fluting of the head with the two peg holes in the middle of the upper and lower blocks. He anchors it with three nails driven into it through the upper block, and glues the belly back on, for good.

Using a spare piece of the maple left over from the wedges for the back, he cuts a bridge. He spends an entire day on this intricate sliver of hardwood, so vital to the sound the violin will give out, for it will plant its two slender bare feet on the smooth skin of the belly of the violin, the left foot directly over the bass bar, the right foot over the sound post, and it will act as courier of the strings' tremblings to the great sound box below. This time, after he has cut the arms and legs with their graceful swirls, he incises, in the body of it, low in the center and upside down, a hollow heart.

Next he slips the little dowel of the sound post through the right-hand *f*-hole, using a spiked setting tool to hold it, and tries it out. It needs a bit trimmed off one end. He is infinitely careful, because this tiny part will be the very soul of the violin. Its duty will be to tell the resonant back the entire truth that has been confided to the sensitive belly by the bridge. He wedges it in place.

The third day he is more agitated than ever. He cuts from a piece of ebony the tuning pegs the strings will be wound around at the head, and then shapes the tapering tailpiece that they will be fastened to at the lower end. In midmorning, during one of his restless pacings, he suddenly goes to a chest in a corner of the room and, kneeling on the floor, rummages for a long time in a disorderly jumble of old designs and sketches stored there. He is singing quietly, the lilting adagio melody of a slow dance neither of the sons recognizes.

At last he exclaims:—*Ecco!* He takes out of the box a sheet of sketches he made nine years ago, when he wanted to inlay the coat of arms of Cosimo di Medici into the fingerboards of a set of instruments the Prince of Tuscany had ordered. On this sheet, besides outlines of the escutcheon and armorial bearings, are small drawings of three naked Cupids, wings spread, baby-fat legs uplifted, bows and arrows aimed at who knows what adored ones? He traces the smallest of these onto the new tail-piece, and on the fourth day he gives the little figure a sparkling life in mother-of-pearl. The Cupid seems lighter than air, as if floating on the zephyrs of the stately dance tune Stradivari has kept sounding.

Francesco, to Omobono when they are alone:—*Dio mio!* The tune he was humming! I remember now! Do you know the score that was sent us from Rome last week? Those variations by Arc-angelo Corelli? I haven't played them, but I read the score. He must have, too. The tune is the beginning of a *follia*—the Spanish dance of madness!

Omobono:—I told you. He is out of his mind.

Giovannini lent a hand as Marisa dressed the mistress in the morning, closing his eyes as the maid slipped off the peignoir. Sometimes a move was made before he had time to close them; sometimes he opened them too soon. The mistress lowered her gaze modestly to the floor.

A velvet skirt seemed too heavy for Marisa. He lifted it over the mistress's head and let it gently down around her.

One morning he said:—That amber brooch on your breast is crooked. Let me fix it.

Another day:—That ribbon makes your décolletage too . . . too forbidding. Here, I'll adjust it.

Once:—Your bust should be raised. Marisa, loosen the cords in back for a moment and I'll lift a little.

There came a time when the mistress herself offered a gambit—said her right shoe hurt her. Giovannini knelt, took her foot up on his other raised knee, removed the shoe, massaged the sole and the arch and the ankle and some of the calf, and then replaced the shoe. Ah! Much better!

Then:—Marisa! You pinch my thigh when you fasten my garter! Let Giovannini do it.

And, once when fully dressed:—My underclothing feels all bunched. Marisa, lift my skirt. No, the petticoats, too, you silly! On the sides, Giovannini. . . . Now in front. A little more. Thank you, thank you, just right.

In the month of August, Stradivari began to notice that his wife was putting up much less resistance than usual to his exercise of his rights. One night he asked himself, Could that have been acting? Certainly not pleasure! Impossible! In September he began to call on her more frequently. He looked forward to creeping into the Moroccan tent. He was extremely puzzled and rather testy with his sons. And he made such a poor violin that he actually had to destroy it.

Meanwhile, Giovannini in public was a model of discretion —cool, distant, civil, courteous. But when the mistress and he were alone, there were squeezes of the hand, thirsty looks, sighs, moist palms, licked lips, more sighs, and finally, one afternoon, a kiss. That touch of lip to lip was the ruin of Francesca Feraboschi Stradivari. The flame had reached the straw.

She became a wanton. She took her *cicisbeo* to bed with her morning, noon, and night. Marisa the chambermaid whispered to Feliciana the cook. Before long the marketplace buzzed with rumors. Sh-h-h! Did you hear? Maestro Stradivari is a *cornuto*.

Within a month poor Giovannini was worn out; he looked like the leavings of a slaughterhouse. He resigned to save his life. Francesca took to the streets. Twice she had dizzying successes. The third man she invited to her bedroom turned out to be a young, newly appointed magistrate—a sparkling blond youth but, alas, a man of honor. The scandal broke. Francesca was laid up on her bed for the rest of her life.

On the fifth day after dictating the letter, Stradivari strings up the violin, all finished in the white. Once again the sons shake their heads. What is this? Is he going to play it unvarnished? He *never* puts strings on an instrument before it is varnished. He sets it aside on his bench and asks Francesco to bring him the belly plate his son has been working on; he sounds it with his knuckle and begins to scrape at it. Francesco finds other work to do.

Two hours later there are noises in the hallway, and Marisa soon comes to the shop door to say there is a woman to see the maestro.

And behold: that woman brushes past Marisa and walks brazenly right into the shop. Francesco and Omobono, expecting the so often promised murder of any woman who trespasses in the sanctum, both gasp.

The woman must think they have drawn in their breath at her beauty, for she flashes each of them a grateful look, and she blushes. Her face might well have been the reason why they gasped. The only time they have seen her was from above, that morning when she crossed the square. The level look is far more stunning. It is not that her features are perfect; her cheeks swell out oddly, her eyebrows are thick. But there is a lovely heat of complacency within, which makes her skin look as warm and soft as rose petals at noon. She is still wearing the black dress and the tasseled shawl. All that black lends power to the radiance of her face.

The sons see that the father has stood up and is swallowing —seems to be drinking the woman's beauty. And how handsome *he* suddenly is! Omobono finds himself furious. Francesco is pale.

—I am Antonio.

He is talking to the little tassels on the shawl, Omobono thinks, telling them that, yes, they pronounced his name correctly when they were waving at him from down in the piazza that morning. *Quale follia!*

—You were going to show me something.

He reaches out his left hand and says:—Come.

To Omobono's mind, the father is nauseatingly suave. She puts her hand in his, and he draws her toward the bench.

He places the violin on its side on the bench, and he says: —This.

She gives a little negative squeal, as if she has seen a grub on a tomato plant, and says:—It is all white. Beh, a white violin.

He says:—Don't worry, it will be varnished.

She begins a question:—Why did you want me to see—

He says:—I am naming this violin for you. Your name is Antonia?

She nods, both to answer his question and as if she half-expected all along that he was going to say what he had said—that he was naming the white violin for her. Omobono sees pleasure already infused into the puzzlement in the woman's eyes.

The father says:—The violin's name is Antonietta. In your honor.

She pouts, says:—You have never even seen me.

—But I have.

And he tells her about that morning—the sound of the clogs, the early sunlight, her face seen from the loggia as if from a balcony in a theater. He says he started making the violin that very morning, he has been thinking of her in every moment of its making. He does not mention the tassels. Omobono grunts out loud with disgust.

The father points at the Cupid on the tailpiece. The woman laughs—a thin little giggle.

The father says:—*Guarda*, I want you to see something.

He turns the violin up and points at the nick beside the purfling.

He says:—A slip of my hand. My hand never slips. Do you know why my hand slipped?

She shakes her head, she does not know.

—I did it in the moment when I learned that your family would not give me a marriage contract.

Omobono intently watches a series of expressions chase each other across the woman's face. The one that rests there finally is a look of incredulity.

—To marry *me*?

All the father says is:—My hand never slips. I am going to leave the little gash there. I am not going to patch it. It, too, is in your honor, Antonia.

She looks thoroughly vexed. Omobono's heart jumps for joy. She says, pettishly, as if she has been insulted:—I must leave.

And she does, in a huff and a flurry. However, the tassels at her back wave a sweet goodbye to all three men.

Stradivari is alone, up in the loggia. It is a brilliant, sunny June day. He has taken the strings off the violin, and has removed the pegs and the tailpiece, along with the button at the bottom that held the tailpiece in place. He is ready to start varnishing his Antonietta.

He is alone up here with his secrets. Among all the elements that contribute to the tone of a violin, he has long known that varnish is one of the most crucial. One cannot imagine that the tone of voice of a coloratura soprano will be affected by the costume she wears, but with Antonietta this will surely be the case. If the varnish is too thick or too hard, the tone will be metallic, shrieking, or, beyond a certain point, quite dead. Too soft, it will be muted, feathery, and thin. Somehow over the years he has found his way to varnish that gives his violins a sweet brilliance no other maker has been able to match. His secret is not in the materials; every Cremona *liutaio* knows what he must use. The secret is in the mix of the ingredients and the exact mode of laying it on. He has written down what he knows just once —on the flyleaf of a Bible that he hides in a place that only Francesco has earned the trust to know of.

He seems at ease. His sons were astonished yesterday to see that he was not at all distressed by the widow Zambelli's abrupt departure. He settled back at his bench and went on scraping at the belly that Francesco had roughed, giving a new lilt to the Corelli dance of the crazed as he hummed it. Omobono sulked all afternoon.

Measuring the ingredients with care, he now mixes a thin varnish of turpentine, oil of lavender, and, to give a yellowish tint, gamboge dissolved in linseed oil. (When she was constipated, which was often, Francesca used to get Francesco to steal from her husband's storeroom small amounts of gamboge in its powdered form; it stormed through her abdomen like a blissful tornado.) He inserts a round shaft into the hole for the tailpiece button as a handle to hold the violin up with, and, using an elegant half-inch camel's-hair brush, he lays onto every part a very thin layer of this morning's mix. Every brushstroke is tender, gentle, loving. The varnish soaks into the grain.

He lets the base coat dry for twenty-four hours. He dresses the violin in four more layers of these filmy underclothes on four successive days. By the fifth day of varnishing he is showing signs of impatience, like that of a man who has been owed money for too long and is beginning to wonder if he will ever be paid.

This morning he mixes a new varnish, using the same oils

as before but adding for color, this time, the resinous red of "dragon's blood," derived from the fruit of a rattan palm from faraway Malaya—a coloring first brought from Asia by Marco Polo, and now rarely supplied by merchants sailing across the Indian Ocean and all the way around Africa; Stradivari found a precious supply of it, years ago, in Venice. He heats the oils a bit and mixes this varnish lukewarm. When it is ready, he applies a thin, thin coat. Now, for the first time, the waves of the back begin to seem to move as he turns the violin.

The great bulk of Avvocato Zucchi suddenly appears on the loggia. The man is frowning like a self-important archbishop.

Zucchi:—You called me a thief.

Stradivari stares at him. What can he say?

Zucchi has papers in his hand. He waves them in the maestro's face.

—Here is your damnable marriage contract.

Stradivari gapes a moment, then rushes forward and throws his arms around Zucchi's neck, all the time holding the wet violin upright in his left hand by the shaft in the tailpiece buttonhole.

Zucchi, canting his head backward in distaste, pushes him away.

Stradivari:—How did it happen?

Zucchi, still displeased:—You would not believe her behavior. She told her family she would kill herself if they did not approve her marrying you. She says she came away from your shop in a trance. She says you were the handsomest man she had ever seen. She says you gave her the most precious gift she had ever had from a man. Tell me, you slanderer, what did you give her?

Stradivari is suddenly in command of himself, and, with a shrug that is like a swagger, he lifts the violin high, as if it were a flaming torch, and says:—I gave her my admiration.

Zucchi holds his nose and says:—*Che merda!*

Stradivari, suddenly cautious:—Is it a decent contract?

Zucchi:—No dowry. What is more, the parents want you to pay them what they call a consolation fee.

Stradivari:—How much? . . . Never mind, I will pay.

Zucchi:—Also, I am obliged to charge you an additional sum of four more ducats.

Stradivari, stumbling over himself in a precipitate lapse of his stinginess:—Wait. Let me hang this violin up. I will come down with you and pay you now.

Zucchi, quickly thawed:—Congratulations, dear Maestro!

Four more thin coats of the reddish varnish and the violin is finished—though the coats must slowly cure, up there in the *seccadour*, for several weeks of benign summer weather. And how exquisite it is as he hangs it up there on this final day!

Under the glistening finish, the maple of the back and sides has a bold, broad curl so fluid that its waves seem to roll, subtly, adagio, in the shifting lights of June. On the back these waves slant upward from the joint at the middle, as if in jubilation. The corners are clean, the purfling sharp in its statement of them. The belly pine has a generous grain, and the *f*-holes are superbly definite, a little more upright than in the "long" violins. He is not entirely pleased with the head, which seems a bit chunky to him; he had envisioned something more feminine. But on the whole, he feels, in his joy, that the violin has a beauty worthy of its namegiver, who on this very day sheds the black of a mourner and appears in the streets in a dress of many folds which shimmer, by chance, with almost exactly the same transparent yellowy red of Antonietta's new clothing, which Antonia has not seen. What a good omen!

Stradivari spends the next days making a rectangular wooden case for the violin, with a recessed space inside exactly the shape of

Antonietta, lined with velvet taken from one of Francesca's expensive French skirts still hanging upstairs. He makes padded clips in the top to hold two bows. He decorates the outside with ornate patterns of roundheaded brass nails.

The wedding is set for mid-July. On Sunday, June 21, the priest of San Sigismondo posts at the church door a notice:

> *I, the Reverend Father Bartolomeo Grassi, Parish Priest of the Collegiate and renowned church of San Sigismondo in Cremona, announce the intention of Antonio Stradivari, of the parish of Santa Cecilia, to contract a marriage with Antonia Maria Zambelli, of this parish. If there are persons who know of impediments of any kind to this alliance, let them come forward.*

On two other holy days, the feast day of St. Peter, on June 29, and Sunday, July 5, these banns are further published.

No one objects, though there are hot gusts of reminiscence in the town about the first wife's rutting in the streets, and much talk of the age difference between the partners—what pleasures will a June bride have with a November groom? Omobono would like to object, but he cannot think of any grounds other than a burning envy.

Ten days before the wedding date, Stradivari takes down the violin, fits it with strings, and plays on it. He also gets Francesco, who is a better violinist than he, to play for him. When he has heard Antonietta's tone, he informs his fiancée that the wedding will have to be postponed until the middle of August. He explains that this instrument named for her must be played at the church that day, and unfortunately it needs time to mature. The tone at present is adolescent—moody and cranky, rather mushy and inarticulate—because the varnish is still too soft. It must have more time to dry. He says that you cannot rush an instrument, you have to give it time to grow up. One must be patient.

Antonia makes the face of someone who seems not quite to have grown up herself, but she agrees to wait until Monday, August 17.

On August 12, Stradivari plays on Antonietta again, and again has Francesco play. Having heard the violin's tone in his shop, he grows agitated and says that they must go to the cathedral. There he stations his son at the center of the choir and then walks to the very end of the nave, where he stands by the font of holy water.

He calls out:—Play!

Francesco launches into the Vivaldi melody that his father has hummed at work.

What Stradivari now hears causes a puckering of his skin, starting in the roots of his hair and working downward on his spine and along his arms to the backs of his hands and the tips of his fingers. Yes! Yes! This sound is *almost* what he imagined on that sleepless night so long ago. The tone is a harvest of hints of the best of all the tones of the past. It has the brilliance of the Maggini violins from Brescia; the sweet, woody, soprano Amati tone; the rounder, more throaty sonority and power of his own "long" violins; and something beyond, something new, powerful, bell-like. Pianissimo whispers are as clear at this distance as forced notes. But there is also something mysterious in these sounds that he cannot name. The edge of the timbre tugs at his heart, fills him with yearning. He has a sudden fantasy of placing a muscular palm on Antonia's hot cheek. He feels his maleness stirring. Tears come to his eyes.

These tears, this hint of lechery, make him furious. He shouts to Francesco:—Enough!

Francesco comes down the nave excited. He calls out as he comes:—It is so easy to play! Did you hear what I could do? By

using the bow in different ways, closer to the bridge and farther away, pressing and then letting its weight do the work? I drew out flute, and horn, and oboe, and clarinet—and a soprano's voice! I found out something, too, Father. You must not attack Antonietta with the bow, you have to be gentle, even playing fortissimo. If you are kindly, the strings vibrate on after you have lifted the bow.

The father, gruffly:—I think the cheeks of the arching must be a little too high. A little too much Amati in the tone. Too sweet.

Francesco:—It is a joy to play.

So many want to come to the wedding that it has to be moved from the church of San Sigismondo to the cathedral. Gossip has fueled a steamy curiosity. The groom is twenty years older than the bride. Will he wear to the wedding the horns that his first wife gave him? Is the bride fated to be involved in a scandal? Is it true, as some say, that she has scattered her favors, like soldi thrown to beggars, among numerous suitors who had not the decency to wait for her to get out of the black? The guests arrive in a merry and mischievous frame of mind, which the soft, warm afternoon intensifies.

By four o'clock the place is packed. Many priests bustle about. The groom stands waiting.

Here comes the bride up the nave! Through her veil, when she kneels beside him before Father Grassi, Stradivari sees lips that could not be more different from those of the earlier time. These seem tender small fruits of the tree of temptation. The mesh of the veil might catch fire from the beams of the flashing eyes!

Father Grassi, a fat and jolly priest, thrilled to be booming in the cathedral, sheds on the words of holy matrimony a lilting, frisky gloss that is on the edge of the suggestive—on the edge, some said later, of the lascivious. This shocks a few wedding guests but titillates the many others who came to the wedding with senses peeled by gossip. Man and wife are soon made one. They stand. Altar boys bring them chairs to sit on.

Now Francesco in the choir beyond the altar plays on Antonietta, the instrument named for the bride with the little dewy Cupid on its tailpiece, Corelli's "*Follia*" variations.* He is accompanied by one of the Guarneri sons on the contrabass.

First comes the stately theme, adagio, that the maestro has been humming over his work:

The first of the variations follows, allegro. The music gradually casts a spell. All rustling and coughing stops. The variations grow sweeter and sweeter, more and more intricate, faster and faster. The guests imagine the stamping feet and whirling skirts of dancers of the *follia*. Flirtations in sound drench the listeners, who are already half drunk on the emotions of a wedding and on the beauty of the veiled bride that they glimpsed as she walked down the aisle, swinging her hips in exultation beneath the train held up by adorable nieces. They begin to hear from the violin the trills of something like seduction. It seems to all but three stone-deaf people in the crowd that the music has started to soar on the wings of the madness of love. *Amor alla follia!* There is a hint of scandal in the air. The voice of the violin is overpoweringly sensual as it sings a dance of desire. Its racing tones seem to ask the bride and groom: What are you waiting for? Hurry! Hurry home! The goal and reward of a wedding wait in bed for you there!

---

*Opus 5, No. 12.

The effect on the crowd in the cathedral is startling. Antonietta is a hypnotist. Arrows from her Cupid's quiver shower into the packed nave. The entire assemblage—excepting the three deaf-mutes—is aroused by the message of the voluptuous strains from the glistening instrument. After the bride, unveiled now in all her dazzling ripeness, rushes incontinently down the aisle hauling her catch by the hand almost at a run, the wedding guests themselves go home in haste, inflamed, the men tumescent, the women moist.

Riots of pleasure in the beds of Cremona ensue, lasting until the small hours of the morning. Wounded marriages are healed in delight. Babies are conceived. Virgins bribe their duennas to let them meet lovers in alleyways. Priests doff their habits and vows and share with each other ecstasies of the forbidden. Closer to home, Omobono hires the simulated passion of a dark-eyed *puttana*, and shy Francesco, alone and naked as a baby up on the loggia, plays a divine solo on his beloved organ.

As for Maestro Antonio Stradivari, he tears down the tenting over the great bed and, with his blushing bride finally in his arms upon it, plumbs in himself hitherto unimagined wells of patience, unselfishness, and masculine gentleness. His sensitive fingertips drink from the tingling wifely skin messages of insatiability. He rises avidly to each new carnal dare of hers, and at last, as the moment of true espousal comes closer and closer, Antonia Maria Stradivari, formerly Zambelli, emits repeated cries in tones almost as musical, as sweet, and as abandoned as those uttered in the church that afternoon by her amazing namesake, Antonietta.

Intermezzo One

After his marriage to Antonia, Stradivari entered what has come to be called his "golden period." In two ensuing decades he produced violins that were greater than Antonietta, violins close to realizing the vision of a perfect instrument that he had had during that restless night after he first saw Antonia walk across the square. Indeed, in those years of his connubial bliss he turned out some of the greatest violins ever made, among them the ones that were eventually named the "Betts," the "Alard," the "Messiah." Those marvels he sold, but he would never sell Antonietta as long as he lived.

When Antonietta was three years old, the War of the Spanish Succession between France and Austria reached its long arm to Cremona as the Austrian Prince Eugene drove to the outskirts of the city and surprised the French garrison, capturing Louis XIV's arrogant commanding general, the Duke de Villeroi. Antonietta, hanging in the storeroom on the second floor of Stradivari's house, was safe through it all. Over the years the maestro took the instrument out, from time to time, and played it for Antonia's pleasure and his own, and its music never failed to excite them both. Antonia bore him five children, each of them conceived, we can guess, with the sweet, seductive tones and overtones of Antonietta still echoing on the bedroom walls. Four children survived; the first of two sons named Giuseppe died at eight months of age.

Stradivari lived to be ninety-three, and with the help of Francesco and Omobono, he built violins to the very end. Early in that final year of her husband's ripe age, Antonia died, and he, still yearning for her company, followed within months. Stradivari and Antonia were buried side by side in a crypt in the Chapel of the Rosary, in the third bay on the right as one entered the church of San Domenico, across the street from the rooms where the voice of Antonietta had so often been heard, singing of the longing, the obsessive itch, and the fevers of the heart that had gone into the instrument's shaping.

In Stradivari's long lifetime he had made altogether some one thousand violins, and when he died there were ninety-one of them, including Antonietta, still unsold in the storeroom.

Thirty years after the maestro's death, a French violinist named Pierre-Nicolas Lahoussaye happened to join the procession of violinmakers, dealers, and performers that was still trooping through the *liutaio*'s old shop. Lahoussaye had spent some fifteen years in Italy, having studied under the great Tartini and having been patronized by the Count of Clermont and the Prince of Monaco, among others; he was about to leave the country for an engagement with the orchestra of the Italian Opera in London. At that time Stradivari's and Antonia's youngest son, Paolo, who had become a cloth merchant, was living in the house and was selling off the remaining violins.

At thirty-three Lahoussaye was still unmarried and was known as something of a rake, compensating for his small stature in his many flirtations, with elegant manners, foppish clothes, and a certain amount of bluster. He tried his hand at eight violins in the Stradivari house that day. The ninth he took up was Antonietta. He noticed the Cupid on the tailpiece but said nothing about it. He had only played a few bars of a Tartini sonata when he broke off and, affecting a casual interest, asked Paolo the price. He was not pleased to be told that this fiddle was Paolo's father's favorite and so would cost forty-five Tuscan gold coins called gigliati, whereas other instruments were going for from twenty to thirty. Nevertheless, bursting with excitement at what he had heard, he paid the sum. He also bought the case Stradivari had made for the violin. A few days later he left for England.

Seven years after that, a fanatical collector of violins, violas, and cellos named Count Cozio di Salabue, of Casale Monferrato in Piedmont, bought from Paolo and his cousin Antonio every one of the then remaining instruments made by Stradivari and his sons, together with all his tools, and his patterns, molds, and labels, and even the drawings that the maestro had kept stored in the chest in the corner of his shop. There was nothing left then in the house on the Piazza San Domenico of the great man's craft, save a few scraps of wood stored up under the roof of the loggia, where the after-echoes of the young widow's clogs on the cobblestones on that fateful morning were perhaps—who knows?—still ever so faintly whispering.

Act Two

1778

Salzburg, March 22, 1778

My dear Wolfgang!

By the time you read this letter, you will be in Paris. I am sending it in care of Baron Grimm, who will know where to reach you.

Be careful, my son. You have been given great gifts, you must not let that city of twinkling lights bedazzle you. I saw Count Kühnburg, the Chief Equerry, yesterday; you will remember that he is a man of rather easy morals, yet even he said that Paris is a bower of temptations, and that you should be on your guard against plausible young Frenchmen, and even more so against the women, who want nothing more than to catch in their cobwebs young men of genius, really in order to get their hands on their money or even to force them into the servitude of marriage. Carry a clean thread into the labyrinth of the city, son, so that you can find your way back out again. You are only twenty-two. You do not yet have the maturity to see through tricksters of both sexes, who by flattery and charm would find ways to subdue you and bilk you. Such a disaster would kill your devoted father!

The French consider themselves gourmets. Do you know what their cuisine reminds me of? To me their food tastes like the droppings of birds. If you say that, the French will reply that you should enjoy them, because their birds are elegant ones: larks, finches, and so on. No matter. Shit is shit. You must hold to your good, weighty German diet. Remember that highly seasoned foods give you indigestion; if you forget, you will soon have to be bled.

Now. First things first. You are going to Paris to make your fortune. The archbishop has been miserly to you in Mannheim. I am deep in debt. Bear in mind that the word talent stands in the holy Bible for a unit of money. Move quickly to make the connections that will pay off. Baron Grimm, of course, comes first. Equally important is Madame la Duchesse de Bourbon, née d'Orléans, who, when you dazzled Paris as a child, dedicated a trivial composition of her own to you. You dedicated two of your earliest sonatas to Madame la Comtesse de Tessé, who gave you a tiny watch and your sister Maria Anna a dear gold toothpick holder. Cultivate also Madame d'Épinay, who has been—sh-h-h!—mistress to Baron Grimm, and who gave your Mamma an exquisite fan.

Be bold, my son. Besiege Mesdames la Duchesse d'Enville, la Duchesse d'Aiguillon, la Duchesse de Mazarin, la Comtesse de Lillebonne, la Comtesse de Wall, la Princesse de Robeck. I know that you find begging repulsive to your modest sensibility, but you *must* approach these people of quality and ask for their protection, and you must do so with a measured gallantry, not forgetting to kiss hands, bow, move your feet discreetly, with toes pointed outward—they set great store by *politesse.* And you must do this *at once.* (But do not forget, son, that even ladies of rank know how to set traps! *Sois sage!*)

I am sending by separate post letters of introduction to the philosophers Denis Diderot and Jean d'Alembert. Also, I am told that Monsieur Voltaire is in Paris; you could present yourself to him, reminding him of your father's acquaintance with him; we met on good terms twelve years ago. It is essential that you become known in the circle of great minds—the nobility adores them *and slips them cash.*

I know that you love me and would not want to be responsible for my early death because of any carelessness on your part. I need consolation for being separated from you, unable from such a distance to hear your voice and your music and to take you in my arms. If you love me, love God even more. Be a good Catholic. Pray and put your trust in God to help you earn money. I will remain until death, no matter when it takes me away, the truest friend you have on earth.

Leopold Mozart

Paris, *le* 26 *mars*, 1778

Mon très cher Père!

We arrived in Paris, thanks be to God, three days ago at four o'clock in the afternoon. You cannot imagine the boredom of the trip. It was clear and frigid for the first eight days on the road, but for the last two it poured and blew the way Punto blows on his French horn: *foomala-foom-foom!* I thought the carriage windows would break from hearing such music. Mother and I sat sopping wet in the carriage. And no one to say a word to! For nine and a half days! The hours were at anchor. *Je m'ennuyais à mourir.*

We are staying for the time being in a single room with two beds at the house of an ironmonger, Herr Mayer, on the Rue Bourg l'Abbé. Here Mamma can at least speak German, though the room is so dark that she can barely see to knit. There is no place for a clavier, so I feel suffocated in these quarters. Madame d'Épinay is looking for better ones for us.

My dearest Papa, I have a request to make of you. Please be more cheerful in your letters. You must not worry your head about me *any more!* I am in Paris, where anything with two legs and a head that doesn't fall off its shoulders can make a fortune! Baron Grimm tells me that if I write two or three operas, I can be sure then of a steady income. I can take pupils, dear little girls, at a customary rate of three louis d'or for twelve lessons. A composer is paid five louis d'or for a symphony written for the Concert Spirituel—the institution, you remember, Papa, that has the King's permission to give concerts on holy days when the Opéra is closed.

It is true that the trip was expensive. Carriage, food, lodging, and tips cost us more than four louis d'or. Right at the moment we are rather hard up. You cannot believe what food costs in France. Did I say food? You were right, Papa. Stewed eels! Larded rabbit! Soup with so much garlic that the bowl levitates off the table and hovers just under your chin.

With Baron Grimm's help I have already made an arrangement with the Concert Spirituel. They want me to compose some choruses for a Miserere by next Wednesday! I have quickly made friends with the concertmaster, Lahoussaye. Believe it or not, he is smaller than I am—a tiny little violinist, merry as a bantam rooster. Even though he is French, he and I are able to laugh together all the time. He offers me free lunches at his rooms and will let me use his clavier to compose on. He has two splendid violins. Mostly he plays on an instrument he has owned for many years, made by Jakob Stainer, but he more recently bought one made several decades ago by an Italian luthier named Stradivari, which he says has a haunting tone, though he likes his familiar Stainer better.

Be happy, dear Father! You know that I love you and want above all else in this world to please you. Write to me about dear Bimperl. Does she tell you—"bark bark bark"—that she misses me? Does she snarl at sister Nannerl? Please don't let her get hydrophobia! I will growl and bite you if you do!

I send you 10,000 kisses, however.

Your faithful son,
Wolfgang Amadé Mozart

Salzburg, April 5, 1778

My very dear son!

You ask me to be of good cheer in my letters, yet everything you write brings me new anxieties.

You say you and your mother are "hard up." I thought that the purpose of your going to Paris was that you would be sending me money, not the other way around. My debts now come to 700 gulden. How am I ever going to repay them? My monthly stipend from the Prince is 20 gulden, and I am forced to rush around giving violin lessons in a city where rates are miserly, to say the least! Only God's mercy has brought me through all these years, caring for you and teaching you and loving you, as well as supporting Mamma and Nannerl and two servants, and paying for the births of seven children and then funeral expenses for five of those seven! Think of this, my dear Wolfgang: *Never once in my life have I spent a single groschen for my own pleasure.* Do not misunderstand me: I adore you and put all my faith in your filial love. I trust you, and know that you will have good sense about finding sources of income.

Another concern. You write me good news about the Concert Spirituel. (I am told that they like sophisticated settings of the psalms in counterpoint. I am sure you have our Latin prayer book with you; you will find all of the psalms in the complete office of Our Lady.) However. I have been asking around about your new friend Monsieur Lahoussaye. People tell me that he is a cheerful poltroon, but that he has a very bad reputation. They say he is a shameless lady's man. As a violinist myself, I have made the distressing observation that many violinists are libertines. Do not let this person lead you into a rose garden—thorns, son, thorns!

There are others, too, with whom you must have nothing to do. Monsieur Hochbrucker, the harpist, is extremely dissolute. Avoid Gluck and Piccini; their rivalry has made them poisonous. Grétry's comic operas may be witty, but he is not a man you should befriend. You can be yourself with people of high rank, but with all others, son, pretend that you are English. Hold back. Your frankness to everyone is a great flaw.

When you have your hair done in your rooms, do not leave your money, or your rings, or the watch that the Elector gave you lying around where the frizzer can see them—or any other servant, for that matter. Do not tell your friends when you have been given money—take it straight to Turton & Baur, the bankers. It is not safe to walk at night with money on your person.

I am worried as well about your going here and there in Paris in all weathers. Springtime in Paris is deceitful. Wear your scarf! Do not sit in drafts. Do not run in the streets when it rains, for the rounded cobblestones in Paris are notoriously slippery underfoot.

Please do not blame me for these cautions, my dear son! Expressing them is the duty of a father who loves his son and counts on him to save him from want and misery in his old age, if God gives him one. I kiss you a million times, my dearest Woferl.

L MZT

Paris, April 15, 1778

Mon très cher Père!

Today I had the most extraordinary experience. Oh, my dearest Papa, you are a violinist, you should have been in my place! I was working at Lahoussaye's clavier, joking with him as I wrote down some music—a sinfonia concertante for Wendling, Ramm, Punto, and Ritter to play at the Concert Spirituel*—it was all finished in my head, I was just scribbling the notation, so I could talk with him as I worked. He was emphatic on the subject of Englishwomen, he came here from London two years ago, he said women on that island are *pommes de terres soufflées*—you know, Papa, those inflated potato slices with nothing but hot air in them!—and that they have hearts of overcooked mutton. He says he found some of them tasty, nevertheless!

He asked me if I would like to play something with him,

*Sinfonia Concertante in E-flat for Flute, Oboe, Horn, and Bassoon, K. 297[b], Appendix 9 in the Köchel index of Mozart's works.

and he got out the score of a sonata for violin and clavier by Joseph Shuster, the *Kapellmeister* to the Elector of Saxony, which I had heard and admired in Munich on the way to Mannheim—remarkable in giving much more voice to the violin in relation to the clavier than we are accustomed to. He played the first movement on his Stainer, and the second, an andante, on the Stradivari.

Oh, Papa! Lahoussaye is a competent fiddler. His tone is round, he has a fine staccato which he plays with a single bowing, up or down, and he can play a double trill quite well. But his cantabile playing is deplorable, because he interrupts the singing tone with sudden squirts and allegro bouncings that jarred on my ears. And as for *his* ears, they must be full of candle wax, as you will see in a moment.

Nevertheless! Two things, Papa. First of all, the bow. There is a bowmaker working here in Paris, named François Tourte, who is just now developing a totally new—and sensational—bow. He cannot read or write, but as a boy he was apprenticed to a watchmaker, so he brings to bowmaking an unmatchable precision. When you were teaching me to play the violin, I remember you always said that my right hand, the bow hand, was the one that would make the *real* music for me. You should hear what this bow of Lahoussaye's can do—subtle nuances I have never heard before! The shaft is made of rare Pernambuco wood from Brazil, which is strong yet flexible—springy, like the handle end of a good whip. Its lower third is slightly thicker than the rest, so there is perfect balance, as I later discovered when I used it to play myself. The gap between the shaft and the horsehair is narrow. The nut, made of ebony with inlays of tortoise shell and mother-of-pearl—*wie schön!*—holds the hair flat, like a ribbon, and it has an ingenious screw that can tighten or loosen the hair to suit you exactly. They say that Monsieur Tourte's daughter sorts the horsehair—only white—and that she discards ninety-nine out of every one hundred hairs, as not good enough! If only I can earn the money to buy you one of these bows!

As to Lahoussaye's dead ear. He said he changed violins as we were playing because he wanted to show me how superior his Stainer was to the Italian violin. My God in Heaven, how wrong he was! I played them both myself. The Stainer has a nice pure little tone, but the sound the other violin, *played with that bow*, made!—a *cantilène* like that of the best Italian sopranos, or like that of my dear Aloysia Weber! Papa, it overwhelmed me, filled me with yearning. It is night now. I am alone in my room. I still hear those sounds, and I cannot put a name to what they make me wish for!

To keep on Lahoussaye's good side, I pretended interest in the Stainer awhile, but then I asked him to tell me about the Italian fiddle. He said he bought it ten years ago in Cremona, in the house where Stradivari made it, from the luthier's son, who told him that this was his father's favorite of all the instruments he had made. Like all great violins, it has a name: Antonietta, this one given by the maker himself. According to the luthier's son, the reason for the name is this: Stradivari made it in the weeks when he was out in the town every night courting the woman, named Antonia, who became his second wife. The son said it had his father's *potenza sessuale* built right into it. It seems Stradivari was something of a ram. The fiddle, by the way, has a charming mother-of-pearl Cupid inlaid in its tailpiece. Lahoussaye showed me a tiny flaw, next to the purfling not far from the fingerboard; the son said this accident had happened one day soon after they were married, when Stradivari and his Antonia had had a quarrel, and she stood in the door of the shop and shouted that she would never let him in her bed again, and in his rage his hand slipped. Lahoussaye laughed and said that the existence of the son, who was born later, proved that she had relented, but he guessed that if the violinmaker was such a potentate between the sheets as the son said, she probably changed her mind ten minutes later. Anyway, the unmended flaw and the fat little Cupid both give testimony to Stradivari's attraction to her.

It is late at night. I still tremble with the joy—and the restlessness—that playing this Antonietta aroused in me. Thank heavens you taught me to play the violin! At this moment I wish I had grown up to be a violinist, like you, rather than being so devoted to the clavier.

Dear Papa, I love you and send you numberless kisses. Mamma has a cold; she will be writing to you. Tickle Bimperl's stomach for me.

Wolfgang

To ALOYSIA WEBER, Mannheim, aged fifteen.

Paris, April 15, 1778

My dear Aloysia:

I must tell you something. Today I played a violin that belongs to a friend, and its tones reminded me vividly of you. It seemed to me that it had exactly your lovely, pure voice, singing those arias I wrote for the diva Anna de Amicis, with horrible difficulties in them that your sweet voice mastered so easily. I played passages from them on the violin, and I heard echoes of your singing them when we went with your father to Kirchheim-Bolanden to perform for the Princess of Orange. How could a violin sound like a clavier? Yet when I played this one, I could hear you playing my clavier sonatas, playing them more to my taste than the great Vogler or anyone else could have! It was as if my fingering hand and my bowing hand were reaching out to your dear hands on the keyboard!

It is two o'clock in the morning. The violin's voice—*your* voice!—still echoes in my head. I feel you close by me. Ah, Aloysia, the mittens you knitted for me kept my hands—and my heart—warm during the frightful cold of our trip to this city, and my thoughts of you will keep my whole body warm through this night.

I send you 123,456,787,654,321 kisses.

Wolfgang Gottlieb Mozart

To ROSA CANNABICH, Mannheim, aged fourteen.

Paris, April 15, 1778

My dear Rosa:

I must tell you something. Today I played a violin that belongs to a friend, and its tones reminded me forcibly of you. It seemed to me that it had exactly your gentle voice, murmuring answers to me when I was giving you lessons. How could a violin sound like a clavier? Yet when I played this one, I could hear you playing the sonata I wrote for you,* rendering it with taste, your timing just right, the grace notes brilliant. I played some passages from it on this violin, and it was as if you were there in the room with me. It was as if my fingering hand and my bowing hand were reaching out to your dear hands on the keyboard!

It is half past two o'clock in the morning. The violin's voice—*your* murmuring voice!—still echoes in my head. I believe that a violin keeps in its belly forever all the music it makes, and now, in a way, *you* are captured! I feel you close by.

Please give my love to all my friends there whose names begin with M—Herren Mannheimer, Moonshine, and Meddlesome; O—Count Oxenhorn, Herr Overhead, and Herr Oboe; Z—Herr Zonca, Herr Zebra, and Baron Zoozu at the castle; A—the Addlegassers, the Addlepates, and the Assholes; R—Maestro Rust, Baroness Rumpled, and the fast-moving Herr Rumor; and T—Herr Tanzmeister the twinkletoes, Herr Tannenbaum the woodenhead, and Father Tantrum who does not exist. And keep some for yourself!

Your behind-first adorer,
Trazom Suedama Gnagflow

*Sonata for Piano in C, Köchel 309.

To THERESE-PIERRON SERRARIUS, Mannheim, aged sixteen.

Paris, April 15, 1778

My dear Therese:

I must tell you something. Today I played a violin that belongs to a friend, and its tones reminded me sweetly of you. It seemed to me that it had exactly your cheerful voice, chatting at the table when your father so kindly took me and my Mamma in. How could a violin sound like a clavier? Yet when I played on this one some passages from the sonata that I dedicated to you,* I felt as if you were right there beside me. My friend who owns the violin told me that it loves sunshine but that it cannot stand bright lights indoors—sounds atrocious when played directly under a chandelier—and when I thought while I was playing of the brightness of your eyes, the fiddle squeaked!

The violin's voice—*your* voice!—still sounds in my ears. The sweet cheerfulness, not the squeak.

Late it become has, o'clock three. If seem you to silly I, me forgive, you if please, that because like mooncalf a feel me made violin. I am os loneyl for oyu that I ncaton sdant ti.

Esteem and a crown of myrtle, Empress Serrarius, from

Julius Augustus Tiberius Wolfgangus Claudius Mozartus

To MARIA ANNA THEKLA MOZART, nicknamed "Bäsle" ("Little Cousin"), in Augsburg, aged nineteen.

Paris, April 15, 1778,
3:30 ante meridiem

My very dear Cozz-Buzz:

Today say I played flayed a fiddle piddle that reminded grinded me we of you too. Oh my, do you want to know why?

*Sonata for Piano and Violin in C, Köchel 296.

Well, I'll tell. Hell, the smell. Yes, *ma chère cousine*, I was playing along perfectly calmly, serenely, tranquilly, even-temperedly, coolly, imperturbably, and even peacefully, when I began to smell—pieoo!—faggh!—whoo!—ach!—the most redolent stink of all. It was a dragon of an odor. I stopped playing. I asked my friend, the owner of the fiddle piddle, if he had let one. He said he had not. I began playing again. Again: ach!—whoo!—faggh!—pieoo! I wondered whether I myself had pooped in my pantaloons, but when I turned around and sniffed behind myself, there was nothing. I played. Once more: faggh!—ach!—pieoo!—whoo!

Then, dearest sweetest smelliest cousin, I realized what it was. Out from the *f*-holes of that fiddle piddle was coming the biggest loudest most thunderous most rumbling fart you ever heard. A smell that would reach to high heaven and make the angels faint. Dear one, I sniffed and sniffed, because it reminded me most achingly of something, somewhere, sometime.

As my nostrils shriveled and my hair began to burn, I realized what I was reminded of. It was of a monster of a poot that you let that time when we were riding in the carriage together to Munich. Ah, dear Bäsle, this fiddle piddle made me feel very close to you and so wish that I was very far from you. In fact, you are now in Augsburg and I am in Paris, but I can smell you from here. This makes my heart go pitter-patter and my ass go shitter-splatter.

I am, will be, was, may have been, would be, had been, shall have been, could be, wish I were, dreamed I was, hoped I could be, insist that I am

Your devoted sniffer,
Stinkgang Smelladeus Mofart

Paris, April 28, 1778

Mon très cher Père:

You will be glad to know that I now have three pupils, at six livres per lesson, or three louis d'or for twelve lessons. The trouble is that the French like to pay for lessons with compliments (*"Oh, quel prodige!" "Incroyable!" "Étonnant!"*) and then withhold the hard cash until the series of lessons is all over. I am told it is not easy to collect it even then.

Furthermore, acquiring pupils is punishing work. I was told that the Duc de Guines had a musical daughter who wanted lessons, so I applied at his house. I was told that I should come back one week later. I did. A servant seated me for an hour in a frigid room, with windows wide open. At last the Duchesse came in, and what a sight she was! Not a jewel on her. A gorgeous blue satin *robe de chambre*. Her hair had been done for the day. Her frisure stood up on top of her head at least a foot high, with a toupee not entirely of real hair but partly of crêpe, with a cap six inches high on top of *that*, and a chignon hanging down behind right to the shoulder blades, with curls wiggling all around her ears. At last you could focus on a tiny face built into this structure, with brilliant eyes and a little mouth full of apologies for keeping me waiting. Extremely courteous. Would I kindly play something on the clavier over there? Naturally she wanted to know if I was qualified to teach her gifted daughter. Please forgive the wretched condition of all her claviers.

I said my hands were so cold they were as stiff as a pigeon's talons. Wasn't there a room with a fire in it?

"Ah mon Dieu! D'accord!" she cried, and took me into a room where she sat down and began to play cards with three men who had come to call on her. Her husband the Duke was nowhere to be seen. She played for an hour, while I sat literally cooling my heels. There was a tiny charcoal fire but here, too, the windows were open, and I thought I would die of shivering and of

headache. At last the daughter came in, and I was commanded to play on a frightful gravicembalo that was all out of tune. Madame and her lovers went right on dealing cards and talking. I was furious and, frozen or not, I began to play my Salieri variations.* You know how difficult they are. The young girl was dazzled. That was my reward, apart from a flood of hollow compliments from those who had not even listened.

I have since given the daughter her first lesson. She is sixteen years old, and to look at her, you would think she had nothing on her mind but lace cuffs and pet kittens and chocolates filled with *crème de menthe*. Not at all. She has astonishing gifts. She plays the harp magnificently and the clavier extremely well. She wants to know everything. She wants to compose. She even wants violin lessons!

I feel shabby when I go to give lessons at the houses of people of quality. You will remember I had an all-purpose black suit with a copiously embroidered waistcoat made in Mannheim, which here is appropriate for formal occasions. Apart from that I brought from Mannheim only my eureka-red Spanish coat and two waistcoats. I was right to leave my braided clothes there; they are no longer *de rigueur* here. But I need two suits. I have found an inexpensive tailor, a dear man with the unfortunate name Douloureux—Monsieur Painful—who promises to make me the suits in a week for only three louis d'or.

The American ambassador, Mister Franklin, is setting a new fashion here. He appears before the King and at the most fashionable balls in his drab brown Quaker coat and knickers. My tailor is going to make one of my suits in this style! Franklin brings fresh air with him, too, from a country that has cocked its snook at the lordly English! Liberty! So much is stirring, Papa. There is talk of war with England. There are rumors of people in provincial cities being collared in back alleys and snatched out of bed to be made into soldiers. There is gossip—

---

*Variations on an Arietta by Antonio Salieri, Köchel 180.

as yet no public announcement—that Marie Antoinette is pregnant. (After playing that violin, I think of her as Maria Antonietta!) My pupils' parents are delighted that there may be an heir. I hope my time here is not cut short by hostilities. I have just begun to enjoy myself!

I kiss you and Nannerl many 1,000 times in a row, dearest Papa.

W MZT

Salzburg, May 2, 1778

My dearest son!

Two suits at Paris prices! My dear boy, do you realize what your father is obliged to wear? Let us start at the feet. My ancient shoes are cracked and stained from walking in wet streets. Black silk stockings? Not for years have I worn them. I am reduced to frayed white stockings on holy days and at other times coarse woollen stockings from Berlin. My pantaloons have split at the seams in the back ten times, and with your mother away in Mannheim and Paris I have had to sew them up myself, with stitches that look like hen scratchings. I hardly dare sit down for fear of hearing a ripping sound, with people thinking I have blown my pants open by breaking wind. Everywhere I go I wear my one puce flannel doublet, the cuffs and elbows of which are in ribbons. And you, my son, wish to dress yourself up like a sultan to give lessons to pretty little girls, and then have your tailor send the dolorous bill to a person in Salzburg whom strangers in the streets constantly take for a beggar! Three louis d'or, you say. *All* that you will earn from twelve lessons to one of your three pupils!

Another thing. *I do not like* your banter with Lahoussaye about "edible" Englishwomen. This fellow may be a concertmaster but he is also a roué. Everyone who knows him says that. And all the talk about the violin made by that indecent Italian, and how the instrument somehow harbors his gross venery. I am a violinist, Woferl. I can tell you that a violin is a violin, and nothing more! Its tone is as pure or as foul as the heart of the person who plays it. *Please!* Remember your mission in this world!

I write this way because I adore you and depend on you.

MZT

Take care of your health, my dearest son. I miss you.

Bimperl cries for you and your mother. When she wants a bit of sausage, she rolls over on the floor, pretending she is a *Bratwurst!* When I have taken a pinch of Spanish snuff, she stands on her hind legs, wanting to lick my fingers. Any other kind of snuff, she makes a sneezing sound and runs away!

Paris, May 9, 1778

Padre mio!

I owe everything to you, my dear Papa. You have nurtured me, loved me, taught me—and scolded me—and if I exist at all, it is as an artifact that you have crafted. I know that. I am a grateful son. But sometimes when you berate me, you are not entirely fair. Let me tell you why your letter of May 2 did not do me justice.

Here is a day in my life in Paris.

I can only get up at seven o'clock, since it is not yet light in our rooms until half past seven. As soon as I am dressed, I sit down to compose. What am I writing? The Duc de Guines (whose charming daughter I am teaching) is a man of many graces (and a great favorite, they say, of Maria Antonietta) who plays the flute (like a nightingale). His daughter Héloïse, as I have told you, plays the harp (like an angel). I am composing a concerto for their two instruments, for which Monsieur le Duc has promised two louis d'or. I am to compose as well an opera in two acts, to be entitled "Alexandre et Roxane"; a poet is now writing the libretto. The Concert Spirituel wants a symphony. Monsieur Noverre wants a ballet, to be called "Les Petits Riens."* I have told you about the sinfonia concertante for Wendling and the others. You seem to think I am doing nothing, but I am juggling hundreds of thousands of quavers and crochets and hemidemisemiquavers in my head all at once!

Very well. At eleven o'clock I go halfway across Paris to give a clavier lesson to a hopeless young lady of thirteen, who, besides having bad-tempered tears running down through the powder on her cheeks half the time, cannot hear the difference between major and minor chords. At one o'clock I have a respite—a cheerful hour, usually, and a light meal, with Lahoussaye. At three I hurry across the river to give a lesson in galant treble and thorough bass to the young wife of a dilettante Dutch naval officer, who promises to pay the high price of four louis d'or for making his wife a great composer in twelve lessons—and he should pay more than that, because his wife is an ass. She has not an ounce of imagination. I have to start a pattern for her, and then I say, "See what a moron I am, I can't think of how to go on. Would you finish this for me?" She gapes and yawns and scratches her scalp, as if trying to relieve an itch in her brain, and then she makes a botch of the rest.

At six comes the one pleasant appointment of the day, for then I teach Héloïse de Guines. She is, as I have told you, a delight. She knows two hundred pieces by heart. Her touch on harp strings and clavier keys is as delicate as raindrops falling on a lake. Because Lahoussaye prefers his Stainer fiddle, he has loaned me his Italian violin, and I accompany her on it. The other day, while I was buying some sonatas by Schobert for the de Guines girl to play, I found a French translation of your

*Concerto for Flute and Harp, Köchel 299. The opera was never written. Symphony No. 31 in D major, the "Paris" Symphony, Köchel 297. Eleven dances for *Les Petits Riens*, Köchel 299[b], Appendix 10; the ballet as a whole was never completed.

book* in a little music store in Montmartre. Now, as I accompany Héloïse during her lessons, I remember how you taught me, and I faithfully follow your instructions in the book! "Merry and playful passages must be played with light, short, and lifted strokes, happily and rapidly, just as in slow passages one performs with long strokes of the bow, simply and tenderly." We are starting violin lessons. Even on open strings she can make a silvery, silky tone on this Antonietta. This interests me. When Lahoussaye plays on Antonietta, the violin gives back a sound that is slightly vulgar and coarse—and in a way it bears out his preference for his Stainer. When I play, it seems to *me*, the violin's tone is pure and dreamy, playful and tender. And this girl draws out a naïve and innocent sound. Yet no matter who is playing, the singing of this instrument causes one to feel restless and wistful, as if yearning for something breathtaking to happen. If you had to fashion me, Papa, why oh why didn't you make me, in your likeness, a violinist?

Sometimes I stay for supper *chez* Guines. Sometimes I go to Baron Grimm. Sometimes I come home and eat with Mamma. After that I compose again, and read, and write letters, and I go to bed at two in the morning.

So you see, dearest Papa, I am not throwing myself away on the strumpets of a wicked city. I work hard, I walk for miles and miles from duty to duty, even in the rain, and as soon as I collect some money, I promise to send you what I can. The French hornist Rodolphe, who plays for the King, has offered me the position as organist at Versailles for two thousand livres a year, on the basis of six months at the palace and six months on my own elsewhere. I could introduce Lahoussaye's Antonietta to Maria Antonietta! But no, I do not like the idea of being a royal puppet, I will decline.

---

*Leopold Mozart, *Versuch einer gründlichen Violinschule* (*Treatise on the Fundamental Principles of Violin Playing*), 1756, published in a French translation by one Valentin Roeser in 1770.

Mamma will have written you about our move to a light-filled house on the Rue Cléry, just off the Rue Montmartre. We are not far from the Grands Boulevards. Mamma goes for exercise to the Luxembourg gardens, and I have been to the picture gallery in the palace. You must understand, my anxious paternal ancestor, that I make every effort to elevate my mind! I am not wasting my time in this city of slippery slopes! I am, in other words, your faithful and clean-living offspring,

Wolfgang God-loved Moozle

Salzburg, May 15, 1778

Mon très cher fils!

What you tell me about the Queen's pregnancy offers great opportunities! When the baby is born, *especially if it is a male child*, there will be great celebrations, with much demand for good music. They may want an opera in Marie Antoinette's honor. (I wish you would stop sullying her name with the suggestiveness of that low-down fiddle's origins!) Make arrangements *now*. French taste seems to me trivial and shallow, but I would advise you to listen to French operas and ape what they like, even if you have contempt for it. This is the way to be a success, Wolfgang, because you must face facts; it is your fate and mine—as creators of an item of luxury, music—to be patronized.

Furthermore, my son, haven't you been much too hasty in deciding against the court appointment? You say you would be a puppet. I would say more like a puppy—you would be petted and fed tidbits from the royal table! You would soon be the darling of the King and Queen, I am certain. Besides what you earned at Versailles, you would have six months each year to pick up other work. It would no doubt be a life appointment, and in time you would be musical tutor to the royal princes and princesses and so be closer than ever to their majesties. If war came, you would be protected. Do not be in such a rush to deny yourself a good life, in which you might even be able to send some money to your aging father. Think it over.

I trained you to be a virtuoso on the keyboard rather than a bow-scraper because it would help you to be a skillful composer. On a clavier you get a greater range of musical experience than on a violin, what with using both treble and bass clefs, chords, harmonic modulations, and all the rest. As a violinist, yes, you would dazzle the pretty girls, accompanying them as they play the clavier, and perhaps even give their mothers at the card table delicious palpitations. Son! Be on guard. A Cupid on a tailpiece is a warrant for folly.

I have received the bills for the suits. I cannot pay them just now. Have mercy on your impoverished father, who loves you more than himself.

MZT

Paris, May 19, 1778

My dearest Father:

Why can't you take me seriously? I must tell you with all the solemnity I can summon that Héloïse de Guines is a remarkable young musician. You did not believe me about Aloysia Weber—but you will see, Papa, she will be a great opera singer. And take my word for it, this French girl can reach similar heights. She learns whatever I teach her with the most amazing speed. I explain something, or I show her something on the keyboard, or on the violin's fingerboard, *once*—she knows it and can do it.

Let me tell you about her lesson yesterday. We were in the same room where I went through that first humiliating audition, but this time the weather was fine, and the room was warm, and a well-tuned clavier had been brought in for the lessons. Imagine the setting, Papa. This is the room where la Duchesse de Guines holds her levees—though this, of course, was in the late afternoon. Here everyone seems to be at ease on a down coverlet of well-being. There are several clusters of furniture, grouped around tables with curving legs, where guests can chat and drink coffee laced with cordials according to whim. The ceiling is high, and it is decorated with pastel dreams of vines and fruits in delicate plaster. At the windows there are silk curtains like waterfalls splashing on the floor; they are capped by valances embroidered with hunting scenes. Canaries sing. Yesterday Madame la Duchesse was wearing a dress of ash-blond silk to which her *couturière* had given a name that suggests its cut—"Indiscreet Pleasures." Her coiffure, also named—"*à la Minerve*"—was capped with ten blue feathers. She was drenched with jewels from the famous Böhmer & Bassenge. As before, three gentlemen, who seem to be established rivals for her favors, were gambling at lansquenet with her, talking and laughing out loud, while at other tables a dozen men and women sat sipping and gossiping.

None of this distracted Héloïse, whose power of concentration is ferocious. We are used to the bother; we work so intensely that it seems we are in a sealed chamber. I set her to sight-reading of one of the Schobert sonatas, and she played the allegretto first movement with note-perfect ease, and, what is more, with sensitive understanding of the shifting whims of the music. I, meanwhile, began to weave improvisations on Lahoussaye's violin around her playing. She became excited by what I was doing, and her touch stepped up to new levels. The cardplayers put down their hands to listen; the gossipers were hushed; even the canaries fell still. For Héloïse and I had begun a dialogue, as she, too, started to improvise, abandoning the Schobert text but still playing in his voice. I tell you, Papa, it took my breath away.

When we stopped, everyone in the room stood up and applauded. I had tears in my eyes. Héloïse had a fierce little smile on her face, which was deeply flushed. Dear Father, please take me seriously! This young woman is a rare musician!

She has made amazing progress on the violin as well. I have Lahoussaye's permission to leave Antonietta with her to practice on. We have only been at it for a couple of weeks, but she can already play in first, second, and third positions, and can move from one to another with ease—glissando, if necessary. We will be trying some duets soon, she first on the clavier and I with Antonietta; then vice versa.

She says she has fallen in love with Antonietta, and having seen how carefully she puts the violin away after a lesson, I can believe her. With a silk kerchief she wipes away the resin dust that has been scraped off the bow onto the belly by the strings, and then she cleans the strings, from bridge to nut, with another bit of silk dipped in almond oil. Then she wraps the fiddle in a quilted satin gown and lays it away in its case, making sure that it is placed where it will not be exposed to drafts.

Now I have a confession to make. After those intoxicating moments Héloïse and I shared, I was invited to stay on to dine, and when the meal was over we were all still in a giddy mood because of what the violin had said to the clavier and what the clavier had dared to answer, and we stayed up late at a different sort of improvisation. Monsieur le Duc and Madame la Duchesse were present, of course, as well as Baron Grimm; one of the three cardplaying rascals, a Comte de Somebody whose name I never learned; two beautiful older women; and Héloïse and her younger sister Blanche. We were set to improvising verses, one line to each guest, in turn, all in the most outrageous sort of smut—at which these French people of quality seem to excel: we passed merrily along to each other uproarious lines about shitting, ass-licking, and acts of a different sort that I'm afraid I cannot repeat to you, my dear innocent Papa. I would never have allowed myself such a sticky tongue, except that I was egged on by little Blanche, who at fifteen had the naughtiest mind of all, and how I enjoyed myself! Be my confessor, Papa, and absolve me of this sin if I will do penance by playing scales for six hours and promising never to utter such trash again. But all the same, I will. Oh, yes, I will. For you see, sir, the holy Saint Amadeus, the patron of stained sheets, of split pantaloons, and of the perfume known as *essence de la commode*, has already given me absolution, contingent on my being even more wicked next time.

Your prodigal son,
W. Amadeus Mephistopheles

To ALOYSIA WEBER, Mannheim.

Paris, May 23, 1778

Dearest friend!

Enclosed please find some new coloratura passages to go at the end of the aria I wrote last February with your voice in mind, "Non so d'onde viene."* You sang it for me, the very first time, after only two days' practice on your own, with no guidance at all from me, *exactly* as I would have wanted you to. This was my first realization of your wonderful gifts, and it also was the first time in my life that I understood how one person could give another a kind of kiss in musical form, as I thought you did to me that day. You will remember the note I sent you last month about playing an eloquent violin belonging to my friend Monsieur Lahoussaye, the concertmaster of the Concert Spirituel. I think what I was trying to say was that the sound I made on that violin gave me the pleasure of embracing you, even though we were far apart. I wish with all my heart that you were here, so that you could sing and I could accompany you, sometimes on a clavier, at other times on this violin which seems to reach out so tenderly to you. How sad I am that my father would not hear of our going to Italy together, when I suggested it, where I might have composed an Italian opera for you, and you could have sung in it for me—enabling us to cohabit unchastely—in music!

You must buy a walking stick, dear friend. It is the latest fashion here. It seems that Madame la Comtesse de Lillebonne turned her ankle one day while out walking her little lapdog, a

---

*Köchel 294.

Maltese terrier, on a leash; perhaps she slipped in its tiny little poop. The doctor who examined her ankle said she must carry a cane wherever she went, and at once it was *à la mode* for all the ladies to hobble with a walking stick to church to confess, to their friends' houses to tell lies, and when taking their pet dogs out to watch them lift their legs. Some of the sticks are topped with silver, some with ivory, some even with gold. Be up to date, mademoiselle!

Why do you never write to me?

I send you 10,000 musical caresses.

Wolfgang

To MARIA ANNA THEKLA MOZART, "Bäsle," Augsburg.

Paris, May 24, 1778

Mademoiselle ma très chère Mademoiselle de la Mademoiselle:

I have no time to write, so I will write. If I have no time to write, why do I write? Because I do not write in time, nor do I time my writing. Why then do I have no time to not write? Because I write this time.

Now that that is clear, I will tell you a story. Once upon a time to write, there was a fiddle. There was also a clavier, but that doesn't prevent there having been a fiddle, does it? Now this clavier was most attractive, for it had inlays of layings-in. The fiddle was beautiful, too, with *f*-holes that looked like a-holes. Do you know what the fiddle said to the clavier? Of course you do not know, otherwise I would not need to tell you. Do you think I should start over again? Once upon a no time to not write, there was a . . . oh, but you know that already. As I was saying about what the fiddle was saying, it said to the clavier: "On my SOL, I LA you with all my heart." The clavier said: "DO you want to FA MI?" The fiddle said: "I DO." The clavier said: "Let's C, I'll give you a key so you can B-sharp and can get into my flat to FA MI." The fiddle said: "Will you bare your bars and B-flat on your back?" The clavier said: "Will you let me unbutton your clefs?" The fiddle said, "E! It makes me treble just to think about it." The clavier said: "We'll FA SOL much that we'll have to take a measure of rest." . . . I don't think we'd better finish this story. It might end with a coda fartissimo.

And so, Mademoiselle de la Mademoiselle, it is time to retire. It is time, not to write, but to end writing in time for the violin to violate the violent clavier. Good night, my beloved spouse-like mouse, please shut your eyes so as not to watch the indecent acts the fiddle and the clavier will now perform.

Adieu, ma cherry,
Monsieur le Mozieur

Salzburg, May 28, 1778

Mon très cher fils!

Your mother writes me that you are a good boy, that you are working hard on the symphony for the Concert Spirituel, that you run all over the city to give lessons, and that I have been unkind to you in my letters. Ah, my Woferl, if you only knew how much I love you! I have submerged my whole being in your welfare. I do not feel that I fabricated you, as you suggested in one of your letters. Far from it. You are a miracle given to us by God, and looking out for your welfare has simply been this poor sinner's way of thanking Him.

To call myself a "poor" sinner is accurate. Why have you not given me an accounting of your earnings? You must have collected from at least three cycles of twelve lessons with each of your pupils—I reckon you should have had therefrom thirty louis d'or, at three per cycle for two pupils, and four for the other. Where has the money gone? It is clear that I have seen none of it. You should have everything you compose engraved and sold; this requires finding a printer and actively soliciting subscriptions. I have repeatedly given you lists of wealthy patrons to cultivate. You write to me about staying up late for word games but not about getting up early to compose the opera and ballet about which you wrote me. And why do you not answer me about the offer of a post at Versailles?

But enough reproach, my beloved little cub! Your sister Nannerl and I have other worries, among them your Mamma's health. She writes so often of headaches, feverishness, and the coughing up of phlegm. Has she some of the black powder that has helped her in the past? Should she be bled? While you are staying up late in the houses of your pretty young pupils, she is alone, with only a candle for company. Nannerl and I feel that you are neglecting her. You have a careless temperament, Wolfgang, with you everything is a merry game. You live each day as if it were a joke. Baron Grimm has written me with the opinion that you are "too good-hearted, too little concerned with the means by which one may become successful. Here in Paris, to make your way, you must be shrewd, enterprising, bold." I beg you, Wolfgang, settle your feet on the ground, try for once to be a son to your Mamma and Papa, who love you without reserve.

I kiss you a million times, and Nannerl blows in your ear to tickle you, and Bimperl licks your hand.

MZT

Paris, June 1, 1778

Mon très cher Père!

In yours of May 28 you asked both patiently and impatiently, I thought, both lovingly and—excuse me—fretfully, about my progress in what you once called this "city of twinkling lights." The lights, such as there are, have begun to seem dim to me.

I am making good headway on my symphony, which will be performed at the Concert Spirituel on the eighteenth day of this month, when I will presumably collect three louis d'or. However, both the opera and the ballet have been disappointments. The libretto for the former was never finished—and I am honestly relieved, because this vile French tongue is so unsuitable for opera. As to the ballet, it turned out that Monsieur Noverre only wanted an overture and a few dances, and I was paid nothing—it was "for friendship"! Monsieur le Duc de Guines, though most cordial to me, has yet to pay me for the concerto I wrote for him and his daughter. Nor have I been paid for the concerto I wrote for Wendling and his colleagues. Nor has the Dutch naval officer seen fit to pay me for two of the three cycles of twelve lessons I have given to his "genius" of a wife. Guines owes me for two cycles. It seems that the banks in Paris glue their stupid clients' money to the walls of their vaults.

My accounting, therefore, amounts to this: I have received nine louis d'or from teaching the imbecile girl, three from the Hollander, and three from Guines for Héloïse's lessons. This makes fifteen altogether, of which Mamma and I have had to pay out nearly twelve for lodging and food.

You ask about the post of court organist at Versailles. Every one of our friends whom we trust—Grimm, Wendling, Raaff, Ramm—and also Madame d'Épinay, Madame la Duchesse de Guines, and Madame la Comtesse de Tessé, all of whom I consulted—*all* of these advised against accepting the appointment. They say that the intrigues and rivalries among the court musicians are enough to bring on suicide, and that the worst fate of all is to become a darling of their majesties, who are dangerously fickle.

The one bright light in all this, which shines with constancy, has been my work with Héloïse de Guines. Papa, this young woman is a phenomenon! Each day, after an hour of technical drill on each of the clavier and violin, we play our wild game of improvisation, she first on the clavier and I on Antonietta, then we exchange instruments. We start with a theme from one of my compositions and break away into variations, answering each other's ideas and weaving in and out around each other's sudden fancies and turns and jumps. More and more people come each day to listen and cheer us on, and now the room is packed each day.

Papa, I come to the point. She and I should go on tour to all the capitals and great cities. Here at last is a sure way to make a fortune! Lahoussaye thinks we should go first to London, where he says there would be a huge subscription for such a novelty—and what is more, he says he will rent Antonietta to us for the tour at only one louis d'or a week. Then: Venice, Verona, Milan, Florence, Rome! Please write at once to our dear friend Lugiati and ask what the highest terms for such recitals might be in those cities. Then, fond Papa, our home ground: Salzburg, Vienna, Mannheim, Augsburg! In Salzburg you would see and hear this little wonder.

I have yet to discuss this with Héloïse herself, but I have spoken about it "behind the screen" with her mother, who is most enthusiastic about making the tour with us. Imagine the sensation! A beautiful young woman who is a daughter of *nobility* on the musical stage with the brilliant young Amadé Marzipan! I guarantee you that Antonietta in my hands, in conversation with either a harpsichord or a clavier under the hands of Mademoiselle Héloïse—or vice versa—will have all Europe throwing bouquets to us on stage. Picture Héloïse at the keyboard: there she sits, straight as a skilled equestrienne, her eyes flashing first toward the violin in my hands, then toward her listeners, a peculiar little smile tightening her lips as the notes from the keyboard under her hands respond to Antonietta and tease Antonietta and lead Antonietta on and then give in to Antonietta! I wish you could hear the gasps and storms of applause *and the kisses* we both get from the crowd in the Guineses' room each day!

Mamma will write to you about this. She hates the boredom and expense and bad air of Paris, and I think she believes that the tour would be wonderful for her health. You, too, could perhaps join us after Salzburg! Please begin making arrangements for that part of the tour at once.

You must conclude, Papa, must you not, that you have a dutiful and loving son, whose name is

Wolfgang Amadeus Musik

Salzburg, June 8, 1778

My dear son!

For two nights I have not slept, and I am now so weak that I can hardly move my pen across the paper. I don't know when I will recover from the astonishment and horror with which I read your letter of the 1st. Do you mean to murder your own father? I have for many years undergone frightful hardships for your sake. Do you remember when I was seeing you off to Munich, and I had a fever and had been vomiting for three days, yet I packed your bag and was up at four o'clock in the morning to see you off, and myself lifted the heavy valise, full of copies of *your music*, onto the carriage, and thereby strained my back, so that I was flat in bed for a month? What form does your gratitude to me take? You stab me with a rapier—you strangle me—you shoot me with a pistol ball—you starve me to death.

It is always the same story—your soft heart that gives in to any appeal, your need to believe every word of flattery, your "kindness" to others which is really a form of vanity, your faith in mountebanks and deceivers, so that you are led into worthless and impractical projects of every sort and allow yourself to pursue daydreams and actually seek out ways of throwing money away rather than saving it for your honest mother and father in their old age. I have tried over and over again to teach you to be suspicious of your own warm and generous nature, which makes you feel that *you* are a member of the nobility, *you* are a patron, *you* have it in your power to support the talents of others.

And who are those others? Please read what I will now write with great care and think about it. Who are those others?

Wolfgang, do you remember your harebrained idea of giving new life to the German *Singspiel* in Munich by writing music for the little singer Mademoiselle Kaiser, the bastard daughter by a count out of a cook, who, you, said, was so pretty on the stage that you wept to hear her crescendos and decrescendos and her slow, true, and clear trills?

Very well. Off to Augsburg, where you have your usual flirtation, this time as the maestro of my brother's crude little daughter Maria Anna Thekla Mozart, with whom, I understand from your mother, you still exchange preposterous love letters.

In Mannheim you come under the sheltering wing of Herr Cannabich, and at once you spread *your* sheltering wing over his tender daughter Rosa, and you announce that you have painted an immortal musical portrait of her in the adagio movement of a sonata!

What follows? Still in Mannheim, you are kindly taken into the home of the distinguished Councilor Serrarius, and suddenly his mincing daughter Thérèse-Pierron is the queen of your heart, and you dedicate a sonata to *her!*

And next, *still* in Mannheim (how restless your poor heart is!), you come under the influence of the reprobate Herr Wendling, who promptly insinuates you into the Weber family. At once the Webers are the most saintly, the most Christian, and incidentally the poorest family on earth, except they are rich in having *two* lovely daughters and your patronage. You fasten on the elder of the two, Aloysia, whose voice, you write, is as clear and sparkling as a mountain brook, and you actually propose going with her to Italy and sponsoring her there as a prima donna, who will sing operas you have not yet written and never will.

Now we come to the climax, dear son. You now propose in all seriousness to be the patron of those who are patronizing you. You wish to take the prodigious Mademoiselle de Guines all over the world so that she and a clavier can converse in public with you and that violin, which I think has turned you into a cuckoo bird. What ever makes you think that Monsieur le Duc de Guines will allow you to go traipsing off to city after city *à trois* with his wife and daughter? The applause at that woman's coffee parties must have made you—and possibly Madame la Duchesse—quite daft.

Wolfgang Amadeus Mozart, my beloved son, you are a composer! Sadly, you are obliged to support your great gifts—and, if possible, your aging mother and father—in various forms of musical prostitution. This does not mean that you have to become involved in actual prostitution! Come to your senses. Save yourself! Spare my life, my dear son. You have very nearly killed me.

MZT

By the way, Bimperl has a new trick. I stand her on the table during supper, and she scratches first at the loaf of bread and then at the bread knife! What can I do but cut her a slice?

To MARIA ANNA THEKLA MOZART, Augsburg.

Paris, June 12, 1778

Ma très chère Cousine-Queen:

I am told that your father is brother to my father who is father to a cousin of one whose father is uncle of one whose father's brother is father of one whose uncle is father of one who shits on all fathers who dip their pens in shit to write their letters. In other words, dear Coz, I have just received a letter from your uncle, your father's brother, my father. Why do I tell you this? Why not? Why do I shit on your nose? Why not? Why do I use the same asshole I have used for twenty-two years to unload from, without fear of its becoming frazzled? Why not? Why do I have a gun in my behind, aimed at all fathers? I ask you, why not?

Do you remember my telling you about a violin that could blow farts all the way from Paris to Augsburg? Today is very it heavy, stuffed it because full shit of is. Bow when the pull strings across the I, streams *f*-holes out stink of its.

This is called music, I mean moo-sick, because it is cowshit.

Od uoy dnatsrednu em?

Forgive me, dear Bäsle. My asshole is on fire today. I would appreciate it if you would lick it to cool it off. If you will be so kind, I will kiss your lips, your eyes, your cheeks, your hands, your elbows, your knees, your thighs, your . . . well, whatever does not have a sign on it, saying DO NOT KISS MY —. You are a dear cousin. If I could not write to you, I would be very angry. Good night! Get in bed and dump a load to keep yourself warm!

Your father's brother's deafening-defecating son,

Wolfgang Amadeus Moo-sick

Paris, June 13, 1778

My dear, dear Father:

I was deeply distressed to read of your pain at receiving my last letter. You must know, dearest Papa, that I was only half serious about that fanciful tour of the great cities with Mademoiselle Héloïse and her kind and elegant mother. I am afraid I was not entirely truthful to you about my own Mamma's views of the trip. She is altogether too ill and weak these days to undertake such an ordeal. And to be candid Madame la Duchesse herself was not altogether persuaded that her tender daughter should be so exposed just now to public view. Héloïse is a bountifully talented young woman, but such a grand tour would have pushed her too hard and too fast—and, as you so wisely point out, would have got in the way of my proper work of writing music.

I tried hard to be angry at you for what you wrote, but I failed. You are right in saying that I get carried away by trivial fancies, and that my greatest weakness is my generous heart's desire to give protection to those who seem to me to need it, when all the time my own greatest need is to be protected from myself! Thanks be to God I am easily turned aside from my follies, because the moment people lose confidence in me, I am liable to lose confidence in myself.

Of course you are right about that little singer in Munich. I think I must have been influenced by the praise all the Müncheners were heaping on her—and she *was* pretty! I was hurt,

Papa, by your sarcastic remarks about my playful intercourse through the post with my Bäsle; writing to her is like being bled, it is good for me. And what was the harm of writing fine sonatas for girls who were kind to me in Mannheim? As to Aloysia Weber, yes, again I was hasty, for though she has a voice that goes straight to the heart, especially when she sings cantabile, she does not yet know how to act and so is not ready for opera. On my advice, she is studying acting now with the actress Signora Toscani—and one of these days, mark my words . . . !

It breaks my heart to read your outcry that I am killing you. You are my Papa! I wept when I had to read your letter about how shabbily dressed you are for my sake. Do you doubt me? Don't you remember how, when I was a little boy, I used to perch on your knees and sing my little nonsense song, "Nannetta Nanon, puisque la bedetta fa, Nannetta, inevenedetta fa Nanon," and when I had finished I would kiss you on the tip of your nose? The rule of my life then and now was and is, *Next to God comes Papa*. I am sworn to love, honor, and obey you as long as we both shall live. Papa! Papa! I *beg* you to go on loving me, for *I cannot live without your arms around me*.

You will be glad to know, after this fuss, that I have not been idle. I have finished my symphony. Yesterday I played it right through on a clavier for our good friend Anton Raaff, for my friend Lahoussaye, who will lead the orchestra, and for Herr Count Sickingen, Minister here of the Palatinate. The symphony is in D major and according to the Paris fashion has three movements, lacking a minuet. Here in Paris there is a mad craving for a bold *premier coup d'archet*, a savage attack of the violins' bows at the very beginning, and again at the ending, fortissimo-unisono, so I have given these to them, though the pother the oxen here make over this is absurd. But I have put a twist on this asinine trick in the introduction to the third movement that will surprise the fools here—at the very first, just two violin desks play piano piano, trippingly, for eight bars, then *crash!*—their beloved *coup!* The Parisians like noisy noise, so I have given it to them! The andante movement, however, is to *my* taste. The performance is to be on Corpus Christi, five days from now.

So you see, *mon cher Père*, I know my duty and I will do it. I kiss your hands 1,000,000 times and I am always and will always be your most obedient son

Wolfgang

To ALOYSIA WEBER, Mannheim.

Paris, June 14, 1778

Dearest friend!

Today I was playing the violin I have told you about, named Antonietta, in company with a young woman who is one of my pupils, and I was astonished by a feeling that the instrument had a forked tongue. It was speaking to my pupil, merrily, because her gifts delight me, but it was also speaking to you, sadly, sadly, because you are far away and I never hear from you. Sometimes I wonder whether life is worth living. I am lonely in Paris, which is no place for an honest German. My mother is very ill—she lies in bed in that most deceitful of conditions: a burning fever that makes her shiver as if she were freezing. I am neither hot nor cold. I feel nothing. You never write to me. Why?

I am composing a scena called "Popoli di Tessaglia,"* which I shall send to you soon. I am writing it for you and for you alone, for your skylark's tongue to sing. Do you know that the lark gives us its exquisite trills while flying almost straight upward into the high air? In my next letter I will send you some ideas on how to render this scene, how the breathing should go, and how it should be acted. I hope it will seem heavenly to you; you will make it so, in any case, my lark. This afternoon I played some passages from it on that violin for my pupil, and I wondered if you could feel on your lips, even so far away, the kisses the violin was sending you. My pupil may have thought the kisses

---

*A recitative and aria set to words from Gluck's *Alceste*, Köchel 316.

were for her, because she was weeping with joy at the end. If so, it was because Antonietta is two-faced! Did I tell you that the violin has a Cupid inlaid on its tailpiece?

The violin's tones not only kissed you, they embraced you, they shot arrows to Mannheim aimed at your heart, they told you the whole tale of my loneliness. Please write to me!

Wolfgang

Paris, June 19, 1778

Mon très cher Père!

My symphony was performed yesterday, and, thanks be to God, it made a hit. When he paid me my three louis d'or, Monsieur Le Gros, the director of the Concert Spirituel, told me that it is the best symphony ever written for him.

I have had a nerve-racking two days, however. Monsieur Le Gros can only afford a single rehearsal of each number for the concerts, and mine, day before yesterday, was a disaster. I have never in all my life heard an orchestra perform so badly. They scraped and fumbled through the entire symphony twice and hardly got a note right. I went home in despair and decided to stay away from the concert rather than face the whistles and catcalls of these disdainful Parisians.

During the night—I slept not at all—I suddenly realized what had gone wrong. The orchestra was like a chicken with its head cut off. What I mean is that the ensemble lacked a leading voice, which should have come from the instrument of the concertmaster, who was conducting on his violin. That was the trouble! He was using *his* violin, the Stainer, whose sweet, thin tones were not equal to the task of dominating and encouraging ten other first violins and eleven second violins, to say nothing of thirty-five other instruments, including woodwinds and brass. As I wrote you the other day, this is a *noisy* symphony, which means all the more that its gaiety and verve depend on the high spirits of the strings. I told you in my last letter of the device with which I have introduced the third movement—strings deliciously piano and then the *coup d'archet*. In the rehearsal the soft passage was horrid, it broke down in disorder, and all one heard was a kind of stammering whisper.

I was up before dawn, and I dressed and rushed across the city to the de Guineses' mansion. I pulled at the bell and rapped on the door and even shouted. Finally a footman in an old dressing gown came to the door. I must have looked wild, because he seemed to think I was a thief or a drunken derelict, and he slammed the door shut in my face. I kept battering at it, and finally the Duke himself opened it in his nightgown and cap. I blurted out that I needed the violin his daughter used for her practice. "At this hour?" he said. "Do you know what time it is? Have you lost your mind?" "Yes," I said, "I have, and the only way I can find it again is with the help of that violin." Shaking his head, he let me in. It turned out that Héloïse had the habit of hiding the fiddle under the skirts of her bed, and she had to be roused, because the maid who had been routed out to fetch the instrument could not find it. The girl came out to me with a sleepy face, her hair down, holding the case in her arms. Forgive me, Papa, I know it will offend you if I say she was like a painting I have seen somewhere here—perhaps in the palace in the Luxembourg gardens—by the Spaniard Murillo, of the Virgin Mother with the holy babe in her arms. In the dim light of the morning, Héloïse seemed to me to be standing before me on her bare feet, like that Madonna, on a thin rind of a magical new moon.

I took the fiddle and ran. On the way back across the city, I pulled up short, deciding to wait until the last moment, just before the concert, to confront Lahoussaye with the need for the change. I even toyed with the idea of letting him begin the symphony with the Stainer, and then rushing down to him from the audience with Antonietta, stopping the orchestra, and making him start over with the other instrument, or leading the symphony myself with it. How dramatic that would have been! But in the end I settled on the less sensational course of demanding the change before the concert. He put up a terrible fight. He was used to the Stainer, the Stainer was his *friend*, the Stainer would have hurt feelings and would not sound right for weeks! But at last he agreed.

Papa! It worked! The orchestra sang! The strings flew like kites over the meadows of my ideas. It wasn't that you could *hear* Antonietta as a separate sound. No, it was that the choir of strings now had an intelligible leading voice and they—and the entire orchestra—followed with a responsive zest and firmness. There was a passage about halfway through the first Allegro that I had expected would delight these Parisians, and yes!—there came, after it, a huge burst of applause. At the end of the first movement, there were shouts of "*Da capo!*" They wanted it played right over again! Of course Lahoussaye went on with the Andante. And then the trick opening of the second Allegro, which had been such a catastrophe at the rehearsal—the violins trickled this time like water in a gentle fountain, and with the explosion of the fortissimo that followed there was an echoing explosion of clapping hands! Paris has fallen in love with me!

I was so happy that as soon as the symphony was over and I had been paid, during the intermission, I left the hall, not waiting to hear the rest of the concert, and went to the Palais Royal and had a large ice. As I ate it I said a rosary, which I had promised to do if the symphony was a success. And then I went home.

Are you not proud of me? For I am your obedient and successful son,

Woferl!

From ALOYSIA WEBER.

Mannheim, June 26, 1778

Dear Wolfgang:

You keep begging me to write, so I will oblige. The purpose of my writing, however, is to request that you stop writing to me. I am offended by all the nonsense you have put in your letters about that odious violin, whose tones, you seem to think, are capable somehow of pawing and fondling all your female friends. What has happened to you? Your natural instrument is the clavier. I advise you to wash your hands and return to it.

If you must write letters, why don't you write to my little sister Constanze? She likes you, don't you remember how she always giggled at your filthy jokes? She may believe your fairy tales about Cupids and singing birds.

In justice I must say that I have been grateful for your concern for my career, and for that I do thank you. Beyond that, all I can say is: *Basta!*

Aloysia Weber

To HÉLOÏSE DE GUINES, Paris.

Paris, June 27, 1778

Ma chère étudiante!

Alas, I will be unable to come for our lesson this afternoon, and perhaps for two or three days more, because my dear mother is very ill and I must be with her. I hope you know how much our "dialogues"—or, rather, those between Antonietta and your Mamma's clavier—have meant to my lonely heart. For the time being I must convey to you in this way, in writing, the embraces that Antonietta in my arms would be giving the clavier under your precious hands—indeed the musical kisses—would it have been possible for the two instruments to converse this afternoon.

Till I see you again!
Your teacher

Salzburg, June 30, 1778

My beloved son!

I write to remind you of your dear mother's approaching name day. You should take the trouble to buy her a present—not an expensive one, a trinket would suffice, it is the thought that would please her. God in His inscrutable wisdom has decreed that she should be separated at this time of her frail health—for your sake, Wolfgang!—from her husband and her daughter. It is you who must give her the comfort and solace that Nannerl and I, at such a distance, cannot offer her.

Congratulations for the success of your symphony at the Concert Spirituel. But, son! Your fantasy of rushing into the orchestra and pushing the concertmaster aside and leading the orchestra with a different violin—this sort of rash idea that you so often have turns my blood cold. You could be killed for such an affront. What symphony, even of yours, is worth a life? If the concertmaster were English, he would challenge you to a duel with swords. If he were Italian, he would lurk at a street corner and shoot you. But Lahoussaye is French, is he not, and a Frenchman would invite you to dine with him and would put poison in the wine. You say you eat often with Lahoussaye. Are you mad? I thank the Great God in Heaven that you thought better of such an impetuous act.

The accounting you recently gave me threw me into a panic. Where is the easy fortune that the shining city of Paris was supposed to guarantee to a person of your talents? It seems that an honest German does not have the guile and craft to outwit those Gallic cheats—and you, of all people, German or not, with your gullible mind and your heart that softens like ripe cheese! Would that we lived in a better world, Woferl, where purity and innocence like yours—quite apart from music like yours!—would be properly honored and rewarded. Sometimes I grow weary of life, and if it were not for you, my dear son, and your dear mother and sister—but especially *you*—I would gladly resign from it.

L MZT

To HÉLOÏSE DE GUINES.

Paris, July 3, 1778

Ma chère étudiante!

Weep for me, dear Héloïse! I have never known a sadder day than this one—it is now one o'clock in the morning. God has summoned my saintly mother to His hosts. She is no more. I cannot describe to you the agonies I have gone through in recent days, the fears and the grief. I could see that she was slipping away. Three days ago I had a priest in to take her confession, administer the Sacrament, and give her extreme unction. I was with her at the end. At twenty-one minutes after five her agony began, and she lost consciousness. I was holding her hand. She struggled with her fate for five hours, and then the flame was blown out by the tiniest puff of a sigh—almost, I thought, of relief. I had never before seen a person die, though I had often wanted to—but how cruel that this first time it had to be my own mother!

I am so worried about my Papa, who may break like a carefully tuned violin string when he hears this news. I cannot bear the idea of his learning it from me in a letter, so I am going to write him only that she is very, very sick, and I shall write the truth to a priest in Salzburg who is a dear friend of the family, Abbé Bullinger, and charge him with the task of preparing my father, face to face, in the warmth of his presence, for word of what God has decided.

Be kind to me, Héloïse. Forgive me for placing a burden on your shoulders, but I do, for now I would be all alone were it not for you. You are all I have. I will tell you something. During these last days, to keep myself afloat, I have begun work on a sonata for you and me*—a sonata for us to play—for your Mamma's clavier and Antonietta to share—through which the instru-

*Sonata for Clavier and Violin in D major, Köchel 306.

ments can caress each other and comfort each other, as if with arms around each other in a sweet consoling embrace. Don't worry—the music will not be gloomy, there will be no hint of death in it. To the contrary, I will make it both merry and deep—like you. I want it to celebrate the marvels of our existence, yours and mine, on God's earth, and of our tender feelings for music, which you and I know to be the greatest marvel of all. There is no declaration of love like that of one instrument's tone for that of another, no bliss like that of one musical sound receiving the hug and the kiss of another. In a few days we will enjoy together the intimacy of this music that I have written!

Wolfgang

Paris, July 3, 1778

Monsieur, mon très cher Père!

Today I must send you news that you will find distressing and painful. Mamma is ill, very ill. Her troubles began early in June, when she had toothache, earache, and a sore throat, which seemed never to mend, and soon she had diarrhea. There was much debate about whether she should be bled. For an internal inflammation of the sort she appeared to be suffering from, the French much prefer a lavage, but Mamma banks on the good sense of our German ways, and she finally let herself be bled on June 11. I can't say exactly how much, because here they measure not by the ounce but by the plateful. The surgeon took less than two platefuls, saying that it was too hot that day to take more. A day later Mamma's head ached, and then she began to suffer from shivering and fever. I gave her an anti-spasmodic powder and urged her to have a doctor come in, but she is terrified of French doctors, especially after having been bled by one to no purpose—so, I'm sorry to say, we waited. On the 23rd I had a bad scare, she lost her hearing. How frightful to lose the sense through which music can touch our souls! With Herr Heina's help, I found a German doctor, an old man of about seventy, who gave her a rhubarb powder in wine. This seemed to heat her even more, and her fever worsened. Three days later the old German came again, and he frightened me beyond imagining by saying, to my astonishment, "If she gets cramps and has to go to the commode in the night, I fear she may not see the morning." Thank God, he was wrong. Finally, two days ago, I was at my wits' end, I thought I was losing my mind, I had plenty of time to compose but couldn't put a single note on paper. I kept praying to God to spare my beloved mother—and finally, in desperation, I ran through the streets all the way to see Grimm and Mme. d'Épinay. They were horrified that I had not come to them sooner, and they said they would send their own doctor at once. But Mamma stubbornly refuses to have a French doctor touch her. This is how things stand, dear Father! All we can do in good conscience is to pray to God and trust that in His wisdom He will allow Mamma to find the path back to health. Who knows what He will decide? Let us hope!

Wolfgang Amadé Mozart

To HÉLOÏSE DE GUINES.

Paris, July 4, 1778

Ma chère étudiante!

I must have several more days in which to make arrangements for my mother's burial, the packing of her clothing, a move of my own into other quarters, and settlement of my affairs. After that I will fly to your home for our next lesson. I told you in my last note about the sonata I had begun for us—for sweet congress between Antonietta and your Mamma's clavier! I worked on it all through the days of my mother's decline. You may be amazed that I could compose serene music under such circumstances, but, you see, I could hear those two instruments in my mind, I playing one, you the other, and this kept me calm, and even quite happy. This is the sixth of a set of sonatas I will be publishing soon,* and it is the only one of them that is in three movements. I cannot wait to play the Andantino with you! It has the most pleasing exchange of kindnesses—and more!—between the two instruments. I would like to play Antonietta the first time we go through it—you will have no trouble at all sight-reading it—and then we should play it again at once, exchanging instruments, so that the violin and the clavier can give each other—and us—completely new sensations of delight in sound while performing the identical musical "acts." And then: again and again, I hope!

I will let you know as soon as I can plan to come.

Ton maître M

Salzburg, July 8, 1778

My dear son!

Today, just now, at ten in the morning, I received your harrowing letter of July 3. Nannerl and I could hardly get through it for our weeping. By now my wife may be gone! Or she may have recovered—Great God above in Thy wisdom and mercy, Thy will be done! I know that you have been a faithful son and have done all you could for her. You should, you should, for she has devoted her life to you, she is so proud of you, she has been an adoring mother.

I cannot bear to think that she may already have been taken into God! If she is no more—if she is gone from our valley of sorrows—then—God knows!—you need friends, my dear Woferl. You need friends *who are honest*—a rarity in this world. There will now be endless expenses: the funeral, the burial itself, and seeing to her things—you will be ruined financially, because you know nothing about worldly matters. There will be Frenchmen who mislead you, who charge you more than they should,

---

*Köchel 301–306.

who delight in cheating a foreigner. Move your mother's most valuable possesions to Baron Grimm's for protection, and lock up the rest of her things tightly, because with your lessons you are away from home much of the time, and robbers could easily break in and steal everything. But see how in my concern for you I have too hastily *given up* on her life! I fear that you waited too long to have her bled. She thought she could lie in bed and get well—resting—dieting—taking whatever powders she happened to have—hoping—postponing. Your letter fills me with fear. Ah, son, we must submit in humility to God's will, whatever it may bring!———

And now, at three-thirty in the afternoon, I know the truth. The good Abbé Bullinger has been here, and I know that your mother has gone to her abode above. I know the truth. I weep as I write, dear son, I weep and weep, but your letter had spaded my mind for the bitter planting of the truth, and now I bend my soul to my Lord's decision. I kneel, and I pray that you—*you*, my son, the embodiment of all my hopes and dreams—will be strong enough to go forward on your own, alert to the mischief in human nature, taking your money quickly to the bank, locking your door against French thievery, on guard against false friends and ambitious young women, so that you will be able to go on writing your exquisite music for your mother to hear among the angels in the knowledge that her little son down on earth, her Woferl, the baby who took milk at her breast, is growing up to be a great composer! Pray, Wolfgang, for the strength to give her that joy in Heaven.

MZT

To HÉLOÏSE de GUINES.

Paris, July 12, 1778

Ma très chère étudiante!

Tomorrow, at the usual time! I will bring my sonata. Practice with loving touch on each of Antonietta and your Mamma's clavier for an hour today, so that the two instruments will be in a ready mood for tomorrow's mutual passion! I am in that mood myself! Are you?

Ton maître Mozart

Paris, July 12, 1778

My dear Father!

Mother is at rest. I arranged to have her buried at the St. Eustache Cemetery. It was a dreary, rainy day, and I stood at the graveside alone but for a shabby priest who was hired by the superintendent of the cemetery to say prayers, and two ragged gravediggers to fill the hole. You were right about French cheats—I had to pay this mumbler two livres and the ghouls with shovels, one! I have arranged through Gschwendner to send to Salzburg all of Mamma's clothing and linen, her watch, her ring and her other jewelry. I am also enclosing the French edition of your *Violinschule* and some music that I thought you would like to see—a copy of my symphony, among other things.

So! God's divine and holy will has been done. Now we must say a worshipful Paternoster for Mamma's soul and turn our minds to other concerns, for all things have their proper time. I have moved to live with Baron Grimm and Madame d'Épinay, in a snug little room with a bright view of mansard roofs and linden trees. I am well and reasonably happy, except for occasional bouts of melancholy.

What has made me especially happy in these last days is that I have finished the sixth of my sonatas for clavier and violin. You remember that I wrote four in Mannheim, one of them—you will rebuke me again!—for Therese-Pierron Serrarius and one (in my mind, though I never formally dedicated it to her) for my beloved Aloysia Weber—and I am glad to say they will all be published by Siéber here. No one was willing to give me what I asked for them, so I have had to settle for fifteen louis d'or. This last one is dedicated—Papa! have mercy!—in my mind, again—to my dear pupil here, Héloïse de Guines. We will have the excitement of playing it together for the first time tomorrow.

You were right in warning that Mamma's death would bring unexpected expenses—and perhaps right in saying that I am a booby when it comes to worldly matters. Before Mamma fell so sick, I had completed a fourth cycle of twelve lessons with Mademoiselle Héloïse, and, learning that Monsieur le Duc had gone to the country for ten days, I applied to the housekeeper to be paid—I was owed for three cycles, nine louis d'or. She pulled out a purse and said, "Pray excuse me if I only pay for twelve lessons this time, I am short of money just now." She offered me three. "Please let us know if this does not satisfy you." I know what they think. They think that, after all, this is just a boy, and a moronic German boy at that; that is the way these French snobs would look at it. This rich man has had my concerto for flute and harp *for two months* and still hasn't paid for it. These stupid Frenchmen seem to think I am still the seven-year-old child that they first saw, when you brought me here to show me off, Papa. I wish I were still in Mannheim, with the Webers, or, better yet, at home with the comfort of your company and Nannerl's. If it were not for this one brilliant pupil here—curses that she is this niggardly Frenchman's daughter!—if it were not for her, Papa, and if it were not for the clavier that she will play tomorrow and the violin I will play, of which you so disapprove, I think I would die. I thank God that I have something to look forward to for tomorrow. This is what keeps us alive—is it not, Papa?—wanting what the next day will bring. And the next, and the next.

Wolfgang

To ALOYSIA WEBER, Mannheim.

Paris, July 14, 1778

My dear friend!

You have asked me to stop writing to you. I will do so—after this letter. I feel that I am obliged in all honor to tell you about an experience that I had yesterday. After that, if you insist—*basta*, as you say.

You and all your family, who were so kind to us in Mannheim, will be saddened to learn that my dear mother died eleven days ago. She suffered undeserved tortures, but her final moments, with her hand in mine, were peaceful, thanks be to merciful God. During the worst of her ordeal, I kept sane by writing a sonata for clavier and violin, the last of a series for which I had composed five before I left Mannheim. One of them, you must remember, I told you I had written, with all my feelings naked, for you!* Do you recall the moments of ecstasy in its minuet? Did you not tell me you felt them, along with me?

So. In my last letter to you, which apparently offended you, I mentioned a gifted young pupil I have had the good fortune to be teaching here in Paris. Her name is Héloïse de Guines. She is the daughter of a duke who is a great favorite of the Queen, she is sixteen years old, she has beautiful features and a strange tight little smile that speaks of mysterious banked fires within, and she moves me to the depths of my heart by her sensitive musicianship. I write freely to you about her in the knowledge that, after all, you hold me in such contempt that these words could not possibly make you jealous. I composed this final sonata of the portfolio for her.

This brings me to yesterday. Read this, dear Aloysia.

It is five o'clock of a benign sunny afternoon. I enter the magnificent chamber in the ducal palace where we have been having our lessons each day with an audience of guests, idlers, fops, cardplayers, and gossips, friends of the Duchess—all of them dazzled by our inspired improvisations, to judge by their applause and embraces afterward. But today we are alone. Héloïse's parents have gone to the country. Her duenna has tactfully retired, confident that the funny little music teacher is a harmless creature.

---

*Sonata for Clavier and Violin in E minor, Köchel 304.

Look at your friend Mozart. His hair has been freshly frizzed a few hours ago. Tucked under his arm is a sheaf of quarto sheets of manuscript music. He is dressed in a brand-new mourning coat that he has had made by a tailor with a name appropriate for the purpose, Douloureux. It is in the Paris fashion, which to our German eyes looks strange indeed, for it is a frock coat of bright red cloth with black buttons, its sleeves, pockets, and lapels trimmed with crape. It makes its wearer look roguish and dashing, as if these Frenchmen think that the death of a spouse or of kin is cause for a profligate frolic.

The pupil is already seated at the clavier. Yes, her hair, too, has just been dressed; it is piled up on her crown with an intricate interweaving of ribbons. She is wearing a simple pale saffron-colored gown, gathered up under her breast with three ribbons of the same colors as of those in her hair; her arms are bare. Her eyes sparkle at the sight of her teacher's new coat, and that fierce smile of hers draws the purse of her mouth into a shape not so much of joy as of some kind of almost painful excitement.

The violin, Antonietta, glistens as it waits atop the black clavier, which is inlaid on its sides with mother-of-pearl and ivory in scenes of arched bridges and moon gates and willow trees in a mandarin's dreamlike garden.

I place the music for the second, slow movement of the sonata on the piano stand and then kiss my pupil's hand. I take up the violin. Héloïse strikes the note A on the clavier, and I tune the strings. We do not say a word. She nods. She is ready, her eyes say, for anything.

And so the music starts. The clavier speaks first, andantino cantabile, declaring itself to its partner in a fairly bold voice:

As the clavier then tries to repeat this first avowal, Antonietta answers extremely shyly, plaintively, on a heartfelt long soft note of appeal, but this quite quickly seems to be transformed into something more like a claim, until, before we know it, Antonietta has grasped the clavier's hand, as it were, and, breaking down all reserve, begins to answer back some of the very words the clavier has just spoken—but then goes on to make something quite new of them!

Antonietta carries on for a few moments, more firm now, yet also gentle and considerate. The clavier answers, all in the treble clef, softly, softly, and when Antonietta joins again, it seems that there is a mysterious alchemy at work which has begun to transform sound into touch. There is a playfulness in this first sweet contact, which ends in two peals, one from each partner, of what seems to be cheerful—yet slightly embarrassed—laughter, rising, staccato. Then, after a groan of realization and surrender, the instruments seem to throw their arms around each other and—at last!—they share (musically) a shy kiss.

This has taken their breath away, and they draw apart and start again from the beginning—this time with somewhat more assurance on both parts, with new warmth and with crescendos that seem physical as well as aural. How can I describe the effect of the caresses Antonietta and the clavier are now exchanging upon this tender virgin, her eyes fastened greedily on the music, her rigid smile infused with the first signs of a degree of pleasure she has never, never experienced before?

After the second musical kiss, the clavier is much more daring, and it makes the next advance, to which Antonietta responds with an outcry of trills and grace notes, each of which is like a tiny catch of breath. This encourages the clavier to do the same thing again, and this time Antonietta answers dare with dare and takes each one further, and further, and further, until there is a moment of almost unbearable bliss, when Antonietta cries out, for the third time, with the long, plaintive, soft high note which at first seemed an appeal but now is clearly a sigh of pure delight. . . .

When we finished playing the Andantino, Héloïse's face was crimson. She bowed her head, and I saw her shoulders shake with sobs. Were they of joy? Or was there some other cause? Did she *know*?

I come now to my reason for writing you this letter. What could she have known, Aloysia? It is time that you understood something about me, my dear friend—something I am astonished you have not had the sensitivity to see long since: that I make love through music. There it is. This is my joy, this is my gratification. You were wrong to berate me for the things I had been saying about the remarkable violin Héloïse and I have been playing. It has spoken as I have wished to speak; it has kissed and hugged on my behalf. My task in life has been—and will always be—to try to give those who hear my music a pleasure that is as poignant, as piercing, as sublime as the greatest physical delight God has given us poor mortals to enjoy.

Héloïse, who is most responsive, may well have understood this, but it not this that I mean she may have known. When I stood there with the violin under my arm and saw her convulsed with sobs, I felt guilty, Aloysia, guilty! For it had come to me, at that climactic moment of perfection in the sonata, that I was making love through that music not with her at all, but with you. I had been deceiving this poor girl, and perhaps myself, God knows, because it came to me in the moment of greatest ecstasy that *you* were the one I wanted this music—this violin's rendering of this music—to delight, to caress, to ravish.

Ah, Aloysia, I am so confused! Since my mother died, I have been so lonely that I have not been able to think straight. I feel shame, desperate, abysmal shame, that I am alive and she is not. I neglected her, Aloysia, in my selfishness and single-mindedness. My head was full of music and of everyday trivialities and of idle laughter, and I gave too little thought to her isolation and pain. I believe that you know, from things I told you in Mannheim, that I never managed to love her as much as I love my father, but I had no right to be so careless, to leave her alone so much.

Now that I have faced how lonely she was, I realize how lonely *I* have been. I tell you this because it may help to explain why I was so cruelly double-dealing, without meaning to be, with this delicate girl here in Paris, and why I have been thrown back onto my helpless admiration and caring for you, onto my need for the lighthearted way you accepted me—and my loving music—when I was in Mannheim. I was never able to express my love for you except in those musical terms, and when I had left you for Paris and was at such a great distance from you, you came to see those terms—unjustly, I feel—as false and cheap and vulgar: "that odious violin . . . pawing . . . fondling." Can you begin to understand me now? In my mind the violin, in offering you my radiant musical love from faraway Paris, was simply trying to cry out to you about my loneliness. I was lonely long before I realized, after her death, that I did not love my mother enough. Didn't you know that I was lonely even at every moment when I was with you, even when I was playing music for you? Ah, Aloysia, will I always be lonely?

Basta! Basta!

Mozart

Intermezzo Two

For some weeks after his mother's death, Mozart stayed on with Baron Grimm and Madame d'Épinay, but it had become clear to everyone that if there was a gold mine in Paris, he was not going to be the one to discover it. Leopold Mozart arranged an appointment for his son at home in Salzburg, as court organist to the archbishop. On the way there, in Munich, Wolfgang called on Aloysia Weber and was treated so badly by her that he bitterly wrote home that she was "false, malicious, and a coquette." Two years later she married—unhappily, it turned out—a court painter named Joseph Lange. A year after that, having been transferred to Vienna by the archbishop, Mozart moved in with the Webers, who were then also there, and he soon took up with Aloysia's younger sister Constanze, as if compelled to do so by Aloysia's having sarcastically suggested it in the last letter she wrote him. He married Constanze in 1782. The marriage was neither rapturous nor disastrous, "neither hot nor cold." Nine years later, at the age of thirty-five, having written some of the greatest music mankind would ever hear but never having found his gold mine, Mozart suddenly wilted away, and died, and was buried in a commoner's grave at St. Mark's Church in Vienna.

Pierre Lahoussaye continued for many years his notable careers as violinist and roué. Besides conducting the Concert Spirituel, he played with the excellent Concert des Amateurs, led the orchestra at the Théâtre de Monsieur, and taught at the Paris Conservatoire. He came to realize, thanks partly to what had happened at the performance of Mozart's "Paris" Symphony, that Antonietta had, after all, a stronger throat and more eloquent tongue than his Stainer violin had. The varnish on Antonietta's back began to chip slightly—a symptom that dealers told him was common with Stradivari violins. This spotty flaking did not affect the tone, and it gave a fascinating mottled effect to the back. On an evening when Lahoussaye had been showing this feature to one of his succession of mistresses in high society, Madame la Comtesse de Ponsard, she accidentally spilled a drop of cognac on the varnish of the belly and hastily wiped it away with the heel of her white-gloved hand, leaving a mark that would be seen there forever. In time Lahoussaye's touch in both his lines of activity began to falter. When he was seventy-eight he lost his hearing, and in his bitter grief at being closed away from all but imaginary music, he sold first the Stainer and then Antonietta to the dealer Lupot, who cheated him unmercifully, paying him only twenty louis d'or for the Stradivari. He died in poverty, in 1818.

Soon after Lupot acquired Antonietta, an agent representing the Betts family of London, who were among the foremost experts in the world on Stradivari instruments and had been watching like sharp-eyed ospreys for old Lahoussaye's Antonietta to come finning onto the market, bought the violin from Lupot for twice what he had paid—still a bargain. The agent set out from Paris in a post chaise, charged with Antonietta and a Ruggieri cello that the Bettses had bought from another dealer, Kölliker. At Le Havre the agent embarked on a packet boat, the *Hirondelle*. In rough waters in mid-Channel this French vessel was attacked and boarded by the crew of a British freebooting ketch, the *Drummer Boy*, and the Betts agent, though shouting over and over that he had a valid British passport, was lashed to a belaying-pin rack and had to watch helplessly as the two instruments in their cases were heaved carelessly with other loot onto the deck of the raider.

By the time the agent reached London on the *Hirondelle*, *Drummer Boy* had dropped anchor in Southampton and Antonietta had been carted with the rest of the booty up to London. The violin was sold at a grubby public auction to a music-hall fiddler for two pounds. This man, who was named Chauster, played in a public house every night after his work at the music hall was done, drank several growlers of stout, and, tottering home drunk, slept with the fiddle—literally took it under the covers with him in bed. He never cleaned the resin off the strings or the belly. By day he smoked hideous Indian cheroots. He was unable to get much out of the violin. Its A string kept going out of tune; whatever he tried, he couldn't seem to make the tuning peg hold properly. The fiddle's tone was thin and cranky. (Small wonder! A choppy English Channel crossing [violins have been known to be "seasick" long after damp and violent sea voyages]; a crash onto a pirate deck; an owner with dirty hands and the breath of a hyena playing scratchy music-hall ditties with an out-of-tune string; a nightly curing in tobacco smoke in a pub, repeated by day in damp and chilly digs; unclean, unloved, misunderstood.) Slovenly Chauster, making atrocious noises on the violin, eventually lost his music-hall job. In order to eat he took the fiddle to a pawnshop, where he got a ticket and one pound six bob.

On a long chance, the pawnbroker took the dirty fiddle to a violin shop he heard about on Brandon Road, by the Newington Causeway, Southwark, belonging to one Henry Lockey Hill. Hill, the reigning member of a distinguished family of luthiers, had learned his craft working for the Bettses, and he had recently heard all about the "lost" Antonietta from one of their apprentices. He recognized the instrument at once and bought it from the delighted hocker for five pounds.

Hill lovingly restored the violin. It had a tiny crack in the back (perhaps from the blow of landing on *Drummer Boy*'s deck), which he repaired. Having been told about the famous nick at the edge of the purfling on the belly, he left it unpatched. When the instrument was whole and sound and glistening again, he advertised it—shrewdly, knowing that the Bettses might stake a claim—on the Continent, and before long he sold it to the Paris violinmaker and dealer Vuillaume for one hundred pounds.

Vuillaume had had Antonietta in his shop for only four days when in came the violinist Pierre Baillot, looking for a great instrument. Then in his mid-forties, Baillot had in his sights the peak of a brilliant career, and he felt ready to step up from a *faux* Stradivari, a handsome imitation made by Vuillaume himself, to the real thing. Baillot had played, early in the century, in Napoleon's private orchestra; he had toured Russia with great success twice; had a few years earlier led sensational chamber concerts in Paris, praised by Mendelssohn among others; and he was now fresh back from triumphs in Belgium, Holland, and England. With the backing of a benefactor of the Paris Opéra who was pushing him for the honored leadership of the Opéra orchestra, he bought Antonietta for six thousand francs, a price which gave Vuillaume a ninety-percent markup.

Having been told some of what had happened to Antonietta, Baillot realized that the instrument would be out of sorts, and it took him several weeks to coax it back to a full, round, clean tone. He did land the Opéra post, and later he became concurrently the leader of the Chapelle Royale at Versailles. He also gave solo recitals and led a quartet, which bore his name, in frequent appearances. Playing the Stradivari, he was universally praised for the pure, noble tone he produced—a tone which was also said, however, to be piquantly disturbing, much as (various listeners remarked after hearing it) brandy, strong snuff, a daring décolletage, candied ginger, a stolen kiss, chutney, Egyptian perfume, a guardsman's mustaches, a flirt's pout, or (as one even said) the velvet curtains in the windows of a bordello might be felt to be disturbing. Baillot took tender care of Antonietta.

Act Three

1830

Music is memory, he says. Most of us have associations, usually nostalgic, that click into place when we hear certain tunes, but with Berlioz the connection is so much more intense that he states it in this extravagant way, as an absolute equivalence. Something happened the other day that bears this out, at least in one sense. He asked me to play some passages from his *Francs-Juges* overture, and when I had finished, I waited as usual for him to start reminiscing.

He said, "I have a pain in my foot."

I asked, "Did you turn your ankle?"

"Yes," he said, "I did. Two and a half years ago."

"And it still hurts?"

"No. It only hurts when I hear that music."

He then told me that when he was writing *Francs-Juges*, he was unsure of the capabilities of some of the instruments. Having written a trombone solo in the overture in the key of D-flat, he began to worry that that would be difficult to play, so he showed the passage to a trombonist at the Opéra, who assured him that D-flat was an ideal key for the instrument and that the passage would be splendid. Going home, Berlioz was so happy with this outcome that he "walked on air, in a daze of joy," not watching his step, and he stumbled on a curb and sprained his ankle. Now—and this will probably be so for the rest of his life, he says—whenever he hears themes from the overture, his foot hurts.

The tie between music and memory works for him in another and a much more important way, however. It seems that when certain images from the past come to him, some sort of crossover from the visual to the aural takes place in his mind, and he begins to hear strains of music. And sometimes when he hears music played that he loves—either of his own or by others—visual memories come to him, which in turn generate new music. This feeds into his process of composition, and this, of course, is where I come in.

We met for the first time last year, under circumstances that made him take to me. It was at a recital of my string ensemble, at which we had the appalling audacity to play Beethoven's then rather recent C-sharp-minor quartet,* which Parisians had never heard. As you know, some of our Paris musical establishment considers Beethoven a barbarian savage. Just the year before, Habeneck had put on Beethoven's Third, Fifth, and Seventh symphonies at the Conservatoire, to howls of protest from the "patriots" in the audiences—but not from twenty-five-year-old Berlioz, who was, he says, electrified, transported, inspired.

He came to my recital already admiring me, he later told me. A fanatical devotee of Gluck, he said he had praised me to friends one night at the Opéra because, virtuoso or not, I did not consider myself above sitting in the orchestra and playing routine accompaniments to *Alceste*, and he told them to listen for a passage I would be playing on the G-string that they would be able to hear right through all the rest of the ensemble. (He didn't know then about my eloquent violin.) And he had also been present on the night of the *Nina* riot, when it had been announced on posters that I was to play the solo in the ballet but I was ill and had to cancel at the last moment—which the management failed to announce. When the scene was almost over and I had not played, listeners began to shout, "Baillot! Baillot! The violin solo!" The entire audience got to its feet, the curtain

---

*Opus 131.

fell, the orchestra members fled, and the infuriated crowd poured into the orchestra pit and threw down the music stands and smashed a double bass and ripped open the kettledrums.

There were about two hundred present the day of our Beethoven recital. We were not halfway through the first movement of that chaotic but magisterial quartet when I could hear coughs and programs rustling and then people talking out loud. Finally almost all of the audience, outraged beyond tolerance, simply stood up and walked out. But Berlioz was one of a tiny group that stayed and heard us right to the end. Afterward he came up to me, slowly shaking his head like a person under a spell. His eye fell on the Cupid on the tailpiece of my violin, and he suddenly squinted as if in pain, and the only words he spoke to me were "I am hopelessly in love."

I had heard from friends at the Conservatoire that the flamboyant young student Berlioz was given to high-flown language, and at the time I thought he meant that he had lost his head and his heart to this mysterious music he had just sat through. But rumors I have picked up since then from those same Conservatoire friends have made me think that something else—and something rather peculiar—was on his mind.

He came to me about two weeks ago with a bizarre proposal. He said he is about to compose his first major work—"a monstrous dramatic symphony"—and he wondered whether I would enjoy doing him a very great kindness. I was charmed by the shameless vanity in his choice of the word "enjoy." *I* was the one who was to get pleasure from the favor! Would I be willing to come, he asked, two or three mornings a week, or more often if it pleased me, to play on my violin for him for just a few minutes each day, and then to chat with him? This would be an enormous help to him, he said, in his work. It would stir up memories, the images of which would stimulate his emotions and start the day's flow of melodies in his mind. He was asking me to serve him a daily mental apéritif!

He then turned on a stream of most eloquent flattery. You

would have thought that there had never been such a great violinist as Baillot. (Alas, I know that is untrue because—*Dieu sauve mon âme*—I have heard Paganini. When he played violent pizzicati with his left hand while still bowing with his right, and when he poured out unbelievable trills of octave double stops and mad runs of whistling harmonics, I thought I was hearing Beelzebub playing a fiddle. I covered my face with my hands and wept.) For his own part, young Berlioz went on to say with bland assurance that he was going to be a great composer, and he begged me to become, in this way, a patron who would help him on the road to his first great success. In other words, my doing him a favor would bring fame to *me*.

I must confess that I was fascinated by the preposterousness of this young man's invitation and by the reach of his conceit. I am old enough to be his father—he tells me he is twenty-six years old—and though I am not quite Paganini I am very much in demand, yet he seemed to expect that I would jump at the chance to take the time, perhaps every morning "if it pleased me," to massage his naïve gifts. Inwardly laughing, I told him I would have to think about it.

As it happens, Berlioz's principal teacher of composition at the Conservatoire, Jean-François Le Sueur, is an old friend of mine, and I told him about the amusing visit I had had from the young tyro. Le Sueur startled me by clutching at my shoulders with his hands and shouting excitedly, shaking me, "You must do it! You must do it!" He spoke then so earnestly of the gushing, turbulent talent of his pupil—fashioning music that Le Sueur both hates and honors, "music that in defiance of my teaching will bring glory to France"—that I was completely turned around. It happens that I have very few engagements for the next month or two, and moreover this is a period when I have been rather bored and restless—and . . . well . . . the upshot is . . . I go to him three or four times a week.

We meet in the small room he rents a couple of streets away from the Conservatoire. It is shabbily furnished; there are no curtains at the windows. Berlioz composes, without the use of a piano, at a scarred and rickety table. He has swiped a music stand from the Conservatoire for me to use, and each day he sets some music on it for me to perform. Often the sheets before me will be orchestra or opera scores, from which he expects me to pick out the significant melodies, from whatever instrument or voice, and make fluent sense of a passage. This is an exercise I *do* rather enjoy.

While I play, he lounges on his bed against the wall on the street side of the room. He wears an ordinary workman's clothes: a long-sleeved linen shirt, a gray vest tied at his waist with a broad sash, a bandanna at his throat, and, on chilly days, a floppy cloth cap on his head. Berlioz has a huge arching blade of a nose, piercing brown eyes underlined with signs of insomnia, a generous mouth, and an enormous crown of curly hair that cascades down into copious sideburns. When he makes a sudden movement of his head, on days when he is not wearing his cap, this wonderful hair shakes out sparks of reddish light.

When I took my violin out of the case at our first appointment, I found myself drenched, whether I liked it or not, in Berlioz's rapturous intensity. He asked me if he might hold the instrument in his hands for a few moments. His eyes hungrily devoured every sweet morsel of its beauty, saving for dessert the mother-of-pearl design of the Cupid. Then, handing the violin back to me, he said, "I have never seen the sea—except there, on the back of your instrument! How lucky you are! I hear the music of the wind on those waves! I myself play the flute, my instrument is that of the forest, of birdsong—quite by chance I began playing the flute. When I was a child, I found an old flageolet one day in a drawer, and I tooted on it so endlessly and annoyingly that my father in despair bought me a flute to take its place, and he gave me Devienne's book of instructions to teach myself by. But I was always in awe of the violin. My uncle, my mother's brother Félix Marmion, was a guardsman for Napoleon, a crimson uniform, huge mustaches!—he played the violin. He lived recklessly, he was cut on the cheek by a saber in Spain, he sped from campaign to campaign—Prussia, Poland—wounded by a gunshot in the foot in Prussia and a lance in the side in Poland, always carrying his violin with him and playing it for glory after each battle. And he played for us, too, when he visited—the violin brought wars, bravery, blood right into our parlor! When my father finally gave in to my begging and hired a musician to teach me the flute, he picked a violinist from the Lyons orchestra, a man named Imbert—and my happiest times were listening to him play his violin for me—he brought me the trees astir in the woods, he brought me on his E string the majestic far crests of the Alps of the Dauphiné. And when my father tried to force me to step into his shoes as a doctor and sent me off to study medicine, bribing me with a new flute, my companion and roommate in Paris was my cousin Alphonse Robert—he, too, a violinist. He brought me sublime relief from cadavers. Ah, Baillot, you will help me! We will do wonders together!"

Carried along like a drowning man on this flood of emotion, I began, as quietly as I could, to tell Berlioz some of the reasons why I love my violin. I spoke of the shades of tone it can give me—all the way from the subtleties of shot silk and thin crystal to a thick, chocolaty sound, and even cries of pain, if needed, though it could never growl or snarl, never be rude or cruel. I said the violin was equally at home with *Eine kleine Nachtmusik* and the harsh Beethoven quartet that Berlioz had sat all the way through; with Vivaldi and with Gluck; with Bach and with Weber. I told him that I am so respectful of my instrument, which is now a hundred and thirty years old and getting stronger every year, that I cannot think of myself as its owner, but only as its temporary custodian.

All this Berlioz took in with a kind of reined-in patience, as if he could hardly wait to speak himself and only heard me out as a courtesy. But he sat up straight, with an expression of a mischievous small boy, when I told him the stories I had heard from the dealer Vuillaume about the British pirates, and the drunken music-hall fiddler in London, and the pawnshop owner's profit. Then I told him that the violin had a name. Antonietta. According to the legend Vuillaume passed on to me, I said, it was named for a woman with whom the great Stradivari had fallen in love at first sight on the day he began making the violin, and whom he never saw again all the time he was working on it.

I was unable to finish the story. Berlioz leaped up off the edge of his bed, the blood drained from his face, and cried out in a kind of groan, "*Sacré nom de Dieu*, the Cupid, I understand!" Then, pacing back and forth, he shouted, "Play for me, Baillot! Play!"

I tuned up. He sat on the edge of the bed, leaning forward tensely.

He had put on the music stand Giulia's prayer, "Tu che invoco con orrore," from the second act of Spontini's *La Vestale*, the fervid, sweeping phrases of which I played with a tremulous bel canto tone. When I had finished, I tucked the violin under my arm and turned to see how Berlioz had responded to his first hearing of what Antonietta had to say. He was unashamedly weeping. I was both thrilled and embarrassed.

FIRST MOVEMENT

This morning I found on the music stand, ready for my reading of it, the aria "O malheureuse Iphigénie," from Gluck's *Iphigénie en Tauride*. We have been at "our work," as Berlioz calls it, for a fortnight. He tells me he is well into the first movement of his symphony, but so far he has been unwilling to show me any of it.

I tuned Antonietta and played the melody of the aria.

When I came to the end, Berlioz remained, as on other mornings, silent for a long time—a time that I have come to think of as the hush of the final snowfall of feeling which adds just enough weight to the drifts on the steep mountainsides of this man's emotions to cause an avalanche. Of words. And here it came.

"That violin has the voice of Iphigenia! Of course the great thing about Gluck was his making the voice, the words in their natural cadence, what counted. Unhappy Iphigenia, there she stood before me in all her misery, Baillot, in my poor room! Thank you! That violin shakes me. How do you make it speak so exactly with Gluck's spirit? I've been a Gluckist, you know, since first I heard his music. He broke with all that Italian operatic fountainwork and gave us simple speech in his airs, almost as if he were writing English ballads. I organized a claque, you know. . . . Listen to me."

He looked grim, seemed to be grinding his teeth. "I am going to be as well known as Gluck. I too am going to break the molds. You will see."

Then he sat back, this twenty-six-year-old boy, relaxing into the complacent look of somebody already famous, and said, "I was only nineteen, supposed to be studying to be a doctor, but I found out that anyone could use the library at the Conservatoire, and before going to the Opéra I would get out the scores and study them and copy passages. Then I would lecture my friends—d'Ortigue, Ferrand, Du Boys, Pons, Gounet, whomever I could bully!—telling them exactly what to listen for, what merits to applaud, what errors to hiss. I bought them tickets, I lied to them, said I'd been given free seats, and I placed them exactly where the music would sound most clearly—not too close to the horns, not in a place on the left side where echoes from the boxes were unpleasant or on the right where the trombones blasted at you, near the front in case the set was a holy forest, farther back if the voices were to be projected from a hollow room in a palace. You never heard such a racket as we made when things were right. We stamped and clapped in rhythm and hooted our bravissimos. But when liberties were taken! Once when this opera that you've just been playing from was being performed, they banged cymbals in the first dance of the Scythians, where

Gluck had written only strings, and as soon as the dance was over I stood up and shouted at the top of my voice, 'No cymbals! Who has the brass to rewrite Gluck?' Then again in the third act, when they left the trombones out of Orestes' monologue, I shouted, 'You cut the trombones! Shame! Shame!' Once when they were playing the sacred march in *Alceste*, Guillon the flautist—I *know* the flute, that is my instrument—Guillon couldn't stand the idea that Gluck wanted an eerie guttural undertone of the lower flute register, so what does he do? Plays his part an octave higher, to make sure the audience will hear him! I screamed. People must have thought I was either a madman or a wild little egotist scrabbling for fame at any price."

In Berlioz's pause at this point in his outpouring, I had time to take sides as to that last sentence. He does not seem mad to me. He is obviously greedy for notice, and if he is as gifted as Le Sueur says he is, he will probably get lots of it—but not without making a great fuss fighting for it in noisy ways. Come to think of it, most of the famous men that I have run across have been both generously talented and offensively self-nominating. It's the way of the world; vanity grabs the prizes and feeds itself with them.

He went on talking: more of the same. About himself—his musical strivings in the time when he was studying medicine. And I wondered, How is this going to help the work he will do today after I leave? What visual images did my playing conjure up that are translatable into melody? Iphigenia right before his eyes in his little room? Yes—but, after that, nothing visual but what he could see at any time in a mirror.

And then I realized: It must be that his "monstrous dramatic symphony" has a hero.

This morning the music on the stand was handwritten. It was a love song, which Antonietta sang, I must say, with haunting beauty. I was deeply moved hearing the sounds that I myself was making with the violin's help. It seems that whenever love is the theme, Antonietta trembles in my hands.

It was over. Snow fell longer than usual.

Then, at last: "My dear Baillot, that is from the scena that I wrote in my third attempt to win the *prix de Rome*, two years ago. They gave me second place, which is useless, besides being humiliating! I tried again last year for the fourth time—they awarded no prize at all! I am going to win it this year. I promise you that. Just wait. No one thinks you are a composer until you've won it, but the judges are all those old square-toes from the Academy who cannot stand originality. To win it, you have to put on sheep's clothing and pretend you belong in their bleating flock. What an ordeal the competition is! First you have to qualify by writing an acceptable exercise—a fugue. All right. If they take you, they sit you down in a hall, and the secretary of the Academy reads you a bad poem. In this case it was *Herminie*, by that hideous poet Viellard—"old man"!—have you ever heard of him?—of course not—an episode stolen, really, from *Jerusalem Delivered*, by Tasso. It's the story of the hopeless love of Erminia, a Saracen, and Tancred, a Christian soldier, who meet in a fight to the death at the walls of the holy city. Once the poem has been read, they lock you in what is called a 'box,' a small room with nothing but a piano and a copy of the poem. At eleven and six, a warden unlocks your door, and you dine with the other competing convicts. Actually, you can receive visitors for two hours each evening, but if they bring you books or papers or even clothes, those are searched carefully to make sure you aren't being fed ideas from outside. You are allowed twenty-two days in this prison to finish your composition. Then, do you know what? This music you have written for orchestra and two voices is played *on a piano* and sung by two people who are reading the music for the first time, and a jury of the six musical members of the Academy casts its votes. But that is not the end of it. The process is repeated a week later even more absurdly, before the whole Academy, not just musicians but also architects, painters, etchers, sculptors, who know less about music than they do about magnetism or the steam engine! Again the ballot box is passed around and the final choice is made. Not until the prize is actually awarded is the composition played for the first time by an orchestra! . . . And now I want to tell you something, Baillot." A long pause.

I prod him. "What did you want to say?"

"This, Baillot: the germ of that song—its soul—the soaring part, you know, starting with the third phrase"—he hummed the phrase—"I heard that in my mind—let's say it infected me—when I was twelve years old."

"I find that hard to believe."

"It's true. I swear it. I have had it in my head ever since."

Again this morning a manuscript score waited for me on the music stand. Berlioz was grave as he greeted me, and he said, "Baillot, I am entrusting something to you today that is very precious to me. It is the opening Largo of my symphony. I want you to promise on your honor that you will not repeat this music on your violin for anyone else's ears."

I promised, and I played. I was stunned. Once again Antonietta reached right into my own heart with the music. I say "again" because when I had finished and had tucked Antonietta under my arm and turned to look at Berlioz, I suddenly realized that I had heard a haunting echo at the very beginning of this song.

"Wait!" I said. "The 'soul' of Erminia's song! Those first bars—isn't that so? The theme that you say 'infected' you when you were a boy?"

Apparently the violin had sounded the depths of Berlioz's feelings, too. He was barely able to nod. There were tears in his eyes. And I thought, How leaky this boy's tear ducts are! Set seasoned food before him, he doubtless salivates; play tender music to him, especially his, he weeps.

After a long while he said, "Your violin is an aphrodisiac."

What could have made him say that? Is *that* what made him cry? I did not think I should answer.

Then he said, "I thank you, Baillot. Or should I say, I thank you, Antonietta? Ordinarily I do not listen to my own compositions until they are finished, but I needed to hear that theme in its new life. One day you will see why. This has meant a great deal to me."

He paused again. Then he said, "Let me tell you about that 'germ.' It has a story."

I put my violin in its case and sat down to listen.

"Toward the end of every summer when I was small," Berlioz said, "my mother and my two sisters and I used to spend three weeks at the home of my mother's father in the town of Meylan, halfway up the great rock dome of St.-Eynard, not far from Grenoble. One day, we were invited to the home of a Madame Gautier up above the town, a small white villa surrounded by vineyards, with a dainty garden, almost in the shadow of a ruined ancient tower—the set, one might have thought, for a sentimental opera. But it had what could never be seen on a stage in a hall: one of the most intoxicating views on earth, down the sloping mountainside and across the valley of the Grésivaudan, with its two wandering rivers, and then to the massed white army of the Alps beyond. I was in a vulnerable state of nerves from taking all this in, when down from the verandah of the villa came our hostess, Madame Gautier, and two young women, her nieces, dressed in white. I was drawn at once to look at one of them, because she was wearing pink slippers!—*petits brodequins roses*, Baillot! I had never in my life seen anyone who dared to wear pink shoes! She was standing on an outcropping of rock in those slippers, with one hand reached out to the trunk of a cherry tree. My heart was beating wildly when I finally got the courage to raise my eyes and look at her face, and what I saw changed my whole life. I have never, to this day, got over the emotion that flooded me then. She was, mind you, several years older than I—seven years, I learned later, she nineteen and I twelve, but what difference could that have made?—because she was not a girl, she was a goddess in pink shoes. She was slim and much taller than I was; she had a crown of black hair over a pale face in which the gaze from two eyes like amethysts brushed across me with something like amusement, paralyzing me. I was a lost soul. After that I felt ill and could not imagine what was wrong with me. Her name was Estelle Duboeuf. In bed at night I kissed the sheet under my cheek and murmured the name and cried, and in the daytime I crawled under a bush, like a poisoned animal, and lay there wondering whether I had really seen the feet in those slippers, or I lolled in a hayfield waiting to die from a ridiculous happiness that I could not control.

"But I was not to be happy for long. My uncle Félix Marmion, who must then have been about twenty-five, was also visiting—the hero with the scarlet coat, mended where the lance had pierced it, his face lit up with a brave scar. Two things were obvious to all the grown-ups: the funny little Berlioz boy was mooning over Estelle, and Estelle's brilliant eyes had no other aim than at the guardsman's head, swollen with vainglory, balanced on a handsome straight neck. Only now can I realize what all the snickers meant.

"One night there was a party. When Uncle Félix danced a waltz with Estelle, I wanted to cover my eyes but I had to cover my ears instead, to shut out the terrible faint triumphant tinkling of his spurs, which pierced right through the music of the orchestra and the shuffling of feet and the clamor of everyone talking at the tops of their voices, and nearly killed me. Later, a game of prisoner's base was announced. Two teams were formed, and the men had to choose partners. Someone shouted that little Hector should be the first to choose. I stood there frozen, looking at the floor, believing that everyone in the room could hear my heart pounding like the hooves of a cantering horse. And then

—I thought I would faint with joy—Estelle took my hand and said, 'Monsieur Hector is *mine!*' At last I had the courage to look up at her face, and I saw it all. She was teasing me—but mainly she was trying to tease Uncle Félix. And everyone else could see what was happening just as well as I, and the whole company broke out laughing.

"I went home, when we left soon after, heartbroken. I began composing melancholy little duets and trios in minor keys. Then one day I found on my father's bookshelves the mawkish verse romance by the poet Florian, *Estelle et Némorin*, and at once *I* was the pining Némorin, and soon I set to music some verses that spoke to my sense of loss in having had to part from my real Estelle:

Je vais donc quitter pour jamais
Mon doux pays, ma douce amie,
Loin d'eux je vais traîner ma vie
Dans les pleurs and dans les regrets!"

He had finished his story. Awkward questions came into my mind. Was it his memory of this faraway Estelle that had made him jump up that first day, so disturbed, when I told of Stradivari's love at first sight for his Antonia? Was this ridiculous puppy love the "hopeless adoration from a distance" that my gossiping friends at the Conservatoire had hinted at? Was this Estelle of Berlioz's adolescent dreams to be the heroine of a serious symphony that would "break the molds"?

Of course I couldn't blurt these questions out loud. I asked instead, "Did you keep a copy of the song all these years?"

"No, no, it was burnt, along with other things I wrote back then. But I remember every note of everything I have ever written."

I recalled his aphorism "Music is memory," and I think I believed him. Still, how strange and childish all this was!

SECOND MOVEMENT

This morning the music on the stand was the duet "Gardez-vous de la jalousie," from Méhul's *Euphrosine.* I had of course played with the Opéra orchestra this famous passage, with its keen probing of dark human feelings, after the manner of Gluck, yet spinning out its musical motives with the crystal purity of Haydn's symphonies. It tested the limits of my skill as I tried to do justice, with double stops, to the eerie chromatic harmonies just before the final outburst of fury.

During the usual wait for Berlioz to react after I finished playing, I assumed that he would speak of tumults of jealousy—more, perhaps, about the dashing Uncle Félix and the goddess in pink slippers.

Instead, in a quiet voice: "After I finished my first big work, a mass, when I was twenty-two, I was in a frenzy to have it put on. I had the nerve to call on the royal Superintendent of Fine Arts, the Vicomte Sosthènes de la Rochefoucauld—he was the one, Baillot, do you remember, who thought that ballerinas' tutus are pornographic and fought, unsuccessfully, thank God, to have their thighs covered! He gave me permission to use the Opéra orchestra if I would pay the musicians myself. Where could I get the money? I had a wild idea. Before I set out from home to Paris, I had found in my father's library the books of Chateaubriand, and in them I had discovered myself. 'The reasoning spirit, by destroying the imagination, undermines the bases of the fine arts.' Yes! Yes! When an idea hits me, I am impassioned, I am overcome, I perspire and have chills, my brain whirls. I try to tell my thought to others. They scoff. They have 'the reasoning spirit.' They tell me to 'think things through.' I feel blocked and empty—but in time I recover my ardor and I know I'm right, I know that my impulsive idea, riding the waves of my passion, will produce something vigorous, fiery, complete! I know it! You will charge me with hubris, Baillot, but I felt so close to Chateaubriand that I thought that if he only knew me, *he* would feel close to *me*, too. So I wrote to him asking him to lend me twelve hundred francs to pay for the orchestra. Absurd? He wrote to say he hadn't the money—but oh, Baillot, his letter gave me something better than money. That great man did not condescend to me. He seemed to recognize me as a colleague, a fellow artist, and I felt for the first time admitted to the company of the Romantics, the enemies of 'the reasoning spirit'—where I belong!"

Not knowing quite how to respond to this outburst, I simply asked, "Were you able to raise the money?"

"Oh, yes," he said. "I borrowed it from my friend Pons, and I have been in debt ever since. My mass was a great success."

What a leap, I was thinking, from Méhul's aria about jealousy to this young enthusiast's claim of kinship with Chateaubriand. Then I remembered the ravishing leaps in the melodic line in the Estelle theme which was to introduce his symphony—and which I had gathered from him was to bear its fruit, in the soaring lines of Erminia's song, in all five movements. This vaulting seemed to be his signature. And suddenly, as if to drive this reflection home in my mind, Berlioz took yet another sudden jump in thought. He sat up straight on the edge of the bed and said with flashing eyes, "This movement will be ecstatic. It's a waltz."

I wondered, Would we hear the clinking of spurs?

Today, to my delight, he had set out the climactic love duet from *Paul et Virginie*, composed by the violinist Kreutzer. I feel a warm kinship to that fine artist, and I try to play as he played in his prime—with broad and smooth phrasing, concentrating on tone, avoiding as far as possible spiccato bowing and fancy double stops and a lot of shifting of the left hand on the fingerboard. Antonietta responds especially generously to this modesty of technique, which is really a sort of kindness to the instrument.

Kreutzer played this way on *his* Stradivari, too! I gave my best —and so did Antonietta—to this dulcet music of Kreutzer's.

After I finished, Berlioz was silent for a very long time. When he spoke, it was in a hushed tone, like that on which my playing had ended. "I read that poem," he said—evidently meaning the silly, sugar-coated romance of *Paul et Virginie* by Saint-Pierre on which the Kreutzer opera is based—"when I was fifteen. . . ." His voice trailed off then, and again I waited.

"I think it is time for you to know," he finally said, "about the engine of this symphony—what drives it."

As usual when he began to talk, I put Antonietta away and took a seat.

"It started three years ago. An English company was to bring two Shakespeare plays to the Odéon. You will remember the hostility France felt to Shakespeare—to everything English in the years after Napoleon's defeat by Wellington. But there was a special hatred of Shakespeare,

This ape of a genius,
Sent on a mission to mankind by the devil.

I remember every detail. It was a September night. I had a free seat in the orchestra. I went with an open mind. Look, I don't know, even today, a whisper of the English language, but I had studied up on the Letourneur translation. The actor Kemble brought the chill air of Denmark onto the stage and made a terrifying art out of the prince's vacillations. But the first sight of the Ophelia! Ah, Baillot, a spear was thrust into my chest. Try to see her through my eyes: a tall floating presence, bare arms of Venus, a head crowned with shining black hair and canted slightly forward on a soft neck—a full mouth above a rather small chin, a straight nose, and *huge* limpid eyes. Her name was Harriet Smithson. She was twenty-seven, and I was twenty-three, and she had not spoken two sentences when I was her worshipper! At the end of the mad scene, I was one of many in the audience who could be heard sobbing. Strong men had to get up and walk out. I see her now. She moves forward on the stage like someone with an absent soul, mindless and as if stricken blind. Her steps falter, she sways, her remarkable eyes are empty! And then, in a voice that is as thin and toneless as an oboe hesitantly and badly played beyond a distant wall, she sings:

'They bore him barefaced on the bier,
Hey non nonny, nonny, hey nonny . . .'

Her veil drops away, real tears from those copious eyes shine on her face, she drifts off like smoke into her mad trance. Oh, *Dieu*, Baillot, if you could have seen her.

"Four days later I went to *Romeo and Juliet*. I had long since wangled a pass to the orchestra of the Odéon, good any time, but Harriet Smithson had created a sensation—Victor Hugo and Alfred de Vigny adored her, Alexandre Dumas had glimpsed 'the freshness of Adam's first sight of Eden'—and I knew there would not again be a 'papered house' to see this Eve act, the ushers would never let me in on a pass, so I hurried to the box office and bought a seat. Just in time. That was the end of me. The contrast, Baillot! The gloom of the North, sunless days and frigid guilt, tears, losses, horror, in the other play—and now, in their place: Italy's bright light, tenderness, sweet pain, embraces even on a deathbed. When the final curtain went down, I knew that my heart was locked away forever.

"I stopped eating. I walked the streets through entire nights. I, who had reveled in my work, was revolted by the sight of pages ruled for musical staves. I became an aimless wanderer. Once, I woke up in a meadow near Sceaux; another time, propped against a haystack on a farm by Villejuif; once even on a snowbank at the edge of the Seine, near Neuilly—had I meant to drown myself? My worship was certainly hopeless. All of Paris was singing Ophelia's praises, the fame of Juliet was on everyone's lips, and I, Hector Berlioz, was nobody. After weeks of this despair at my invisibility to those soulful wide eyes, it came to me one day that I must show Harriet Smithson that, to the contrary, I *was* someone—a cynosure like her!—and I decided to do what had never been done in Paris: put on, for her notice, a concert at the Conservatoire devoted entirely to the work of one composer. *My* work.

"It took half a year and all my resources to arrange. Cherubini, who ran the Conservatoire, was a bitter old man. He had caught me, once, going into the building by the wrong door, and he rejected my petition for the use of the hall as the impudent effrontery of a bad boy. It took me weeks to get him overruled by Rochefoucauld. Then, if I wanted the concert to be noticed enough to reach the ears of my Ophelia, my Juliet, I would have to enlist the newspapers—not easy for someone who was still just a student. But I did it! I had to go deeper than ever into debt to pay for the music copying and for the musicians.

"Never mind. The concert, when it finally took place—an overture to *Waverley*, the 'Et resurrexit' from my early mass, a piece I called 'The Greek Revolution,' and my *Francs-Juges* overture—was wonderfully received by the critics. The British actors, alas, were off in the provinces, and when they returned to Paris to stage *Richard III* and *The Merchant of Venice*, I bought tickets again, saw my angel, went back afterward to the stage door, was turned away rudely by the doorkeeper, sent several notes and letters which never reached Miss Smithson, and at last learned roundabout that nobody in the company had ever heard of a concert by the unknown young—what was his name—Bouliot?

"I didn't give up. I went to great trouble to find out about her. That she was born in Ireland, three and a half years before I was born. That she was adopted by a priest and raised a strict Catholic, but that his health failed and to support herself she went on the stage. That she was guarded from sin by a brother, and that when she traveled, it was under the sharp eyes of her mother and a hunchbacked sister. And that she had a manager, named Abbott, who dictated every step she took; it was he who had engaged her to play Ophelia with Kemble.

"I kept writing letters, in which I tried to do justice to what I felt for her. Miraculously, somehow, they began to reach her blazing eyes. For a long time I heard nothing. But then, one day—I could hardly believe it—a letter came, written in a feminine hand, saying that my appeal was a touching one. The final words were: 'Love like yours is fragile, sir. I will put you on probation. Let us see what time brings. Then perhaps we might meet and . . .' The letter broke off in that way. Can you imagine what I felt?"

He leaned back on the bed and stared at the ceiling.

Finally I asked in a quiet voice, "What happened? *Did* you meet her?"

"Never. . . . Never. . . . I kept writing, but there was not another word from her. I tried to get in touch with her through the Englishman who acted as her interpreter, a fellow named Turner. Do you know what he finally told me? He said there was gossip and laughter among the actors. The 'probation' letter had not been written by her at all—it was the work of that gibbous freak of a sister—and its purpose was to get rid of a stage-door looby who had become a nuisance to the great actress! This was the response I got, Baillot, to the most important emotion of my life. . . ."

THIRD MOVEMENT

He was waiting for me this morning, in quite a different mood from yesterday's, with two passages from *Der Freischütz* on the stand—the dreamy pastoral melody, "Durch die Wälder, durch die Auen," and Agathe's rapturous aria as she watches Max approaching under the moonlight. As I took Antonietta out from the case, Berlioz stood beside me, saying, "Weber is the only composer whose music makes me desperately homesick. How sane he was! D major for serene landscapes and C major for the forces of good in this world! Four years ago I heard he was passing through Paris—dying of lung trouble, they said—and I spent three days hurrying around the city trying to catch up with him. I just missed him wherever I went: at Auber's, at a music shop, at Catel's home, at the Conservatoire where he was calling on Cherubini. At the Opéra they told me he had just left to go and see Rossini, but I *hate* Rossini's music and I couldn't bear to follow him there. Weber left for London and died soon, so I never had a chance to tell him how much his music of life in the village and the woods—life at the core of my memory—meant to me. . . . Play this for me!" he said, subsiding on the bed.

I did, and Antonietta rose to Weber's robust rural sounds with a sweaty resonance which surprised me (a city person through and through) but which evidently thrilled Berlioz, because when I finished he stood up at once, without the usual melancholy soak, and began to pour out a rapture of nostalgia.

"Look! It's early in the morning! I see the village women washing their linen in the stream near the stone house, moving together to a rhythm of a folk tune they're singing; the little islands of soapsuds float away rhythmless on the clear water, swooping now and then on eddies. Ah, Baillot, listen! There is a cow in a barnyard lowing its bassoon lament. On a slope above the village two flocks of sheep graze, quite far apart, and by one of them a shepherd plays on his pipes an old, old *ranz des vaches*; then there's a silence as wide as the sky; then the other shepherd answers from his distance with the same sad tune. The farrier is beating out a red-hot horseshoe on his anvil, and his strokes are cousins to the tolling of the bell in the church tower calling the faithful to mass. My sister Adèle, my favorite, my pet, eleven years younger than I, frets and whimpers, stirred out of bed by our scolding mother. Now you can hear the men ride off on a chase, the horses' hooves syncopated, the wild calls of the tenor hunting horns supposedly driving the prey but really shouting the male exuberance of a race across an empty field. In the church—listen!—the voices are soprano and alto, with a psalm,

'As the hart panteth,' set to the lilt of a thousand-year-old folk song. *Sacré vierge!*—that's the sound of my flute as I try in the loneliness of my room to give the psalm that I hear from the church an obbligato! Out the window I can see the ice of the faraway peaks glistening in the early sunlight. A mist hangs on the Bièvres lowlands. There's a breeze whispering its secrets in a poplar beside the house. The flute angers a magpie, which caws its raucous shout at me from the stone wall at the foot of our garden. . . ."

On and on he went, and I had the feeling that even though he called out to me by name every once in a while—look, Baillot!—listen!—I was not really there in his mind. Antonietta's Weber had taken his hand and led him home to his boyhood.

Once more he had set out music of the countryside for me and Antonietta to play: the beautiful arietta, "Intendo, amico rio," from Gluck's *Il rè pastore.* And once again he flew back in his talk to the village of La Côte St.-André—to the morning when, as he put it, music for the first time showed him its naked face: the morning when he made his first communion. He was twelve years old, he said—the same sensitive year, it struck me, in which he idolized his *stella montis*, his Estelle. "My sister Nanci and I went together at six in the morning, led to the rude chapel of the Convent of the Visitation by the almoner. The air as we walked was soft. I was excited by the thought that for a moment I would be in the bright hot light at the center of a ceremony. Religion to me, up to then, had been a jumble of chanted words, dry images of a heaven that seemed nothing more than what one could see in a dusty old painting. In the church I was the only boy in a flock of girls in their long white dresses. The priest called me first, as if God were greedier for a male child than for all the beautiful virgins. Just as I took the wafer on my tongue, the choir—also made up of young girls—began to sing the Eucharist. Those high, silvery, quavering voices went right to my heart! I knew for the first time the meaning of the phrase 'God is love.' There was also something giddy, though, something heady and profane, about my response to those reedy voices—a sense, which I have never lost since that morning, of the complexities and ambiguities that may be embedded in the most pellucid of melodies. It took me years to learn why I had felt this. It was a decade later, in Paris, that I heard Dalayrac's opera, *Nina, ou la Folle par Amour*, about a young girl driven mad by love, in the mistaken belief that her lover had been killed in a duel. You know *Nina*, of course; I remember that horrible riot in your honor. I suddenly realized when I heard the tune of Dalayrac's lovely, heartbreaking song from that opera, 'Quand le bien-aimé reviendra,' that in the artless way of the country churches that melody had been used for our communion hymn —no doubt because it was 'so sweet'!"

This morning I found the adagio movement of Beethoven's Sixth Symphony on the music stand, and Berlioz told me why he wanted to listen to its "gigantic calm." *His* slow movement, he says, is to tell a story of the serene country life of his boyhood home. "I will call this section 'In the Fields,'" he said. Quite by chance, however, as we chatted before I played, I came to sense that deep down, under the quiet of the last few days, under this pastoral mood, there was a stifling smoke of some sort, an emanation of the heat in the boiler of "the engine of the symphony." And without knowing what I was doing, I stumbled on what it was.

As I was tuning Antonietta, my glance fell on the tiny hollow place chipped out from the side of the purfling on the belly, and I realized that I had never pointed it out to Berlioz. "Look," I said, "do you see this little flaw in my Antonietta? I think of it as a 'beauty spot'—a mole, you know, that accents and humanizes what would otherwise be too perfect to be beautiful. Can you guess how it got there—and why it has never been repaired? Vuillaume told me this. It seems that just when Stradivari was cutting the channel for the purfling, a spiteful friend of his, who knew about his infatuation with this Antonia he had never met, came bursting into his shop to tell him that his angel was a slut—that she had been seen under a full moon the night before in an open field, in the arms—not just in the arms—in the clutches—*flagrante delicto*—on her back, you know—under a young lieutenant. Stradivari was so shocked by hearing this that his hand jumped and he dug this flaw. And in his rage he swore never to repair it. That's what Vuillaume told me."

By this time I was used to Berlioz's flare-ups in response to things I said—his jumping up and walking around, his face going white, his tossing his head with a shivering of the reddish hair. I was therefore not alarmed, after I had told that story, by his lurching up and coming close to me, with his jaw stuck out, his face right in mine, his huge nose like a machete. "I wish you hadn't told me that," he said. He turned away and paced back and forth, and finally sat on the edge of the bed and said, "Baillot, sometimes your aim is too good." He looked at the floor. I knew enough to wait him out. Finally he said, "I hadn't wanted to tell you this. Two months ago I was floundering around, I wanted to start my symphony, but my mind was sterile, I felt hollow and lazy. I remember the exact moment this happened. I was sitting over there at the table, with an empty sheet of ruled paper in front of me. I could hear pigeons in their obscene conversations on the roof. There was a knock. I shouted to whoever it was to come in. It was Harriet's interpreter, Turner. He stood gloating over me like a triumphant upperclassman hazing a new matriculant—what can make a man behave this way?—is this the English hatred of us French?—and said, 'I thought you ought to know this. Abbott—her manager, you know—Abbott is a fox. He got the best of her. He's a wily one, he tricked the camelback sister; they say he invited Harriet and the little monster to his rooms for supper, and somehow he mesmerized the cripple and got her to go out to the farmers' market to buy some leeks for the soup, and while she was gone—*alors!* . . . And after that it has seemed to be simple—in Harriet's dressing room during intermission—an act between the acts, you know—while the unsuspecting hunchback is sitting in the audience! You can hear them through the thin walls murmuring and . . . well, the whole company is talking about it.' "

I realized the peculiar message Berlioz was conveying to me, perhaps just what he had not wanted me to understand, if indeed he understands it himself: that there is a vein of rage in his genius—that a clinking of spurs can impel him to create. "And after that," I quietly suggested, "you were able to start work on your symphony?"

"Yes," he said, frowning but sounding relieved. "After that you began playing that violin for me, and it all came quickly."

FOURTH MOVEMENT

When I arrived this morning, Berlioz was dressed in different clothing from what he had worn on all the previous days: he was in gray trousers under a long house coat, and on his feet were old slippers squashed at the heel. He looked bedraggled, and I had the impression that his symphony was taking a strange swerve of some sort. It turned out, however, that his senses were, if anything, more finely honed than ever. When I tuned Antonietta, he said, "Your A is much too low."

His saying this surprised me. Over the last few years the standard concert pitch, the level of the note A above middle C that is built into tuning forks, had been steadily pushed upward, mainly, I think, by composers, and the reason I was surprised by his remark is that I had read an article that he had written opposing this rise, on the ground that the higher pitch was straining singers' voices in reaching for upper notes. I had thought it would please him that I was using a fork from several years ago. I said this.

"Yes, I did write that," he said. "But I want a higher pitch for this symphony—to give it the brilliance it needs."

I tightened the A peg ever so slightly and re-tuned the other strings.

The music waiting for me on the stand was the eerie fairy music from Weber's *Oberon*. Its greatest subtleties had been given to the woodwinds, and I worked hard to thicken Antonietta's tone into a fluty sound that would please Berlioz.

When I had finished, he said after a few moments, "Have you ever taken opium?"

"Once," I said, "when I had broken a leg. A doctor gave me some."

"Did you have dreams?"

"Not that I can remember. I think I had too much pain."

He fell silent. I put Antonietta away.

"Two years ago," he finally said, "not long after my mind was set on fire by Shakespeare, I had another searing experience: I read Gérard de Nerval's translation of Goethe's *Faust*—and how deeply I read it! I read it over breakfast in the morning, I read it while I walked in the street, I read it between the acts in the theater, I read it by candlelight in bed at night. I dived into the book and was drowned in it. That hero stands for all that I want to be—erudite, gentle, free, wild-hearted, in awe of Nature, brave, a gambler with destiny, an explorer trying to find the richest outer limits of our life on earth!"

And a bargainer with Mephistopheles over life in hell, I thought but did not say.

I visited Berlioz late that afternoon to tell him that we were going to have to call a brief interlude in "our work." If he wanted Antonietta tuned higher, I was going to have to ask Vuillaume to overhaul the violin and make the changes he and a very few other experts were daring to make on the old Cremona violins in response to the rise in pitch. I had postponed these repairs longer than I should have, terrified that something might go wrong. The problem was that increased tension on all four strings caused by the rise in pitch put a dangerous amount of extra pressure through the bridge onto the belly, and also on the juncture of the neck with the body.

At first Berlioz was angry. How dared I break the rhythm of his days? But, as so often happens with him, his mood changed rapidly and soon he became quite excited—and anxious—about what would be happening to "my friend and helper" Antonietta. Could he go with me to Vuillaume's workshop to watch the work?

We set off together the next morning to the luthier's establishment at 46 Rue Croix des Petits-Champs, and within an hour the craftsman was at work. Once the strings had been removed, I could hardly bear to watch Vuillaume's first operation, but Berlioz craned and put his face so close to the leaf-thin, razor-sharp knife in Vuillaume's hand that the luthier had to wave him away. With great care Vuillaume inserted the knife in several places between the belly and the sides, first in the C-curves, then along the upper and lower bouts. Finally, with a hideous cracking sound—at which I put my hands over my ears but not before I heard Berlioz let out a scream as if he had been stabbed—the belly came away from the body. On that first day of work, Vuillaume removed Stradivari's bass bar and replaced it with a longer, thicker, and stronger one, and he cut a slightly sturdier sound post. On two following days, as Berlioz, fascinated, asked a thousand questions, Vuillaume took off Antonietta's neck and reshaped and reattached it, slanted at a slight angle downward from the body of the violin. He then cut a new fingerboard, nearly two inches longer than the old one, to make possible the playing of much higher notes on all the strings. He supplied a new bridge, taller and more arched than the old one. And finally he put the violin back together, and when the glue was dry, the following day, he strung it up with more powerful strings than I had been using, all but the E string wound around with very fine silver wire.

And the day after that I took Antonietta home, and in fear

and haste I tuned the strings, using a new, higher fork, and I anxiously began to play, from memory, Berlioz's Erminia theme. The tone was emaciated and resentful. I was shaken by a terror that Antonietta had been raped and ruined. But I forced myself, in my love for the instrument, to be patient. I played various sorts of music for three hours, and slowly, slowly, Antonietta warmed to my care—and there finally came a moment when I stopped and shouted out loud for joy. Not only had Antonietta not been hurt, the violin unquestionably had an entirely new resonance and power! I could hardly wait to return to "our work."

This morning he had placed on the music stand the strange, dark wedding march of evil Lysiart and Eglantine, from Weber's *Euryanthe*. I was able, with my new throaty Antonietta, to give full vent to the harsh thrumming of the procession and of the hallucinatory passage that follows. I saw Berlioz's look of astonishment at Antonietta's tone.

When he began to speak, there was at first no sign of the malevolent ghostliness of the music he had listened to. He spoke fondly of his father. "I had only two years of schooling as a boy, from six years old till eight, at a seminary which was like a jail. After that my father tutored me at home—and taught me everything I know. He was so gentle! He did not push me: he led me. He beckoned to me along the path of poetry, and I ran breathless to catch up with him. La Fontaine! But oh, above all, Virgil! . . . Let me tell you about one morning's Latin lesson. It was a cloudy, oppressive day in August, his study was dark, I could hear a bluebottle buzzing around the room. I was translating the fourth book of the *Aeneid*, and I felt torn apart by Dido's savage grief at being abandoned by Aeneas. She mounts the pyre on which she has meant to burn all the memories of her betrayer—especially 'the bed she knew so well'—and she stabs herself with the sword the Trojan gave her as a gift.

Three times she tried to lift herself; three times fell back—.

I felt as if *I* were dying. My father, to encourage me, pointed at the next line:

Quaesivit coelo lucem, ingemuitque reperta,

and my heart broke as I blurted out,

'. . . *her rolling eyes went searching heaven*
And the light hurt when she found it, and she moaned.'

I threw my hands over my face and sobbed. I have never forgotten the pain of that sorrow."

On my way home after our session, I thought about how his mind had so quickly bridged the distance from a wedding march to suicide, from love—admittedly a sinister sort of love—to death, from evil joy to pure grief. And I wondered, What was he brewing in this movement?

Once again, this morning, a manuscript score. Once again, a dark, throbbing march.

"I wrote that for my *Francs-Juges*," he said after I had finished. "It never got anywhere, you know—my poet friend Ferrand's libretto baffled the Opéra jury. This piece was called 'The March of the Guards.' "

One of his long silences.

Then: "You have to be patient with me. . . . It's hard to forget things. . . . When I was six or seven, a cousin of my father's drowned in a swamp—I used to picture him being sucked down in a quagmire, struggling, shouting for help. . . . And then, later on, I think I was fifteen, my best friend Imbert, the son of my music teacher, said a solemn goodbye to me one day

—and he went off and hanged himself from a branch of a linden tree."

Another wait.

"The poet André Chénier was a hero of mine, do you know about him? He was guillotined by Robespierre, you know. The year after Imbert died, I found in my father's library a poem Chénier wrote in prison in the days before the march in the tumbrils, and I set it to music:

'Await me elsewhere, Death. Begone from here!
Console those hearts that guilt and fear
And cold despair devour.
Pallas still keeps green bowers for me;
Love, its embrace; Muses, their melody.
It is not yet my hour.'

"You know, Baillot, they say that during the march in the carts, Chénier and his fellow poet Roucher recited Racine! Imagine the courage and defiance! And I made a note on my score—this I found in Chateaubriand—that as Chénier climbed up on the scaffold, he raised his hand to his forehead and cried out, 'To have to die, when I have so much in *here!*'"

Again Berlioz stopped.

"Has it occurred to you," he then said, "that your Antonietta is bisexual?"

Used though I was to his kangaroo mind, this jump astonished me. "What do you mean?"

"I was thinking this when I heard some of the things Vuillaume told me when he took the violin apart. He said that the gentle, sweet vibrations of the soft, swelling pine front are held in check yet somehow excited by the stiffer and bolder pulsations of the maple back. The bass bar presses against the belly. . . . The ribs are shared—Adam, Eve. . . . And the resulting tone—well, I mean, the strings are a choir: soprano, alto, tenor, baritone."

Next came the most peculiar jump of all. With hardly a pause he said, "Something exciting has been happening to me. I've been supporting myself, you know, trying to pay off my debts, by giving music lessons—among others, lessons in guitar playing at a school for girls run by a Madame Daubrée. My friend Ferdinand Hiller teaches piano there, and so does an eighteen-year-old named Camille Moke, who struck me, the first few times I saw her, as a shallow flirt, a real coquette and a tease—black hair, blue eyes, a lush figure that seems to hover rather than walk, lightly, lightly, as if the earth's gravity has somehow been gelded and has no lust for such a divine body as hers. Her father, in Ghent, gambled his money away, and her mother left him and moved to Paris and set up a lingerie shop. I've never seen this mother; Hiller says she is fiercely protective of Camille, as if she intends to save the girl on the shelf for sale one day at a price far higher than the shop's entire stock of fancy underwear would bring. Hiller fell for Camille, and he saw at once the convenience of her giving piano lessons at several addresses in the city far from the mother's sharp eyes. Since my sessions and hers at Madame Daubrée's often coincided, he asked me, once he had reached an understanding with her, to be his go-between, telling her where around the city to meet him. Sometimes he borrowed my room. He apparently made a bad mistake: told her that I was so madly in love with an English actress that I wouldn't even look at her. One day I stopped her in the main hallway at Madame Daubrée's and hastily whispered the address and time Hiller had given me. In the most natural way in the world, as if she simply wanted to thank me, she ran her fingers lightly down the back of my right hand. Another time, she reached up and gave my face a fleeting touch with the back of *her* hand. Then once she said, 'I know your room by heart. I can see you, leaning over the table at work—and then . . . lying on the bed!' The other day she pressed into my hand a note asking me to meet her the following afternoon at a tavern on the left bank for an innocent cup of coffee, and she set a time. I meant to go, she'd pricked my curiosity, but I got so absorbed at my desk the next day that I completely forgot. I really forgot. That 'indifference' of mine apparently pushed her over the edge. Yesterday she handed me this note."

Berlioz took a crumpled piece of paper from his pocket, smoothed it out on his knee, and handed it to me.

It said: "*I will come to your room at five o'clock tomorrow. Please be there.*"

"This afternoon," I said.

"This afternoon," Berlioz said, with eyes of a stunned ox.

FIFTH MOVEMENT

Because of some rehearsals, I was unable to be with Berlioz for three days, until this morning. As had happened several times before, he had posted a manuscript score on the music stand. Berlioz looked as if he had been dragged like a harrow across a field.

"I think I've told you," he said, "how shaken I was by *Faust*, two years ago. The images in the play were so sharp and so stark that I at once started spinning melodies. My first idea was to write a ballet, and one of its dances was going to be from Goethe's thrillingly gruesome Brocken scene—that's the draft of the dance there on the stand. I couldn't get backing from the Opéra for the ballet, so I wrote six songs, instead, to verses in Nerval's translation. I had them printed before they had even been performed, and I don't know what possessed me, I sent the sheets to Goethe. Never a word from him. My friend Hermann tells me he heard from a malicious cousin of his in Berlin that the songs were laughed at. Goethe gave them to that old windbag Zelter—Zelter had the audacity to *rewrite* Bach's *St. Matthew Passion* last year, that's what *he*'s worth!—not that I like Bach . . . Anyway, they say he told Goethe my score was nothing but coughing, snoring, croaking, and vomiting! Well, now I have to gulp telling you this—when I looked at them again, the songs weren't good enough to satisfy *me*, and I've called in all the copies I could find. But this on the stand is music for the ballet; this is more serious, Baillot. This comes straight out of me. Play it for me, won't you?"

I did. Antonietta had never sounded so eerie. A chill ran down my spine.

Berlioz sighed. "I want to tell you about one of the most horrible moments of my life," he said. "I didn't sleep at all last night, thinking about it."

Could it be, I wondered, that his meeting the other day with the young flirt had turned out to be a catastrophe? I had held back from asking him about it when I first arrived, thinking that Antonietta would pull this out of him soon enough. But no. As it turned out, it was something else.

"My family did all they could to prevent me from going into music. My mother thought anything to do with theaters was sinful, and my father naturally wanted me to follow in his footsteps as a doctor. The first time I went home to La Côte from Paris, when I was twenty, I thought I persuaded Father to let me drop medicine, and I told my sister Nanci that, and she went straight to my mother, and of course Mother got a wind up like a mistral. The next year I was turned down for the Rome Prize competition, and I got in trouble with my father about my debt to Pons, and he cut off my funds and called me home and told me I was to be a doctor and nothing else. He was icy cold to me. Father saw how crushed I was. I couldn't eat. Father loves me, and he suffered for me, and after a bad night he called me to his study, where we had had so many happy hours together, and he said I could stop my medical studies, after all—but I mustn't tell Mother! I was so elated that like a fool I ran to Nanci again and poured out my joy to her, and, being a woman, she felt she had to break the outrageous news to Mother—without telling me, of course.

"I was walking in the garden. I heard a shriek. Mother came ripping out of the house and approached me like a cat with its back arched. Her hair was disheveled, her face was that of a witch. She shouted that she would not allow me to go back to Paris. I was so horrified that I must have looked firm and hateful. At that she fell to her knees on the gravel path, and with her face flooded with tears, which she wiped off by smearing her face on my pants leg, she *begged* me in the most abject way not to bring disgrace on the family with the sin of performing in theaters. By now I *was* firm, I was in a rage—perhaps partly at myself for having reduced her to such a revolting, sniveling state. I tried to stare her down. She got to her feet, her fingers bent into claws, and she screamed, 'May God damn your soul to rot in hell!' And she ran off wailing to the cottage next door." Berlioz groaned, almost as Antonietta had groaned playing his frightening music. "Baillot!" he cried, "think what it means to be cursed by your mother!"

Never has Antonietta uttered such frightening sounds as I had to draw out this morning, when Berlioz gave me the appalling Wolf Glen music from *Der Freischütz* to play. Along came the fearful moment when the ghost of Max's mother appears, trying to warn him of the danger of making the magic bullets, and I heard Berlioz break into a strange moan that harmonized with the music—but was this awful obbligato of his a groan of pleasure or of pain? I could not tell. I think this doubt disturbed me even more than the music itself.

He was inappropriately—shockingly—grinning when I finished. I was very upset. I took my time putting Antonietta away.

"But you haven't asked me about Camille," he said. "Don't you care what happens to me?" He looked mischievous—like a small boy ragging someone bigger—a little afraid.

"Of course I do," I said, trying to be careful.

"I have never been so happy in my life," he said, lying back on the couch. "I am all new. This little creature comes to me every afternoon. She loves me! She says it straight out. I've never had a woman tell me that. She's a tiny thing, you know, she's as light as a spirit, I call her Ariel! She's not a nothing, though, she won't fade away. She's a wonderful musician, Baillot—Kalkbrenner told Hiller she was the best pupil he had had in years. The strangest thing: your Antonietta, sounding out that grim music just now, seemed so sweet to me! It seemed to me that in this new mood I'm in, I heard the *truth* from that violin for the first time. I'm writing terrifying music right now, my last movement is pouring out of me so easily. The truth? The truth is that what I thought was love—for Ophelia, for Juliet—was just a daydream. I *pity* Harriet Smithson, Baillot, I despise her. She's a whore."

"*LE PROGRAMME*"

He finished his symphony two weeks ago, but he had asked me to keep coming to see him, to keep playing snatches of music for him. Really I think it is the violin, not me, that he has come to need early in the mornings—like strong coffee. Just a very few minutes of hearing its tones seems to tune him up for the day.

He told me this morning that he has already made arrangements for a concert to get the symphony heard. He has talked Bloc, the director of the excellent Orchestre des Nouveautés, into taking him on later in this month. But Berlioz says that that orchestra, though it is ample for the *opéras-comiques* it has been accompanying, isn't nearly big enough for what he calls "my gigantic symphony." He opts for large scale on principle. He was talking the other day about some vocal music he had composed sounding "starved to death" when a soloist sang it, but with a chorus it was glorious. "Fifty voices," he said, "are always better than one." So he says he is inviting eighty additional musicians, mostly from the Conservatoire, to make an orchestra of a hundred and thirty to swell out the sound. And of course he is begging me to join in. He says he wants above everything else to have Antonietta's voice in the ensemble. I tell him that my positions at the Opéra and at Versailles make my taking on other engagements extremely tricky, but he begs and begs. I told him I would think about it.

At my saying that, he opened the tap of his charm. He knew that it was no use flattering me; bribery was the better course. So he said, "Would you like to read my score?"

After all the weeks of "our work," after all the music and all the talk, after all the breathtaking jumps and non sequiturs and avowals and confessions, I was dying to see what this creature had written, and my face must have shown it—because *his* face at once got the lazy look of a tiger's just after its lunch. His vanity is enormous, carnivorous.

He got up, crossed the room, opened a chest, and got out a big pile of manuscript, which he placed on his desk. "*La voilà!*" he said.

I sat down at the desk and started to read.

To say that I was amazed is not nearly strong enough. I have read so many orchestral and operatic scores that I can hear the entire sound as my eyes fly over the pages, and what sounds I heard! It was music, the purest of music, wildly alive from the very first bar to the very last. How could a boy of twenty-six know so much about instrumentation? Yes, this broke all the molds! Its novelty was shocking. The pace made me dizzy. The changes of mood from movement to movement made it a drama indeed. And the score was so muscular, so lean, there was not a fat phrase in it. Monstrous, yes—a monstrous epigram.

I stood up and turned to Berlioz when I had come to the end of the terrifying—just as he had said—the terrifying last movement, and I was speechless. I threw up my hands and shook my head from side to side, to show my amazement.

He understood. He burst into tears and went over and kissed the top of Antonietta's case.

. . .

What a shock I got this afternoon! The concert is to be nine days from now, on the Sunday of Pentecost. I have arranged to play. There will be just one rehearsal, day after tomorrow. I practiced for three hours this morning—we are putting on Salieri's *Tarare* at the Opéra, and I went through the score—and afterward, on my way to have a meal at a bistro near my house, I bought a paper, *Le Figaro*. The May weather has been splendid, and I sat at an outdoor table, ordered a pot-au-feu, and opened the paper. At once a headline jumped out at me:

ÉPISODE DE LA VIE D'UN ARTISTE
SYMPHONIE FANTASTIQUE EN CINQ PARTIES

It was a puff for the concert, and it had obviously been written by Berlioz himself. It began: "It often happens that a composer sits down at his piano, teases the keys, strikes out some chords, and tosses some notes on his ruled paper—without having had, during all his work, the slightest glimmer of what one could call in artistic terms an idea. . . ."

This leaves the discovery of the meaning of the music, if there is any, to chance. Not so this time. "M. Hector Berlioz, a young composer with a fresh imagination, wants to play a more candid game." He himself will "analyze his inspirations. . . . The following program"—or synopsis—"of the music should be thought of as if it were the spoken text of an opera. . . ."

The first movement has the headline DAYDREAMS—A LIFE OF PASSION. "The author imagines that a young musician, afflicted with the spiritual sickness that a famous writer has called '*le vague des passions*,' sees for the first time a woman with all the charms of the ideal creature he has dreamed of, and he falls desperately in love with her." Strangely, this "dear image" always haunts him as *a musical idea*, which stands, in twinship with his mental picture of her, as a double *idée fixe*, or obsession. This will be heard in each movement. In this one he moves from "a melancholy daydream, broken by fits of meaningless joy, to one of delirious passion, with its elements of rage, of jealousy, its return to tenderness, its tears . . ."

A BALL follows, during which his soul is troubled when he sees "the dear image" again.

The third movement is called IN THE FIELDS. Two shepherds carry on a dialogue of a *ranz des vaches*, and the artist feels peaceful. Although he is lonely, he has hopes of soon being less so. "But what if she deceives him?"

Then comes MARCH TO THE SCAFFOLD. At last, knowing for sure not only that his adored one doesn't respond to his love but that she "is incapable of even understanding it and moreover is *unworthy* of it," the artist tries to kill himself with opium. But the dose is too weak, and it plunges him instead into a sleep with the most horrible visions: he dreams that he kills his beloved and is marched to a scaffold and *watches his own execution*.

Finally there is a DREAM OF A WITCHES' SABBATH. He sees himself at this affair, surrounded by "a ghastly troupe of ghosts, sorcerers, devils, monsters of every kind, gathered for his own funeral. Strange noises, groans, bursts of laughter, far-off shouts." The beloved melody is heard, but it has become "trivial and grotesque. . . . *She* has come . . . a roar of joy at her arrival . . . she joins the devilish orgy." A funeral ceremony. The sabbath dance.

So many thoughts rushed through my mind as I read this weird argument of his symphony. I felt angry. How absurd it all was! Why had he done this? Was it to attract a big audience with sheer prurience? The ridiculous worship of Harriet Smithson that he had told everyone about was by now such a common subject of gossip in musical circles that no one could mistake what he meant. This "program" would certainly titillate concertgoers.

His need to be in the public eye made him shameless. He wanted to have Gluck's final fame at twenty-six! I thought of all his importunate ways of getting attention: his shouting in the audiences at the Opéra when he was nineteen, his writing arrogant articles in the papers, his pursuit of Weber all around Paris, his wild idea that his kindred spirit Chateaubriand would stake him to a concert, his sending his songs to Goethe—and all the rest. But this, somehow, was worst of all.

I was struck by the falsities in the program. The *idée fixe* had nothing to do with Harriet; it was Erminia's song. It was derived from—its "soul" was in—the tune he had written in his childish hankering for his Estelle. The march—I had recognized it at once as "The March of the Guards" from *Francs-Juges*. The witches' dance—from his *Faust* ballet. Who could tell what other previous rags and tags had gone into this pastiche?

And what of his not one but three passions: for Estelle, Harriet, Camille? And perhaps a secret fourth: for his angry mother?

Above all, this fabrication wasn't in the least needed. I had heard the symphony in my mind. It held, in its pure musical state, drama enough. No matter what fragments he may have drawn from past work, he had welded everything together into a solid, dazzling, bizarre intaglio, whose pictures each listener could imagine to suit himself. I had been gripped by the recurrences of the Erminia theme in all the movements and had been moved by the different brilliant colors he had given it. The waltz had elated me, the march had disturbed me, the last movement had frightened me. Wasn't the music enough?

And yet . . . I recalled the tears, the grins, the earnestness, the mischief—the play, the depth, the strong vibrations of feeling in this young man during all those mornings. The emotions may have been misguided, but I couldn't think him insincere in the ways he expressed them, either in words or in music. He is all of a piece; he lives his life and writes his music as a Romantic.

I remembered how gravely he had said, "It's time for you to know about the engine of this symphony." I had to grant him, at a minimum, that he meant what he said and felt what he felt.

I walked home briskly, elated in spite of myself. I can't wait to see how the concert goes.

I turned up at the Théâtre des Nouveautés for the rehearsal a bit late, having had business to attend to at the Opéra. I came in on a scene of pandemonium. One hundred and thirty musicians, eighty of them strangers to the theater, were milling around like a mob in a revolution. There simply wasn't room for all of them to sit down and perform. Berlioz called out that the violins would have to play down in the orchestra pit, while the rest played on the stage. Then I heard him shouting at the stage manager, "You promised there would be plenty of chairs and music stands!" The stage manager bawled out to the carpenters to hammer up some benches. Stagehands were sent to the cellars to find music stands. A third of the instrumentalists so far had no place to sit; those who did quarreled with the regulars of the theater as to which ones should have precedence at the desks. "Candles! Candles!" someone was shouting. "We need light!" There was no room for the extra kettledrums. The double-bass players complained that they didn't even have room to swing their bow arms. A French hornist and an English hornist fought a little Waterloo. The conductor Bloc ran around with sweat pouring down his face.

All the while, the directors of the theater sat in seats halfway back in the hall, somber as a jury at a murder trial.

With half the afternoon wasted and the musicians beginning to call out that they wanted to go home, good-hearted Bloc finally managed to bring something like order to the crowd. He had a last-minute consultation with Berlioz—too late to run through the whole symphony, he said, but in order to "give the directors at least some idea of what they are getting into" he would conduct "A Ball" and "March to the Scaffold."

After the march, which I could tell created a sensation among the instrumentalists, I saw the directors whispering to each other and, one by one, shaking their heads. Finally the chief director called out an announcement for all to hear. The concert was cancelled.

1832

He is back from Rome. He has written me a note, saying that while he was in Italy he revised the *Symphonie Fantastique* and wrote a sequel to it, which he calls *The Return to Life*—"a spectacle, a novelty!—part music, part spoken narrative." He is polishing the latter now, for a concert at which both will be performed; would I care to come in the mornings again with my violin to help him out? He gave me an address: Rue Neuve St.-Marc, No. 1.

This morning I went, impelled by both curiosity and affection. What an astonishing apartment I walked into! In contrast with the drab room he had previously rented, this one had, among other things, a chest of drawers finished in matt white paint, with gilt handles; chairs covered in some sort of slightly worn corded material in primary colors; a bed with crossed spears at the head, gripped at their juncture in the talons of a griffin; a statue of Cleopatra on the chest, holding up an oil lamp; an iron clock, painted black, evidently not running; and under the bed an upside-down Roman helmet on a little base, for a night potty.

Berlioz greeted me with a warmth that struck me as extravagant, considering the fact that he had not bothered to write me a single letter from Rome. He saw me gaping at the furnishings, and he said, "Believe this or not, Baillot. Until the day before yesterday, this was Harriet Smithson's apartment. Yes, she's in Paris, Baillot. She has moved to the Rue de Rivoli, and she's opening soon at the Théâtre-Italien—but don't get the idea that I will be going to see her plays. I want to put on my concert; I can't risk falling off my tightrope on *her* account!"

His having taken Miss Smithson's rooms bowled me over, because the last I'd heard, he was planning to marry Camille Moke. I had seen him, off and on, before he left for Italy. I knew, of course, that, as he had promised to do, he won the Rome Prize on his fifth try—with a cantata on "The Death of Sardanapalus," about a king who refused to abdicate and died in a fire he set himself. He was still locked in his cell working on this, he told me afterward, when he heard gunfire break out in the city. In three days of rioting and fighting in the streets, "*les trois glorieuses*," which Berlioz belatedly joined "more or less for the fun of it," Charles X, the last of the Bourbons, was forced from the throne and Louis Philippe was installed as the Citizen King. "I had set the revolution to music before it happened," Berlioz said of his piece on Sardanapalus, seeming almost to claim he had overthrown the Bourbons himself.

I had heard that he became engaged to Camille, in the face of opposition both from his own parents, who thought Camille "common," and from Madame Moke, who apparently wanted a more lucrative marriage. In December his *Symphonie Fantastique* was finally performed—I was unable to play—with young Franz Liszt on hand. The "program" had done its work, and despite what seemed to me a mediocre performance, the audience was thrilled and critics raved. Harriet Smithson was not in Paris. Berlioz told me later that he dined after the concert with Liszt, "who gave me a swelled head."

We parted later that month, when he left for Rome, sealing his engagement to Camille by giving her his Rome Prize gold medal. He promised to write to me but, as I say, never did.

I said, "But I thought—"

"I know, I know," Berlioz said, full of his headlong energy. "We'll have time for all that. But we have to get to work!"

There was his "we." *We* had to get to work. I got Antonietta out.

"Ah, my beauty!" Berlioz said. He touched the back of the violin with his fingertips, and said, "Look at those waves!"

As I tuned up, he sat in one of the padded chairs.

The music this morning was the enthralling sea music from Weber's *Oberon*—the mermaids' song, the storm, Reiza's outcry: "Ocean, thou mighty monster!" I saw when I had finished that Berlioz was transported with delight at hearing Antonietta's voice again.

"The first song in this new piece of mine," he said, "is one of the ones I wrote with Goethe in mind:

'The wave murmurs; the wave stirs;
A young fisherman sits nearby.'

"Do you remember my saying, once, that the back of your violin was my first sight of the sea? Well, I have seen the real thing now. On my way to Rome I sailed from Marseilles to Livorno on a Scandinavian brig. One of the passengers was a roughneck from Venice who once served in a crew for Byron in the Adriatic—said Byron dressed him in a uniform with gold lace, and told about wild orgies the poet started. Our first days at sea were magical, but we were becalmed off Nice for so long that I thought the city a huge magnet that was holding us in its field and might even pull the metal fastenings out of the brig's planks. But then an icy, fierce *tramontana* blew down from the rocks of the Alps and kicked up liquid Alps. The crazy captain would not shorten sail. One gust heeled the vessel right over on its beam ends and knocked the captain off his feet. The Venetian tough, putting on a one-man mutiny, grabbed the wheel and shouted to the crew to furl sails. This saved us. I had decided that if I must drown I would do so as quickly as I could, trapping my arms in my heavy coat so I would not be able to swim—I'd go right to sleep in a cradle of waves."

Today he had me play from manuscript the revision he had just finished of the second song, "The Chorus of the Shades," from his strange new work, which he is now calling *Lelio*—for the narrator of *The Return to Life* who is also, I assume, the imaginary hero of the *Symphonie Fantastique*. In other words, Lelio = Berlioz. The song begins:

The chill of death, night of the tomb,
Endless sound of the footsteps of time. . . .

When I had finished, he covered his face with his hands, as if frightened by what he had heard. Finally he shook himself, almost like a wet dog, and with an obvious effort to take command of himself he said, "You were wondering, yesterday . . . Let me tell you the whole story."

I sat to listen.

"I stopped off for a leisurely stay with my family at La Côte on the way to Rome, and I worried about Camille's silence. Her mother had formally accepted me as her daughter's fiancé, and Camille had given me a ring to bind us. But only a single tepid letter came—until one day I got a foul one from Hiller, saying that I was not missed, that my beloved was blossoming in public like a flower ready to be picked. Since I had more or less stolen Camille from Hiller, I thought I could dismiss his spiteful letter as his only way of hitting back. When I arrived in Rome, though, two months after having left Paris, there was not a word waiting for me. I seethed for a week and then decided to hurry back to France to find out where I stood. The director, Vernet, said I would lose my standing with the Academy if I did so, but I left anyway. By the time I reached Florence, I had come down with a quinsy, and I took to bed in the Hôtel des Quatre Nations, on the Arno. I had brought along my scores, and I spent the time as well as I could, revising 'A Ball' from the symphony. I had been there a fortnight when a letter at last reached me, forwarded by Vernet.

"It was not from Camille. It was from her mother. It announced to me in words like cannonballs that Camille was about to marry Monsieur Pleyel—you know him, Baillot, the piano-maker—old, ugly, but apparently just right for Camille: rich! The old woman had the nerve to beg me not to kill myself. How can I describe my rage? I decided to go straight to Paris, disguise myself as a lady's maid, go to the Moke house pretending to deliver a letter from 'the Countess M,' pull out a pistol and blow both women's brains out, and then snatch off my wig and, yes, shoot myself in the temple. I bought a maid's uniform from a French dressmaker across the Arno from my hotel, acquired some strychnine and laudanum to use in case my pistol misfired when I turned it against myself, and took off up the coast in a coach. At Pietrasanta, a village along the way, we changed carriages, and the bag with my assassin's costume was left behind. I had to buy another in Genoa. On the Corniche road near Nice, late at night, the driver stopped the carriage for a few minutes, and I could hear seductive swells of the Mediterranean beating and sucking on the cliffs below. It seemed that the sea was calling to me, inviting me. I was hypnotized. All I could think of was the storm in the brig on the way to Livorno, when I pictured being rocked to sleep in the waves. Early in the morning, when we stopped at a small harbor, I broke away from the carriage and jumped off a quay. But, as you see, I didn't drown. Some men in a fishing smack saw me and hauled me out in a net, boating me as if I were a huge mullet.

"The frigid kisses of the sea chilled me back to my senses, thank God. I wrote Vernet, saying I had, after all, not left Italy. Could he forgive me? He did—and here I am—alive, Baillot! *Lelio: The Return to Life*: it's Berlioz, you see, *his* return."

My guess had been right. And his return to "life," I was thinking as I sat in that room, was a return to the Harriet Smithson he has never even met.

I had to stop my visits to Berlioz for a few days because I was engaged for a recital with my quartet in Provence. On my return, my concierge handed me an urgent note from him: It was "imperative" that we meet at once. How easy it was for this boy to issue commands! . . . And for me, pretending that I had made the choice of my own free will, to obey!

I went to his rooms this afternoon.

Berlioz was waiting for me, all steamed up like a railroad engine trembling with its pent-up power on the tracks. "I need you—I need Antonietta—in my concert," he said in a rush, his wheels skidding. "I think that she—you know whom I mean—might be there. I'm looking for some way to lure her there. Your violin had such an important part in the making of the symphony—she *must* hear its voice."

"Among a hundred and thirty instruments?"

"No! Listen! I have a plan. The Estelle theme at the very beginning of the introductory Largo—it's given to muted violins, pianissimo, remember? Instead we'll give it this one time to Antonietta, solo. Boldly played, but bel canto, you know. The soul of the melody that haunts all five movements—the melody that is in her image, Baillot! She will *have* to listen from then on. Baillot, you have helped me so much—help me once more, I beg you."

I temporized. I said that the directors of the Opéra had not been pleased by my running off to Aix. I would have to see.

But I knew I would arrange to play, because this time he had not commanded—he had implored.

For this concert he had the luxury of three rehearsals. He had got permission to use the great hall of the Conservatoire, which seats more than a thousand. In rehearsal the music of *Lelio: The Return to Life* resounded with Berlioz's volcanic energy, and its passages of spoken narrative led the hearer along the tangled path of his emotions toward each song, but in my judgment, which I naturally spared him, this long piece was by no means a match for the revised *Fantastique*, which was more and more coruscating with each run-through. He was delighted with the way Antonietta sounded in my solo playing of the Estelle theme at the very beginning. "It will seduce the whole audience," he said. But I knew that he had something more particular than that in mind.

The night of December 9. Good weather. The audience is beginning to drift into the hall. Berlioz is fussing about. I have never seen him look so elegant. He is in formal clothes: a cutaway coat of black velvet over a yellow vest, a white foulard neckpiece with a pattern of quavers, black satin trousers with the gold chain of his watch fob dangling down, black silk stockings and black shoes with shiny metal buckles—I doubt that he can afford silver. His hair is a chandelier of red sparkles. He comes up on the stage to say a word to the actor Pierre Bocage, who will take the part of Lelio; he pats me on the shoulder as he passes me.

From where I am sitting at the concertmaster's desk, I have a clear view of the whole house. I spot many notables taking their places in the boxes. Liszt and Hugo are sitting together in the box next to the center one where Berlioz will have the place of honor. Over there is the leading tenor of the Opéra, Adolphe Nourrit. I recognize the Polish pianist Chopin. Alexandre Dumas. The men from the papers—Janin, d'Ortigue, Fétis; others, too. George Sand looking forbidding. The assistant concertmaster beside me points and whispers the name of the German poet Heinrich Heine. My heart jumps as I see a face like a burning ember with wild smoke for hair: it is Paganini! What will he think of my playing? I can't bear even to guess, and I tear my eyes away—the novelist Eugène Sue; the Deschamps brothers; the rich Ernest Legouvé. . . .

As people have come into the hall, they have been given copies of the "Program" of the *Fantastique*, and almost all, as they take their seats, start reading it.

But where is *she*?

Yesterday, Berlioz excitedly told me that he had stopped the previous morning at Schlesinger's music shop, and while he was telling the publisher how much he wanted to have Harriet Smithson in the audience for his concert, an Englishman entered, bought something, and was about to leave when Berlioz asked Schlesinger who that was. Schlesinger said it was a man named Schutter, the correspondent for an English paper, *Gaglignani's Messenger*—and, oh! he knew Miss Smithson! Perhaps he could get her to go to the concert with him. Berlioz hastily gave Schlesinger two tickets to a box, and the publisher ran after Schutter, and through the shop window Berlioz saw Schlesinger talking with Schutter and gesturing. Then Schutter took the tickets. . . .

The house is almost full. There is the usual hum of an audience settling down. I see Berlioz appear in his box. He holds up his hand in a signal to the conductor to wait a few minutes. . . .

There she is! She floats into the box where Hugo and Liszt are seated, right next to Berlioz's. And what a radiant sight she makes! She is in a simple, gauzy, sleeveless pale blue gown, gathered to a high waist by a twisted silk sash, evidently with cameos of some sort as shoulder clasps holding up the drapery over her breasts. Her dark hair is gathered on top of her head. Her huge eyes shine with excitement at the stir her appearance causes. There is a loud buzz of talk, and almost every head in the house turns toward her. She must think it is all because she is a famous actress. She leans forward slightly in an acknowledging bow. She demurely sits and at first looks self-consciously down at the "Program"; then Victor Hugo leans over and speaks to her, pointing to the printed sheet. She begins to read. . . .

I place a silk kerchief on my left shoulder and tuck Antonietta between it and my chin. A long pause to let silence creep like a hungry cat into the hall. I remain seated as I start to play. Slowly,

slowly, Antonietta projects the hesitant melody to the farthest reaches of the great space.

I want Antonietta with these notes and those that follow to justify all the months of "our work." The passage is marked largo. The bow languishes, the stops of my callused fingertips pressing the A string onto the ebony fingerboard step along in response to the notation very, very slowly—at a stately and measured and interrogatory pace. Hours, days of dreaming, years of hope stretch out on the limpid tones of a few measures. It is up to my violin to make the first appeal seem to last to the end of time. I know in a corner of my mind that Antonietta is being asked to send a ridiculous message. A man who is still a callow boy wants me to offer up to a single pair of disenchanted ears, through this wooden box in my arms, the ineffable yearnings of his lack of experience. And whose imaginary ears, exactly, does he want to reach? Those of a princess in pink slippers reaching out a hand to lean against the trunk of a cherry tree? Those of a make-believe brokenhearted virgin stepping toward footlights, her eyes empty, to sing a mad song? Those of a tease from an underwear shop? Those of a bitter woman with fingers curled to scratch and with damnation on her lips? I feel the absurdity of the appeal my violin is being asked to make, but at the same time I want the message to be lofty, mature, true, and overpowering as it injects the purity of Berlioz's beautiful gifts into those real ears, with the hair lifted away from them, in the box at the back of the hall. I remember the mornings. I remember all the roundabout ways in which this glorious music was made. I remember the many masks on that young face: of rapture, mischief, agony, nostalgia, grandeur, fear, and, rarely, deep and sure calm. What really moves me, I realize, as I do my best to draw out their meaning from these few measures, is the mystery of this young man's astonishing act of creation. I watched it all and understand none of it. I drown myself in this marvel. . . .

When my brief but (in another sense) my very long solo ends and Antonietta subsides into the ensemble of the Largo, I steal a glance at the boxes. I see that the actress, blushing, has turned her head and is looking at Berlioz, whose anxious ivory face is turned toward hers. The two are so close to each other they can almost reach out and touch each other. I feel a rush of happiness. I am swept up, as the audience is, too, in the tides of the Allegro of "Reveries—Passions." Without forcing the bow I feel the intensity of Antonietta's voice when we come to the soaring *idée fixe*—the image of the beloved, whoever she may be—and I feel an upsurge of energy. It seems that the whole orchestra is exhilarated by the tension of the two dramas—the turbulent one of the music itself that they are playing, and the other, being driven by the appeal of their performance, back there in the boxes at the heart of the theater. As we play, we become more and more fired. The waltz: a wild lift of spirits, then doubt. When at the end of "In the Fields" the second shepherd fails to answer, even I feel unbearably lonely, and I see that Miss Smithson's head is bowed. The terrible march—the theme of the beloved cut short by the doom chop of the guillotine. And then the chilling revelry of the witches—I hardly dare to look at the boxes to see the effect on that woman of the shrill, distorted love theme this time.

It is over. I hold Antonietta on my knees. Harriet Smithson is wiping tears from her eyes with a handkerchief. Her head is turned toward Berlioz.

Intermezzo Three

During the performance of *Lelio* at the concert, the actor Bocage, seated at a table in midstage with the orchestra around him, sadly declaimed, immediately after the "Song of Bliss," "Oh! why can't I find that Juliet, that Ophelia, to whom my heart calls out?" After these lines Harriet Smithson could have no doubt that she was the heroine of the evening and the inspiration for two sensational works of art. The next day she sent word to Berlioz that she had been deeply moved. He asked then to meet her—"in the name of pity; I dare not say of love"—and a go-between arranged a formal introduction. Three days after their meeting she sent a message: "*Eh bien, Berlioz, je vous aime.*" The pronoun *vous* spoke of a love at a certain distance.

There followed one of the most bizarre courtships in all the annals of romance. Berlioz's family refused to permit him to marry this actress—meaning harlot—whose career, in any case, was deteriorating fast. (Abbott had dropped her when she had demanded a salary equal to that of all the rest of the company put together.) Berlioz applied for legal *sommations* which would prevent his family from disinheriting him, even if he married against their will. Harriet broke her leg stepping down from a carriage. When Berlioz tried to comfort her in her rooms at the Hôtel du Congrès, the "damned hunchback" let it be known that she wished she were strong enough to pick him up and throw him out the window. Berlioz's father wrote Harriet not to put any hope in his will; he would sell everything rather than leave his son a house to share with her. The couple got a marriage license, which the crippled sister grabbed out of Berlioz's hands and tore up. Harriet wondered then if they should postpone the marriage, and at that, Berlioz took an overdose of opiates to kill himself, then was sorry he had and took ipecac to throw up. Harriet refused to go for a new license. Berlioz took an eighteen-year-old mistress. Harriet relented. Banns were published. And in October, 1833, the two were married.

Berlioz was astonished to discover that Harriet was a virgin. Harriet bore Berlioz a son, Louis, and for a time they enjoyed parenthood, but the marriage, alas, did not take many years to rot. Berlioz wandered all the time in his forest of memories, where visual and musical images worked on each other; he was an absent husband even when he was in the room with Harriet. Harriet's career crumbled. Once having won the hearts of all good Frenchmen, she now became a laughingstock as a pantomimist. She grew fat. She never learned to speak French properly. She became an alcoholic. Berlioz took a mistress, this time a long-standing one, and he and Harriet separated. In 1854, after a series of strokes, Harriet died.

All this time, Berlioz was storing up sharp-edged visual memories to be transformed, in due course, into memory's other self.

While Berlioz was courting Harriet, Baillot made a recital tour through Switzerland and Italy and undertook an act of creation of his own—the writing of *L'Art du violon*, a book that still stands today alongside the exemplary works on violin playing by Leopold Mozart, Kreutzer, Auer. His health began to fail toward the end of the decade, and after he died, in 1842, Antonietta disappeared. That is to say, dealers had no idea where the violin was; it dropped out of their meticulous listings of the whereabouts of the great Brescian and Cremonese instruments, records they kept in case one or another of them might at any moment come on the market. Most likely, an amateur fiddler in Baillot's family took possession of the violin for his or her own pleasure, perhaps not even realizing its value. This is just a guess.

In 1872 a manufacturer of steel pen nibs in Birmingham, England, named Joseph Gillott, who was famous among all who cared about fine handwriting for his superbly flexible "swan bill" and "magnum bonum" nibs, suddenly died. A few days after his death, a Birmingham solicitor charged with the settling of Gillott's estate called at 28 Wardour Street, London, on George Hart, the pre-eminent English expert of the day on old violins. The lawyer told Hart that Mr. Gillott had lived an enigmatic life of obsession. For some reason his mind had been removed from its hinges and become fastened to a violin of his dreams. He had almost ruined his nib business by turning all his profits into the purchase—very secret, through a network of agents—of innumerable fiddles, evidently in search of his ideal. Would Mr. Hart come to Birmingham and make a survey of the accumulated instruments and appraise their value for the estate?

At the Gillott factory, a senior nib man led Hart through several clanking machine shops, past a furnace with a cauldron of white-hot metal, through corridors letting onto offices and storerooms, until, at the far end of a warehouse, they came to a locked door. Hart's guide inserted a key, which squealed so loudly on being turned that Hart wondered when the door had last been opened. When it did swing back, Hart saw before him an immense storeroom table, on which there was a higgledy-piggledy mountain of fiddles reaching almost to the ceiling—mantled in dust, without strings or bridges, some of them with their backs or bellies gaping away from their ribs. On the floor there was a hill of bows like a mound of bones. Hart hardly knew how to begin. He saw sticking up from the heap the scroll of a head that looked far above average; he carefully drew out a viola, dusted it off, and upon examination recognized it as the work of Giuseppe Guarneri, son of Andrea. He put it aside.

It occurred to Hart, before he tackled the job of culling other treasures from the heap, to ask the nib executive whether his employer had bought any violoncellos.

The businessman had no idea what that word meant.

Any giant fiddles, any whales?

Ah! Yes! And the guide led Hart to a basement storeroom, where, at the far end, beyond a wilderness of discarded stamping machines, obsolete lathes, chipped plaster statues, three ancient pianos, and stacks of paintings and empty gilt picture frames, were five or six rows of—at least fifty—"whales." Among them Hart positively identified, on inspection, some true giants, by Bergonzi, Amati, Cappa, Landolfi. . . .

Then the nib executive held up a finger. He said he had just remembered something. He was proud to aver that he had been a particular trustee of the late Mr. Gillott, and the said gentleman had once whispered to him in confidence that he had a "bevy of specials—real beauties, Mr. Trull," at his home. "He made them sound, sir," the guide said to Hart, "like houris in a harem." Hart said they must by all means go there at once.

They rode in a buggy to Edgbaston, Gillott's estate; the house was a neo-classic monster of garish yellow brick. The nib man led Hart through darkened rooms with sheets spread on the furniture, up creaking stairs to Mr. Gillott's bedroom, and there, in a big glass-doored mahogany chifforobe against a wall—where, from his bed, the fiddle fancier must have been able to gaze lovingly at his "specials" as he drifted off to sweet dreams of purflings and *f*-holes and tailpieces—were displayed a dozen magnificent specimens. Taking them out, Hart quickly recognized among them, without any question, two Amatis, a Bergonzi, two Guarneris, and six Stradivaris, all in gem condition. It was on a closer look that he noticed, on one of the Stradivaris, a Cupid inlaid on the tailpiece; whereupon he at once checked further and saw the famous flaw in the purfling. He had found what he and other dealers had long listed as "the missing Antonietta Strad."

The better instruments from the Gillott collection were auctioned up in London at the house of Christie, Manson & Woods. Notable violins were bought that day by the Earl of Harrington and Lord Dunmore, among others. The Antonietta, carefully restored, was bid for and won at a price of £625 by a violinist with something of a reputation in the Midlands, one George Haddock, of Newly Hall, near Leeds. A former pupil of Vieuxtemps, he played Antonietta for two decades in numerous provincial recitals.

Upon Haddock's death, the violin passed by way of the Hill family's shop in London into the arms of a wealthy dilettante fiddler named Harold Duxley Billington, scion of an estate near Honiton in Devonshire. The Hills handled it twice more in the nineteenth century, selling it in turn to two collectors, each of whom retired the violin from active use. In a gala auction held at the Putticks firm on Queen Victoria's sixtieth jubilee, in 1897, the violin was sold abroad, at £1,050, to a German philanthropist for the benefit of a child prodigy named Adolph Ehrhardt, who at thirteen had grown just enough to handle a full-sized instrument. This boy was soon playing concertos with the Berlin Philharmonic and other symphony orchestras, and his patron bought him a Guarneri del Gesù with a bolder and larger tone than Antonietta's, suitable to outride the blare of a modern orchestra of more than a hundred instruments.

In 1911, Antonietta was accordingly sold through the Paris agent Gand to Sergei Pavlovich Diaghilev, the patron of the Ballets Russes, who bought the instrument for a brilliant young Russian violinist, originally from St. Petersburg, named Pavel Andreivich Federovsky. Federovsky had been a pupil of Leopold Auer at the St. Petersburg Conservatory, along with Elman and Zimbalist. He had soon been drawn into the Diaghilev circle and was eventually chosen as concertmaster for the Paris seasons of the ballet. He was later appointed to the lustrous post of concertmaster of the Imperial Opera, back in St. Petersburg.

For almost a year after acquiring the Antonietta Stradivari, Federovsky complained that the violin had been horribly polluted by the showy vulgarity of the playing of the Ehrhardt boy. It seemed to take forever for him to purge the "Wagnerian gassiness" from the instrument and to be able to play on it in the Auer manner: striving above all for purity of tone; reining in virtuosity with a seemly reticence; giving plenty of scope to his innate Slavic intensity but carefully keeping on the near side of sentimentality; and, to achieve a flowing sostenuto grandness of voice, using the "Russian bow grip"—applying pressure on the nut of the bow with the second joint of the index finger. Antonietta finally more than obliged. One day Federovsky exclaimed, "This violin likes me!"

Act Four

1918

C. F. RAMUZ

One of the young women came up from the laundry at the foot of the hill to tell me that there was a phone call for me. Stravinsky had a telephone, of course, but I did not. He had found in the directory the number of this *blanchisserie* near my house in the Lausanne outskirts and with his bluff charm of a boyar had talked the proprietress into sending one of her bare-armed nymphs up the hill to summon me whenever he called. I walked down the slope in my shirtsleeves, felt slippers on my feet, chatting with a sturdy Lisette.

There was the usual bustle in the laundry: the drubbing of linen on corrugated washboards, the muffled splashing of sudsy water in tubs, someone rattling a poker in the coals under the boiler, the clatter of flatirons being set down on their metal holders, and, like the murmuration of a flock of warblers, the prattling and giggling of the women. As soon as I picked up the earpiece of the phone, however, all activity stopped, out of courtesy crossbred with curiosity; it was as if they were all playing that children's game of statues in which, when the music stops, everyone must freeze as they are. All the ears, pink from steam, listened. I shouted, "*Allô!*" A *brise* was blowing down off the Alps that morning, and now all you could hear was the flapping of the wash drying on lines stretched between posts up above the flat zinc roof.

As usual, Stravinsky had a thousand things to say in three sentences. I could picture him, in his study at the top of the house, nestled between two kettledrums and a Hungarian cymbalom, the piano to his left, his desk across from it as tidy as a melody by Haydn, a cigarette in one hand, a strong cup of coffee and a little glass of marc at his elbow. He stacked his words up on each other as tightly as the huddled notes in some of his complex chords.

"What?" I shouted. "Slow down!"

I made out from his babble that an old friend of his from St. Petersburg, fleeing the Revolution, had with great difficulty made his way through Poland and Austria and eventually to Switzerland. He spoke the man's name.

"Repeat! I can't hear you!"

"What difference does a name make? I need your help."

It came out next, without his actually saying so, that he was terrified that this dear friend would expect to be housed by him. I could imagine Stravinsky toting up the expense of such a visit in his head. I grasped at once that this outlay must be avoided like typhus. It would be for me to find a house for the friend. Near Stravinsky, if I would please. He adored Federovsky. "Ramuz, wait until you see his wife."

"Ah! This man not only has a name, he has a wife."

"And two children. This morning. You must find the house this morning. They arrive this afternoon. Please. Have mercy on Federovsky. A cheap house. Near here."

And he told me to be at the Morges station at three-fifteen to help him meet the family—in other words, to carry the luggage.

"You must hang up now," I said. "I am going to have a busy day."

But no, he wanted to tell me that he couldn't sleep the night before, his stomach made noises all night like a bear grunting, he had had a letter from Diaghilev, the ballet company was disintegrating, and also word had come that his concert in Milan had fallen through, and his wife Ekaterina's cough was worse. . . .

What could I say? We were all having a hard time. The war had cut off my royalties from France and Germany, we were hemmed in by all sorts of shortages and rations, it was hard to find milk for my children. I had had to move from my lovely house at Treytorrens and into this cottage near the laundry.

I realized that for Stravinsky things were even worse. He kept saying this was the hardest time of his whole life. He had lost his homeland. I had known him here in Switzerland for four years, and I remembered how exhilarated he had been by the benign February Revolution the year before this. When the news of it came, we climbed the Petit-Chêne together. A violent north wind was blowing against us, like wild tidings of Russia's change coming down to us. We saw two women whose long skirts—sails aback—had wrapped themselves tightly around their legs and had arrested both of them for a few moments in strange poses. His imagination feverish, Stravinsky pointed at them and said, "Look at that picture, Ramuz! Those two! Your motherland and mine!"—assuming with his characteristic generosity, I suppose, that my little Switzerland must bulk as large in my mind as huge Russia did in his. The wind tore great gasps of emotion out of his mouth. Russia was being reborn!—the Russia of Pushkin, Gogol, Moussorgsky, a holy Orthodox Russia, pre-European, a peasant land, a Russia of great basso voices and of the sound of clanging bells! He must go back; his place was there. . . . But he did not go back, and then came the October Revolution. The dream faded. He saw himself as an exile. He would never see St. Petersburg again. No more money could come from the family estates or from rents in St. Petersburg or from sales of his music. His wife and one of his daughters were ill. The war, meanwhile, was destroying Diaghilev's magnificent company; there would be no more commissions, no more fees for performances. Stravinsky's music had been published exclusively in Germany; there would be no more royalties from any of his work. Money was mother's milk to him. The teats were going dry; he howled with hunger and colic and panic.

All the same, he was so alive! His excitement about the arrival of these friends, these Federovskys, was that of a little boy. He *was* a little boy: I had often thought that this must be the secret of his genius. He was open to life as only a small child could be. Every sight, every sound, every taste, every touch made him vibrate with amazement and delight and terror. And every chord of his music caught those vibrations in its net.

As always, he rattled on and on. On my end, there was time only for interjections, monosyllables. The nymphs lost interest. One of them began to sing. Soon they were all back at work. . . .

I was at the station before Stravinsky. When he came breathlessly along the platform, I saw that he had dressed up to meet his friends. Had I found a house?

I had. A nice little vineyarder's cottage right among the terraces. Four would be slightly cramped in it, but it was economical.

Stravinsky failed to thank me. He looked impatiently up the tracks, suddenly furious at Switzerland because this train was five minutes late.

Soon it came. A door swung open from a compartment in one of the cars. A very tall man stepped down and turned to lift his two children out; then down came a woman with a black velvet hat that sprouted a purple ostrich feather.

I ran to the doorway of the compartment; from within, a porter handed me a great number of cases and boxes and parcels. I suddenly felt myself rudely pushed aside by the tall man, who reached up to receive from the porter a rectangular wooden violin case with a pattern on it of rounded brass nailheads. Federovsky turned away with the case clasped firmly under his arm.

I had been too busy to see how Stravinsky had greeted the family. I now could take them in. Federovsky made a gaunt formal figure. I judged that he was about the same age as Stravinsky, thirty-five. He was wearing a black homburg. He had on rimless pince-nez glasses, behind which there were tears. I saw that Stravinsky's eyes, too, were brimming. I had often envied in my friend this wonderful Russian accessibility of feelings. What a strange pair they made, Stravinsky so tiny, his friend such a tall wooden post!

At first they spoke Russian, very fast; but when I turned to them, they changed, with immediate good manners, to French, which—the second tongue of the Russian upper classes, a lingua franca for casual talk—they all spoke beautifully, though with lilting guttural vowels and r's rolled on the ends of their tongues. Stravinsky told the couple that I was Switzerland's greatest writer. Federovsky bowed to me stiffly from his waist. As we talked, he kept calling Stravinsky by what must have been his St. Petersburg nicknames: Guima, Guimochka.

I finally had the courage to look right at Madame Federovskaya. I guessed that she was about thirty years old. A delicate veil hung down from the dizzy hat; I could make out, through the veil, a creamlike skin, a gossip's slightly amused lips, sapphire eyes under black brows. I saw why Stravinsky on the phone had alerted me to the sight of her.

Now Stravinsky was down on his knees in the dust of the platform talking as an equal with the little daughter. His head was at the level of her head. He called her Manichka. He was asking her whether she had understood what the clickata-clickata of the railroad train's wheels was saying to her.

"Yes," she said. "The train was saying, 'Hurry! Hurry! We are going to Uncle Igor!' "

Stravinsky clapped his hands. "Brava! You understand everything."

PAVEL FEDEROVSKY

I had forgotten what a peacock he is. Or, rather, bantam rooster. This tiny cockerel came along the platform dressed like his idea of a boulevardier. Bad taste. A dark blue jacket, known I think as "*un sporting.*" *Brown* trousers. Gray spats. A Riviera straw boater seated on his oversized ears. A monocle! He obviously thought himself very ducky. It was for Anna, of course. At once he started the old tricks for her. I knew it meant nothing. He would flirt with a veal cutlet if he thought it was female. But it nettled me. He is so obvious. Charms children with his childishness—but he snubbed the boy Sasha and got on his knees to the miniature woman. I had been at first so touched to see him. We were both lost souls. Our lovely city, vanished, erased from our lives!—the Neva! the canals! the beautiful embroidered curtain at the Opera! And, oh! Stravinsky's father singing Boris—his cry of pain: *O, gospodi, Bozhe moy!* We go far back, Guima and I. We worked together. So hard, so well. To get the orchestra just right. I spoke to him of *Firebird, Petrouchka, Sacre*. His music of the Russian soul. He was suddenly angry. Sick of hearing about those old things. Bah! Very rude to me. But to Anna: smooth as an ambassador. He makes a statement to her. Sets his lips in a smile that is a little kiss of the afternoon air. Bends his head slightly forward. As if: I have spoken, do you understand me? Waits for her reply. Leans expectantly forward, like a *maître d'hôtel* taking an order from an honored guest. She answers. He puts his hands over his huge ears. His monocle falls out on its ribbon. Her words, her voice give him too much pleasure. He can't stand such pleasure. Later, at the little hut the Swiss writer has hired for us, she says to me: Isn't Igor charming? We have a short quarrel. She defends him. I bellow. "No, no," she finally says, "I was *laughing* at him. He is so naïve! So conceited!" To this I agree. Anna's and my quarrels don't last long. I asked Guimochka there on the platform: What do you hear from Diaghilev? He was our God! Again the maestro cut me off with a sharp tongue. Sergei Pavlovich did not invite him to go to America with the ballet. Two years ago! Very very angry.

IGOR STRAVINSKY

I remember my first sight of her on a winter day in St. Petersburg. Seeing these two through my tears on the station platform in the bright sunlight by the edge of the lake, in the warm spring air, I suddenly felt cold. I was walking to the library of the Conservatory. The ochre of the houses was trimmed with white on all the ledges and sills. The canal in front of our house had been frozen solid for weeks. It was white, and the streets were white. A very fine snow was falling, like sugar tossed out from a huge pewter-capped shaker over the city. I turned onto Nevsky Prospekt. I was almost blinded by the whiteness, and yearned for something black to come along. Here came a sleigh drawn by a roan-red horse with bells on its harness, tossing its head and breathing plumes of steam. The driver sat high. Under the welcome black hood of the sleigh I saw the pale face of a woman wrapped in a black fur—a face so sad that I thought at once of Anna Karenina. I thought, This woman is going to kill herself. The sleigh was gone in a moment.

The face haunted me. Later I met the Federovskys at one of the "Evenings of Contemporary Music." In candlelight I could not find a trace of sadness on the face, and I guessed that it must have been nothing more than the snow, the cold that morning that had put a tragic mask on it. I decided: This woman is an empty bucket. When I got to know them, I saw how flimsy she was. The worst of it was that, married to a hypersensitive musician, she was totally immune to music, was tone-deaf, often could be heard humming off key. She walked into a room like an actress coming onto a stage, her arms slightly lifted, aware that the audience was looking at her and wondering about her, and when she spoke it seemed as if the lines had been memorized, the words somehow did not belong to her at all. Her gaiety was like a costume she put on for a scene. The only true, sincere sadness was on Pavel's face.

How happy I was to see him now! How I love him! He made sure that the orchestra played *my* music. He himself plays the music he reads on the page; he reads the mind of the composer. He is not one of your "interpreters." I hate "interpretation," whether by performer or conductor, for it is nothing but a form of boasting. Pavlochka is a delicate machine. He stood there on the platform so stiffly, and I knew that he loves me as I love him, and that he was thinking—as I was—about our city, our beautiful St. Petersburg, which might as well be Atlantis at the bottom of the sea, Pompeii buried under molten lava.

They have delightful children. I sensed, at our first greeting, that young Sasha was too proud and sensitive to open up to me at once, so I had a few words with Manya, who is just as bold as her mother.

RAMUZ

Federovsky played his violin for us at Stravinsky's house. We were in the blue room, a place of such a blue that it seemed we were high in the sky on a perfect day. The two wives sat on the couch; Anna Federovskaya's eyes blazed in perfect unison with that azure light, while poor ailing Katya Stravinskaya's skin looked like linen bleached by laundry bluing. When Federovsky first took his violin from the case, Igor, with his appetite for sensation, asked to hold the violin for a few minutes; he drank its beauty, uttering little yips of delight. Look! What about this Cupid on the tailpiece?

Federovsky said that Diaghilev had bought the violin for him and had told him its history, which he had got from the dealer Gand in Paris. This was a rather famous Stradivari, known as "the Antonietta Strad." The maker named it, Federovsky said, for a woman he madly loved after merely glimpsing her face one night at a concert. Stradivari was making this instrument at the time. He was a widower, and the day after the concert he wrote to the woman asking her to marry him. Since he was rich, she eagerly accepted. But a few days later—here Federovsky showed us all, one by one, a little chipped-out place near the decorative line at the edge of the fiddle's belly—a few days later, while Stradivari was working on the violin, a strange man burst into his workshop and shouted that the woman was pregnant, out of wedlock; she was an alley cat. In his alarm at that news, Stradivari's hand slipped and caused the chipped place, which he vowed never to repair. It turned out that the man had lied—he was in love with the woman himself. Stradivari married her, and the liar committed suicide. Stradivari left the blemish there, as a reminder that no one in this world is perfect.

Igor was excited by this story and clapped his hands in delight. When Federovsky began to play, however, he sat limply in a straight wooden chair at his desk, idly sketching on a pad, seeming not to listen, apparently indifferent—but I could tell that his invisible antennae were quivering. There was nothing fancy about this recital: Federovsky was playing simple Russian folk tunes. I, an outsider at such a feast, was entranced; I could imagine what this music was doing for the four exiles.

After about half an hour Federovsky put away his instrument, and the two men, aroused by the absolute Russianness of the sounds still echoing in the room, began to pour out memories with such passion and shared intimacy of feeling that I must admit I found myself a little put out. I felt as if the closeness to Stravinsky that I had enjoyed for three years might now be in danger (though I realized that even in sharing these exclusive reminiscences with Federovsky, he was still reaching out to me in one way. With his perfect manners he kept to the French tongue).

In his good moods Igor had often talked to me about Russia, usually on a rather abstract plane, analyzing *Dead Souls*, or talking about the untranslatability of Pushkin, or explaining the meaning of the Tatar incursions into Russian Russia. Or, sometimes, dropping anecdotes. Such as: Stasov's memory of Tolstoy, when, as the great writer was lecturing on the need for absolutely pure passive non-resistance and non-violence toward all God's creatures, for the sake of peace on earth, a member of the audience asked what a person should do if attacked by a tiger in the woods. "Do the best you can," Tolstoy said. "It doesn't happen very often."

But this, between the two men who had lost their motherland, was on an entirely different plane. They threw simple images and sounds at each other, quite in the mood of the folk tunes the violin had sung, images and sounds of all that was lost and gone. Stravinsky stopped sketching. There was a fierce intensity in their recognitions; they knew each other's codes; their laughter was heartbroken. The women were silent. I felt out of sorts, not on their account but on my own. The violin had done this to all of us.

STRAVINSKY AND FEDEROVSKY

S: The bells, Pavlochka, the bells at Nikolsky Sobor. *De dong dah dah dong de dah.* They made my scalp tingle—long before I knew about overtones, you know. The vibrations of the deep ones went right through me, they made my bones sing.

F: The noise of the droshkies—

S: Oh, my God, especially the ones with iron tires, on the streets paved with wooden blocks, remember? The hooves on the wood and the rasping of those wheels?

F: Ai! And the wheels of the streetcars pulled by horses, the squealing of metal on metal when they took a curve!

S: For me the best sound was the shouting of the men selling things in the street. Carrying their trays on their heads—remember how they kept their balance by slinking, you know, walking smoothly, you know, like Javanese dancers, or like prostitutes?

F: The whores on Nevsky Prospekt at night! When I was a student, I thought when they came up to you and asked for a cigarette—*paparosi*, they said, so sweetly, reaching out a hand—I thought that that was all they really wanted! I would give them one and walk on.

S: I never thought *that*. But listen: When I was little, at the Champs de Mars—

F: Sleighs pulled by elks, do you remember them, in winter?

S: Ha! Yes! But always at the Champs my father bought ice cream for me from one of those vendors. *Morozhnoyeh! Morozhnoyeh!* I knew all the vendors' chants, I still know them, I could play them for you one by one. Ah, Pavlochka, those tunes you were playing for me . . . When I first came here, I was homesick—I guess I am always homesick, even when I am at home!—the war was just beginning, and I felt very far from Russia, and in my homesickness I read our wonderful folk poems. It wasn't so much the stories the poems told that moved me. It was more the lilt of the simple Russian words, the uneven fluttering and chattering of the syllables—those were almost music in themselves. So I gathered some of them like flowers, first in *Pribouatki*—Ramuz here translated it into French for me, with me; then *Les Berceuses du Chat*; then some choruses for women's voices; and then, of course, *The Wedding*:

Hear the Bridegroom saying,
"I would sleep now."
And the Bride replying,
"Take me with you."
Hear the Bridegroom saying,
"Is the bed narrow?"
And the Bride replying,
"Not too narrow."

FEDEROVSKY

Whatever we start talking about, he works it around to himself before long. He's a genius, we know he is. He feels the need to remind us. I don't need the reminder, I know it already.

I had been disgusted by his sitting there while I played for him, drawing some kind of picture. Not listening at all, it seemed to me. After we talked, I took a look at what he had drawn. I was interested to see what kind of a sketch my Antonietta would inspire—if he *was* listening. It was a scene in the Garden of Eden. You could tell because the woman was reaching up for an apple on a tree with a snake in it. The man and the woman were naked. Adam had an erection. Eve was wearing a Swiss one-thousand-franc banknote as a fig leaf.

RAMUZ

We three decided to take an afternoon off. I led them up the hill past the bonemeal factory to the little pink-faced Café Crochettaz, embedded in a steep hillside in that Cézannne landscape. We sat on the terrace, looking out over an iron railing onto a bay of the lake, which glistened in the still air like satin. We ordered three liter flasks of wine from the local vineyards, and some cheese, and a long loaf of bread, and we sipped and talked. The way a man eats and drinks tells all you need to know about him. Here were these two old friends, the tall and the short, showing me the truth about themselves in the way each in turn picked up the knife and peeled some rind off the semi-hard cheese to cut away a slice, then broke off a chunk of the bread, and put the cheese on it, and took a bite, and chewed, and drank.

Stravinsky was all out in the open, doing these things. His eyes shone; he flicked the knife decisively, broke the bread with a loud crunch of the thick crust; his first bite was followed by two or three chews, then a pause, and a little groan of pleasure, then faster chewing. He held the wine in his mouth a few seconds before swallowing it. This was a man in love with sensation, reaching out at every moment for extremity. You could see a wonderful simplicity in him, though; it was the ordinary things in life—bread, cheese, wine of the country—that thrilled him; he experienced each of them as absolutely extraordinary. I knew very well the brittle sophistication of his mind, yet at the same time he was a primitive. He was savage and civilized. He was saint and sinner. You could tell it all from the way he chewed, the brief pause as if he had stopped to offer thanks to God, the little sensual groan, the speed with which his liter of wine disappeared.

Federovsky—slicing, breaking, drinking—showed himself to be much less stiff and withheld than I had first thought him. There was a strange mixture of robustness and tenderness in him; we had heard this mix, to be sure, in his playing of the violin. And there was a comical streak in him, too, which showed itself in slightly overblown facial expressions, puffs of his cheeks, grotesque frowns as he tore the bread or stuck the knife upright in the cheese after cutting a slice. He rolled his eyes to heaven each time he swallowed wine. Nor did it take him long to finish *his* liter.

Nor me, either.

We ordered more. And then more.

FEDEROVSKY

There were several people on the terrace. All were drinking and talking. Our being out in the open muffled the chatter. I saw Stravinsky looking across again and again at one of the other tables. He was ogling a busty woman. You could see that she was enjoying herself. A vein stood out on her forehead. Her face was as pink as the façade of the inn. She laughed often. From the way Stravinsky looked at her, you would have thought her breasts must be full of the lovely Vaudois wine we were drinking.

Perhaps I was mischievous. While Igor was staring at her, I asked him about his wife's health. He did not stop peeking over at the other table from time to time as he answered.

STRAVINSKY

When I was nine, we began going for summers to a large estate that belonged to an aunt on my mother's side, at Pechisky, in the Ukraine. I was a miserable child; my mother openly favored my oldest brother, Roman, and he and Yury—also older—bullied me, and my father had the temperament of a wild boar. I used to mope and yearn for a gentle sister. Well, there at Pechisky I found her, or at least a substitute for her: my first cousin Ekaterina Gabrielovna Nossenko. She was a year older than I was. Katya and I played together all day every day, and we became dearest friends, and we decided—before we even knew that our sexual organs had any other use than to piss with—that we would get married and sleep in the same bed all the rest of our lives.

Fifteen years later we did marry. There was an Imperial edict forbidding marriage between first cousins. We found an old soak of a priest in a village near St. Petersburg who with a little persuasion in cash and vodka would marry people with his eyes closed. We went there and were married with just two witnesses, two sons of Rimsky-Korsakov who were close friends of mine. They held the crowns of wedlock above our heads as we knelt after paying the bribe. Their father, my beloved teacher, gave us an icon back in the city that evening which has blessed our marriage ever since. Did you notice it in my study? Katya and I are closer than lovers, you know. Just as she was when we were ten and eleven, she is still my dearest friend. She has, by the way, the most beautiful hand as the copyist of scores. She copies everything for me. She can never do enough for me.

However. There is a curse on my family, Pavel. TB. Some

time in the past a succubus had intercourse with our genes. TB killed my maternal grandfather, who was the Tsar's minister of agriculture. It has run through the family ever since. Katya's mother had it. Katya has it. I spent five months in a sanatorium at Sancellemoz with it. Two of our daughters seem to have weak lungs, one is quite sick. This is why we began coming to Switzerland—for the thin air up high.

Yes, Pavlochka, Katya is failing. Just when the world is falling apart and there is no more money!

RAMUZ

Three more liters! . . . And another three, why not? . . . As we grew drunk, the two men withdrew from me once again, wandering off into their Russianness. Their voices sank deeper and deeper. There were no sequiturs; there was no connection between what one said and what the other answered. They kept laughing and laughing like a French horn and a trombone, but their gaiety was so gloomy! Or was it that their gloom was so hilarious? Or was it that their faraway happiness made *me* gloomy?

STRAVINSKY AND FEDEROVSKY

F: There was a peasant who sold cabbages in the street near our house. Old man. Had a wagon and an old, old horse. Every so often the man would put his fingers in his mouth and whistle. Right away the horse would piss. S-s-s-s-s!

S: My great-grandfather Ivan Ivanovich Skorokhodov died when he was one hundred and eleven years old. Want to know how he died? He was a creative man. We have creative men in our family, Pavel! He created by servicing women. I write music, he screwed. Well, he couldn't help himself, he was full of love. Now I will tell you how he died at the age of one hundred and eleven. His family tried to confine him. Locked him in. They thought his creativity was bad for him. He knew better. He died by falling off a wall one night, escaping from the house because he had arranged a rendezvous down the street.

F: Know how I got my job at the Opera? I saw a hunchback. Right by the Mariinsky Theater. Across the street. I ran across and touched his hump with Antonietta's case. I almost got the violin out to touch him with that. I gave him a ruble. The very next day they made me concertmaster!

S: Something awful. When I was a boy. I tasted my own *govno*, Pavel. I translate that word for you, Ramuz, you ignorant man, don't know the best language of all. *Merde*, Ramuz. P-f-f-f. Bland. No taste hardly at all. I have tasted worse food in a thousand restaurants.

F [*his face suddenly radiant*]: Ah, Guimochka, Guimochka! The Swan Woman in that story of Afanasyev's! "Let her body glint through her wings, and through her body let her bones appear, and from bone to bone let the marrow run like a flowing string of pearls!"

S: *Bozhe moy!* Federovsky! Ramuz! Help! Where will the money come from?

RAMUZ

So we got talking about money, or, rather, the dire lack of it. We were all frightened. What impresses me, as I piece together what followed, was Federovsky's clarity of mind. He was just as drunk as Stravinsky and I were, but he had soon built up a perfectly formed idea. He began, as I remember, by saying that we needed some simple way to get money. We must keep it simple. Simplicity always wins, he said. We start, he said, with a prime number. The number three. Very simple. It is we. We are the *alpha, beta*, and *gamma*. First of all, he said, Ramuz is the greatest writer in Switzerland. Second: I, Federovsky, he said, am the greatest violinist who has ever sat at this table at the Café Crochettaz—at least, facing the water; perhaps a greater violinist had sat at this table facing the pink wall. Third: Stravinsky is the greatest composer on earth. We must use our triad of greatnesses. Prepare and perform a musical play!

All right. Where? There has been a Revolution, there is a war. All the great opera houses are dark. This must be a simple piece. For a small space. Few instruments. Tiny cast. You could put it on in a town hall. Or in a tent. Anywhere. You could go like gypsies from town to town. Money, *chers maîtres*! Not much. Enough. Enough for a simple life. Hurrah! Simplicity wins!

Stravinsky groaned. You could not tell whether this was a groan of thankful prayer, like the one that came with chewing delicious bread and cheese, or a groan of despair, that came from hearing Federovsky say, "Not much." Finally he said, "An operetta about what?"

Without a moment's hesitation Federovsky said, "Afanasyev! A tale by Afanasyev!"

I said, "But it has to be in French."

Stravinsky said, "Naturally."

STRAVINSKY

I began worrying about money. I was afraid that we were building up to an expensive chit with all the wine we had ordered. We were intoxicated. *In vino*, however, *veritas*. I suddenly had a brilliant idea. I told the others I had thought of a way we could pool our talents to make some money. We could write a small traveling show—a play with music. With a modest ensemble of instruments, a cast of three or four, a minimum of scenery, you could go from city to city, putting it on in small theaters. I even had the beginnings of an idea for what it could be. Federovsky had been muttering earlier about a story by Aleksandr Nikolaevich Afanasyev. I loved those stories of peasants always being tricked by life, and I knew that Ramuz would love them, too, because his own work is a poetic rendering of his beloved Vaudois peasants of the vineyards; he was always calling them God's prey.

And I had the thought that though the Afanasyev stories were profoundly Russian, we—Federovsky and I—were now cut off from Russia, and we would be collaborating with Ramuz, so we must make this piece something international, universal, or, better yet, local wherever it might be performed.

FEDEROVSKY

It came time to leave. Stravinsky obviously considered himself to be in love with the woman at the other table. She was now, like us, drunk. Stravinsky couldn't tear his eyes away from her. Especially when the waiter came with the account for our long afternoon. While Ramuz and I dug deep in our pockets, he was far away, drinking the wine of her bounty. He was deaf to two distinct pronunciations of his own name. Ramuz said to me, "You will have to get used to this. I am." We two paid.

On the way home we climbed a series of stone stairways up a hill of terraced vines, which had so far put out only their tender springtime verdure. Pure ranks of a delicate yellow-green. The rows on rows of the bulwarks of the terraces steadied our fuzzy minds with their neatness and regularity. To Stravinsky they apparently loomed like a giant score, stave on stave packed with little leaves of music.

"Ah, my friends," he said, "look at that! Music establishes the order of things!"

RAMUZ

Both men performed for each other. We were in the blue, blue room. First Stravinsky played his recent very Russian music: passages from *Pribouatki, Renard, The Wedding*, and the touching sweet lullaby he had written for his little daughter Mitoucha—a song he had asked me to translate into French. "*À ma fillette,*" he had written at the top of the score in his notebook. The expressions on Federovsky's face while his friend played were like those he had displayed over bread and cheese and wine at the café—cheeks blown out into sudden balloons, eyebrows scurrying up and down his forehead, lips pressed together so hard as to twist his nose: delight, amazement, nostalgia, painful joy, despair.

When Stravinsky had finished, Federovsky took out his Antonietta and quite literally answered what Stravinsky had been playing. Stravinsky had often told me that in spite of the obvious Russian folk flavor of these and many earlier compositions of his, he had never "quoted" or even "paraphrased" actual folk tunes. But now, with a brilliant speed of mind, Federovsky juxtaposed passages from Stravinsky's Russian-flavored things—going back to the earlier ballets, as well as the pieces he had just been playing—with strikingly similar lines and phrases from folk music. I was curious to see how Stravinsky would take this. His bluff was being called. But in the most respectful and appealing way. And by a man who obviously knew every note Stravinsky had ever written. Stravinsky sat again at his desk, his face illegible, sketching idly on a pad.

Illegible—until I saw the moisture gathering on the lower lids of his eyes.

When Federovsky put the fiddle down, Stravinsky, after a long silence, broke abruptly into the story of a day last year when he returned home after a long and very wet lunch at my house in the Lausanne suburbs and found a strange personage in a tailcoat and a top hat in his garden. He thought he must be drunker than he had realized. Seeing things. He asked the apparition what in the world it was doing in a pretty garden on a sunny day in such a costume. It was a real-life man, who said in a sepulchral voice he had been summoned because there was a death in the house. He was a mortician. And yes, Stravinsky rushed inside to find that his "second mother," Bertha, the East Prussian woman who had nursed him from childhood and was now nursing his children, had died. "When I was very small," he said, "she must have put a lantern in the hall and left my bedroom door cracked every night, because to this day I can't sleep unless a narrow beam of light lies across my bed." She had learned to cook all sorts of Russian food, and she sang the same German lullabies to the little ones that she had sung long ago to him. She had lived for love of the whole family, but especially, as he knew, for love of him. She had burst a blood vessel and abandoned him.

FEDEROVSKY

I had had the strange thought, as Stravinsky sat at the piano, that there was something diabolical about him. Anyone who could get at the heart of what was Russian in a song by putting the melody for the voice in the key of G major, with an occasional wobble toward E minor, on top of a repeated F-natural diminished seventh in the bass, so that the whole mass of sound leaned toward the key of C—he *was* a devil!

And then I had another thought, while I played my violin and watched him sit there drawing a picture, pretending he was on another planet. Listen to this, Stravinsky, I thought. The very soul of music is in the sound a violin makes, the sound *this* violin makes.

It was after both of us had stopped playing and he had told his story about the loss of his "other mother" that I put those two thoughts together.

"Guima! I have it! I know the story we should use! Do you remember Afanasyev's story about the soldier who gives the Devil his violin—his soul, really—in exchange for wealth and happiness? And recovers the fiddle, at least for a while, by getting the Devil drunk?"

Stravinsky stood up and threw his arms around me. "Yes! Yes!" he shouted. "We'll be rich!"

Being so much taller than he, I looked over his shoulder while he was hugging me and saw the sketch he had made this time.

It was anatomical—a pair of breasts, shaded into the round, opulent, the nipples prominent, the areolas generous.

As he backed away, I pointed at the sketch and asked, "Is that a synopsis of the woman at the café? Her finer points, let's say?" Then I touched his arm and added, "Or . . . Bertha?"

He clapped his hands and said, "Bravo! You understand everything."

As if I were a clever child.

RAMUZ

Stravinsky told me, when I was alone with him the other day, that Federovsky is one of the few people on this earth that he trusts. (He did not take the trouble to add that I am another.) He says the violinist is like a priceless leather boot that has been carefully oiled for years—evidently thinking of those handsome, shiny Russian boots that are so flexible that they wrinkle down the wearer's legs like loose stockings. "He exactly fits my foot," Stravinsky said. This seems to mean that that old boot Federovsky is pliable and useful to Stravinsky—a sound basis for trust, I suppose. Before long, however, there is a modulation, and soon we are singing in the key of Anna. Stravinsky speaks of the mystery that lurks in a woman who is stupid, shrewd, gentle, bold, and stunningly beautiful. "Federovsky is a good fiddler because he is always reaching for his wife's mystery on that instrument of his."

I realize that Stravinsky often talks foolishly, and that sometimes he is rude and hurtful (doesn't he trust *me* after all this time?), and that he seems selfish and boastful, and even, sometimes, ruthless. But I have known for a long time that he has a skin as thin as the surface tension of water, and that he constantly and desperately needs warmth and comfort and support. His scars itch all the time. Federovsky told me the other day about his friend's deepest wound, which he suffered at the first performance of *The Rite of Spring*, five years ago, in Paris, at the inauguration of the Théâtre des Champs-Elysées. Pierre Monteux had put the orchestra and dancers through sixteen careful rehearsals. Federovsky was Diaghilev's concertmaster, and he says that the musicians were fascinated—overwhelmed—by the complex music. But at the very first measures of the prelude on the opening night there came hoots from the cheap seats in the balcony. The shouts of outrage soon spread throughout the house. Stravinsky fled from the hall and ran backstage in an agony of chagrin. There was soon an uproar as defenders began to bawl at the hecklers, who redoubled their protests. Part of the trouble came from the choreography—Nijinsky's first effort in that line. The great dancer not only knew nothing about music, he could only count with his legs. The full fury of the hurricane came with the "Dance of the Adolescents." The audience remembered Nijinsky's pornography of the year before, when the faun fucked on stage, and now the pubescent dancers in this scene began to hop like lascivious toads. I imagine that Stravinsky must still hear, ringing in his ears, the screams of hatred of that audience. He makes a partial payment every day of his life, I suppose, on the tax that this world levies on those who are blessed and cursed with merciless originality.

STRAVINSKY

There came a moment while Federovsky was playing so winningly those many quotations from my work, and showing how superior they were to crude Russian folk tunes, that something clicked in my mind. Violin . . . Violin . . . And then I had it! Afanasyev's story of the soldier who trades his fiddle with the Devil for a magic book that will bring him riches. The soldier gets his fiddle back in a card game with the Devil when he gives the Devil too much wine to drink. And then he wins a Princess with its music. All three of us are excited about this idea of mine. Ramuz will write the narration, I will write music that will feature violin solos, and Federovsky will charm the world with my music on that instrument of his—which I think the Devil may indeed have owned at one time. Oh, yes, I shall write music that will rouse a Princess from her stupor!

RAMUZ

We were at work in the blue room. We have agreed to call our piece *The Soldier's Tale.* I showed him my verses for the narrator's first reading, beginning:

Entre Denges et Denezy,
un soldat qui rentre chez lui.

Quinze jours de congé qu'il a,
marche depuis longtemps déjà.

This called, Stravinsky said, for the march of a weary man, and he was composing it. He had settled on a skeletal orchestra, over which Pavel's violin could have sway. He had chosen from the four orchestral families—strings, woodwinds, brass, and percussion—two spokesmen each, treble and bass, a kind of octet. Violin and double bass; clarinet and bassoon; trumpet and trombone; and drums, high and low.

Federovsky told me later of his astonishment at how slowly Stravinsky worked. I was used to it, from our labors together on *Renard* and *The Wedding*. It seemed as if every note, every chord, every movement of sound had to be heard, weighed, discussed, given unanimous approval, and praised to the skies—or at least to the blue ceiling that was the upper limit of the universe in which we worked. It was a great concession on Stravinsky's part to allow others in the room with him as he composed; he usually insisted on total absorption in solitude. But this, he generously kept saying, is a collaboration. We were all drinking Armagnac; as the day wore on, the praise began to sound like gargling.

Stravinsky would try everything on his piano, which was muted with pads of felt so that no barbaric ears outside the room could hear what was going on; then he would have Federovsky play the solo phrases on Antonietta, and he would listen with his head tilted, his big ears cocked. Sometimes he whacked a few thumps on one of the several drums that huddled around him as servants of his love of emphasis. Sometimes he stopped to listen to his four children chirping and squealing at play in the garden below, for although he scowled or even screamed at most noises that penetrated into his workroom while he composed—dishes clattering in the kitchen, the cawing of a picket line of jackdaws, or, alas, Katya's coughing—these sounds of the jubilant young energy of the fruit of his semen seemed to act on him as a psychic caffeine.

In this starting-and-stopping way he wrote a few measures, and then suddenly, to our amazement, it was time for afternoon tea.

FEDEROVSKY

Precision has a high price. With Stravinsky it is the energy that is spent on neatness. The rest of the house was cluttered with the trash of Katya's and his acquisitiveness. Ramuz had warned me. Stravinsky, he said, is a man of prey. I must keep my packet of cigarettes in my pocket. Otherwise, it would soon belong to him. Never put a box of good Swedish wooden safety matches down on a table. In fact, if you value it, hold on to your hat in his house. All the tables and sideboards in other rooms were crowded with the booty of a predatory life. I had seen the jumble. Glass paperweights from Murano. An ashtray from Maxim's in Geneva. Two old quill pens. A tiny bronze Sphinx. A miniature cuckoo clock . . .

But his desk! It was like a military parade ground. Everything had to fall in, dressed right. There was the row of colored inks, red, green, blue, yellow, and two blacks—India ink and a Chinese tablet. Different erasers of various sizes for various sorts of obliteration and amnesia of what was rejected. Shiny steel instruments, as orderly as the scalpels on a surgeon's tray: two rulers, a compass, a penknife, a metal scraper for erasing ink. And, set apart but lined up like everything else, three of the little five-wheeled rollers he had invented himself to draw staves with.

And his score! He drew all the stems of chords and the lines marking the bars with a ruler in rigid verticalities. The notes themselves were small and round, perfect grapes to make a brandy of sound. The title "Marche du Soldat"; the designations of instruments, at the left of the staves on the opening page; the clef and rest marks; the instructions and signs for tempo and volume—all were set down with a calligrapher's fastidiousness. The tempo was indicated by an exact numerical setting of a metronome. Various colored inks made these things extra clear.

There was a paradox here. On the one hand, this excessive neatness. On the other, the seismic, chaotic power of the music that the tidy notes held in their spell. Even with this thin little orchestra, the music he was putting down hinted at the huge demonic force that the tired soldier would soon encounter. Music can establish the order of devilish things.

In the ninth measure, in midmorning, he made a tiny smudge in the trombone stave. He cursed and took a new sheet and started over again, laboriously copying out all the parts, while Ramuz and I twiddled our thumbs.

STRAVINSKY

I don't know what got into me. I said to Federovsky, "I suppose you think your wife is the Princess of our piece. She's all right, but she is unable to pee in a straight line. Did you know that, Pavlochka? Her water describes a curve as it goes down into the pot. Don't worry, I haven't seen this with my own eyes. I deduce it. She is the sort of woman who pees in an arc. That is to say, everything she does, every move she makes, is a little bit on the elegant side, a bit too grand. Do you follow me?"

Whereupon Federovsky said, and I can hardly blame him, "And you, Igor Fedorovich, are the Devil of our piece." But I noticed that he wasn't really angry.

I said, "The Devil takes many forms. Sometimes He is a blacksmith's apprentice, sometimes He is the ticket taker who charges money for permission to kiss a virgin, sometimes a woman will knead Him into the dough of the bread she is making. And sometimes, Pavlochka—be careful, Pavlochka—sometimes He lives right in the belly of a violin. He is what gives the fiddle that awful soul you talk about."

He looked down at his violin, which he was holding under his arm, and he raised it up and tapped on its back with a knuckle, and put his ear down to it. "Not at home," he said. "I think He has gone to make a visit to your brain."

I said, "My brain has no room for visitors. It is jammed to capacity with just two things: intervals and rhythms. No, Pavlochka. He is certainly at home in that box of yours when you play. I can smell the resin burning."

FEDEROVSKY

I forgive him. He is fragile. His petulance is the glue that holds him together. I remember his confiding in me long ago in St. Petersburg about his terrifying father. He told me that on a day when the great basso was to perform, he was always in a rage. Nervousness. Sometimes the temper would erupt in public. Guima spoke of one time out in a street in Bad Homburg. He thinks he was eleven. He did some small thing that tripped off his father's temper. Perhaps he spat in a gutter. His father commanded him to get out of his sight—go back to their hotel. Igor did not march right off like a good soldier. He grumbled. Then his father exploded in a street scene of bad language that gathered a large crowd of passersby.

"To one who cannot possibly win," Guima said to me when he told me this, "winning becomes important."

But what *is* it he wants to win?

RAMUZ

Tea came to pacify. Tea came *à la Russe*, in glasses nestled in silver holders with handles. Never a cup of tea in this house; *stakan chai*—a glass of tea. Weak enough to see a sailboat on the lake right through it. Stravinsky, who is fascinated by the power of small words, remarked that the one for this drink is a rare bird. What other word, he asked, is virtually the same all over the world? From the Mandarin Chinese, *cha*, or, at Amoy, *tuh*, where the dialect changes the *ch* to *t*. Russian, *chai*. French, *thé*. Italian, *tè*. German, *der Tee*. Portuguese, *chá*. Spanish, *tè*. English *tea*. Even in Hungarian, that island of language, Stravinsky said, the word is *tea*, pronounced tay-́ah.

From there I moved to the tantalizing problem of how to make what one writes universal, for we had said that we wanted to find a way, in shaping our soldier's story, not just to be "international" but to reach into mankind's ear. Quite beyond using a word like *tea* that anyone anywhere would be able to make sense of, how could we find words—or actions—or music—all three, really—that would reverberate in *everyone's* mind *everywhere?*

"What we have to do," Stravinsky said, perhaps thinking of Federovsky's remark about a visitor in his head, "is to work back down from the cerebrum to the brain stem, and depend on what we find there that may be useful. The urges, I mean. Instincts. The basic needs and desires that were in us long before we reached the stage of even wanting a culture. Those are what I reached for, you know, in the *Sacre*."

"Folk tales," Federovsky said. "The stuff in folk tales. Of any country, you know. Many things in them are interchangeable."

"My brain stem can't spell," I said.

"Ah. *Alors.* After we've drawn from down deep, we have to put our wits to work. We have to mark staves on a page and put in the notes—in the right places. For me, that is the supreme pleasure in life. The work of making sense of the wild sounds in my dreams. Imposing the order of music on the threat of chaos. I live for that. Nothing else matters. Performances always disappoint me. By that time I have long since heard the music in my mind as I made it. The work itself was and is my greatest joy."

FEDEROVSKY

This must be true. I remember that after every performance of his work in the Paris days, he was furious. It didn't matter how the music was received. He boiled with his father's anger. Something was always wrong. He had heard the oboist flat a note that was supposed to be natural. The conductor had imposed his personality on the music. He wanted to assassinate someone in the audience who had a bad cough. There was no pleasure for him in success; he had had his pleasure long before.

Today as we were working you could see the fun he was having. Once, he struck a very strange chord on the piano, one that he was trying out. He turned to us with ecstatic eyes. "Did you *feel* those *vibrations*?" Then he said, "When Beethoven had lost his hearing, he used to hold a stick between his teeth, and as he played he would lean forward and touch the stick to the wood of the piano, so he could feel the vibrations of his originality in his head."

Guima struck his strange chord once again, fortissimo.

RAMUZ

He calls his work "the supreme pleasure" of his life. Most of us would put a different thrill from that at the top of the list, and we would surely agree which one it should be. He appears to have women on his mind all the time, yet the sex act evidently gives his senses a lower order of delight than does the joyful task of setting down a few bars full of untamed chords. He put the alternatives to us vividly one day, speaking of the varieties of the creative urge in his family: "My ancient great-grandfather," he said, "used to create by having sex. I write music." I have noticed that in the presence of women the focus of his interest always comes to rest sooner or later on the shapely reservoirs of their mother milk; on the nurture, I suppose, that he knows those beautiful vessels can give to infants—that they still can give, in fantasy if in no other way, to the sentient, creative infant that lives on in him.

STRAVINSKY

Federovsky's violin has the most sensuous tone. I asked him to run over some of my draft material this morning, and I felt bewitched. I began to think back on last night, and the violin made my mind run free in the meadows of our missed opportunities. Ramuz took us to Lausanne, and we had a fine dinner at the Grappe d'Or. Then Ramuz led us through many back streets to a little café in the suburbs, where there were no other customers besides a couple of old mole trappers warming their insides in preparation for their dawn round of their traps in the vineyards. They wore rabbit-fur hats indoors, and they held in their unshaven jaws the stubby-stemmed pipes that Ramuz says are called "mouth burners." The many nips of brandy that they had taken made them cordial, and they invited us to join them. So it was brandy for us, too, on top of a great deal of red wine we'd had with dinner. In our wooziness, Federovsky and I could understand very little of the slangy dialect these men spoke with Ramuz, but we did gather, after some time, that we were all five headed out from there to a friendly whorehouse the trappers knew about.

We entered a dimly lit room in which shabby satin covered everything—except the half-dozen girls, who were naked from the waist up. The madam was a shrewd hussy with a black mustache; she saw that we were drunk, and that money could be extracted from us without subjecting her girls to anything more drastic than sitting on our laps from time to time. We bought wine for everyone. We sat around and had a hilarious hour. All of us, women and men, laughed until we cried.

At one point the madam, already tipsy herself, and perhaps carried away by what must have seemed to her our willingness by then to believe anything, said, "Messieurs, I didn't always look the way you see me now. I was beautiful once. And I was rich, too. I was invited everywhere. Poets from all over Europe sang of the parts of my body in great detail." She lowered her voice to a whisper. "I have held in my arms the Kaiser of all Germany. The Crown Prince of Liechtenstein. The Prince's adolescent son. Grand Dukes . . ."

We howled with laughter.

So I stirred myself this morning from the enchantment of listening to Pavel's violin and of daydreaming about the slender, not yet spoiled figure of a particular one of those grisettes last night, and I suddenly heard myself saying, "Look here! Why should the Devil always be pictured as a man? Ramuz, in one of our scenes He should be a She. Let's have Her appear as the madam of a brothel. That woman last night—model the Devil on her. I could have killed you two for agreeing to pay what she charged—for what? For nothing! She *was* a demon. I could see the flames in her eyeballs."

RAMUZ

I have taken some days away from the others to finish the narration. I followed and did not follow Afanasyev. The tale will go like this:

A poor soldier has two weeks' leave, and he is on his way home. On the banks of a stream he meets an old lepidopterist, chasing butterflies with a net. They get talking. The old man (we suspect who He is) persuades the soldier to trade his fiddle for a magic book, and to spend three days with Him. . . .

As the soldier straggles into his native village—not much more than a crossroads in the country, a frontier post, with a church tower in the distance—he realizes that three years, not three days, have passed. A cattle merchant comes along (we can guess about Him!) and, seeing the magic book, tells the soldier how to use it to make a fortune. . . .

The soldier, at home, is rich but bored. The madam of a brothel (what could Her true name be?) comes to see him. She fishes from her basket a series of pictures of Her trollops to tempt him. Then She takes an old fiddle out of the basket. He recognizes it as his. But when he tries to play it, he can't get a single sound out of it. He hurls it out a window and tears the magic book to shreds. . . .

He is at a card table in a room in a palace, gambling with the court violinist (a demon of a virtuoso), who has somehow taken possession of the soldier's fiddle. The King's daughter is sick; the King has promised her hand to anyone who can make her well. The soldier loses and loses at cards, but he keeps filling the violinist's wineglass until the fiddler passes out. The soldier recovers his violin. . . .

He plays it beside the Princess's sickbed. She rises. She dances, to his music, a tango, a waltz, and a ragtime, and then she throws herself into his arms. The Devil sneaks up behind them dressed as Himself—with pointed ears and a long tufted tail. The soldier plays such dizzying music on the violin that the Devil ties Himself up in knots, and the lovers drag Him away. . . .

The soldier takes the Princess to his home village, but as soon as they go through the frontier post at the crossroads, a potentate in a brilliant scarlet cape (yes, it is He), who has got hold of the soldier's fiddle again, appears and casts a spell on the soldier with it and leads him slowly away. . . .

I showed this narration to my two partners. To my astonishment, Stravinsky—laying bare, I thought, a sentimental streak that he had kept utterly secret up till then because it was exactly the sort of thing he pretended to despise—asked if we couldn't have a happier ending. Couldn't we drop the final curtain when the Princess hugs the soldier after her three dances?

Federovsky hooted, and I said, "That's not the way the Devil works, Stravinsky."

He said, "But we could make more money with a happy ending."

So it wasn't softness of heart, after all; he was just being true to himself. Federovsky and I managed to talk him out of this nonsense.

STRAVINSKY

These two fellows live in the clouds. They seem to have no idea that stage productions cost money. It is left up to me to be the practical one. How can we employ actors? Pay a scene designer? Buy costumes and scenery? Hire a hall? When I heard the other day that that great patron of the arts Werner Reinhart, of Winterthur, was visiting Lausanne, I wasted no time inviting him to visit me. I told Ramuz to be on hand, and after I entertained Reinhart for an hour on the piano, Ramuz and I told him all about our wonderful novelty—a concert with narration. Ramuz, damn his tongue, stressed over and over that this was a tiny gem, a cameo, a miniature. What had to be the result of this trivialization? Reinhart could not help looking at the project through the wrong end of a pair of opera glasses: it almost disappeared from his sight, it was so small. He gave us a miserable three thousand francs.

I knew we would need much more. I made Ramuz rack his brains for the names of angels, and finally he thought of a rich woman who also happens to love music, a certain Madame Auguste Roussy, of La Tour-de-Peilz, and I signed a letter to her which Ramuz drafted, asking for fifteen thousand francs. It turned out that she did not love music nearly that much; we got zero francs from her. I then crawled like a beggar to the Infanta Beatrice of Spain, who lives not far away, and to whom I had already described our musical tale one day; nothing from her but humiliation. I lost sleep. I could not compose. Desperate, I wrote to Reinhart.

Miraculous! Today a draft for fifteen thousand came as if on the wings of a dove to the bank in Lausanne. Now I hear music in my head again.

FEDEROVSKY

We sat down today to continue work on the fifth scene.

Guima said, "I had a beautiful dream last night. I was walking along a road. I came on a woman sitting on the ground by the roadside. Her legs were crossed under a huge skirt with spangles on it. I could see that she was a gypsy. Baubles hung from her earlobes. She had curly hair; ringlets straggled down by her cheeks. She held a small child in her lap. She was sitting with a straight back, her torso turned slightly to her left, in order to be able to play a violin with her arms lifted clear of the child's head. She had invented a haunting tune to amuse her little one. She played it over and over again, with long strokes of the bow.

The child was entranced. Each time the tune ended, it would clap its tiny hands. The tune was still ringing in my head when I woke up. It still is now."

And he proceeded to write the theme down, giving it first to the trumpet, then to the bassoon, as part of the "Little Concert" that we were just then working on—the music that announces the soldier's now having the craft to waken the Princess, after the violinist-Devil has drunk too much and has fallen asleep.

At one point he broke off his work and said to us, "I don't often dream directly onto the score like this, but I often do useful work on my pillow. In St. Petersburg, I remember, when I was finishing up *The Firebird*, I had a dream of a solemn council of some dim past tribe of pagans, sitting on a circle of blocks of stone, their eyes fastened on the spectacle of a young woman dancing herself to death as a sacrifice to the god of spring. You know how I used that dream, of course. Sometimes I hear melodies, but not often. The pictures in my dreams are all in color. That gypsy last night had brilliant blue eyes." He looked at me as he said this, and I knew that the woman in his dream was my Anya.

Later in the day, writing the tango to which the Princess dances, he used the theme again, giving it to the violin. As soon as he had put it down on paper, he wanted me to play it.

Stravinsky listened with his eyes closed, his head tilted back. His face was blissful. When I had finished, he said straight to me in a matter-of-fact way, seeming to know that I would understand, "I dream about her quite often."

I said, "Lucky fellow."

He said, "Yes. This time she gave me music."

But I decided not to be angry. He is so single-minded. Most men trade caresses with the women in their dreams and wake up wet. For him, they sing or perform on an instrument!

And besides, he forgot in his dream that Anna is tone-deaf. Poor thing, she would play a violin wretchedly.

RAMUZ

We had a little contretemps today. Stravinsky, who is drawn to big sound, has not used the violin much in the past in delicate solos or in what Federovsky speaks of as "the concertante role that our playlet requires," inasmuch as the transactions with the Devil all have to do with the fiddle; so, along the way, Stravinsky has tended to ask for help and advice about the violin from Federovsky. As we work, he is constantly asking Pavel to play solo strains, or even brief phrases, as soon as he writes them down. Then he asks Pavel what he thinks. Are certain double stops and triple stops playable? Sometimes he asks Pavel to take a piece home and try it several times and come back the next day with suggestions.

Federovsky is wonderfully tactful in his comments. He keeps saying he is amazed by the way Stravinsky exploits contrasts of the instruments one with another in his score; by the fact that they are never blended in conventional terms with each other but serve to show each other off; and by the interplay of tempos and pitches and timbres which make such a small handful of instruments sound so rich and so orchestral. Then he will shyly suggest a very slight strengthening of the violin's voice in a particular place, for the sake of the drama. Or a tiny quickening of tempo, just here. Or a more challenging jump in pitches, of a sort a violinist can easily negotiate, in this other place.

Stravinsky never takes Federovsky's suggestions. Never. Not once has he done so. He shouts that Pavel has missed the point! That was not what he had in mind! How could Pavel be so *deaf*? Sometimes he is very sharp and rude.

Until this morning, Pavel has always accepted these rebuffs with a touching good grace—the mere performer yielding to the creator who knows what he is doing.

There is a background, of course, to what happened this

morning to make that sweet control crack apart for a moment. Five of us—we three and Katya and Anna—sometimes lunch together and often have tea together. For three years I have seen what happens to Stravinsky whenever he is near a beautiful woman, and Anna is certainly beautiful. The dynamic personality dissolves into gelatin. Great Igor becomes a shy gnome. His eyelids droop, as if marvels hurt his eyes. He blushes. He speaks to the beautiful one in a tightened voice that sounds like a clarinet; to everyone else he trumpets. I am so used to all this that I assume Katya must be, too. Unfortunately, the contrast between poor sick Katya's looks and Anna's in recent weeks has grown more and more shocking as Katya's health has deteriorated while Anna has bloomed in the soft Swiss air. Stravinsky has taken to smirking at Anna. It is all too clear that he has utter contempt for her mind, yet he cannot help having a visible glandular response to the glow of her skin, her slightly mischievous mouth, her eyes as deep and blue as the lake under the spring sun. His flirtation, in other words, looks utterly cynical unless you know, as I do, that it means nothing. Pavel may also have come to know this, but to a devoted husband, which he obviously is, such knowledge may not be of any real use.

This morning's was a case in which Stravinsky had again asked Federovsky to take home a passage—this one in the crucial "Little Concert"—and come back with his reactions. He made what sounded to me like a sensible minor suggestion, and he played some notes to show Stravinsky what he meant.

Stravinsky said, "*Nyet*, Pavlochka, that doesn't give me an erection."

I had heard Stravinsky use this offhand expression several times before when something didn't seem any good to him. This was apparently the first time Federovsky had heard it.

Pavel's voice was like a series of pistol cracks as he asked, "And exactly what does give you an erection?"

"You know what! You know who!" Stravinsky shouted back,

infuriated by his usually docile friend's sudden show of spirit, and as always deadly accurate in the aim of a barb.

Federovsky went white. He stood up and seemed nine feet tall.

Then I saw Stravinsky collapse back in his chair, with his arms flopped over the wings, and he groaned. Then he said, "Pavlochka! Pavlochka! You are my oldest friend in the world!"

I believe that Federovsky knew perfectly well that this was a lie, because Stravinsky had often proclaimed that his dear Katya was his oldest friend on earth. The gaunt man sat down and quietly said, "You asked for a suggestion, and I made one."

"And it was ridiculous," Stravinsky said.

Federovsky was silent.

I love these Russian storms. They fly through like summer squalls, and the sky is—or seems—cloudless afterward.

FEDEROVSKY

In my discomfiture—for I was embarrassed that Ramuz had had to witness such vulgarity—I suddenly felt my nose itch, and I sneezed. Instead of offering me a *Gesundheit*, Stravinsky threw me a hostile look, rose, nearly knocking his piano stool over, and hurried out of the room.

"What is *that* about?" I asked Ramuz. "What is *he* so touchy about?"

"That is about germs," Ramuz said.

Then he told me of Guima's terror of infection—his fear of anything that can rob him of energy for his work, or, far worse, interrupt it altogether. He smokes too much, and in the spring when he was working on *Petrouchka*, he had told Ramuz, he came down with nicotine poisoning, and he was terrified that he wouldn't be able to finish the ballet in the ten weeks before the Paris season was scheduled to start. After the scandal of the opening night of *Sacre*, he came down with typhoid fever, which left him weak and musically sterile for months. In the winter two years ago, when he and Ramuz were working on *Renard*, he developed a horrifyingly painful neuralgia in his rib cage, and Ramuz had to suffer through aeons of the maestro's bad temper and atrocious rudeness before they could finish.

I had noticed all the many little silver pillboxes scattered around the house; I realized that he knew exactly what remedy each one held, and I had seen him dip into this one and that one now and then, as if in little ceremonies of exorcism.

"Katya tells me," Ramuz said, "that he thinks all water, even bottled water like Évian, carries dysentery. So he uses wine to brush his teeth with."

"While he is at it," I said, "he could use a bit of it to rinse out his mind."

RAMUZ

I was summoned to the phone at the laundry. As I picked up the receiver and turned the little crank on the wooden box of the telephone to let the operator know I was listening, a hush fell; all the bare-armed naiads struck their poses to listen to scraps of what I might say—tidbits to be rehashed at once in gossip and gusts of laughter such as I often heard on my way back up the hill.

Our "triad of greatnesses," as Federovsky had dubbed the three of us, had finished our work of making, and we had begun to think about all that had to be done to get the piece on a stage. We had reserved the modest little Théâtre Municipal in Lausanne in mid-October for the first performance; then we would go on to Geneva, Winterthur, Zurich . . . and who knew where else? Casting was on Stravinsky's mind now, and we got talking about the role of the Princess.

"You don't seem to understand, Ramuz," Stravinsky said. "Her three dances are the heart of the piece. How can you be so casual about this role? You baffle me."

"Who said I was casual?" I felt like teasing him. "We could get one of the girls from that whorehouse the mole trappers took us to. Don't you remember how royally that little one wiggled her hips?"

A swift wave of something like sighs flew around the laundry.

Stravinsky exploded. "Ramuz! Be serious!"

"Do you have a better idea?"

Stravinsky's voice now became a murmur; I had to strain to hear him. "Do you think," he said, barely above a whisper, "do you think we could teach Anya to dance?"

"Anna *Federovskaya*?" I shouted.

"Sh-h-h!" he said, as if afraid I could be overheard even on his end. Was Katya in the next room? Again, a murmur: "I have thought of her as the Princess all along."

"Have you lost your mind, Stravinsky? This is a musical performance. That woman is anti-music. She is to music what a dark cloud is to the sun."

Now the voice was huffy. "Have *you* a better idea?"

"You should be ashamed. It's your wife, not Federovsky's, who is ill and needs to be roused from her lethargy by beautiful music."

"Is that your better idea? Katya!" The scorn in Stravinsky's voice was strident and alarming.

"In the name of friendship, I will forgive you that shocking sarcasm. Your shame in having dreams of Anna caused it. . . . Don't apologize to *me*," I said, as if he had been trying to do so. "Apologize to Katya." I paused again, but all I heard was a kind of growl—perhaps he was clearing that foul cruelty from his throat. "As a matter of fact," I said, "I do have a better idea: Natasha Panayev. She's in Geneva, you know. You wouldn't have to teach *her* to dance like a Princess." For she had been a ballerina at St. Petersburg, occasionally prima; she was now in exile here in Switzerland with her husband, Pyotr, who had been an assistant regisseur of the Imperial Ballet. "She's still quite lovely," I said. "You wouldn't have to coach her to *look* like a Princess, either.

I remember your telling me yourself that whenever the black swan raised his wings near her, she would look as if she'd faint from the underarm odor, but then she would raise her chin and dance on—isn't that exactly the demeanor of a Princess? What's more," I went on, "Pyotr could be our director—and wouldn't be a bad Devil, come to think of it."

There was a long silence. Then: "We will go to Geneva tomorrow."

FEDEROVSKY

Stravinsky gave a jerk on the bellpull at the front door. An ugly little woman, evidently the Panayevs' housekeeper, opened it. Her mouth gaped, and she involuntarily crossed herself, as if she had suddenly seen three awful Magi, or perhaps even a hellish parody of the Holy Trinity. We must in truth have made an odd sight: little Stravinsky, looking literally half my size because I was standing on the first step of the entranceway while he was still at ground level, wearing his monocle and spats and with a bizarre array of percussion instruments hanging from his belt all round; Ramuz in his Alpinist's cap with a pheasant feather cocked out from it, carrying sheaves of sheet music and text; and I, lugging my big rectangular violin case and no doubt appearing sour as a ghoul, for on the train trip to Geneva the maestro had been saying over and over what a shame it is that my Anna is tone-deaf; had it not been for that, *she* would have been our Princess. Oddly, he seemed to be saying that to annoy Ramuz, not me. How boring he can be!

We were shown in, and Madame Panayev came floating across the floor with a dancer's gliding steps. I realized at once that Anna would indeed have made a preferable Princess. I saw Stravinsky openly shudder as he looked at her. This woman gave a picture of an organization of no longer young muscles under exquisite control in every movement, a sinewy product, alas, of years of rigorous discipline. The long-stemmed neck was a set of poised cables; the cheeks and jaw worked in bunches as she spoke; strong arms, raised to coif, had drawn the black hair severely back into a bun at the rear. She was elegant, sure enough, and even regal; Stravinsky had been right about the proudly lifted chin. But could she languish, pale and sweetly enchanted, in need of Antonietta to rouse her from her couch?

Her husband came into the room after her. He was suave, dapper, silky, with black eyebrows that swooped out and up and away from the crest of his nose. Yes, a goodly Devil.

Soon the room reverberated with Stravinsky's ebullient energy. He had Ramuz tell the story of our *Tale*, but he could not resist interrupting along the way to point out the charms of it all. Then, rearranging the furniture in the room so as to set up his toys of percussion within reach of the piano stool, he started us off on a skimpy run-through, with Ramuz explaining at each stage what was happening. I played the violin part and, where I could, that of the clarinet. As Stravinsky pounded the piano and banged at the drumlets, he used his voice to tootle and bumble the sounds of the trumpet and trombone and bassoon as best he could. I saw that the Panayevs looked more and more perplexed; then, dismayed; then, positively outraged. Until . . . until we came to the three dances, and Antonietta began to sing the tango. At that Madame Panayev floated up from her chair, almost as if from a trance on a sickbed, and, nearly but not quite dancing, she began to sway with the waves of sound from my—or the soldier's—magical violin, subtly, smoothly, her arms becoming weightless, her torso fluent and free, and as the tango melted into waltz time and the waltz drifted into ragtime, I saw her transform herself, clothed in those understated movements, those pulsations of pleasure, into a soft, awakening, ethereal, and, finally, wildly erotic princess. Stravinsky saw this, too, and as we played on he shouted, "Brava! Brava! Brava!"

The Panayevs agreed to take part.

RAMUZ

With all his apparent—or feigned?—helplessness when it comes to the simple tasks of daily life, Stravinsky is a remarkably efficient organizer of our production. Perhaps the profit motive is what fuels his motor so that it runs like a Hispano-Suiza. The pleasure of composition is behind him, and he is short-tempered and brusque; his powerful engine makes noises that sound like backfires. I have learned simply to nod when he asks my opinions. This saves the energy of defending myself from his quarrels.

For some time he has had Ernest Ansermet, the conductor of the Geneva Symphony, lined up to lead the music. A student of Bloch, Nikisch, and Weingartner, this tall fellow, whose head seems to come to two very odd-looking points, at the top of his swept-up hair and at the end of his Vandyke beard, has been a friend of Stravinsky—as he has also been of Debussy and Ravel—for several years. He toured North and South America with the Diaghilev ballets last year, and he brought back from the United States and gave to Stravinsky some sheet music of American Negro jazz, which entranced Igor. Never having heard jazz, only having read these scores, he had great fun trying to emulate the style in the Princess's ragtime dance.

With the Panayevs enlisted, Stravinsky poked around and signed up three stagestruck students from Lausanne University to be our actors: a paleontologist named Elie Gagnebin to be the Narrator, a student of belles lettres named Gabriel Rosset for the Soldier, and a serious would-be actor named Jean Villard-Gilles to take the difficult role, part spoken and part mimed, of the Devil—not Panayev, after all; he will be helping us as our regisseur. With Ansermet's advice, he has found a clarinetist, a bassist, and a trumpeter from Zurich and a bassoonist and a percussionist from Geneva; Federovsky, of course, will be the fiddler.

We are ready to rehearse.

STRAVINSKY

To my mind, enjoyment of our *Tale* must come through eye and ear all at once. I want the orchestra to have nearly half the stage, at the left, the scenery and actors to be at right center, and the narrator to the far right, outside the set. I do not believe in listening to music on gramophone records. I think one should listen to music while watching the musicians perform. The sweep of the string players' bow arms and their flying fingers, the sight of the wind and brass players hastily taking the breaths that will give us magnificent sounds, the pounce of the percussionists after their patient long rests, and the supple, metronomic, histrionic movements of the conductor—all these conveyed by the optic nerve reinforce the delights that the tiny drumsticks in our ears can give us.

With this staging, the actors' miming will be meshed, will be *in time*, with the visible and audible music—and, now and then, with the movements of and sounds from the narrator's mouth. We need, though, taking up about half the stage, a vivid and plausible series of settings, so that what is happening will seem both real and unreal at the same time—as real and unreal as the music. We need to see the Princess swaying voluptuously in her palace bedroom as we simultaneously see Federovky's cobra wrist sliding the bow down the string and hear Antonietta singing a song of witchery and venery. How lucky I have been to persuade the painter René Auberjonois to design the sets and costumes! I have long admired his work. His sketches, so far, have been superb: reality and fantasy copulating before our very eyes.

RAMUZ

Anna Federovskaya came to the rehearsal today. Stravinsky is always at his best at these rehearsals, but her presence seemed to key him up to an even higher than usual pitch of exuberance.

The instrumentalists were not with us yet, so he played the piano; Federovsky of course took the violin parts. Igor was dazzling in his joy in his own music; he thumped on the piano as if it were a robber trying to steal his gifts; he shouted new ideas to the mimes; he would leap up on the stage to demonstrate a gesture or a grimace; he sipped enough *Kirschwasser* to guarantee a howling headache later—and all the time, I could see, his invisible feelers were reaching out to the beautiful woman sitting in the fourth row with me. He never looked right at her, but he was obviously throwing his energy right into her lap. One thing I noticed. While she was watching, he never once corrected Federovsky's playing, as he would not hesitate to do at other times.

Pyotr Panayev, as nominal director, served as a loyal sedative to the maestro. Calm, tactful, modest, and watchful, he would give quiet suggestions which would sometimes subtly negate a foolish suggestion Stravinsky had just made. And Stravinsky didn't mind; he would laugh and pummel the piano into submission.

I could tell that Federovsky was very much aware of his wife's presence. He posed, with the tones he drew from Antonietta, a great measure of the mystery of her beauty, her brashness, her delicate kindness, her fine-tuned responsiveness, and, yes, her stubborn thickness of mind—the complex mystery I remembered Stravinsky having spoken of with such reverence and yearning and contempt.

We came to the Devil's whirling dance in the fifth scene. Young Villard-Gilles could not get the hang of it. He couldn't let himself go. Panayev tried to direct him with words.

Then Stravinsky shouted, "I'll do the dance! The Devil is dressed as the Devil in this scene—I'd have a mask on—you wouldn't know—I'll do it!"

I liked this idea, and I said so. Stravinsky had after all seen the dance in his mind as he wrote the dizzying music.

Panayev quietly said, "Let's think about it. Could we go back to the Princess's three dances? The tango first?"

Perhaps because of Anna's presence, Stravinsky accepted this check without a word. He said, "Pavlochka, the tango."

As Antonietta sang—mysteriously, mysteriously—the tango's step, st-step, step, *stop* . . . step, st-step, step, *stop*, we saw Natasha Panayev transform herself before our eyes, once again, from a tense, wiry, severe middle-aged woman into an adorable, languid, and highly sexed young belle, clearly of royal blood, roused from her torpor on the couch to open up like a flower in a breeze and move full blown, finally, in the ragtime, with giddy, carnal abandon. And again we heard Stravinsky shouting, "Brava! Brava!"

This ended the rehearsal. Stravinsky came straight to us in our seats, and he said to Anna, "Do you think you could learn to dance like that?"

And she said, "Do you think you could learn to dance like a Devil?"

Stravinsky guffawed, clapped his hands, and awarded her, too, a "Brava!" And he added, "You understand a few things."

FEDEROVSKY

The *Tale* will be told tonight in Lausanne, and Guima has been atrocious all day. Katya says he is always like this before a performance, as bad-tempered as his father was before singing. He is still hot under the collar because everyone overruled him, in one of the rehearsals some days ago, and decided that Pyotr Panayev, and not he, should do the Devil's dance. He has gone to the bathroom six times this afternoon. "Fear of ridicule is my most dependable laxative," he bitterly said as he trooped off one of those times. Just now I heard him, behind a closed door, shouting at Katya because a shirt stud had rolled under the chiffonier. If he is this bad before the show, what will he be like after it? Will he hate me because he thinks I have used too much vibrato in the dances? Will he swear at my darling Antonietta for not sounding exactly like the gypsy's fiddle in the dream?

RAMUZ

The theater is already full. The curtain will not go up until nine o'clock—a late hour for the Lausanneurs, but the show lasts less than two hours, and we thought it best to make the evening seem full by delaying the start. Stravinsky has got his crowd. He has been at some pains to drum up attendance by the many Russian aristocrats who have colonized the suburb of Ouchy; he went himself three times to call on various nobs and snobs, to make sure they would come. The Grand Duchess Helen is here, crusted with diamonds. Critics have come from Zurich and Geneva. I am as jumpy as a dog with fleas. If there is the slightest criticism of our piece, Stravinsky will surely blame it on me; he will say that the narration spoiled everything, even the music.

He and I, in our boiled shirts, our crisp white ties, and our crow's-tail coats, are in the front row; he insisted on taking the center aisle seat because he said he might have to flee. Anna Federovskaya, lambent in a shimmering shot-silk gown, takes the seat directly across from him on the other side of the aisle. Pallid Katya sits just beyond her.

The clarinet sounds an A, and the instrumentalists go into their cacophony of tuning and of trying things out.

STRAVINSKY

The report from the box office is good. Reinhart certainly doesn't expect us to pay him back; we have plenty left from his backing to pay off our actors and musicians; we three will share the gate. As the composer, I suppose I am entitled to at least sixty percent; then I suppose Ramuz is entitled to, let's say, twenty-five percent; Pavel is, after all, only playing his fiddle, perhaps fifteen percent is even too much for him.

I wish the audience were not so restless. This late start may have been a mistake.

"Ramuz, get up there and tell Ansermet to begin."
"Be patient, Maestro. Be patient."

FEDEROVSKY

We have got off to a good start. Young Elie Gagnebin as the narrator is very clever at making the Soldier sound like a Swiss youth from the vineyards, a Vaudois peasant in uniform—an irony to begin with, a *soldier* from this proudly unwarlike nation—and he makes the lepidopterist sound like a rich old dilettantish professor from Geneva University with a demon under his skin. I can't see the mimes from here, because the wing of the stage set stands between the mimes and us instrumentalists, but I have a full view, straight out on either side of Ansermet as he conducts, of the faces of the audience, which more or less mirror the mimes, and I can see how taken up the people are by the oddness of the tale.

And the music! It is so complex. How exultant it is—yet at the same time sinister, threatening—but sophisticated, world-weary, cynical—nonetheless naïve and energetic and decisive and joyous! It is Igor Fedorovich Stravinsky's personality distilled into a spiritous liquor of sound. It is hellishly difficult to play; the Devil is at home in its chords. I have to count the rests extremely carefully, because the slightest error in timing in this jumpy score makes a screech where there should be a howl, or a groan where there should be a moan, or flatulence where there should be a soulful sigh. And he has given me tricky double and triple stops, often piled on each other in a dreadful hurry. But I have practiced and practiced, and I know almost all of my part by heart.

Ramuz is pale. He looks frightened nearly to death. He does not want to be pounced on by a Stravinsky who hates performances and has a keen nose for scapegoats.

But look at Guima. He is entranced. Every so often he nods, as if to say, "Yes! That's right! That's the way it is supposed to be." He obviously loves what Ansermet is making of his music.

He glances now and then across the aisle, to where Anya and Katya sit. Sometimes he leans forward a bit as he looks at them, evidently wanting to see their faces: are they having a good time? Or *is* it "they"? Is there just one face that interests him?

Federovsky! Pay attention to the score! . . .

Now we are playing the pastoral music of the next scene—I see in the faces of the audience the image of the Devil as a cattle merchant, propped on his cane, waiting to trick the Soldier . . . the "Airs by a Stream" . . . the madam of the brothel producing the pictures of her strumpets and then the mute fiddle . . . the "Royal March" to the castle . . . the card game with the court violinist . . .

Like Stravinsky, I keep looking at the faces of those two women. My Anya, I am sorry to see, is interested only in what the narrator has to say; she has told me at various times that, for her, Stravinsky's music is like the cries in the monkey house in a zoo, the sound of a handful of pebbles thrown against a tin drum, the shouts of the fishmongers at the market, the crepitation of cockroaches in a drawer, the croaking of jackdaws in tree-tops, and God knows what other babble and twaddle. She knows the whole story to come. She looks bored, even drowsy. And how beautiful she is in this somnolent state! She *is* a Princess in need of a magical tonic—but not, alas, one of music. I have the bad thought, but shake it off at once, that Stravinsky, looking at her as he does now, may have in mind a different sort of tonic. . . .

Now there is a look on the other face that I have never seen before—never, perhaps, taken the trouble to see. As the court violinist—the Devil Himself—tells the Soldier about the sick Princess whose hand is promised to whatever healer can rouse her, I see Katya's face begin to glow, her eyes to shine. Perhaps these are merely the hectic flush and the brilliant stare of the consumptive, brought on in this warm theater by a reminder of her own sickness. But no, as the "Little Concert" begins, she obviously hears in the bold grammar of the music the voice of a friend, a voice long heard by day and by night, by night and by day, of a true friend—whose music has a healing magic.

Now, with the first notes of the tango, the curtain rises on the scene of the Princess lying on her couch. I am amazed by the radiance of Katya's face. I am moved to call on Antonietta to make this tango the most restorative, vivifying music ever heard. And it suddenly occurs to me that Guimochka must have written this bright, cheerful, apparently thoughtless yet magically healing music with a deeply sad, a wishing heart. I play now with all *my* heart, for him and for his oldest friend.

I sense a kind of murmur hovering over the audience. Natasha Panayev must be rising from the couch; I can imagine the grace of her movements, languid and weak at first, as the music I am playing works its curative wonders. Katya's eyebrows are lifted. She stirs in her seat. I have a moment's foolish hope that she will rise herself and start to dance.

We have come to the coda of the tango. I render with care and with a full bow the tune that came to Guima in his dream, the tune played by the gypsy woman for her child, the gypsy woman who was—or was she?—my Anya in the dream:

This is the moment, as I saw in the rehearsal, when Natasha Panayev—throwing out her graceful arms to praise the Devil's mortal enemy in heaven, rising *aux pointes* and seeming to float weightless and free as the air around her, on tiptoe—breaks through to the peace of full health. And this is the moment when I see, for the first time in my experience, that Guima's Katya is supremely, serenely beautiful.

RAMUZ

It is nearly over. The Devil is going to bag the Soldier, after all. I have felt wave after wave of relief, as I have realized what a good time Stravinsky has been having. He has been bouncing in his seat like a four-year-old. The audience has obviously been enthralled; the music is apparently coming at him exactly as he had imagined it; the mimes have been flawless; even my narration coming out of the mouth of that student seems to have pleased him.

The music ends with a series of sinister drumbeats.

Wild applause breaks out. The audience rises to its feet. In their curtain calls the mimes all offer elaborate gestures of acknowledgment in Stravinsky's direction. So does Ansermet. The instrumentalists all bow to him. There are cries of "*Compositeur! Compositeur!*" I even hear "*Auteur! Auteur!*" They want us up there.

But instead of going up on the stage to take a bow, he crosses the aisle. Oh, God in heaven, he is going to make a fool of himself in front of all these people, who are staring at him and clapping for him, with that woman.

I should be used to this man's surprises. He walks right past Anya Federovskaya and goes to his Katya. He takes her hand in his and raises it to his lips.

Intermezzo Four

The dream of packing the *Tale* into a gypsy wagon and touring Europe with it, and making money, even if "not much"—this soon burst like a soap bubble floating in the air. Theaters had been reserved in several towns, and posters had already gone up on billboards. But within days after the opening in Lausanne, the malign hot breath of Spanish influenza, which was wilting the whole of Europe, swept into Switzerland. Stravinsky, both Panayevs, two of the student actors, and all of the musicians save Federovsky came down with it. Katya became perilously ill, and all four Stravinsky children had fevers. Somehow the Federovsky family was spared.

This sickness could kill a stallion of a youth in three days; most of those who survived passed the crisis within a week. Eight days after Stravinsky fell ill, Ramuz wrote to Zurich reporting that the composer still had a violent fever; the engagement there would have to be cancelled. And so, in time, were all the others that had been planned.

When Stravinsky got back in touch with Diaghilev and the revived Ballets Russes two years later, Diaghilev would have nothing to do with the *Tale* because it was not a package he had wrapped himself. The work was performed under other auspices several times over the ensuing years, notably in Paris, in 1924, but no showing ever measured up, in Stravinsky's mind, to the modest one that night in Lausanne.

. . .

Stravinsky's hand holding Katya's for a kiss after that performance seemed a kind of fulcrum on which the hopes of her life were poised for a moment in balance, thanks to the curative music still echoing in her ears; but from then on, the weight of her illness tilted any hopes she may still have had onto a relentless downward slant. There was no music, no magic of any kind, from then on, that could sweep her up into a tango, a waltz, a ragtime of recovery. Instead she kept fading—but very, very, very slowly—which made the decline all the more painful.

In 1921, while engaged with performances in Paris, Stravinsky met a woman veiled in a mystery as potent as but quite different from Anna Federovskaya's—different because this person, with all of Anna's other charms, was far from stupid. Her name was Vera de Bosset Soudeikine; she was the wife of a stage designer who was close to Diaghilev. Stravinsky and she found themselves in perfect harmony with each other, and during the eighteen years still left to Katya, who never lost her place as Igor's oldest and dearest friend, he and Vera, who had become the dearest and deepest love he had ever known, met surreptitiously, off and on, and kept alive the fires of their passion and mutual respect.

Katya died in 1939, and the year after that Stravinsky, who was in the United States lecturing at Harvard and giving some concerts, married Vera, by then long since divorced from Soudeikine. For the three decades of the rest of his life, Stravinsky, recognized as the greatest composer of his time, was enlivened, amused, protected, and constantly spurred to a headlong gallop by his second wife.

It was she who, when he died, in 1971, decided that it would be fitting for his funeral to be held in Venice, and for his body to be borne over glassy waters in a crape-trimmed gondola to the island of San Michele, to be buried there near the grave of his first sponsor and second-best friend, Sergei Pavlovich Diaghilev.

. . .

Federovsky rejoined the Ballets Russes orchestra during its London season in 1920. After a performance in Monte Carlo five years later, during which Federovsky played solos on Antonietta in a revival of *Schéhérezade* so airily that the dancer Danilova seemed to float off the ground in her leaps for as long as fifteen seconds at a time, Leopold Stokowski, then vacationing in Monaco, approached him and offered to buy him away for the Philadelphia Orchestra; the first seat in his second violin section had just fallen open.

Federovsky, restless and ready to make a change, accepted, and he moved with his family to the United States and sawed away for Stokowski. Antonietta responded churlishly, Federovsky felt, to Stokowski's orotund orchestral voice—particularly in the overblown arrangements, as wild as flights of hot-air balloons in violent windstorms, that he made of Bach's magisterial organ music. But later, after Eugene Ormandy, who had started life as a violinist, took over the Philadelphia, Antonietta sang with renewed pleasure in that conductor's voluptuous renderings of late-Romantic music. Federovsky died in 1955.

Anna Federovskaya, still a beauty at sixty-two, soon married a tympanist seventeen years younger than she, a man who, daily punishing his thumpety drums till every drop of anger was leached out of him, returned to her each evening with a touch as soft as that of a powder puff, and kept on loving her right up to her ninetieth year, when the radiance that he had gently nurtured was finally snuffed out.

After Federovsky's death, Antonietta was auctioned by Christie's in New York, for $65,000, to a rich young scientist and amateur violinist named Felice Frank, who, as the son of a concert pianist, had had a certain amount of musical taste drummed into him early. He lived a sybaritic life in Westport, Connecticut, on the fat royalties from a number of patents on medical devices and machines that he had invented—one of them a delicately automated iron lung, which could keep polio and accident and coma victims alive, it seemed, for centuries. He also kept Antonietta's vital signs going by playing second violin, rather pokishly, in an amateur chamber group that met in Fairfield every Wednesday night.

In the sixties, Frank heard about a brilliant but poor young violinist at the Juilliard, named Gaspard Montvieux, who had been drafted as a replacement at first fiddle for the distinguished Sugar Hill Quartet. It happened that all three of the others in that ensemble had magnificent instruments—a Stradivari second violin, an Andrea Guarneri viola, and a Grancino cello. To balance the foursome, Frank generously lent Antonietta to the young recruit and bought himself a Guarneri del Gesù to replace it. In time, he became not only the patron but also the lover of Montvieux, and one day in 1969 both men were instantly killed when a college student who was taking two trips, one to Boston and the other on acid, and who seemed to think he was flying an airplane, swooped over the median divider of the Merritt Parkway and hit Frank's BMW head-on at seventy-five miles an hour. All three bodies were carted off by ambulance to a hospital—DOA. The super-totaled BMW, which had been thrown six feet into the air and had rolled over three times, was illegally trucked away, with the connivance of a state policeman, by a scrap-steel dealer from the Naugatuck Valley; Antonietta was locked in the trunk. The dealer also took what was left of the assassin's Toyota pickup.

Neither Frank nor Montvieux had relatives on the East Coast, so it was several days before anyone realized that the Strad was missing. The booking agent for the Sugar Hill Quartet took up the chase and finally ran down the state cop who had taken the payola from the scrap-steel man to let him steal both wrecks, and he arrived at the huge automotive graveyard off Route 7 when the BMW was eighth in line, with only a couple of hours to wait before being compacted in the place's huge hydraulic auto press. The agent watched as the trunk was cut open, just in time, with a blowtorch.

The ancient violin case was split open. Antonietta's back and belly were both broken, and the neck was twisted grotesquely to one side. The agent wept at the sight, and the mechanic, with his blowtorch still flaming, said with feeling, "Holy shit." It looked as if that wooden carcass would never make music again.

To complicate matters, Felice Frank had never taken the trouble to draw up a will. The agent, basing his claim on the fact that recordings of the Sugar Hill Quartet had listed the Antonietta Strad as its first violin, got a court order to have the injured Antonietta remanded to the Wurlitzer musical-instrument house, in New York, pending eventual determination of ownership and for assessment of the damage and supervision of repairs, if they should be deemed worth making.

Mrs. Wurlitzer showed the wounded violin to the shop's resident luthier, Fernando Sacconi, and asked him if there was any possibility of restoring it.

Sacconi examined the wreckage for only a minute or two. Then he said in his soft-spoken way, "Do you remember the Red Diamond Stradivarius? It was what year?—about twenty years ago. The violin belonged to Sascha Jacobsen, concertmaster of the Los Angeles Philharmonic. So he was caught on a beach road in a violent wind storm, his car stalled, he got out in water up to his waist, holding the violin over his head. He was pulled toward the sea. Some people on a nearby bank rescued him, but the violin was washed out into the waves. A lawyer taking a walk on the beach the next day found a fiddle case half buried in sand. His wife told the director of the Philharmonic about it—so it was the Red Diamond. Jacobsen took it to Hans Weisshaar—you know about him, Mrs. Wurlitzer. Look, it was like this: both the top and the back were warped, the two pieces of the back had come apart, the purfling had come unglued and had swollen out of the channel, the ribs were twisted, the blocks and linings inside were all unattached, part of the neck was missing—waterlogged, slimy, sand all over everything. Oh, and the label that Stradivarius put in with his own hands in 1732 was torn into three pieces! All right. Hans took a month drying it out slowly with the help of a humidifier. He built molds to correct the warping. Etcetera, etcetera. Anyway, he took nine months working on it—and when he had finished, it sounded better than it had before. Truly. Look, Mrs. Wurlitzer, if Weisshaar could do that, I can do this."

And he did. It took him seven months. Montvieux's colleagues on the quartet, summoned to hear the restored Antonietta played, attested that its tone was absolutely as full and deep and sweet as it had been before the accident.

On the way home, the violinist said to the cellist, "It didn't sound quite as . . . I don't know . . . sexy? Is that what I mean? . . . as I remembered."

The cellist said, "Maybe not. I couldn't figure out what I was hearing that was new, till it hit me. I was thinking, My God, what that violin's *worth* now, after what it's been through. I began to hear the sound of money. I thought, Man, that's the ringing sound of a cash register. I see scores for it—what's it called?—Antonietta?—from now on with dollar signs on the staffs instead of clef signs. Either of you catch what I mean?"

The second violinist said, "Funny idea. Is that what they've meant all these years when they talked about a rich tone?"

The courts ruled that the violin belonged to Frank's only living relative, a sister from Monterey, whom he had loathed. She had no intention of paying for the repairs, and when she was told that the violin would certainly sell for a price in six figures, she snapped her fingers and said, "Fire away! Sell the goddamn thing."

Antonietta was bought by an English newspaper magnate for $175,000. He earned points as a benefactor of the arts by making it available for use by young soloists with the Royal Philharmonic, the BBC Symphony, the Academy of St. Martin-in-the-Fields, the English Chamber Orchestra, and the orchestra of the Covent Garden Ballet Company.

Act Five

1989

1. Panoramic helicopter shot, from the west, of Makoniky Head on a bright summer midday. Its steep, sandy bluffs give it an ochre face. Vineyard Sound is a rippling blue. A few fluffy good-weather clouds drift overhead.

MUSIC OVER: *First movement of Arnold Schoenberg's violin concerto.* The viewer may wonder why such forbidding music has been chosen to complement such a ravishingly serene day. The answer, which may eventually make sense to those who watch the program: it was chosen as the theme for the episode because it is, in heart and mind, mathematical music.*

TITLE & CREDITS blossom against the view of the promontory, which, as the lens slowly zooms in, soon fills the entire TV screen. At top center, on the crest of the bluffs, shining in the sunlight, stands what is generally agreed to be the most sensational house on the island, the famous "Hat Hut"—much larger than the name suggests—designed by Eero Saarinen, that daring craftsman of oddities, who, for example, gave TWA an eagle for a terminal, and in this case thought Makoniky Head needed a hat.

As the house grows larger and larger on the screen, the MUSIC *swells in a crescendo. Could a music of numbers be hinting that this bizarre structure is a countinghouse?*

---

*Opus 36.

The last credit—the name of the director—fades with the eye of the camera still closing in. Now a tiny figure—the figurative king, coming down from his countinghouse?—is seen descending the stairway that zigzags down the tall cliff from the house. The focus keeps moving in, until the man on the steps is seen, life-size, trotting down in exuberant haste.

This person appears to be about fifty years old, and the viewer immediately gets the impression that, as the presumptive owner of that magnificent house, he must have some inner magnetism or grasping power that is totally invisible out where his skin shows. He doesn't look at all royal—certainly doesn't look like a major player in leveraged buy-outs or a super-winner from insider trades. He does not seem self-assured; he is not smoking a cigar. He has a small blah figure and a skim-milk face. It is hard to tell at first glance what sort of man he really is, because his eyes, behind mirroring sunglasses, are hidden from the viewer. His mouth might be considered sensitive. He is wearing a wide-brimmed palm-leaf hat from the West Indies, which he may have bought because it has roughly the same shape as the mass of the house on the heights. He has on bathing trunks, in sizzling orange-and-pink checks, with legs that droop down almost to his knees, and he is shod in black soft-leather space shoes. He has a towel over his shoulder striped in shades of green and mauve which clash violently with the colors of his swimsuit.

MUSIC *gradually fades into sudsy sound of the smallish waves seen breaking on the Lambert's Cove beach. . . .*

2. As the man walks along the beach, he scans (camera taking his POV) the groups of bathers, some of whom, glistening with tanning oils, are frying themselves under the August greenhouse sun, while others, pale and prudent, huddle with hopes of long life under brightly colored beach umbrellas. The man raises his hand in a casual salute to a few select friends, who wave back eagerly, obviously wishing he would stop and talk with them.

A couple, in the shade of an umbrella, comes slowly into view. The woman, perhaps fifty, wears a white terry-cloth bathrobe and a wide-brimmed garden-party hat, which is tied under her chin with a purple Givenchy scarf. She shows through this feminine disguise a distinctly executive mien, confirmed by the set of her prognathous jaw. Her eyes, though, have a happy, dreamy look, perhaps because the man beside her is exactly the tycoon who, the viewer would have thought, should be the owner of that house on the heights. He is massive rather than fat, and either he is totally bald or someone shaves his head for him; he would appear to be something of a brute were it not for his sparkling, gentle-looking eyes, which paradoxically make him look all the more forceful: there may be a useful brain within the brawn.

FLORA LOMBARD

Hello, Spenser! Come talk with us. But take those miserable glasses off, darling, so we can see what bad things you're thinking.

3. Close view of Spenser; he has stopped walking. A girl in a mini-bikini drifts down toward the water beyond him. The woman's command has made Spenser blush, but he leaves his glasses on. He turns and comes up the beach toward the umbrella.

SPENSER

Hi, Flora! Imagine seeing you out here with the natives.

He hesitates and looks at the man.

FLORA

Darling, this is Spink Farley. He's up for the week.

SPENSER

I heard, I heard. [He turns to Farley.] Look, this is some coincidence. I was talking about you just this morning. I was asking Andy Willsworth up for the weekend—you know, he's the President and CEO of Consolidated Broadcasting—and he said, God, he'd heard you were up here visiting Flora, and he's dying to meet you. You two guys really ought to know each other. Flora, you'll have to come over on Friday night.

FLORA

Friday, Friday. I *think* it's copacetic. I'll buzz you, darling. How nice!

Spenser walks on along the beach.

4. Flora and Farley watch him walk off.

FARLEY

Who in the hell is *that* little hummingbird?

FLORA

I'm sorry, I didn't really introduce him, did I? He's Spenser Ham. You mustn't be put off by that getup, darling. I guess he's color-blind. He's a pussycat. He's so sweet and so kind. His wife died two years ago, and he carries on so bravely—his upper lip isn't even stiff. He gives just the best parties on the island. You'll meet *everybody* on Friday.

FARLEY

But who is he? What does he do?

FLORA

I guess he buys and sells companies. You know. That sort of thing. I'm surprised you haven't heard about him.

FARLEY

I've heard about this Willsworth who he says wants to meet me. He's one of the new guys—very double-knit—hipped on beating the Japs, you know, on that new high-definition technology, or whatever it's called, for the tube. From all I hear, a terrible meatball.

FLORA

Never mind, Spinky. Never mind. It'll be a lovely party.

CUT TO:

5. Spenser Ham on the terrace (the brim) of the house on the bluffs, a short while later, speaking into a walk-around phone. Beyond him is a shimmering sweep of one of the most beautiful moneyscapes in the world: the verdant prime real estate of West Tisbury, Chilmark, Menemsha, and Gay Head on the left, then a wide reach of the blue tablecloth of the Sound studded with many triangular stand-up white napkins of yacht sails, and, on the right, the outer Elizabeths—Pasque, Nashawena, and Cuttyhunk—steaming like dream islands in *Victory*.

SPENSER

Mr. Willsworth? Hello. My name is Spenser Ham. . . . Yes, that's right, on the Conover takeover. . . . Yes, I was a player on that one, too. . . . I realize we haven't met, and you may think this is forward of me, but something's come up. I have a house up here on Martha's Vineyard, you may have seen it in *Vanity Fair* a couple months ago. . . . That's right, odd shape, no question. The point is, is that I was on the beach just now, and I ran into Spink Farley, I'm sure you know who *he* is. We had a long talk, and I can't remember how, but your name came up, and Farley said, God, was he dying to meet you, and this may have been presumptuous of me, but I offered to ask you up here for a visit while he's here. You two guys ought to know each other. The mutual advantages—well, I don't need to get obvious. Look, I know this is short notice, but Friday night I've got some other people coming you may know or want to know—there'll be at least two network anchors, Millson and Kerry, and of course we have a whole mafia of writers, and then Flora Lombard, the designer, you must know her. . . . You have opera tickets? Couldn't you change them? . . . Sure. . . . Island Air has direct . . . A Lear? Fantastic. . . . Okay, check with your lady and let me know. Name's Jenny, right? I saw her picture in . . . You've heard Farley's an asshole? Not in my book, Mr. Willsworth. . . . Well, yes, there's that—that's a definite plus, I thought you'd cotton to that. . . . All right, then, I'll hope for the best. . . .

Soft MUSIC *comes up: reprise of the passage from the Schoenberg concerto, played however so faintly that* we also hear the smooth strokes of the cylinders of a powerful automobile engine, during FADE INTO:

6. POV of the driver of a big car, whose headlights (we see a silvery Mercedes logo at the front of the hood) sweep up toward a gate with a guardhouse beside it. There is no guard on duty —security here is presumably state-of-the-art electronic. The driveway swings to the left, and, *with the* MUSIC *suddenly swelling*,

the massive crown of the Hat Hut looms into view. MUSIC *fades* as the car pulls up by steps that rise onto the hat brim and stops. The camera swings out alongside to watch Flora Lombard, in flowing pale blue chiffon slacks, and Spink Farley, wearing a red blazer and white sailcloth trousers, alight from the car. An attendant takes the car off to park it. The couple sweeps in through the open doorway.

7. We now see what the two take in as they enter a breathtaking oval room, big enough for an indoor tennis court and two stories high. The ceiling is lined with zebrawood. Well-fed sofas are scattered about like a dozing pride of lions. The paintings on the walls are recognizable. We get glimpses of Chinese jade figures and recent books by Vineyard authors on polyurethaned tabletops. A Steinway concert grand lurks to one side, serving as an ideal platform for three world-famous jade pieces: "Eight Immortals Crossing Sea," "Heng O Flies to the Moon," and "Monkey God with Magic Fan." The piano has no bench for a performer to sit on. A soft suffusive light, which seems to have no source at all, flatters every face.

About thirty people are standing around having drinks; their chatter floats up over their heads like mesquite smoke from a grill. The women wear long dresses or slacks, and most of the men have jackets on, though a few, no doubt writers, are in open-necked unironed shirts; one fellow, a documentary film-maker from L.A., is in a T-shirt with TRUTH IS A WHORE printed on it.

Spenser Ham greets the Willsworths. He is wearing a hair-raising linen jacket in the flaming red and dark green tartan of the Scots clan Bruce—to which, whenever people ask him about the startling plaid, he offhandedly claims a distant kinship—over melon-yellow duck slacks. He looks as if his legs might walk off in one direction and his torso float off in another.

SPENSER

Hello, you two. Let's not waste any time. Come on over and meet Andy and Jenny. [To Farley, with a wink:] She's something else. Ever see a living Barbie Doll?

Spenser elbows his way through the chatting guests. The camera lens (Spenser's POV) glimpses faces and the mike picks up snatches of talk: a wife has left her husband for "a certified eunuch"; a film is "Guinness-world-record boring"; a writer (says a gloating writer friend of his) has had a "six-month block, hasn't written an effing word"; etc. Partway through the crowd, the camera backs away and catches Spenser's right hand, as he passes, patting the full curve of the left buttock, enveloped in pale blue silk, of Gert Millson, wife of the fabled anchorman. No, it is not a pat, it is a sweet little rubdown. We see Ms. Millson's face turn in a reflex of annoyance, but the eyes melt as soon as they recognize Mr. Ham; she is honored.

Spenser, reaching the Willsworths, introduces Flora Lombard and Spink Farley to them. Andrew Willsworth is a tall, slender, good-looking man who has taken the measure of Martha's Vineyard and dressed himself, sans jacket, in a winner of a dark green short-sleeved shirt and sleek black jeans. His tall, thin wife, Jenny, has frizzed hair, a rubberized-plastic face, sharp breasts, and arms that apparently don't bend easily. Spenser leaves the couples together.

FADE TO:

8. Round dining tables, set like polka dots out on a lit area of the hat brim. Dinner is being served. Camera zooms down on Flora Lombard at one of the tables, on Spenser's right. The camera lens takes the liberty of peeking under the tablecloth, where it sees Mr. Ham's adventurous right hand is on Ms. Lombard's left

thigh. She appears not to be noticing this. She is improving her dinner partner.

FLORA

You're such a sweetie, Spense darling, but you're vulgar. I was trying to figure out why, I was talking with Spinky about you, and I finally doped it out. You know what it is? There's no music in your soul.

SPENSER

What are you saying? I should hire an orchestra for a dinner like this?

FLORA

Ah, darling, that's just what I mean!

9. Farley and Willsworth have lingered after the meal out on the brim. They are standing in shadows. Beyond them in the light, the help can be seen clearing the tables. For a moment the camera brings into focus at a distance the face of one of the caterer's assistants: a young fellow with a bright red beard and a corona of red hair gathered behind in a ponytail; then his image fuzzes out and the two men come back into focus. Farley is smoking; the cigarette looks stark as it sticks out of his naked head.

WILLSWORTH

Look, this has to be in confidence like you wouldn't believe. I'm putting my life on a platter for you to carve up.

FARLEY [with evident distaste:]

You can trust me.

WILLSWORTH

I haven't much choice. Those bastards I was talking about have put together a mountain of security—not junk bonds, they have a zillion acres of virgin Sequoia forests, and some bank help, *solid* stuff—and Filcher is muttering about offering fifty-four to buy us out. That's eight points above the market. The bottom line is, is that these guys don't have the first glimmer of what goes on in broadcasting; they just want to sell off our affiliates, dismantle us, and run off with the fucking money. This Ham character made sense getting you and me together. Because the truth is I need a white knight to come in here and rescue us from those killers. We have lots to offer you, and if you moved in on us, we could keep some integrity in our outfit. Ham must have understood that. So what I'm asking you, Spink, would you guys want to consider a friendly buy-out? We're not a bad bargain.

FARLEY [He talks with the cigarette drooping out of the corner of his mouth.]

Well, I'd have to see the numbers, and I'd have to go back to my officers and board. We'll look at it. Let's say, in theory it's not impossible.

WILLSWORTH

Jesus, I hope you'll give it a try. . . . What beats me, how'd this Ham fella know we should get together?

FARLEY

Flora tells me he's a genius.

Brief reprise of the Schoenberg music during FADE TO:

10. Next morning. Now there is just one table out on the hat brim. Spenser, Willsworth, and Willsworth's wife are having

breakfast. Two maids are serving it. Spenser is giving Ms. Willsworth a deep look which seems intended to strip her of her salmon-pink blouse and her bra, presumably so he can see whether the dollmakers supplied this imitation woman with realistic nipples.

SPENSER [to Willsworth:]

How was it? Was Farley as bad as you thought?

WILLSWORTH

Remains to be seen. He holds his cards right up against his chest. But—

SPENSER

But you're glad you came up?

WILLSWORTH

I appreciate the gesture. It was kind of you.

JENNY WILLSWORTH

Yum! This sea air! I slept like a fossil. Oh, Spense, I'm *so* glad we came.

SPENSER

Then maybe you two would do something for me. I need your advice. I want to get a little music into my image. I feel a lack there. I'm like tone-deaf. I just don't know where to start.

WILLSWORTH

Hey, there are some wonderful collectibles in the music world—you could start that way. I was noticing your jades, you know, and of course the pictures! The Gauguin, the Renoir, and is that a what? A Utrillo? That one of the gray Riviera-looking house? You've got a lot of appreciation going there, those things'll always bring a killing. But in music you can get some wonderful buys: original autograph scores—and, even better, old instruments! I happen to know a guy, by the way, Ducket Jones, he buys for the music schools and museums. I'll give you his number, he'd be your man. Definitely.

CUT TO:

11. Spenser Ham in a telephone booth in Edgartown. It is a cloudy, threatening afternoon. Smart shops across the street. Tourists strolling—among them some yachting types wearing yellow rain gear. Girls eating ice-cream cones. Spenser drops in a coin and dials for an operator.

CUT TO:

12. An office filled with a dazzling glare. Through big windows palm trees can be seen, automobiles sparkling in the sunlight. A phone rings. A man behind a desk in a pleated white short-sleeved shirt picks up the receiver:

MAILLON

Allô! Maillon *ici*. . . . Collect—you say Monsieur Bifteck? Yes, yes, I accept.

BACK TO:

13.

SPENSER [into the pay phone:]

Pierre! Hello. This is Beefsteak. . . . Okay, listen carefully. I want you to buy me twelve thousand shares of Consolidated Broadcasting. Move with deliberate speed—know what I mean? Spread it out over a couple weeks. . . . Yeah, there's a blockbuster of a buy-out in the works, but it'll take a while. I don't want to make waves. In the bank's name, as usual, of course and then into the code account. And I want you to use half a dozen different brokers. And even with them, you know, buy a few hundred at a time. . . . Understand me? . . . No, I don't know when I'll be able to get down. . . . Be prudent, huh? This is a firecracker. The SEC'd be on my case in a minute if they knew how I . . . Sew up those Swiss lips of yours, okay, Maillon? . . . Good man.

CUT TO:

14. A crowded room in the "Large Galleries" of Sotheby's in London. The people here are circulating among a number of glass display cases in which are shown rows of supine violins and a few cellos. The camera finds, at the center of the room, a featured case, in which a single violin is suspended upright by its scroll. The instrument glistens, bathed in bright yet misty light. The lens zooms in and seems to move right through the glass into the temperature-controlled space within as it brings the viewer close to the violin's exquisite back, its waves of maple grain flecked with patterns of chipped varnish. The camera then slips sideways, pauses for a long stare at rippling maple ribs, and continues on around for a frank look at the violin's belly. After a few moments the focus tightens and, starting with the scroll, which has the beauty of the uncurling head of a new fern, slides down the strings to the bridge and then, enlarging the detail even more, stares at a fat, licentious Cupid inlaid in the tailpiece. A ten-second hold. Now the frame moves to the left, across the tight pine grain, pauses on an oblong stain where a splotch of the varnish appears to have been burnt away, and glides to and follows upward the graceful triple line of the purfling, swoops in with it at the C-curve, and finally, on the upper curve of the belly, arrives at the only ugly place on the whole instrument—a little wound in the wood.

All through this close inspection, and during what follows, we hear *soft, thoughtful passages of music from a Hindemith sonata for unaccompanied violin.**

The lens now draws back to search the many faces of those who are trooping past the display case at this pre-auction viewing. This is a polyglot crowd. They are here from all over the world, but we can see from the expressions on their faces that they have a single mind: they all covet this glorious object. One need not be a violinist to yearn to own the Antonietta Strad. These people all know about the law of supply and demand. They are obviously well aware that there is by now a finite (and diminishing) number of Strads on this earth—about six hundred and fifty, according to the catalogue most of them hold in their hands—and that any one of the nearly five billion human beings on the planet would be very lucky if they possessed one, especially one so handsome and storied as this. The faces wear a look, above all, of computation, of rapid appraisal of the value of this fiddle in units of currency. The viewer can see, glittering in their eyes, dream symbols of pounds, dollars, francs, marks, yen, and various sorts of Arabic tender. There is a palpable sense, as well, that these people have been quite aware of the TV camera staring lustfully at Antonietta's naked back, at her belly with its tiny scar. As the lens swung back, just now, to look at them, they became self-conscious and put on their best behavior, betraying their awareness that life in the modern world no longer imitates art; it imitates TV. The lens therefore looks at them, they know, searching for the raw essence of the life of the era in which they find themselves. Will they measure up?

CUT TO:

15. The ferry *Islander* warping into the docks in Vineyard Haven harbor. As passengers disembark, the camera closes in on a short man, descending the gangway, who is ably disguised as a day-

*Opus 31, No. 2.

tripper. He gets in a taxi. The taxi is seen rolling up State Road . . . on the straight stretch of Old County Road, with its proud parade of tall pines . . . under the light-flecked canopy of oak trees arching over Middle Road. The taxi stops at the mouth of a dirt driveway; the pseudo day-tripper gets out, tells the driver to wait, and walks up the driveway. Around a turn he comes on Spenser Ham, standing in the road kicking at the dust. Ham is wearing his Bahamian hat and mirroring sunglasses.

SPENSER

Did anyone on the ferry recognize you?

BOLEN

How would I know? Don't be so paranoid. No one spoke to me.

SPENSER

We're going to have to change the routine. Anyway, what are these hot items you have?

BOLEN

I have two. Samson Pitts and his United Lymphomilloid are putting Comary Limited into play. It's hostile as hell.

SPENSER

My God, David and Goliath.

BOLEN

Yeah, it'll be leveraged up to the teeth. I'm told Comary is toying with a couple of possible defenses, to try to ward off the buy-out. Maybe a PacMan.

SPENSER

Where the eater is eaten by the very one the eater planned to eat?

BOLEN

Exactly: they're considering a fat counter-tender. Either that or they may try a poison pill. They talk about issuing preferreds as a dividend to shareholders, each share convertible to forty shares of U Lympho if Pitts is successful with his takeover. This would dilute the hell out of Pitts's control. But my source tells me that Pitts has some dynamite countermoves up his sleeve and that it's an absolute shoo-in that he'll succeed, no matter what Comary tries. You can move on this one, and if you move now, you'll get in way ahead of the arbs. And it'll be so early it won't look fishy to the SEC. Comary stock is bound to go up twenty points, maybe as much as thirty. Here's a printout with all the numbers.

He hands Spenser an envelope.

SPENSER

Good, Bolen, good. And the other one?

BOLEN

It's a lollapalooza of a telecommunications takeover. Northwest Sempervirens is moving in on Consolidated Broadca—

SPENSER

Hell, Bolen, I know all about that one.

BOLEN

Yes, sir.

THEN:

The "day-tripper" is seen getting back into the taxi.

CUT TO:

16. Takeoff of a British Airways Concorde from JFK. Its nose cone is in drooped position, like the beak of a predatory bird; the tripled wheels on their long struts look like talons which the great hunter slowly tucks up under its wings as it climbs into the air. It swoops out over the calm sea.

Loud MUSIC OVER *the takeoff: passage from the second part of Alban Berg's violin concerto, "To the Memory of an Angel." Listeners will pick up from this music the whiff of peril that many people get in the first moments when a huge metal machine so unnaturally pretends it has feathers.**

17. As the craft splits the sky at twice the speed of sound, soaring ten and a quarter miles above the ocean, the camera rides inboard, its lens moving (a flight attendant's POV) along the tight tube of the passenger cabin. We see on the faces of the passengers that any sense of danger they may have felt on takeoff has been left [*with the music*] far behind, replaced now in their minds by a feeling of velvet pride—the complacency of knowing that this is not only the swiftest but also the most expensive of all the ways of crossing the sea. Spenser comes into range in a red leather seat to the right of the aisle, alongside Ducket Jones in the adjacent blue window seat. Jones looks the part of a museum mole: wan, thin, waxy, with rimless glasses and a hopelessly lopsided mustache, which looks like a swift dismissive stroke by a Chinese calligrapher's brush. He is leafing through a glossy publication.

The camera swings around and kibitzes over Jones's shoulder.

---

*Eloquent takeoff music. Berg wrote this piece in honor of death—as a heartfelt requiem for eighteen-year-old Manon, daughter of Gustave Mahler's widow Alma and the architect Walter Gropius. This second section of the concerto depicts her actual throes. Right after composing this music, Berg was stung by an insect, the sting became infected, and he himself died of blood poisoning. Have a nice flight!

He turns a page of the big booklet—a Sotheby's catalogue—and on the new page the viewer can read a bold heading:

A Highly Important Violin by Antonio Stradivari, Cremona, 1699

On the page opposite the text that follows there is a color picture of the back of this violin.

Jones reads to himself for a few moments. Then:

JONES

Listen to this, Mr. Ham. "There is a legend, which we have not been able to confirm, that the Antonietta Stradivari was, on one or perhaps two occasions, played by W. A. Mozart." Imagine that!

SPENSER

So I suppose that jacks up the price?

JONES

Sir, at an auction you can't think about ways to shave the price. The bidders are the ones who jack the price up—and you're one of them.

SPENSER

This whole thing goes against my nature.

Jones reads silently again. Then:

JONES

This is a beautifully documented instrument. There are airtight certifications from Jean Baptiste Vuillaume—he was a famous violinmaker and dealer in Paris—and actually three of them at widely differing times from W. E. Hill & Sons, the best London dealers. A thorough provenance. And all sorts of anecdotes. The fiddle was named for a mistress of Stradivarius's, and apparently there's a nick near one edge on the belly that was caused, while Stradivarius was making the instrument, by his hand jumping in rage when someone spilled the beans that his mistress had told a gossipy friend he had gone impotent, so it got all over town. They also say Berlioz was taught to play the violin on this one by a fiddler named Baillot. Wonderful supporting material! Sotheby's is careful to say they can't vouch for the absolute verifiability of any of this—but I can tell you that this is the kind of thing that will make the bidding hot.

SPENSER

I don't want to hear about it. How deep am I in for, to get this thing?

JONES

The catalogue suggests two hundred to two hundred fifty thousand pounds. And I have to say, Sotheby's knows the market inside out.

SPENSER

Pounds? Come on. Give me dollars.

JONES

Well, that would be . . . the higher figure would be . . . about a third of a million.

SPENSER

Christ. I could kill that Flora.

He tilts his seat back and shuts his eyes to go to sleep.

CUT TO:

18. Sotheby's large auction room. The auctioneer, a fleshy man with thick black-rimmed glasses, is at a podium that looks rather like a pulpit. Every seat in the room is taken. The camera picks up Spenser and Jones about halfway back. Two swarthy men in burnooses sit in front of them. Also notable nearby are six Japanese men in identical blue suits; they are all wearing neckties with the same paisley pattern. Jones is whispering to Spenser:

JONES

That's Pfinsmann, the German dealer—the fat one. Oh-oh, I see Biller—he's bound to be here for Glover Pound; Pound's the collector in Santa Barbara, that's bad news for us.

SPENSER

Can it. You make me nervous. Listen, how do I bid?

JONES

You don't. *I* do. You sit still, Mr. Ham. I must warn you: don't even raise an eyebrow.

SPENSER

Look. We've come a long ways for this. You better not mess up. I want this goddamn violin.

JONES

You'll have it, sir, if you're willing to go the distance.

SPENSER

Get it.

19.

AUCTIONEER [in a BBCish voice:]

Item number twenty-three. A highly important violin by Antonio Stradivari, Cremona, 1699. Bids will begin at one hundred thousand pounds sterling. If you please, ladies and gentlemen.

He looks out. The bidding, seen from Spenser's POV, is rapid. After each signal the auctioneer names a figure ("One hundred ten thousand," etc.). One of the burnooses dips, fluttering its white drapery, price up ten thousand; one of the Japanese men stands up and bows, price up; Jones raises his left hand and twiddles a finger; Biller juts his chin out; Pfinsmann scratches his ear; Jones's finger moves; all six of the Japanese stand and bow one after the other in a rapid succession of tens of thousands; a classy-looking woman—from Paris? Rome?—wiggles her hat; Jones waves his whole hand. . . .

As the bidding proceeds, involving numerous other bidders, MUSIC *is heard* OVER, *pianissimo at first, then louder and louder, until the viewer no longer hears the auctioneer but only sees his mouth move: a reprise of the passages from the Hindemith sonata for unaccompanied violin that was heard earlier, during the Sotheby viewing. Finally, as the* MUSIC *fades out*, the auctioneer lifts a gavel, holds it up while he waits, sees no further telltale movement, gives two warnings, then:

AUCTIONEER

Sold, at two hundred forty-five thousand pounds.

And he whacks the gavel on the podium. At once he announces the number of the next item, but most of the crowd stands up and shuffles toward the doors. On the way by, several of the more knowing shake Jones's hand and congratulate him. The viewer sees that Spenser is outraged by Jones's obvious pride and the greeters' misdirected envy.

CUT TO:

20. An old Douglas DC-3 landing at an airstrip near Freeport on Grand Bahama Island. [NOTE TO DIRECTOR: For God's sake, let's try not to have the boring cliché landing—plane's underbelly, then pulling away to hear squeak and see puff of smoke of wheels hitting tarmac. Maybe have a truckload of Bahamian police in their wonderful white uniforms and white pith sun helmets and lots of gold braid, racing alongside the landing plane with the evident intent of arresting drug smugglers. This would hint at a subtext of positive social comment. Something, please!]

The plane comes to a stop; the propellers stall out. Among the passengers descending the ramp is Spenser, carrying a violin case. His West Indian hat, which must have looked absurd in the rain in London, is jauntily at home here.

CUT TO:

21. A room in the Lucayan Beach Hotel. Spenser tips a bellboy, who leaves. Spenser then puts the violin case on a king-size bed, opens it, takes the violin and bow out, pulls open a dresser drawer, and puts both the violin and the bow in it. He goes back to the case, closes it, picks it up, and leaves the room carrying it. He is careful to make sure the door is locked.

CUT TO:

22. Spenser, with the empty violin case, pausing in a hallway at a door, on the crinkled glass panel of which are printed the words BANQUE DE CHINE SUISSE. He opens the door and walks in. A receptionist, obviously expecting him, gets up and leads him into Maillon's office. Maillon rises to his feet.

MAILLON [using the code name even face to face]
Monsieur Bifteck! *Enchanté!*

SPENSER

Have you got it?

The two men remain awkwardly standing.

MAILLON

It was not easy to find so many hundred-dollar bills—out of sequence, *entendu!*—in twenty-four hours. You tell me only last Tuesday you do not know when you come down. This—so unexpected. You have never withdrawn money before.

SPENSER

I took a bath on a deal in London, so I thought, This damn gravy is just laying here, I might as well skim a little off.

MAILLON

Isn't it risky? The *douane*?

SPENSER

I'm told the customs guys never bother with baggage from here. And if they do, it's beautiful—I just say the money is roulette winnings from the casinos, and I slip a bit to the guy. Happens all the time, as you well know, Pierre.

Spenser puts the violin case on Maillon's desk and opens it. The two men begin packing bundles of money tightly in the violin-shaped cavity.

SPENSER

How you doing on the Consolidated Broadcasting stock?

MAILLON

Parfaitement, Monsieur! Little by little . . .

SPENSER

Now, listen carefully. I have a new tip. I want you to buy—in the same way, by easy stages—forty thousand of Comary Limited.

MAILLON

Comary. Ah, yes. We will do. . . . May I ask . . . your information on these?

SPENSER

You mean you want to piggyback a bit and buy some shares for yourself? Go ahead, Pierre, these are both sure things, but just don't overdo it, you hear? Just a tiny sip.

MAILLON

Merci, Monsieur. You are very kind.

CUT BACK TO:

23. The hotel room. Spenser places the violin case on the bed, opens it. The camera closes in to leer for a few moments at the stacks of bills. Spenser's quick hands remove them and repack them in his suitcase, sandwiching them between two suits and several shirts and a pair of pajamas. He opens the dresser drawer, takes Antonietta out, pats its back as if to congratulate it, and puts it into the case with care. The camera holds for a time on the violin in the open case, swings to peek almost longingly at

a corner of a stack of bills that shows in folds of clothing in the suitcase, then looks back at Antonietta. At this point the viewer, remembering the high price the violin commanded at the auction, and aware of all that cash, warmed by Bahamian zephyrs, that was packed into its case, may think of Antonietta as, above all, an object of value—perhaps as the centerpiece of a commercial interrupting this very program. But then the lens tightens down on the Cupid on the tailpiece. And now the thought is apt to be that the little love god may be learning to shoot ambiguous arrows at those who hear it play, which will arouse in listeners both sorts of cupidity—greed and desire.

FADE AND DISSOLVE TO:

24. The living room of the Hat Hut. Broad daylight. Spenser is supervising the construction of a glass case, against one wall, in which to display Antonietta. There are two workmen. Spenser is snappish, fussy, bad-tempered.

SPENSER

No, you idiot! You'll have to put the humidity control out of sight. In the base. Hide it with a grille.

The workmen, island born and bred, give each other significant looks, which the viewer will easily be able to translate as follows: "It's going to take us a good little while—like, say, three weeks, maybe a month, maybe a *year*?—to find the right grille, huh?" And the answering look: "Bet your ass. Could be never."

CUT TO:

25. Spenser in his office, high in the crown of the hat. Through a window of one-way glass (specified by Saarinen so that from the outside there would be an illusion that there are no windows at all in the huge hat) Spenser looks across at the low green hills

of Naushon and Woods Hole; sport-fishing boats nibble like white mice along the rip of Middle Ground shoal in the Sound. His desk, wrapped around within the curve of the crown under the window, is machine-ridden. At the center sits a big, old-fashioned Lanier No-Problem word processor, as stately and durable as a 1927 Packard touring car (don't make 'em like *that* anymore), flanked by: a Quotron monitor, parading a constant flow of green stock market prices; an AT&T telephone console with fifty buttons and a recording device; a Konica fax machine; a four-color Canon copier; a Sharp Wizard organizer; a 25-inch Zenith TV set; an RCA VCR; a Sony CD player; a Radio Shack weather radio; and a Braun clock set in a piece of simulated tree trunk, at which a mechanical woodpecker repeatedly pecks in time with the clock's jumpy second hand.

Spenser is writing checks for Vineyard causes: the struggling hospital, the Land Bank, the Mayhew Seminars, the Boys and Girls Club, the lobster hatchery, three town libraries, Community Services. . . . He spreads a begging letter on the desk in front of him. The camera closes in, and the viewer sees that the appeal is from the Martha's Vineyard Historical Society, and it is signed by Coverly Patterson, the host of the top-rated public-TV series "Our Proud Land," who summers on the Vineyard. Spenser writes another check. Then he looks up a phone number in the island NYNEX directory, and dials.

SPENSER

Is this Coverly Patterson? Oh, hello, this is Spenser Ham. . . . You know about me? Thank you. I certainly know about *you*, sir. I've been watching you for years. Look, I've just written a check in response to your fine letter about the Historical Society. I just wanted you to know how very much I care about Vineyard history—about history altogether, as a matter of fact. I'd love to hand the check to you in person. . . . Well, it's for ten thousand. . . . No, no, no, I just wish it could be more, we all have an obliga—but let's see, I'm giving a small dinner next Wednesday night to unveil a little surprise I picked up in London day before yesterday—something with a lot of lore—speaking of history. Of all people, you'd really be— Why don't you and Mrs. Patterson . . .

Hint of the Schoenberg theme, then FADE INTO:

26. The living room. Cocktails before dinner, much as at the last party. Camera swings around toward the glass case against the inner wall. Spenser is showing Antonietta to Flora Lombard and to Coverly Patterson of "Our Proud Land." Patterson knows how to deal with cameras; he squares around to show the better side of his face, with its sculptured brindle beard and big black eyebrows. Camera closes on the display case. Antonietta, glistening in indirect lighting, is mounted on a stand which slowly revolves. In front of the stand the sumptuous Sotheby's catalogue is open to the spread which announces the violin and shows the suggested price:

£200,000–£250,000

Camera BACK to the three:

FLORA

It's beautiful, darling, but what's that ghastly hole in the base for?

SPENSER

The temperature control and humidifier are down under there. No sweat, Flora. The workmen are chasing down a good-looking stainless-steel grille to cover the hole. They promised it in two or three days.

COVERLY PATTERSON [to Flora:]

Spenser has been telling me some of the background of that beauty—what a treasure!

SPENSER [to Patterson:]

I'm sure we can dig up more on the fiddle's history. I have a fellow, Ducket Jones, a real violin scholar, I'm sure he can help a lot. [To Flora:] Cov is thinking of doing one of his programs on Antonietta—you know, about how so many priceless things wind up in America.

FLORA

How nice for you, darling.

SPENSER

Oh, no, jeepers, I wouldn't be *on* it.

FLORA

Isn't our Spense a cutie, Mr. Patterson? He really is a shrinking violet. It's not an act, you know. But, Spense, you can't just keep a Strad cooped up in a case. I know something about this, darling. A Stradivarius has to be *played*. It's like a great Arabian stallion, darling—it has to be *exercised*.

CUT TO:

27. The polka-dot dinner arrangement out on the brim, as before. (Among the caterer's help, serving guests, we see for a brief moment, almost subliminally, the face of the young man with a red beard and the shock of red hair tied in back in a ponytail.) *Under the* MUSIC *of Bartók's Rhapsody No. 1 for Violin and Piano, played very loud*, Spenser stands and says a few words, which are drowned out by the music, whereupon Coverly Patterson rises

and Spenser hands him a check. Several quick flashes of light; camera draws back to see photographers from the *Vineyard Gazette* and the *Martha's Vineyard Times* taking pictures. Coverly Patterson has promptly presented the better side of his face. Spenser waves off the photographers, appearing to be infuriated that they have intruded on this very private evening.

CUT TO:

28. Spenser, writing a letter at his word processor. [The viewer may be surprised that this rinky-dink character doesn't dictate letters to a secretary; of course he *has* a secretary. The conclusion must be that he likes to mind some of his own business—and to have others mind all of theirs and none of his.] Stock market quotations are whizzing by on the Quotron screen. As Spenser works, his voice reads what he writes, OVER:

SPENSER

Dear Ducket. You will be pleased to know that the fiddle is a smash hit with the sophisticates up here. However, I have decided to put on some recitals, so we can do more than just look at the damn thing. Now, I realize this is a bit out of your line, but I am sure you will know where to turn. I want you to hire a violinist and an accompanist for me. I want them to be really A-number-one professional level, I want them to be women, I want them to be young, I want them to be lookers. (My theory is there's more than one way to appreciate music.) They will get $500 a week and will have free room and board in my house. They will play for guests after dinner, roughly once every two weeks. Lots of beach life, will meet celebs, chance to get ahead in the world, etc. I want them soon. Your fee will be $2,000—or $4,000 if they are *real* lookers. Sincerely yours.

29. Bright Sunday morning. Steps of the Whaling Church in Edgartown. Worshippers, entering, are dwarfed by the huge, fat white pillars, like upended Moby-Dicks. Spenser briskly ascends the steps, and the camera follows him up the center aisle. He takes an aisle seat in the tenth pew from the front. Parishioners lean and whisper to each other, noticing him, impressed by him. We see his face—this time without the mirroring sunglasses—which is humble, shiny as an apple, clear-eyed, as open to possibility as a check on which no figures have yet been entered. He nods discreetly to several people; those so honored raise their chins a little.

30. Later: Collection is being taken up. Spenser drops a hundred-dollar bill (camera to close in on fingers letting it go; the viewer should feel the Bahamian warmth of the money right through the TV screen) into the plate. This is noticed. Eyes turn. The collecting deacon, a native islander, ducks his head and shuts his eyes in a brief murmured prayer of thanks. A deaf person would be able to read his lips: ". . . and the greatest of these is charity. . . . But, Lord, where do you suppose the little pip-squeak gets that kind of money?"

CUT TO:

31. Bolen, seen earlier as an imitation day-tripper, stepping down from a small commuter plane at the Martha's Vineyard airport, dressed this time as a member of the Edgartown Yacht Club—navy-blue double-breasted blazer from J. Press, open-necked pale yellow L. L. Bean lisle shirt, featherweight khaki slacks, discreetly soiled white Topsiders. He gets in a taxi . . . which is seen on the South Road speeding toward Edgartown . . . aboard the *On*

Time, the tiny car ferry to Chappaquiddick . . . parked at the mouth of a Chappy driveway. . . .

32. Some distance up the driveway, out of the waiting taxi driver's sight, Bolen and Spenser are talking.

BOLEN

. . . and, because Farley seems to be stalling, Willsworth's bunch is considering a scorched-earth defense. You know, just ruin the damn company, give themselves some golden parachutes, and bail out and to hell with it. Anything to block the Sempervirens syndicate. They have win fever. It's now more important to win than to save the lousy business; it's only the fourth-best outfit in broadcasting, after all. Farley knows this, and he's really getting it together now. Sir, it's time to buy a lot more. The arbs'll be gnawing at this in a week or so, and you can work with them—you know, everybody staying under the five-percent-disclosure limitation. The price'll go through the ceiling. Buy, Mr. Ham!

SPENSER

I told you last time that I knew all about this one. I trust you don't expect a percentage on this.

BOLEN

What are you saying? Hey, you're hearing stuff right now that you didn't have before. Whoa. Do you know the meaning of the word "insider," Mr. Ham? Ever heard of the SEC? I could blow you right out of the water.

SPENSER

And cut your own dingus off doing it? [He thinks a while. Then:] All right. From now on, two percent on deals I'd known about, where you top off the data.

BOLEN [after a pause:]

Mmm. Okay. I'll take two.

CUT TO:

33. Spenser at the wheel of a jeep, on Main Street in Vineyard Haven. He is in a hurry. He parks his car in the slot reserved for the handicapped, gets out and crosses the street to a public telephone, drops in a coin and begins talking.

SPENSER

. . . so listen, Maillon, I want you to buy thirty thousand more . . .

LONG FADE with dim sounds of Spenser's order trailing off, then another voice, a woman's, also on a phone, intermixing with his and finally emerging alone:

34. And FADE IN on Mrs. Coverly Patterson, at home, in negligee on a chaise longue, with a breakfast tray on her lap, holding a pink telephone.

FRAN PATTERSON

Another thing, Flora. Your friend Spenser Ham? He has a lover. Do you think it's a man or a woman?

FLORA

What do you mean, he has a lover? How do you know that?

FRAN PATTERSON

I know it because just by chance I've seen him talking three different times in three different pay telephone booths. All over the island. Doesn't even want his servants to know—

FLORA

My God, I guess you're right. The little sneak!

CUT TO:

35. Utter stillness. Front hall of the Hat Hut, view through to the living room in subdued light. A buzzer is heard in the distance. Footsteps. Expensive brown brogues—Gucci?—with fringed flaps bouncing over the insteps, in rapid paces toward the door.

Door opens. Two women.

The viewer's immediate reaction has to be: Spenser Ham owes Ducket Jones at *least* four thousand dollars. Wow.

One of the women is holding a violin case. Both have put their suitcases down. Both are in layered sweat-shirtish tops and wrinkled dark slacks. They are wearing running shoes. In these drab clothes they are world-class knockouts.

THE VIOLINIST

Hi. I'm June Speckman.

THE PIANIST

Vera Flamm.

SPENSER

Come *in*, girls!

36. Spenser's hand flicks a light switch. Beyond the hand and the arm, Antonietta's glass case is seen filling up with light. Camera sees the light creep up on the delicately sculptured faces of the two women as they move toward the case. Closes in on

June. Her cheeks glow; her lips are parted; her eyes dart from detail to detail. Awe shimmers on her face. Certain abstractions are reified—they can almost be seen with the naked eye—in the thrills that stir and flush on her fine face as she responds to Antonietta's beauties, and to the very idea of a Strad! The viewer sees in her responses hints of what it means to be a gifted young person totally dedicated to a craft—traces of years of hard work; self-discipline, patience, stamina, physical endurance; a yearning for unattainable perfection; a generous empathy for anyone who may listen to her playing, a consequent urge to use it to excite and delight; a willingness to subordinate her tastes, when she plays, to a composer's will—but also a stubborn wish to be loyal to her own secret truths.

Camera veers to Spenser's face, as if curious to know whether he is catching any of this. The viewer will have to be the judge.

It is the pianist who speaks first:

VERA

Mr. Ham? Can we play something *right now*?

JUNE

Please, Mr. Ham?

37. Spenser twirls a combination lock, swings back a panel of the glass case, takes Antonietta out, and hands it to June. He places a straight chair at the piano; Vera finds it too low; he fetches a big Rand McNally world atlas and puts it on the chair—just right, Vera, sitting, nods. *Then the two begin to play, by heart, the slow second movement of Hindemith's Sonata in C for Violin and Piano.** The knowledgeable listener will hear at once

---

*Composed in 1939. No opus number. When Hindemith's opus numbers reached 50, in 1930, he decided that a linear chronological counting of his pieces, which kept being debuted in public very much out of their compositional order, made no sense. And 50 seemed to him a nice round number on which to stop.

that these two women are not just four-thousand-dollar lookers; in fact, their physical beauty has suddenly become objectively irrelevant—though perhaps not to Spenser Ham, to judge by the glimpses at him that the camera now and then takes. These are superb musicians. The camera moves from one person to another. At the first sounds from Antonietta, June looks for a moment as if she had had the wind knocked out of her, then her face opens, softens, and begins to glow as if filled with the warmed blood (Spenser appears to be thinking) of sexual arousal. A viewer, insulated from her by the glass of the cathode tube and therefore perhaps more detached than Spenser right there on the couch, cannot help being moved, not only by the music itself, but by her sudden pure surprise and joy at being able to make sounds she has obviously never attained in all the years of her work. *As the movement suddenly breaks into its fast and witty scherzo in 5/8 time*, Vera waggles her head with Hindemith's rhythms, and her fingering on the keys is crisp. Spenser's Steinway, freshly tuned and voiced, happens to be a splendid instrument, too, and though Vera noticeably reacts to this, her face is turned to what is more important—the sounds she is hearing from Antonietta in June's arms. Visible in her glee are signs that these two women have become very good friends.

VOLUME UP *as June treats Antonietta to Hindemith's recapitulation of the earlier slow passages of the movement, now heard in a swift perpetual motion of sixteenth notes, glinting like sunlight on the beating of a hummingbird's wings.* Anyone who is listening is bound to tremble with delight.

38. Spenser is showing the women their rooms. There is one for each, with a shared bathroom between. As they are looking around, greatly pleased with what they are seeing, a manservant glides in beyond them with their bags. The view from the bedroom windows is to the eastward, up toward the Tashmoo Pond opening and the magisterial summer houses on West Chop.

SPENSER

I have to make a phone call. Then how about we take a swim?

Sounds of enthusiastic agreement from the musicians.

CUT TO:

39. Spenser in his office, on the telephone.

SPENSER

Andy! How you been? Listen. I want to talk to you. A little birdie told me you guys at Consolidated had gotten kind of uptight about the Sempervirens move. . . . I just decided ten minutes ago I'd like to buy you. . . . Friendly, absolutely. Sure, white knight. . . . You think I sound as if I'm *on* something? Come on! . . . Well, the fact is I've just been listening to—to some good news. . . . Hell, yes, I realize it'll be expensive, but Andy, I know a buy when I see one. . . . I have absolutely no interest in managing your outfit. . . . Just hold on and give me a few days to get my act together. . . . Do you want to hear a really weird coincidence? You remember the steep cliff down to the beach from my house? Well, the steps down from here were all cut from a single bole of *Sequoia sempervirens*. One tree trunk, three hundred feet of steps. I'm not shitting you, Andy. I had it built two years ago. I bought the damn wood from those pirates. . . .

CUT TO:

40. Three figures are seen from a distance, descending the very steps Spenser was talking about. Zoom in. Spenser is in his awfuls.

June is in a blue tank suit; Vera wears a pink bikini. Spenser looks as if he is thinking of giving Ducket Jones a bonus.

SPENSER

You know something, girls? I'm sure as hell glad I bought that fiddle.

JUNE

Oh, Mr. Ham, are we ever!

SPENSER

Please. The name is Spenser. You can call me Spense.

MUSIC *up during a* FADE: *the first movement,* tempo di ciaccona, *of Bartók's Solo Violin Sonata. This fervid, restless music, with its wild leaps in pitch and volume, and its insistent discords, completely drowns out* the spoken lines in the next two takes, which are, in effect, mimed.

41. A curve in a driveway somewhere on the island. Spenser, in his hat and mirroring shades, is interrogating Bolen, who appears to be some kind of repairman, in a soiled green jumpsuit with a company logo on the chest. The conversation looks urgent—evidently a new morsel of inside information. *The* MUSIC *suggests an overlay of restless impatience on Spenser's usual cool demeanor, and a reciprocal irritable nervousness that seems to pollute Bolen's servility.*

42. Spenser in a phone booth near Poole's fish market, alongside Menemsha basin. He places his order with Maillon—*and perhaps because of the agitation of the* MUSIC *his state of mind seems ruffled.* He nods, and later shakes his head in an impatient no, as if his interlocutor could see him. He hangs up.

MUSIC *fades*, CUT TO:

43. Nighttime. A messy living room, dimly lit, in a run-down summer cottage which looks as if it's made of papier-mâché. Eerily, *the same violin sounds that dominated the previous takes—those of the Bartók unaccompanied sonata—are now heard again, badly played on a rotten fiddle. After what the listener has heard from Antonietta, not long ago, and from the virtuoso on the recorded music-over of those two takes, this sound is thin, tinny, stingy—it seems an envious, whining complaint*. Camera snoops around: daybed, with a rumpled blanket on it; a table against one wall, cluttered with dirty dishes and magazines; a big padded armchair with stuffing spilling out of gaps in the fabric. In this armchair a young woman sprawls, in a Madonna T-shirt and jeans, with bare feet. Her eyes swim; she is on the moon. Two men lie prone on the shabby green carpet, holding beer cans and talking to each other and laughing. From them the lens swoops up a pair of legs in torn jeans and up a bare chest, to frame the head and swinging bow arm of the violin player, and his yellow instrument. It's the guy with the red beard and red hair pulled back in a ponytail. He's completely zonked.

ONE OF THE MEN ON THE FLOOR

Can't you play anything but that shit?

REDHEAD [without stopping:]

Hey, Jocko, listen up. This music is *real*.

Jocko grunts.

REDHEAD

You like monster movies?

JOCKO

Yeah, I like 'em okay.

REDHEAD

Then you got to like this. This is *horror,* man. It's so real. Can't you hear it? I think the guy wrote it just for you and me.

CUT TO:

44. Spenser walking past the International Bazaar in Freeport, Grand Bahama, pointing out to June and Vera, who flank him, the Moorish golden dome of El Casino, one of the island's gambling houses. All three are in tourist clothing. They seem not to have a care in the world. From time to time, they stop and peer in shopwindows. At one of them, a chic boutique, the camera catches them from behind, with their reflections vivid on the plate glass, while ghostly mannequins loom beyond the mirrored glare. . . . Now the lens stares at them fullface, from inside the shop.

SPENSER

Tell me something, you two. What does the expression mean, when you say that a guy has "music in his soul"?

The two women look at each other across Spenser, and laugh.

SPENSER

No, come on. I'm serious.

VERA

It means he's sexy.

JUNE

No, Vera, give him a break, he wants to know, it's much more than that. [She stops to think a moment.] It means that he has a feel in everything he does for the proper balance between basic instinct and good order. Think of his soul as a membrane in his mind. It has staves on it, and there are notes on the staves—and the notes are his actions. If he *really* has music in him, the actions—the notes—are connected one to another in a satisfying way, and the links between them make chords and sequences and melodic patterns. I don't mean that they have to be sweet or anything like that. The combinations of notes may be harsh and complicated—you may have noticed the rough kinds of music I like—but they have to have a pattern that makes sense, they have to be *interesting*.

SPENSER

Hell's bells, you mean I didn't have to buy Antonietta? That nothing like that was the point?

VIOLINIST

Ah, Spense! I don't know you well enough to make a total judgment, but I'd say that the action of buying that violin was written down as one of the few whole notes on the score of your soul.

SPENSER

Well, thank you, whatever that means. That's too fancy for me. I know I like to hear you playing on that damn box—or I like to *watch* you, anyway. . . . But right now, we have to go back to the hotel. And I'm going to have to borrow the fiddle from you for half an hour. I promised to show it to a friend of mine downtown.

CUT TO:

45. Hotel room. Spenser is transferring stacks of bills from the violin case to his suitcase. When he is finished, he fetches Antonietta and the bow from a desk drawer. This time, in his

euphoria, he kisses the back of the violin. He puts it gently in the case, and for a few moments the lens hovers over it. Antonietta glistens in the brilliant tropical light. The varnish of its beautiful back and ribs must be feeling the delightful warmth of all those tropical banknotes! The violin looks as if it has begun to feel very much at home in the twilight years of the twentieth century.

CUT TO:

46. A roulette table in the hotel's Monte Carlo Casino, that night. Players, in tropical dress, are around the table. We hear:

CROUPIER

Place your bets, ladies and gentlemen!

The camera closes on Spenser. He is handing a hundred-dollar bill to each of the musicians.

SPENSER

Good luck. If you win a heap, you can buy me a new soul.

We watch the women lose the money. We see that they have never done anything in their lives as ridiculous as this, but that they nevertheless care terribly each time the croupier's rake pulls away their chips. They are stunning in their naïve greed.

CUT TO:

47. Spenser's office in the Hat Hut. The viewer may be surprised to see Bolen sitting right there, not in disguise—he is dressed, in fact, in the pinstriped charcoal-gray uniform of the person he really is, an executive (and in fact a managing director) of the investment banking firm of Farraday, Simmer. Bolen himself is

obviously surprised to have been summoned, skipping all subterfuge, directly to Mr. Ham's house.

SPENSER

The point is, Bolen, is that this time you and I are aboveboard. Couldn't be cleaner. So we can deal right out in the open. And for once I'm letting you in on something, instead of the other way around. But bear this in mind. At the moment—so far—there are only two people in the world who know about this move, and you'll be the third. If there should turn out to be a premature fourth, or if you should start getting so greedy for yourself that the arbs pick up the signals, I'll personally come to Manhattan, you goddamn little crook, and deball you. Is that clear?

BOLEN

You have an understandable way of putting things, Mr. Ham.

SPENSER

Okay. Here's what's up. I'm going to buy Consolidated Broadcasting.

BOLEN [obviously shocked:]

You *are*? With *what*, may I ask? You must know how steep it's going to be.

SPENSER

This is where you come in. We'll start with secured financing. You know the list of my companies. I want you to scout out reasonable collateral that I can siphon off of them. Give me complete numbers on that. Ought to be damn good—maybe enough so we can do without too much outside leverage. But we may have to use some junk, too, and there I want you to dig up the best risks on the market. I don't want any of that old pumped-up Drexel Burnham Lambert crap. Find me . . .

As Spenser continues to give directions to Bolen, we hear, softly at first, then coming up to drown out the talk, MUSIC OVER: *Schoenberg's Phantasy for Violin with Piano Accompaniment.* The piece's declarative melodies in the violin part, followed rather docilely by the piano, seem to suggest a new level of assurance in Spenser's ordering up of more and more numbers from Bolen.*

FADE INTO:

48. *June and Vera, practicing that very composition in the living room.* We see that there is now a proper bench—a fancy black-leather-upholstered one, capable of being raised and lowered—for the pianist. The pleasure on the two women's faces, as they play, speaks to the viewer/hearer along with the music.

Spenser walks into the room, pauses, listens a few moments, then approaches, holding his hands up in a command to stop.

SPENSER

I wanted you to know, girls, I've just sent out eighty invitations to the first recital. Next Wednesday. It'll be out on the grounds. There'll be a clambake first, and then you come on. I'm having a little stage built with plenty of room for the piano and both of you, and don't worry, there'll be super lighting. I'm wondering. Should we have printed programs?

JUNE

Isn't that a bit heavy? Why don't you be our announcer, Spense?

---

*Opus 47, Schoenberg's last instrumental work.

SPENSER

Oh, I couldn't do that!

But he says this in a way which makes the viewer realize that he probably will do it—and that it hasn't taken the violinist many days to get a pretty good read on her employer's mind.

CUT TO:

49. A luxurious corner office high in a tower in downtown Manhattan, with a sweeping view of Battery Park and the tip of the island and the Statue of Liberty down the bright waters of the harbor. This office is neo-minimalist in décor: a wide reach of bleached oak flooring, one pallid sofa on iron feet, four Italian molded chairs with seats generously cupped in the shape of the human fundament, and on the stark white walls three Jackson Pollocks. All of this seems to push the eye to the desk at the far end of the room—a huge slab of black lacquer with nothing on it but a single telephone. And behind the desk is the man we have seen as a subservient day-tripper on a dusty island driveway, and once even as a repairman in a soiled green jumpsuit: Mr. James Bolen. Here he sits in the lair of a managing director of the investment banking firm of Farraday, Simmer. He is in shirtsleeves; he wears suspenders with pictures of mermaids on them; the gems in the cuff links of his striped shirt look very much like sapphires. The phone on the desk purrs. Bolen picks it up.

BOLEN

Who? . . . What do they want with *me*? . . . All right, send 'em in.

Two men enter.

FIRST MAN

Mr. Bolen? I'm Wilson Curn, Deputy Chief of Investigations for the SEC. And this is Bruno Morano, Assistant U.S. Attorney here in Manhattan.

BOLEN [Waves to the men to sit down.]

What can I do to help you?

CURN

Exactly, Mr. Bolen. We've come to ask for your help. And we think you'll give it to us—

BOLEN

Of course! Of course!

CURN

—because Mr. Morano here has papers we are prepared to serve on you, with complaints which, if proven in court, could land you behind bars for most of the rest of your living days.

BOLEN [cool:]

I beg your pardon? Complaints?

CURN

We have indicted three of your suppliers of information, Mr. Bolen. Their names, in case you're interested, are Timberly, Kurtz, and Frankfort. [Bolen has turned pale.] Shall I say they've been singing your praises? Their songs have also suggested that there may be some even bigger fish in the sea than yourself, if you'll excuse the expression. . . .

Once again, MUSIC *drowns out a conversation: the beginning of Bartók's Rhapsody No. 1 for Violin and Piano. . . .*

CUT TO:

50. The living room of the Hat Hut. Spenser is talking with three islanders; all are standing. The man Spenser addresses seems to be the boss; he is in work clothes and wears rubber boots.

SPENSER

So what time'll you dig the pit?

CLAMBAKE BOSS

Early. We have to start the fire around ten o'clock, so the stones get really hot.

SPENSER

Maybe we better go out on the grounds—see where you want to put it.

The three move toward the door. As they pass the glass case, one of them, the young man with the red hair and beard (his eyes seem clear as a north-wind sky this morning), pauses and ogles Antonietta. Those clear eyes linger on the combination lock.

CUT TO:

51. Bolen on the phone at the black-lacquered slab in his office.

BOLEN

Mr. Ham? Jim Bolen.

SPENSER [thinned out by the phone:]

The name is Spenser, Jim. Do you have some numbers for me?

BOLEN

Yes, sir. Uh, Spen-sir. I was wondering. I got an invitation to your "Stradbake." I'd like to come—we could talk numbers afterwards—but I was wondering. Where should I stay? Is there an inn—?

SPENSER

Oh, hell, Jim, you'll be my houseguest. We're doing business with each other, aren't we? By the way, I've asked the Willsworths, too. Maybe we'll be able to nail the deal down.

BOLEN

Thanks, Spenser. I'll be there.

CUT TO:

52. *June and Vera rehearsing again, playing Hindemith's Sonata in E for Violin and Piano.* Spenser is sitting in one of the leonine couches, listening. *They come to the end of the short second movement.*

SPENSER

You guys are terrific. But the stuff you play is so—I don't know—I start from square one, with music—the stuff is sort of out of my ballpark. I love it when you play, but with me it's all eyes, you know. For me, it's watching. What I do like to watch is . . . is, well, partly, how you move, you know—your . . . frankly. . . . But no, sorry, forget it. Can I say this? The main thing I notice is how much you two love what you're doing. You glow. That really turns me on.

JUNE

Ah, Spense. If I could only explain to you how thrilling it is—with this! [She holds Antonietta high.] I have to struggle a bit with this lovely violin. Or, rather, I have a feeling that the violin struggles against me—that, like you, it might prefer a different . . . well . . . ballpark. But I'm stuck with my convictions, and I'm afraid I force them on Antonietta—and on you and everyone else. I'm hung up, let's say, on a few composers. Schoenberg, Hindemith, Bartók. There are others I love to play—Webern, Berg, some others—but those three are my favorites. They don't at all share a system, each went his own way, but I guess what they had in common—for me—is that they were, in a modest way, like Bach: they weren't satisfied with what the past gave them; they had to *invent*, they had to break new ground that was suitable for their century, their world. Schoenberg and Berg and Webern discovered the music for *our* world. The music we deserve in our world of numbers. They were a jump ahead of where we are now, when—all up and down the line, Spense—numbers have begun to beat the shit out of words. Ugly to say that? It's true, Spense, it's true. Think about it. Everything's programmed. The President of the United States doesn't think—he just asks what the polls are telling him. Look at all our bugaboos. The national debt. Interest rates. God, Spense, you're a number man. You showed us that machine in your office, with all those stock prices whizzing by. These musicians saw all this coming. They could count. That's really it, for me. The incredibly predictive math in their music. Ever heard of Babbitt?

SPENSER

Sure. Sinclair Lewis.

JUNE

No, I mean the composer—son of Schoenberg, metaphorically. He's jogged Schoenberg's musical numerology a few steps—or maybe I should say powers—further along. Listen. Babbitt's real father was an insurance actuary, so the boy grew up on figures. He was a math professor before he got serious about composing. He was the one who introduced all the terms from mathematics to explain the twelve-tone system that Schoenberg helped to invent: "pitch class," "source set," and all the rest. And, what's more, like the pop-music guys, he's taken to composing on the synthesizer. Final musical victory of the binary system. Things are getting really bizarre: the number one and the number zero have all the power now, they run all the programs in all the devices. What would be left of the power of words if we were reduced to just two of *them*? "Yes"? "No"? Where would we be, Spense?

SPENSER

Sounds as if you hate the music.

JUNE

No, no! Not at all! I respect it. I honor it. I feel that it's the absolute truth of our world. Music, you know, tells us the history of its times.

SPENSER

But you don't exactly love this stuff, do you?

JUNE

The truth is marvelous, but it's not always lovable, is it? Do you find our world lovable all the time?

VERA [interrupting:]

Never mind, Spenser. Don't pay any attention to June. You're dealing with a couple of fanatics—'cause I agree with her absolutely. We know what we like. You'll just have to accept us as we are.

SPENSER

Yeah, well, all I can say is, good luck tomorrow night!

CUT TO:

53. Spenser and Bolen walking in from the front door of the Hat Hut. A manservant follows, carrying Bolen's bag.

SPENSER

Great day like this, we better get right down to the beach.

BOLEN

Can't fight that idea!

THEN:

54. A guest room, where Bolen has just changed. Camera picks him up as he leaves the room in flowered trunks. Watching his departure, the camera has in its line of aim the overstuffed chair on which Bolen has hastily tossed his jacket as he undressed. Focus tightens on the chair. Something—perhaps his closing the door with a slight slam—causes the jacket to slip off the back of the chair and fall to the floor. Camera closes on inner breast pocket, which has been exposed in the fall. We see the black tip of some kind of electronic device, and a thin wire running from it up into the lining of the jacket near the lapel.

The MUSIC *Spenser heard the two rehearsing now comes up*, and we see:

55. The recital scene. The evening is foggy. *June and Vera are performing the Hindemith E-major sonata on a crude spotlit stage, left.* Camera sweeps to the right over a wide meadow, with a thicket of sapling oaks beyond it. Many round tables, littered with paper

plates and plastic glasses, are scattered on the grass, with guests disposed around them, the lights over the stage glimmering dimly on them through the mist. To far right, the clambake crew, which includes the redhead, is cleaning up its gear; we can hear occasional faint clattering of their pans. We also hear many guests, who, it seems, have taken that third, and even perhaps fourth, drink, talking loudly. MUSIC *up, as if in an effort to shush these intrusive sounds. The piece comes to an end.* There is a spattering of halfhearted clapping. *June and Vera next play Anton Webern's "Four Pieces,"* each quirky part of which, peppered with silences, lasts only a matter of seconds.* By the time this selection is over, almost all the guests are talking with each other; they have stopped listening. *The performers close the program with the Schoenberg "Phantasy" we have earlier heard them rehearsing.* At the end there is no applause at all, and June and Vera stumble down off the platform and hurry, almost running, into the house.

CLOSE IN ON:

56. One of the tables. This is obviously the table of honor. Spenser, Flora Lombard, the Willsworths, the Coverly Pattersons, and Jim Bolen.

FLORA

You just can't have them play such *hostile* music, darling.

SPENSER

It's their shtick, Flora, I can't help that.

PATTERSON

Why no American composers? I mean, someone like Virgil Thomson? Or, goodness, Copland! Or if you're going to insist on this atonal or twelve-tonal or whatever assault

---

*Opus 7.

on our ears, there's a fine American tradition in that line. Why not Babbitt? Or Cage? At the very least.

BOLAN

Heck, I like country music. You know, a little Nashville on Martha's Vineyard? Why not try that?

CUT TO:

57. June's guest room. Vera is on one bed, crying. June, sitting on the edge of the other bed, has Antonietta on her lap, and a string of Christmas-tree lights, which she must have asked Spenser to get her, in her hands. She wants to dry the fog out of Antonietta. She carefully inserts a couple of the tiny bulbs deep in each of the *f*-holes. Then she plugs the string in. The little lights twinkle.

JUNE

I know, Vera, it was awful. But let's wait and see what happens. I believe in this fiddle, and I believe in the way I played it—and the way you played, too. I'll bet that more than you think got through to those creeps. Let's just see what tomorrow brings.

There is a knock on the door. Spenser walks in without waiting to be admitted. Vera sits up, daubing at her eyes with the backs of her hands. June stands.

SPENSER

Listen, girls. It was damn good. . . . I mean to say, look, the whole thing was my fault. I did a big boo-boo. Having the clambake was just plain dumb. Half the people were fried. Never mind. We'll have a proper recital next time—inside, and first thing. Before drinks.

JUNE

Thank you, Spense. You're a nice man. But will anyone come?

SPENSER

Don't worry. We'll get 'em. I have an idea how. Tell you later. . . . You won't forget to lock Antonietta up in the case, will you?

JUNE

When I'm sure it's dry.

VERA [snuffling:]

Thanks, Spense.

FADE TO:

58. Next day. MONTAGE of quick images:

¶ Spenser and Bolen working a hard sell on Willsworth in the living room of the Hut.

¶ Flora Lombard telling Spenser on the phone that she will invest a quarter of a million in ConBroad, "for your sake, darling."

¶ Coverly Patterson buying a 60-foot yawl at the Martha's Vineyard Shipyard; he doesn't quarrel over the asking price.

¶ Anchorman Rod Millson (whose face we saw at the Stradbake), in his house at Edgartown, arguing on the phone with his agent about what he should get in his next year's contract: he wants two million six; his agent thinks two and a quarter is already through the roof.

¶ Randolph Sorr, the author (he was there), writing a check at the closing on his purchase of six acres on Edgartown Great Pond.

[The images now come faster and faster:]

¶ . . . woman signing off on a mortgage at the Martha's Vineyard National Bank; man talking significant numbers into a phone; pair of hands counting out fifty-dollar bills; Spenser's Quotron spinning out market quotations, which move at great speed across the screen-within-the-screen . . .

FADE TO:

59. Spenser again walking past the International Bazaar in Freeport, carrying the violin case; camera follows him to door of Banque de Chine Suisse. . . .

60. Nighttime. Spenser's room, this time in the Oceanus. Lights are dimmed. Spenser in a king-size bed, with June and Vera under the covers on either side of him. No sign of pajamas or nightgowns. Sheets are discreetly drawn up over the musicians' breasts. The three are passing a joint back and forth. They take deep draws. They are laughing their heads off. This goes on wordlessly for some time.

THEN:

SPENSER

Hey! Hey! You want to know why they're all going to come to the next recital? Why they're going to be breaking the doors down to get in? [He throws his head back and laughs hard.]

JUNE [giggling:]

Why, Spensie? I wanna know why!

SPENSER

Because I'm going to buy you girls the biggest audience you ever had.

JUNE [horrified:]

You're *what?*

SPENSER [with bursts of laughter:]

All right, you don't like that, my first idea to draw a crowd was to have you gals play a recital topless.

JUNE [furious:]

Fat chance, big boy. For*get* it.

VERA

Spenser, that's so gross!

SPENSER

What's so bad about that? Look at you now.

JUNE

Come on, Spense, we're just having some fun. We like you. But in front of those stuffy people on the Vineyard? Have you lost your mind?

SPENSER

We could do a lot worse, believe me. But listen. I got this other idea in the casino last night. I was playing blackjack, remember?—and the house's golden arm dealt me a ace down and a king up, and I gave you two a peek at the ace over my shoulder, remember? Bang!—it came to me right then. What a ace recital we're going to have!

June and Vera look uncomprehendingly at each other across Spenser and rock back against their pillows, feeling weightless again, giving up giggles that rise like bubbles in soda water.

SPENSER

Here's what I'm going to do. I'm going to invite everyone, it's to a recital, the Strad and the Steinway, see—numbers music, like you say—and I'm going to tell them there'll be—surprise, surprise!—a number issued to each person at the door when they come in. Like lottery tickets. And at the end, after you finish wowing them with *your* numbers, there'll be a drawing, twenty-five-thousand-dollar first prize, fifteen-thousand runner-up. How you like them cookies, huh? Think they'll come?

June looks just as angry as she did when she heard Spenser's original idea.

JUNE

I can't be*lieve* what you're saying, Spenser. You want us to be in some cheap damn game show? Let's get out of here, Vera.

SPENSER

Don't be in such a hurry. You haven't heard the kicker. I'm going to pay you each ten thousand dollars for this one.

JUNE

Christ, Spenser. Can't you see that just makes it *worse?* We're musicians. There's no way you're going to hire us for your shitty show-off act. So much money. It's disgusting.

SPENSER

It just shows how much I value you.

JUNE

So you've put a price on us, just like on everything else? You really are a numskull. It's so *vulgar*. Come on, Vera.

Vera gives up a tiny residual giggle, over which she evidently has no control, but she leans forward to get up and leave at June's urging. Something muddy has happened to Spenser's face at the word "vulgar"—his lips are bent out of shape. But very soon they relax and modulate into a grin; we see that a fast little note is about to be imprinted on the stave of actions on that membrane in his mind.

SPENSER

Wait!

He crawls out of bed, over Vera's body. He is wearing boxer shorts. He goes to the bureau and opens a drawer. He picks up in both hands several stacks of hundreds, and holds them up for the two to see. And:

SPENSER

Here it is, kids. Fresh lettuce! All yours . . .

MUSIC *comes up*:

61. *The two women are rehearsing again in the living room of the Hut. They are playing Milton Babbitt's vivacious, riddling "Sextets," with its teasing pitches and pregnant silences and explosive bursts from ppppp to fffff and back again.* Vera is crying. June notices:

JUNE

Snap out of it, Vera. So maybe there won't be another recital. Don't take it so hard. It's just a job. He hasn't fired us yet.

VERA

That's not it. That's not it at all. Damn it, I don't know how to tell you this, June. It's my mother. She went—it was about a month ago—she went for a Pap test, and bingo: positive. Cervical cancer. And bad. She doesn't have beans. Not a bit of insurance—she didn't work, you know, so she'd have had to buy some sky-high individual policy. She's not old enough for Medicare. What I'm saying . . . Oh, fuck, I can't say it.

JUNE

You need that money he offered us.

VERA

I need it. I really need it. I have to help her, June. You've got to help *me*.

JUNE [after a long pause:]

Of course, Vera. I'll tell him we'll do his lousy show.

Sound of MUSIC *comes up again: reprise of the Babbitt.*

62. Camera has moved outside and above ground level, staring for a moment at the part of the Hat Hut from which the music is presumably coming. Then it draws back and back (copter shot) and up and up and up, until the whole of Martha's Vineyard spreads itself out, a great green triangle with many ragged indentations of the variegated blues of its ponds. MUSIC *fades,* and we hear voices in a rapid AUDIO MONTAGE:

¶ I got your invitation to a "Chamber Music and Pot," darling. I'll be there. I'll wear my lucky pants!

¶ Do you know Ben and Judy Munson, Spense? We'd asked them to dinner that night? May we bring them?

¶ Did you think to ask the Doolittles? They're crazy about modern music.

¶ Yeah, I heard about it! Would you be willing to ask Spense for us if he'd—?

¶ Where can I get tickets? . . . It's by invi*ta*tion?

¶ Coverly promised to see whether . . .

¶ Whit Kerry said he'd ask . . .

¶ You going? How'd you . . .

And much more such, the sounds rising like waves of heat radiation from—it seems—the whole island.

Voices finally FADE TO:

63. Dawn, a few days later. The POV is that of the camera out on the hat brim. June in her tank suit and Vera in her bikini hurry out of the Hut and disappear down the stairway over the cliffside. . . . We see their dolphin-like exuberance in an early-morning dip. The beach is otherwise deserted. . . . They climb back up. . . . The camera follows them in the front door, along the hallway. As they start through the living room, June suddenly stops.

JUNE

Look! My God!

She points at the glass case. The access panel hangs open. The violin is not there.

JUNE [starts shouting:]

Spenser! Spenser! Spenser!

Both women dash upstairs. They burst into Spenser's bedroom and wake him.

JUNE

Spenser! Wake up! Do you have Antonietta?

SPENSER [groggily:]

Certainly not! Get out of here!

JUNE

It's gone, Spense! I locked it up last night. It's gone!

CUT TO:

64. Spenser on his cellular phone, a few hours later, out on the brim.

SPENSER

Flora? Listen. I'm having to call off the recital.

FLORA

Word get around? The State Lottery Commission move in on you?

SPENSER

No, no, nothing like that. The violin's been stolen.

FLORA

Oh, darling, that's horrible! I'm so sorry. When did it happen?

SPENSER

Some time after midnight last night. June—you know, the violin girl—says she locked it up just about then.

FLORA

Are the police any help?

SPENSER

It had to be a pro. No fingerprints at all. And someone who knew how to puzzle a really good combo lock. Tricky stuff. God, Flora, I've got about two hundred people invited for Wednesday night. Both girls are on the phone. They have my list, but I don't know if I wrote 'em all down. People have been calling day and night to wedge friends in. Would you tell anyone you see? . . .

SMASH CUT TO:

65. Bolen's office. Jim Bolen stands by a window, staring out. The view to the south is obscured by mist. Curn of the SEC and Morano of the U.S. Attorney's office are seated by the lacquered slab.

BOLEN

What kind of a plea are you offering me?

CURN

Depends. We're going to have to see how much more you can get for us. Your first tapes were excellent. But we need more. We have to be rock solid. When will you be seeing Ham again?

BOLEN

I was supposed to go up day after tomorrow, but he called off the affair he'd planned.

CURN

Do you think he's getting suspicious? Of you?

BOLEN

No, he had to cancel for other reasons.

CURN

When you do go up, is there any danger of his discovering you're wired? You say he has a slew of servants. And those girls, those musicians. Could any of them—

BOLEN

I wasn't born yesterday, Mr. Curn. . . . Now, about the plea . . .

JUMP CUT TO:

66. Manhattan. Subway station at Sixty-eighth and Lexington. Evening rush hour. A train comes in with a roar. Doors slide open. Noise, as people pour out, of footsteps, and of generators under the subway cars. *Through the clatter and the shuffling, thinly at first, then gradually coming* UP AND OVER, *we hear strains of the Bartók Solo Violin Sonata, which we have previously heard.* Walking camera (POV of one of the exiting passengers) moves along the platform. *Although imperfectly played, the* MUSIC, *in a steady crescendo, develops a magnetic power.* The lens picks up, from a distance, against the station wall of soiled tiles, blocked now and then by hurrying figures, the sight of a man playing a violin. As the POV passenger approaches, he sees that the violinist is a flaming redhead, dressed in a plain white T-shirt and jeans. At the player's feet, an open violin case. The POV eyes see a woman just ahead reaching in her pocketbook as she goes past the violinist; she drops a quarter into the case. The POV passenger himself pauses, and we sense that he, too, is dropping a coin. Camera holds on the violinist as the rest of the crowd goes by, with quite a few of New York's usually numbed and indifferent homegoers responding to the hypnotic appeal of the violin, tossing coins as if into a lucky fountain of wishes in a faraway dream city. . . . The station is gradually emptied. The violinist stops playing, bends forward, literally tosses the violin down into the case, its back

falling right onto the stack of change. He clips the bow in place, closes the case without removing the coins from the back of the violin, picks the case up, and leaves.

CUT TO:

67. Maillon's office, Grand Bahama.

SPENSER

How much do you have in my account now?

MAILLON

Something over one hundred twenty million.

SPENSER

Now pay attention, Pierre. I have to put that money to work. I'm taking over Consolidated Broadcasting, and I don't want to resort to any more junk than I have to. I want you to wash that money clean for me. Send it to your headquarters in Geneva and set it up in half a dozen different numbered accounts. Then move them in small takes to twenty different banks in the States, all in the Northeast, deposited in my name. I don't want you to send statements to me on any of this through the mail; I'll come down sometime and check over all that paper myself. That clear?

MAILLON

Not to worry, Monsieur. Your money will be *nettoyé à sec*—how you say? Dry clean? Beautiful!

CUT TO:

68. Lincoln Center, Manhattan. Sunny afternoon. The redhead has set himself up on a sidewalk near Avery Fisher Hall. *He is*

again playing the Bartók. It may be surprising to an out-of-town viewer to see how many disenchanted New York pedestrians drop coins in the violin case—*the* MUSIC, *even though it is badly played, seems to pull the change right out of pockets and purses.* Camera takes long view of a thin, wiry man approaching; it is one of those telelens pictures of a walking person who never seems to get any closer. At last the viewer sees that it is, of all people, Ducket Jones. (It will not be until after the show is over that the viewer will be struck by what a wild coincidence that was; then he/she will shrug and think, Oh hell, that's television for you.) *The* MUSIC *is insistent*; it seems to be the engine of Jones's walking. Now he is closing in. He walks past the violinist without turning his head. Five or six paces beyond the redhead, he suddenly stops. He turns back. He cocks his head, listening; then we see him move in to look more closely at the violin. Camera takes his POV, and zooms in on the near side—the belly—of the instrument, which moves up and down with the redhead's bowing; focus closes tight on flaw near the purfling on the belly. POV backs away, drops to the case at the player's feet, draws away to look at Jones. We see him casually take out his pocketbook; he slips out a dollar bill and drops it in the case. He walks nonchalantly around the corner, camera following him. As soon as he is out of the redhead's sight, though, he runs. He hurries into the lobby of an apartment building, where he talks a doorman into letting him use a phone. . . .

CUT BACK TO:

69. Redhead has moved to the steps of Avery Fisher Hall. Siren is heard OVER *his Bartók.* Patrol car appears, overhead lights flashing. Redhead drops the violin into the case, abandoning it, and runs. Two policemen jump out of the car and chase him. One of them overtakes him within a block, puts him up against a parked car, reads him his rights, cuffs him, and walks him back to the patrol car.

THEN:

70\. Headquarters of the 20th Police Precinct, West Eighty-second Street. Redhead being booked. Ducket Jones, who is carrying the violin, is elucidating the charge to the duty officer.

FADE TO:

71\. Ducket Jones on the phone in an apartment, which we assume is his. Antonietta, in the open case, is on a coffee table in front of him.

JONES

Well, it was just instinctual, you know. The boy played sloppily, but the tone—it just had to be a fine instrument. Then I saw the little chipped-out place.

SPENSER [his voice in thinned telephone timbre:]
Good work, friend. Is the fiddle okay?

JONES

The back is badly scratched, and the whole fiddle's horribly dirty—resin and, I don't know, sweat and grime. With your permission, I'd like to turn it over to Wurlitzer to be restored. Of course it'll have to be on hand for the trial. But that won't be for maybe a month or two. They say it can be returned to you in the meanwhile. How far do you want to press the case?

SPENSER

All the way. Every inch of the way. I want the son of a bitch put away in the joint. Behind steel bars.

CUT TO:

72\. Maillon's office in Freeport. He is on the phone:

MAILLON

How dare you, Monsieur? . . . What do you say your name is? Boolen? . . . Don't you know we have secrecy laws in the Bahamas? It is strictly forbidden for me to give you that information. . . . I would have to refer you to Geneva. . . . Ah . . . Ah . . . I see. . . . *Alors*, yes, yes, in that case . . . Yes, I cooperate. . . . He was here last week. . . . Code name for our use, Bifteck . . . Yes, I give you numbers. . . .

CUT TO:

73. The living room of the Hat Hut. Ducket Jones is seen entering; he has brought Antonietta from New York. Spenser greets him. June and Vera are beside the Steinway. Jones takes the case to the piano and places it there. He steps back to let June open it and take the instrument out. Spenser and Vera crowd in as she lifts it and turns the back up to look it over. There is no sign of the scratches. The belly glistens as it did when June was giving it TLC. She nods to Vera, who sits at the piano. *They begin playing Hindemith's "Meditation," from his* Nobilissima Visione, *and we can hear—we can see from June's zest as she plays—that Antonietta's voice is as rich as ever.*

SPENSER [elated, OVER the MUSIC:]

We're on, kids! I'll send out the invites for next Wednesday.

JUNE

Oh, God.

MUSIC *comes to an end*, THEN:

74. June puts Antonietta in the glass case and locks the access panel. (We see that a new, larger, and more complex combination

lock has been installed.) Spenser flicks a switch; the lights in the case go up, and the violin slowly revolves. The four stand and admire it in silence. As they stare at Antonietta, the camera stares at them. Look at them. They are satisfied by their roles. They must know that the program they are in (or whatever it is) is preposterous, yet they seem to feel completely at home in it. Maybe they are happy just to be on camera, since they must know that TV sets the patterns of life these days. The camera closes on the woman who plays the role of playing Antonietta. It is possible to see in her handsome face, along with her adoration of the violin, signs of traits which may, in the cruelty of time, cut ugly lines in her skin: the stubbornness that makes her insist on playing such unsparing music; a fierce ambition; an undercurrent of doubt whether she has all the gifts of a champion. The viewer will wonder, Is this good acting, or is it the truth of the woman?

CUT TO:

75. The main doorway of the Hat Hut. A sunny midafternoon. Guests are arriving. We see that quite a crowd of them is backed up, out on the brim. The bottleneck, in the doorway, is caused by Spenser, who is himself issuing to the invitees, one by one, bits of paper with numbers printed on them. The camera CLOSES on his hand, giving them out, and, with glimpses at the slips, we see that he has gone to the very great trouble of arranging the numbers in random order, presumably for the sake of a gambler's sense that confusion equals a fair shake. Lens backs off to see Flora Lombard take a number from Spenser and accept a kiss on her cheek.

SPENSER

There's a seat with your name on a card on it, in the front row.

FLORA

How sweet. Draw my number, darling!

76. Camera walks (Flora's POV) into the living room. It is already jammed. Except for the piano and its bench, and a table off to the left of them, the furniture has all been removed, with its burden of stealable jade and books; even the pictures have been taken down from the walls. We are, in short, in Spenser Ham's approximation of a burglarproof concert hall. The guests are seating themselves in rows of folding chairs; soon the chairs are all taken, and quite a few people are obliged to stand back against the walls and even in the hallway. All are in their summer best—except for two men, seated far back, who are wearing dark business suits; one of them has a briefcase on his lap. The oval room is full of a hum of expectant conversation.

77. June and Vera are nervously waiting in the Hut's elegant downstairs bathroom, which has Magritte figures in bowler hats—mute, enigmatic witnesses of folly—scattered up and down its wallpaper. June is warming up, playing runs and arpeggios on Antonietta. Spenser comes in, so pleased with himself that he appears to be six inches off the ground, a flying messenger of good news—Mercury on winged feet. Touching down by the dresser, he bends over and pulls out of a drawer two big bundles of cash, one almost twice as large as the other. June turns away from the sight of the money; she cannot hide her repugnance. Vera, on the other hand, squeezes out a tentative smile at Spenser.

SPENSER

Ready, my angels? I'll announce you, and then you're on.

Spenser leaves the room, and we hear, out there, a sudden cry of delight, a choral yip like that of many people having simultaneously taken a bite of something delicious; the audience must have seen what Spenser is carrying.

BACK TO:

78. The living room. Spenser walks across behind the piano to the table at one side. He sets down the stacks of money. On the table is a big lottery drum full of bits of paper; in his exuberance, Spenser, grinning, gives the drum handle a turn, and the slips flutter within. The audience laughs and claps. But Spenser, suddenly serious, raises a hand as if to take an oath, promising the whole truth.

SPENSER

Good afternoon, friends. I want to welcome you all. We've gathered for a very special recital this afternoon—and I think we're in for a marvelous treat. Our musicians are June Speckman, on the Stradivarius, and Vera Flamm, on the Steinway. They'll play just one number, Hindemith's Second Violin Sonata in D. This is difficult music, both to play and to listen to, though Ms. Speckman tells me that this music is much more merciful, as she put it, than what she and Ms. Flamm played for you last time. She tells me the composer wrote this when he was only twenty-three, before he'd turned more bluntly away from the past and became more strident and shocking. I shouldn't try to say any more, because I'm way over my head with all this. I'm just telling you what she said. But anyhow, I know that this is music these two musicians care a lot about, and that's what matters. I think you'll find that in their hands it's beautiful. And I'm positive you'll find that they themselves are very much so.

APPLAUSE, the sound of which continues as:

79. In the bathroom, June and Vera have heard Spenser's introduction. We can see that June is grateful that he has at least had the tact not to mention what will follow. She tucks Antonietta under her arm, and she and Vera go out.

More good-natured welcoming APPLAUSE.

80. Beside the piano. June—her face is crimson—nods to Vera; she is ready to start.

Vera's face is seen; in contrast to June's, it is as white as a page of sheet music as she nods a response to June. She looks down at the keyboard.

The MUSIC *begins.* In the first few bars,

the knowing listener hears a delicate tremor in Antonietta's voice, different from, superimposed on, June's vibrato. This is a report, one can guess, of a quivering of her nerves; perhaps she is angry at the position Spenser has put her and Vera in. Before long, however, we sense that her musicianship has begun to take control; the tone smooths out.

As the duo continues, the camera turns away, from time to time, to look at faces in the audience. Spenser is enthralled; there is a touching simplicity, even a kind of purity, in his frankly visual enjoyment of the performance; the music flies far over his head like a jet stream only remotely affecting his internal weather. We see in his gaze, however, how much he has come to like those two for what they really are. On Flora Lombard's face there is a look of cynical amusement; she knows what has brought people into this room. Coverly Patterson obviously hates the foreign music so much that he can't even look at the performers, and one can guess that he thinks the lottery drum seriously untraditional at a New England chamber music recital. Bolen has cheeks of wood. On quite a few faces it is hard to differentiate between the responses to what is seen and heard and what is expected to follow. It is clear, though, that for the moment some in the audience are borne off by the music into thoughts that have little to do with what is on the table off to the left. Perhaps—besides being stirred by the bizarre power of the music and the real beauty of the players—they are moved by the way the violinist and the pianist seem, as they play on, less and less aware of anything but what Hindemith is telling them.

BLURRED CUT TO:

81. The final movement of the sonata, a fast-moving scherzo, which is almost a kind of dance. We see that by this time a sea change has set in. Hindemith's news for the performers no longer matters much, for all have begun to listen instead to what the violin itself has to say. *As the scherzo spins on*, we see the faces in the audience turn more and more often to their left. Spenser, lured by Antonietta into the secret places of his own nature, looks keyed up to a new level of joy over his munificence. Flora opens and closes the big pocketbook in her lap, as if to make sure it has plenty of room for possibilities. Coverly Patterson, glancing leftward now and again, seems grudgingly ready to allow a minor revision in the lore of New England musical salons. Bolen, probably without knowing he is doing it, pats his left inside breast pocket, where he's wired, and then the right breast pocket, where his wallet is. Antonietta urges big dreams. Many in the audience have begun shamelessly making eyes at Lady Luck. One can readily see that some are contingently considering choices—

whether a Jaguar wouldn't fit better on the Vineyard than a Daimler, for instance—while others, more estate-minded, are reviewing prospects in the wheat, silver, and uranium futures markets. Soon every eye in the house is riveted on the table off to the left.

The music tumbles to its conclusion. Wild APPLAUSE breaks out. The Antonietta Strad has done its destined work. Everyone is clapping in honor of the beautiful money.

82. Spenser stands and goes to the table. *He* is clapping for *his* musicians. As he turns to the audience, the camera CLOSES on his face, on which the violin has brought out a rapturous look of prosperity and self-satisfaction. We see, shining in his eyes—at last!—a conviction that on the staves on that imaginary membrane in his mind there is written music at least as coherent, wise, and of this world as anything an impoverished kid like Hindemith could write.

SPENSER

Could we have two volunteers, to come up here and make certain that this drawing will be absolutely fair and square?

At once, with alacrity, before anyone else can stir, the two men in business suits rise and step quickly up the center aisle. The camera follows them from behind, so that the viewer cannot see their faces. Clearly visible, however, is a look of surprise blooming on Spenser's face; the recently heard melody suddenly seems to be leaking out of his soul. When the men are close to the table behind which Spenser stands, the one holding the briefcase puts a foot up on the edge of a chair, balances the briefcase on his upraised thigh, opens it, and takes some papers out, which he hands to the other man. The camera moves around to take in the two men.

MORANO [offering the papers:]

I have been instructed to serve you with these, sir. You have the right to remain silent. Any statement you make can and will be used against you in court. You have the right to be represented by an attorney. [The viewer sees Morano trying to keep from smirking as he delivers the obligatory final *Miranda* statement of Spenser Ham's rights:] If you are indigent and cannot afford a lawyer, one will be appointed to represent you.

The audience, which obviously thinks that Spenser has staged this as part of his show, breaks out laughing and clapping. During Morano's mumbling, however, Curn has moved around behind Spenser. He looks down as he opens the jaws of a pair of handcuffs.

Morano picks up the money on the table, and the two men, each taking one of Spenser's arms, march the arrestee down the aisle and out of the room.

83. The camera swings and looks at the audience. There is a kind of explosion of the communal spirit as the guests realize that there will be no drawing. The money has vanished. Swollen hopes are on the rocks. All that Antonietta had roused in these guests is suddenly released in a flame of outrage. The room vibrates with frustrated avarice. There is a mass growl. People are on their feet. Many valuable things in this house are surely going to be smashed.

But suddenly we see that June has taken Antonietta under her chin again. The camera zooms in for a sudden close look—what does this mean?—at the Cupid on the tailpiece. And we hear, clear and decisive above the uproar:

This is the first bold declaration by the violin of the Schoenberg theme music of the program. June has Antonietta speak, to begin with, sharply. Vera accompanies, forte, playing a piano reduction of the orchestral score of the concerto. The cheated audience is still on its feet, and at first the music is interrupted by angry shouts. Now we see June play with exultation. Antonietta counts out the composer's tonal digits, which are arranged with systematized care. There is a strict discipline in the sounds that ring out from the violin now, and with remarkable speed, within a few measures, the hubbub subsides. Flora Lombard in the front row, shaking her head in bewilderment, sits down. Others settle down near her. Soon the entire audience is seated again.

Now there comes another subtle change in the timbre of the music from the violin. Gradually the afternoon air softens. We become aware of the brightness of the light pouring in the windows. Fury slinks out of the room. There soon seems to be a tug at everyone's senses of something that feels like yearning. The camera turns to the audience. The faces—so soon!—are beginning to show that these listeners are drifting off into summertime daydreams, fantasies about pleasures of kinds that money just can't buy. Who would have imagined that anything by Arnold Schoenberg could be *erotic*? But look! People are giving each other melting glances. Some couples are actually reaching out to hold hands. . . .

One more recital number in the long life of Antonietta, an encore, is proving to be an overpowering success. . . .

84. Helicopter shot. The Hat Hut fills the screen. We see three men emerge arm in arm from the front door and hurry out over the brim. They walk briskly down a few yards of the driveway and get into a black limousine, which slowly pulls away.

As the Schoenberg theme swells into full orchestral clamor, the camera view pulls up and out, up and away, in reciprocal symmetry with the opening shot of the program, until, finally, we see exactly what we saw at the very beginning: an azure sky with cotton clouds, the serene promontory, and a stretch of the silver-blue sea riffled with numberless wavelets.

FADE OUT AUDIO

BLACK OUT video

Finale

Spenser Ham thought at first that he was being arrested on a charge of sponsoring illegal gambling, or something of the sort. It took only a quick glance at the papers in his hands to disabuse him of that idea. He was taken to the Dukes County jail in Edgartown.

It happened that the notorious redhead, whose name was Bill Stroop, had been remanded to the Dukes County jurisdiction for trial because his theft of Antonietta had been committed on the Vineyard, and for one night he and Spenser Ham were, so to speak, brothers in their toils. They were in separate cells, however, so they were deprived of a conversation in which both of them, for quite different reasons, doubtless would have used colorful language.

The morning after his arrest, Ham was released on his own recognizance by Judge Philip Bronson, pending his arraignment in Federal Court in Boston. June Speckman and Vera Flamm had left the island. One of the first things Spenser Ham did after he reached home was to write two checks for ten thousand dollars. All of his bank accounts, however, had already been seized by the government.

He showed up for his Boston arraignment with his attorney, Blaine Sopher, of the New York firm of Will, Burnham & Sopher. Ham was charged with seven felony counts, the most serious of which stemmed from various instances of his insider trading, and from some impressive income tax evasion. Sopher was later able to arrange a plea bargain for him, under which he avoided trial by acknowledging guilt on three relatively minor counts. He was eventually sentenced to two years in prison, and he was fined fifty million dollars—which Wall Streeters seemed to consider a humdrum punishment for a humdrum offense.

Spenser Ham's inside source, Bolen, whose cooperation with the investigators had helped bring indictments against four other men besides Ham, was sentenced to only three months in prison and was fined a pittance of two hundred thousand dollars.

Thanks to the fact that Beverly Robbins, a member of the Board of the Boston Symphony, was in the audience at Spenser Ham's recital, the violinist June Speckman was invited to audition for the orchestra. Spenser Ham had asked Blaine Sopher to try to pry loose enough money to cover his checks to the musicians, and it was also at Ham's request that June was allowed to play Antonietta for her audition. The decision on whether she will be hired is due soon. If she is in fact hired, Vera Flamm hopes to move to Boston with her and find work as a teacher of music theory and piano in one of the many colleges in the area. Sopher did succeed recently in clearing the ten-thousand-dollar checks. June, who stubbornly said she wouldn't take money for an occasion devoted to money, endorsed her check over to Vera. The resultant twenty thousand is paying for radiation treatments for Vera's mother.

Spenser Ham's lawyers arranged to have Antonietta put up for auction by Parke-Bernet in New York. I am happy to say that I, the author of this book, am now the proud owner of the instrument whose biography I have been at such pains to record. I was able to make this purchase (the price was $440,000) with the funds advanced to me for this book by my publisher.

And I promise, dear reader, that that whopper is the very last lie I will ever tell (in this book, anyway).

NOTE

I want to thank Linda Ciacchi, who at the time of this writing is a doctoral candidate at the Yale Music School, a Prize Teaching Fellow in Yale College, and a first violinist with the New Haven Symphony Orchestra, for her perceptive help in scouting out from Yale University's network of libraries, for me, a large number of informative works, among which I should mention a few in particular. It goes without saying that none of the many books and monographs and magazine articles that I perused for background can be held responsible for the liberties I have taken.

Among numerous works on the history and construction of violins I should take special note of George Hart's *The Violin, its Famous Makers and their Imitators* (1875); Edward Heron-Allen's *Violin Making as it was and is* (1884); and Joseph Wechsberg's delightful book *The Glory of the Violin* (1972). The most authoritative of several works on Stradivari's craftsmanship (very little is known about his life) is that by W. Henry, Arthur F., and Alfred E. Hill (1902), of the London family of luthiers, restorers, and dealers. Among sources of instruction on the subject of violin acoustics, I had the benefit of writings by Carleen M. Hutchins and Isaac Vigdorchik. Mozart's letters have been edited by Hans Mersmann and translated by M. M. Bozman (1928), and far more completely by Emily Anderson (1938), and I revisited books on Mozart and his music by W. J. Turner (1938), Alfred Einstein (1945), and Erich Schenk (1959). I had the help of Berlioz's memoirs, translated by Rachel and Eleanor Holmes (1932), and biographies of him by W. J. Turner (1934), Jacques Barzun (1949), and D. Kern Holoman (1989). Besides Stravinsky's autobiography (1936) and selected letters (1982–85), I am grateful to C. F. Ramuz's *Souvenirs sur Igor Strawinsky* (1946); to a study of Stravinsky and his compositions by Eric Walter White (1966); to four of the several works on Stravinsky written by Robert Craft with the active help of the composer (1959, 1960, 1962, 1966); and to *Stravinsky in Pictures and Documents*, assembled by Craft and Vera Stravinsky (1978). And I think I must have left the Key West library's massive *New Grove Dictionary of Music and Musicians* in shreds.

A NOTE ABOUT THE AUTHOR

John Hersey was born in Tientsin, China, in 1914. He began taking violin lessons there when he was eight years old, from a White Russian emigré, who later moved to the United States and played for decades with the Boston Symphony. Hersey's family returned to the United States in 1925. He studied at Yale and Cambridge universities, served for a time as Sinclair Lewis's secretary, and then worked several years as a journalist. He has had published fifteen books of fiction and nine books of reportage and essays, and has won the Pulitzer Prize for fiction. He is married and has five children and six grandchildren. He divides his time between Key West and Martha's Vineyard.

A NOTE ON THE TYPE

The text of this book was set in Garamond No. 3, a modern rendering of the type first cut by Claude Garamond (1510–1561). Garamond was a pupil of Geoffroy Troy and is believed to have based his letters on Venetian models, although he introduced a number of important differences, and it is to him we owe the letter which we know as old style. He gave to his letters a certain elegance and a feeling of movement that won for their creator an immediate reputation and the patronage of Francis I of France.

Composition by Crane Typesetting Service, Inc.
West Barnstable, Massachusetts
Printing and binding by The Haddon Craftsmen, Inc.
Scranton, Pennsylvania
Music examples by Irmgard Lochner
Typography and binding design
by Dorothy S. Baker

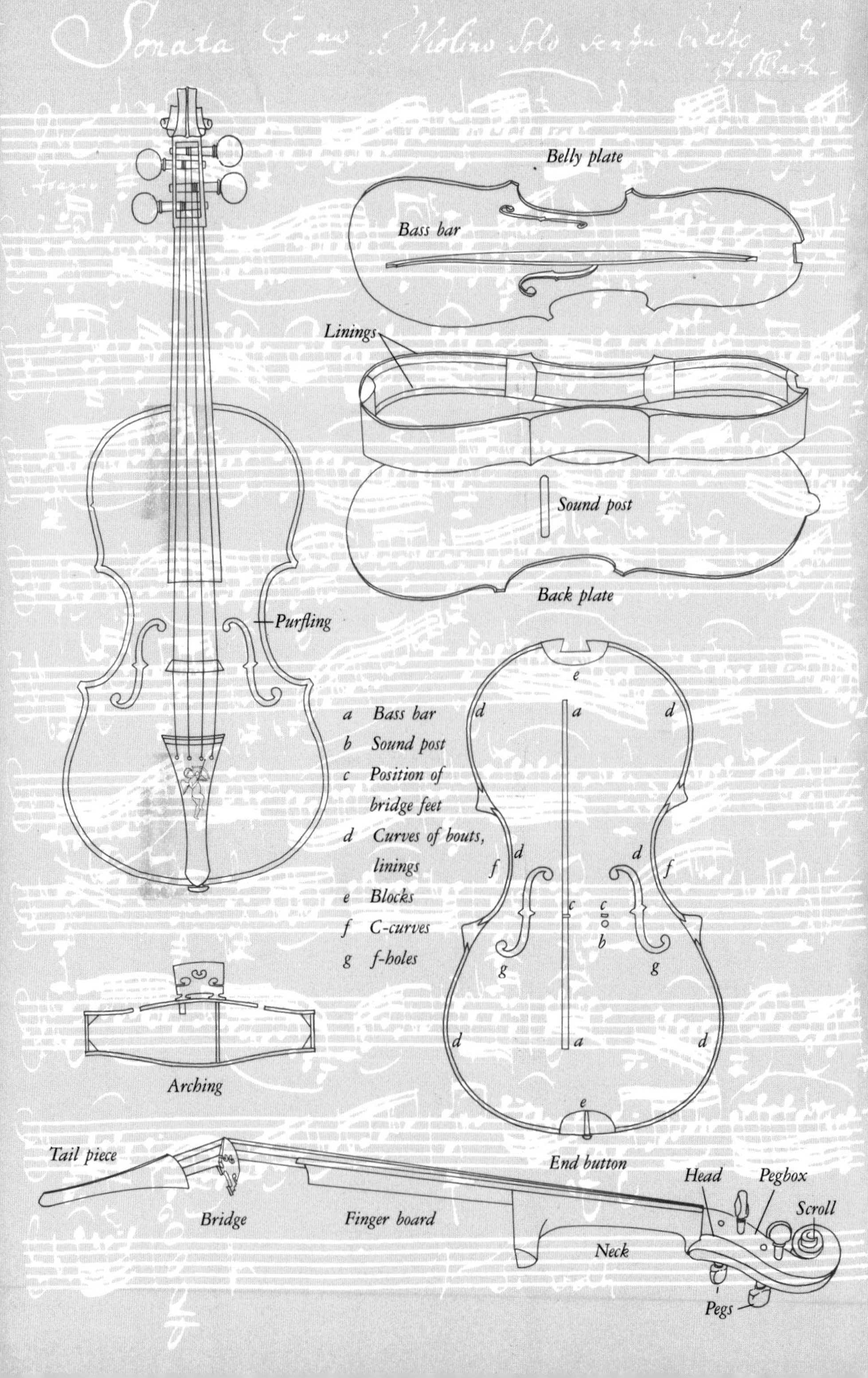

Belly plate

Bass bar

Linings

Sound post

Back plate

Purfling

a Bass bar
b Sound post
c Position of bridge feet
d Curves of bouts, linings
e Blocks
f C-curves
g f-holes

Arching

Tail piece

Bridge

Finger board

End button

Head

Pegbox

Scroll

Neck

Pegs